Lake of Slaves

Brian Duncan

Lake of Slaves
Brian Duncan
Copyright © 2014 Brian Duncan.

ISBN: 978-0-9915032-9-2

Front cover photo by Calin Tatu / Shutterstock
Back cover photo by Giovanni De Caro / Shutterstock
Maps by Philip Laino
Artwork, design and layout by Lighthouse24

In the 1880s the area around Lake Nyasa is being devastated by Arab slave traders and raids by Angoni tribesmen (related to the Zulus). Livingstone's 'Lake of Stars' has become a 'Lake of Slaves'. Into this desolation come a handful of British administrators, traders, and adventurers, who fight the slavers, initially with little success. One of these is Alan Spaight, who is embroiled in the fighting as soon as he arrives in the fledgling British Central Africa Protectorate.

Alan becomes a coffee planter, but his military experience and commitment to combat slavery repeatedly draw him into the conflicts, helped by a mission-educated African named Goodwill, a former slave, who escaped to return to his village.

From 1891 the new Consul, Harry Johnston, brings in British officers and a contingent of Sikh soldiers, and the tide slowly turns. Although there are some fictional characters, this is a true story of the eight years of bitter fighting that ended the slave trade in Nyasaland.

tribal aristocracy, a descendant of the original group of warriors that fled Zululand in the 1830s. Goodwill's mother, Nsofe, was a Nyanja, captured by Angoni tribesmen in a raid on her village. She was only sixteen at the time, and was taken with other captives to the highlands, where she was formally given to the young man who had led the raid. Her fate was to live with this foreign tribe for the rest of her life.

The Angoni were cattle herdsmen who followed the customs of their Zulu ancestors. They were disciplined and warlike, with a strong hierarchical social structure. Even so, they had been diluted by acquisition of women and children from weaker tribes. It was their practice to descend to the lowlands along the Lake shore, usually at harvest time, to rape and pillage. The lakeside tribes were no match for them and would flee at the first sign of the Angoni warriors, who would then raid the granaries and make off with their captives.

Nsofe had three children before her husband died of a fever. As a widow from an inferior tribe she was vilified and victimized; some of the older women blamed her for her husband's death. After long deliberation, and fearful of the consequences, she decided to escape to her home village. Goodwill was thirteen at the time. His name was Nditi, and he had already gone through the Angoni initiation ceremonies for young warriors. He was reluctant to join his mother in her flight, wanting to stay with his friends. But he understood her reasons, and could not bear to be parted from her, nor from his younger sisters.

So he went with them. They left in secret, in the middle of the night. It was a long and hazardous journey to Nsofe's village, walking on seldom used pathways, fearful of being re-captured by Angoni warriors. At nights they huddled beside small fires, far from any habitation. Fifteen days later they reached their destination and found the old village in ruins. The huts had collapsed and weeds were rampant on their remains. A few people lived furtively in the surrounding forest; they explained how Yao slavers had recently taken away the able people, leaving only the elderly and those too young to walk to the coast. Between the Angoni raids and the depredations of the slavers life was meagre and precarious.

Nsofe settled in her former village with her children. They were later joined by a few others who had eluded the slavers. She raised her children as Nyanjas, and made them speak ChiNyanja, although for a couple of years they were more fluent in ChiNgoni, the Angoni language. Their village was a two hour walk from the Presbyterian mission at Domasi, north of Mount Zomba, in the Shire Highlands. She took Nditi and his sisters to the school there. Later they all worshipped in the church and were taught English and other subjects. For seven years they lived in peace, and the children absorbed their education with enthusiasm. At home they ate well from crops they grew and from the goats and chickens they raised. The three children were baptised in the mission church – as Goodwill, Mary and Mercy.

Goodwill learned the traditional village crafts. His favourite occupation was to hunt with his elderly uncle, who had managed to elude the slavers. The old fellow had deep knowledge of the large mammals: elephants, lions, buffaloes and leopards. However, his greatest expertise was in hunting small animals: duikers, hares, rats, mice, guinea fowl, and francolins. He built many different types of trap, and used his intimate knowledge of the habits of these creatures to lure them.

The Angoni tribesmen still made sporadic raids into the Shire Highlands, but they were somewhat reluctant to come near the mission at Domasi, even though the staff were unarmed. The slavers, too, were still active; they had native scouts who assessed where there were sufficient potential captives for a profitable raid. Nsofe's village, though she did not know it, had again become a target. When the raid came it caught them by surprise. They fled in all directions. Nsofe dragged her youngest daughter Mercy into a far clump of bushes where they lay silently until the slavers went on their way, satisfied with a good haul.

Now Nsofe huddled in the darkness of her looted hut. Mercy, lay beside her, having wept herself to sleep. They knew that Goodwill and

Mary had been taken as slaves, but when they returned to the village they dared not remonstrate with their headman. He had too much power over them. It was a miracle that they managed to escape.

— • —

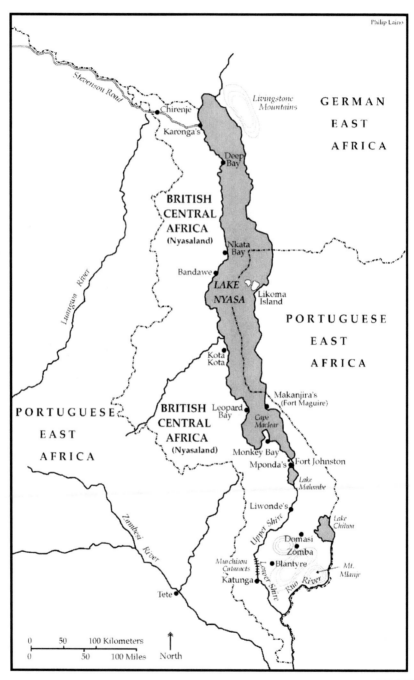

Philip Laino

Stevenson Road

Chirenje

Karonga's

Deep
Bay

GERMAN

EAST

AFRICA

Livingstone
Mountains

BRITISH
CENTRAL
AFRICA
(Nyasaland)

Nkata
Bay

Bandawe

LAKE
NYASA

Likoma
Island

PORTUGUESE

EAST

AFRICA

Luangwa River

Kota
Kota

Makanjira's
(Fort Maguire)

BRITISH
CENTRAL
AFRICA
(Nyasaland)

Leopard
Bay

Cape
Maclear

PORTUGUESE

EAST

AFRICA

Monkey Bay

Mponda's

Fort Johnston

Lake
Malombe

Liwonde's

Lake
Chilwa

Upper Shire

Domasi

Zomba

Munchison
Cataracts

Blantyre

Mt.
Mlanje

Zambesi River

Katunga

Lower Shire

Ruo River

Tete

| 0 | 50 | 100 Kilometers |
| 0 | 50 | 100 Miles |

↑
North

Map 2. British Central Africa - Nyasaland (1890-95)

2

Shire River - August 1887

A young man stood on the foredeck of the paddle steamer *James Stevenson* as it plied up the Shire River, north of the Zambesi. Looking at the wide expanse of marshy land on both banks, teeming with game, he thought, 'This is the real Africa'. Elephants, buffaloes, zebra and kudu – he could see them all, in their primeval state.

He turned to the skipper, who was standing amidships by the helm, and called, 'Where are the people – the African villagers?"

Dougal Skinner took his pipe from his mouth and pointed vaguely to the banks. "Taken into slavery, most of them. Aye, there's precious few left, and they lead miserable lives."

The fair-haired young man thoughtfully stroked his short Van Dyke beard and said, "That will change, won't it? The missionaries, the traders – they'll change things won't they?"

Skinner snorted politely at the idealism. "Don't you know, Mr Spaight, there are forty-six white men where you're going – the area around Lake Nyasa – and nine white women. Do you really suppose they can have any effect. Good Lord, man – the area's the size of Britain. Even with the losses through slavery and diseases – and tribal fighting – there are thousands of heathen savages up there. The missionaries aren't allowed to fight the slavers, and you traders would be pissing against the wind – if you'll pardon my French."

— • —

It was August 1887 and Alan Spaight had sailed on the *Walmer Castle* from Tilbury, in England, to Cape Town. He was coming out to Africa to work for the African Lakes Company, formed to support the missionaries in the area around Lake Nyasa. He would work as a trader, selling calico, beads and wire, and buying ivory.

The whole voyage had taken three weeks so far and he enjoyed all of it. He made some good friends – mostly British people and South Africans. He shared a cabin with two men who had been playing cricket in England, for a South African provincial team – they were good company. There were plenty of deck sports, and several dances.

He read as much as he could about life in Southern Africa – there was an excellent little library on the ship – and he borrowed books from other passengers. He met a man who had been on a hunting trip up the Zambesi from its mouth to Tete, the Portuguese town, and had to cut short his trip because he contracted a bad dose of fever; he was liberal with advice.

Alan continued his voyage on a coastal steamer, the *Badger*, from Cape Town to Quelimane on coast of the Portuguese administered territory in East Africa, just north of the Zambesi River. It was rather uncomfortable, mainly because of the heat. They encountered some very stormy weather – it was said to be quite common along the coast. His new employers, the African Lakes Company, had a representative in Quelimane, who showed him some of the trade goods while he waited a few days for a ship that would take him to Chinde in the Zambesi delta.

Quelimane was the southernmost town in the coastal area controlled by the Portuguese. It had little to commend it – the few Europeans who lived there looked very unhealthy, their complexions pallid, with a curious yellow hue. They seemed to Alan to be lethargic, like time-servers in some prison colony. He wondered if this was something that would happen to him if he lived in tropical Africa.

In these times, voyagers up the Zambesi River had difficulty entering the delta. There were no landmarks in the featureless swamps, and the channels were often closed by formidable sandbars. Until recently it was the custom to go inland from Quelimane up the Kwakwa River, and then cut across to the Zambesi. Then a hitherto unknown delta channel was found at Chinde.

The Portuguese controlled the Zambesi River, but the British had negotiated a right of passage up to the tributary Shire River. The rusty coastal steamer that took Alan there held only four passengers – the other three were Portuguese officials who spoke no English. The heat was intense and the mosquitoes attacked him with a vengeance, despite the repellent he had applied. Chinde was extremely dirty, teeming with flies and other insects. The local Africans seemed lacking in any energy, though cheerful enough.

From Chinde four small paddle steamers belonging to the ALC brought trade goods up the Zambesi and then the Shire River into the Nyasa country; Alan now voyaged on one of them. The passenger accommodation was primitive, the food basic, the heat and humidity oppressive. The Zambesi and Shire valleys were renowned for the ferocity of the mosquitoes. At that time the insect was not a proven vector of the malaria parasite, although it was suspected of having something to do with the fever. Most visitors to this part of Africa sooner or later contracted malaria, or its dreaded variant blackwater fever.

Alan was the only passenger on the *James Stevenson* from Chinde. They probed up the delta to reach the main body of the Zambesi, then forged slowly against the current to the entrance of the Shire River. It took two days to reach Chiromo, where the ALC had a depot in what was little more than a large village. The company had built a jetty on the river bank, to which was moored another paddle steamer – as they approached the skipper informed Alan that it had broken down.

When he disembarked he introduced himself and found they were a mother and daughter, Marge and Jess Kennedy. They wore white cotton dresses with long sleeves. Their broad hats were covered with nets, making them look like a couple of bee-keepers. Marge was short and stout, with an accent that Alan immediately recognised as Scottish, and placed to the north of Edinburgh; she soon confirmed that they were from Perth. Jess was also short, but slender, and he glimpsed through the netting a ready smile and lively brown eyes.

They told him they were on their way to the Shire Highlands where Marge's husband Jock Kennedy had started a coffee plantation. He had formerly worked as a Church of Scotland lay missionary in Blantyre, the embryonic settlement in the highlands. Jess told him that she had worked for a year as a nurse at an Edinburgh hospital and hoped to do similar work in the new territory.

"And what about you, young man?" asked Marge. "You've heard all about us."

"I've joined the African Lakes Company as a trader," he told them. "It's a Scottish company that was started ten years ago, to support the missionaries in this part of Africa. This is their boat. They import calico material as a currency to pay labour, such as those that build the mission stations. They also purchase ivory and export it."

"We know something of the ALC," said Marge. "My husband had his supplies brought in by them." She pointed to the paddle steamer. "So we are to be fellow passengers up the river. We've spent three days here and are anxious to move on. The mosquitoes are dreadful, aren't they Jess."

Her daughter nodded. "We were told it's a very unhealthy place. My father warned us not to spend too much time here – but we had no alternative."

They went on board a few minutes later. There were four cabins on the little steamer and Alan already had the best one. He offered it to Marge, but she would not have it. The fourth would be unoccupied, so the women were able to use it for some of their belongings. The skipper, Dougal Skinner, had accommodation near the stern, but told them it was so hot that he usually slept on deck. Canvas awnings covered most of the deck area, and there were chairs from which they could watch the crew stacking the timber for the ship's furnace.

They set off in the afternoon. The river was quite low at that time of year – the dry season – and they encountered numerous sandbanks, on some of which the ship got stuck. Alan watched fascinated as the crew used long poles, and sometimes an anchor and winch, to pull the steamer away. It had a very shallow draft and had been designed for these conditions.

Crocodiles basked on the banks, and groups of hippos were common – the local Africans had to be careful of them; they could upset their canoes. The passengers were glad to be in a larger ship. They soon saw plenty of game in the bush along the river – groups of elephants, waterbuck, eland, kudu, and great herds of buffaloes. The birds were magnificent, especially the fish eagles that roosted in the trees along the river bank and dove into the water to catch their prey.

The paddle steamer travelled very slowly. For the first fifty miles both sides of the Shire were in undisputed Portuguese territory, but thereafter the British had claims, which increased in legitimacy the higher upstream they travelled. It would take three days to reach their destination at Katunga – a village where the ALC has a trans-shipment depot.

"It's amazing to think that only thirty years ago this was virtually unexplored country." Alan was standing at the rail with Jess. "David Livingstone and the early missionaries came along here just like us."

"Except that they didn't know what lay ahead."

"True. It's such a shame that the river isn't navigable all the way up to Lake Nyasa, because of the cataracts and rapids. We're going to have to walk up to the highlands, just like those early explorers."

Jess sighed. "At least we know that at the end of the journey we're going to be at higher elevations, and that the climate will be more temperate."

The early missionaries had established several settlements in the highlands, including Blantyre, named after Livingstone's birthplace in Scotland. It became the headquarters for the ALC in 1879, when the company built a house and storage sheds about a mile from the mission station. The first British consulate was based there in 1885, though it later moved north to Zomba.

"I've heard you call the ALC 'Mandala'," said Jess. "Why is it called that?"

"They told me it's because the glinting spectacles worn by John Moir, one of the general managers, reminded the Africans of the sun reflected on water, which they call 'mandala'."

At dusk the steamer moored by a large sandbank. Dougal explained that it was safer than the river bank; no one was likely to swim across at night for fear of crocodiles.

"I need to explain the rules for this little ship." He had a strong Glaswegian accent, and was quite shy and diffident. "No one goes ashore at night, and no one comes aboard. I have a shotgun, and, if I need help I'll ask you, Mr Spaight, so I would be grateful if you would keep your rifle handy."

He must have noticed some fear in the expressions of Marge and Jess, because he held up his hand. "I do not wish to alarm you, ladies, but we have to make sure that none of these local Africans think they can take advantage of us. My steamer boys will keep a look out. At dawn they go ashore to do their ablutions. We stay on board. Now, anyone wanting to have a shower can use the small bathroom below; it has only cold water. If you want hot water, for washing yourselves or your clothes, you can ask one of the steamer boys, who will bring you a bucketful. As regards eating – you will be served three meals on the forward deck. I'm afraid it's simple fare..."

Marge interrupted. "Are we permitted to cook something for ourselves?"

"I would prefer that you do not come into the galley."

"Are we allowed to sleep on deck?" Alan asked.

Skinner nodded. "Make sure you use your mosquito nets."

He retired to the stern, where Alan later saw him sipping whisky and smoking a pipe. The three passengers ate supper on the forward deck. It was set on a trestle table by one of the steamer 'boys', who doubled as a steward. Their plates were filled with rice and chicken stew, which they were beginning to realise was the standard fare. A bowl of bananas was provided by way of dessert, washed down with tea served in tin mugs.

After they had eaten Marge invited Alan to smoke. He lit up his pipe, and Marge laughed when he told them that the smoke would not deter the insects.

"You said earlier that you spent time in India, Mr Spaight. Please tell us about it."

He invited them to call him Alan, then told them how he had served in the British Army in the Sudan campaign of 1885. He was seconded to a Sikh regiment and went with them to India.

"Was that unusual?" asked Mrs Kennedy. "I mean, to change regiments."

Alan shrugged. "I suppose so. During the Battle of Tofrek – in the Sudan – the fighting became very confused. The battle lasted only about twenty minutes, and I found myself fighting with the 15th Sikhs, who were alongside my own regiment – the Berkshires. When the battle was over, the CO of the Sikhs asked my colonel if he would let me go over to them, on secondment. Later, when we left the Sudan, I decided to take the opportunity to go with them to India. I spent two years with them."

"But you left the army?"

"Yes. I resigned my commission. Now, here I am in Africa."

"What do you think of it?" asked Jess.

"It's a lot different. Far fewer people, and they seem rather – more primitive. I'm not sure if that's the right way to describe it. The only real Africans I've seen – in Quelimane and Chinde – have been almost naked..."

Marge laughed, and said, "Thanks heavens the steamer boys wear uniforms."

"The wild animals are quite different," Alan added. "They seem more primeval here; I suppose because they wander freely over the countryside, often in full view. In India they are difficult to see because they are generally hidden in the jungles, and stay away from human habitation."

"It all seems rather dangerous," said Jess. "The crocodiles and hippos are menacing presences, and no doubt there are lots of snakes and other horrid things that we don't see."

"What will your lives be like?" he asked, concerned that they might be underestimating the hardships ahead.

"We know the highlands are cooler and the climate is generally much nicer," replied Marge. "My husband says that we'll like it. He came out three years ago, and after serving two years with the mission at Blantyre he purchased a thousand acres near Zomba. It's about forty miles north of Blantyre. Jock has planted fifty acres of coffee, and will plant more this rainy season. I think it will be a hard life, but we will have opportunities that are hard to find in Scotland. Imagine owning so much land – and it cost him only a few bales of calico."

He asked Jess where she would do her nursing. "In Blantyre," she replied. "The only hospital is there, but it's too far to travel from the farm every day, so I'll stay with the McPhails – the doctor and his wife. She's a nurse and has a baby, and I'll help to look after it for my board. I'll go home for the Sabbath."

The two women said their goodnights and went below. Alan set up his mosquito net near the prow, and laid his sleeping bag on the deck; he spread a canvas sheet under it, expecting dew in the morning. Then he lit a last pipe and admired the great vault of stars above. It seemed quiet until he realised that there was a rippling from the river running past the hull, and the orchestra of insects played constantly in the background. Now and then an animal cried out, and he imagined that an antelope might have been caught by a predator.

He saw a shadowy figure approach from amidships. It was Jess, carrying a roll of bedding. "I've come to join you," she announced, laughing shyly.

"I'm delighted," he said, surprised that Marge had allowed it.

As if she had heard his thoughts, Jess said, "My mother said at first that I could not come up here – it would be a scandal at home! Then she said she trusted me – and you. Oh, it's so much cooler here – I couldn't bear it in the cabin. Besides, I like talking to you. I like the way you don't complain. You're usually cheerful, and I think one needs to be."

He helped her to string the lines to support her mosquito net, and spread a canvas on which she laid her own bedding. "You're a brave girl," he told her, "to come out to this wild country."

"Och, it's not so bad – at least on this ship. I feel quite safe with the water around us." She paused. "Do you have a girl – someone you left behind?"

Alan laughed. "No, no one like that. How about you?"

"No, and my father has told me that I will not have many prospects here in Africa."

"There are very few white men; no more than fifty. That's less than in a small village in Scotland."

She giggled. "Perhaps I'll have to go back home."

They were silent for a while before she commented on the stars, and he gave her a tour of the constellations, based on his limited knowledge from navigation courses at Sandhurst. They then realised that they were sleepy and said goodnight.

Before she fell asleep Jess thought about the young man lying not two paces from her. He was the sort of man she liked; not forward and full of himself, but not quiet and introspective. He was easy for an unsophisticated girl like her to talk to. Yes, she decided she liked him.

—•—

3

Lower Shire River – August 1887

Alan always woke early, but the steamer boys were already at work before he opened his eyes to a streak of light on the horizon. They were climbing into the ship's dinghy, and he watched them paddle to the bank. Jess was still fast asleep as he hung up his blanket and net, which were damp with dew.

He strolled back to the galley, where Skinner was brewing tea. The skipper handed him a mug and pointed to the sugar.

"I see the lassie slept on deck," he said. "Brave girl – she'll be sought after in the highlands here."

"How much longer will you do this work, Mr Skinner?" Alan asked.

He coughed and prepared a pipe with much deliberation. "Not much longer. I had a calling – that brought me here – but there's no sense in wasting my health. I've had two bouts of fever and one more will be enough. I've told the Company that I won't stay after they find a replacement."

"You'll go back to Scotland?"

"Aye. I have a wife and three bairns waiting for me."

He shouted to the men on the shore, calling them to return quickly. He muttered, "They'll spend all day chattering and fooling around, given the chance. We must be on our way."

21

When the dinghy returned the men went about their tasks. Two of them stoked the furnace to build up the steam pressure. One of them swabbed the decks, using buckets of river water. The cook started preparing breakfast. The other two men set about polishing the metal work. All of them were smiling and laughing, and Alan wondered what made them so cheerful. He supposed their lot was better than their brothers on shore; at least they were assured of food and somewhere safe to sleep.

Skinner told him that the local tribes had been decimated by the slavers, who carried on their trade with the connivance of the Portuguese officials. "We'll soon be in Makololo country," he said, explaining that they were the dominant tribe in the approaches to Katunga. Alan had read that they were descendants of men brought from the interior by Dr Livingstone. They settled along the Shire River and conquered and absorbed the local tribes. The main reason they flourished was because of their hatred of slavery; it enabled them to attract people from neighbouring tribes who suffered from attacks by slave traders.

When Alan returned to the foredeck he found that Jess had gone. She re-appeared later with Marge, and all three ate their breakfast together. It consisted of maize porridge, without milk or cream, and hard-boiled eggs. Marge explained that she had suffered terribly from the heat during the night; in future she planned to sleep on deck.

They spent the day in the shade of the awnings. Marge read a novel and wrote letters. Jess and Alan made entries in their journals and wondered if they were saying the same things. A couple of hours later they stopped at a 'wooding station' – a village where the people had cut firewood to fuel the steamer. They stayed there for half an hour while the wood was carried on board and stacked.

The view from the deck was the broad floodplain of the Shire, a vast expanse of long grass. The vista was broken only occasionally

Alan said he was surprised that rice was so readily available. "The natives grow it all along the coast – for trade," Skinner replied. "They like to eat it, but it's more valuable than maize, so they generally only partake on special occasions."

The mosquitoes had come out in force and were whining around the passengers. Marge and Jess were in their beekeeper costumes and even wore gloves so that their hands were not stung.

"Have you had malaria?" Marge asked Alan.

He told her that he'd had an attack in India. "Very unpleasant – and the quinine has a taste that I will never forget."

"We've brought some with us," said Jess. "Do you think it's the mosquito bite that causes malaria?"

"I think it might be. The two go together. As you know, the Romans thought it was in the air, in the swampy areas – like here. But perhaps it's something – a kind of poison – the mosquitoes carry. Most Europeans in India think there's some connection, and they all dress like we are now – to avoid being bitten."

Alan helped the women to set out their bedding, and then withdrew to the stern for a smoke to allow them to go through their retirement routine in some semblance of privacy. When he eventually came to the foredeck, all he had to do was remove his breeches and climb into his sleeping bag under the mosquito net. They held a conversation for perhaps half and hour, and then Alan heard a lion.

"Did you hear that?" he asked them.

"No, what?"

"Lions – listen – it's a sound like 'Oomph'". He gave a modest imitation.

They were quiet, and within a few minutes heard it. "I expect they're hunting – some of them driving the prey towards the others. The sounds are their signals to each other."

—•—

27

The next two days passed in much the same way. They noticed a gradual change in the landscape as the flat low marshlands and plains changed to more hilly country. There were more trees too, cladding the hills and sometimes spreading down to the river bank. The trees became denser, until they could be described as a forest. The dry grass among the trees was sparse, and there were fewer animals to be seen. At night they could see fires in the hills, like coral necklaces, and during the day there were plumes of smoke rising into the clear blue sky.

Alan enjoyed the company of the mother and daughter. Marge was intelligent and good-humoured. She had a very pragmatic outlook, not seeming to be dismayed by the many interruptions in the voyage. Jess was lively and cheerful, and took a keen interest in all that was happening.

At mid-morning on the fourth day they reached Katunga, their destination, a large dusty village. From here a track led along the river side which could be used by porters to carry loads past the Murchison Cataracts. However, the African Lakes Company preferred to take their goods to Blantyre, their headquarters in the Shire Highlands, where they were stored and then re-distributed to other depots.

Waiting at the jetty was a short wiry man in khaki shirt and trousers, with a floppy broad-brimmed hat, which he removed to wave, revealing thinning red hair.

Jess jumped up and down. "There's Pa," she shouted.

In due course Alan was introduced to Jock Kennedy, and to Mark Harris, the Mandala representative, whose job was to supervise the unloading of the Company's steamers. He said that a party of thirty porters would walk with them, with two *capitaos*, or 'boss boys' as Harris, a South African, called them. These two men were armed with Snider rifles and wore Company uniforms.

"It's a three day walk from Katunga to Blantyre," Jock Kennedy told the new arrivals, "mostly uphill! I've arranged *machilas* for the ladies, and Mark has one for you, Spaight."

He discovered that a *machila* was a sort of hammock, carried by four men; it was reputed to be very uncomfortable. He did not like the idea of being carried by other men – almost as if they were slaves – so he walked with Jock Kennedy, while the two women lay in their hammocks. At first they laughed and joked about this strange experience, but they grew quiet as the bearers got into their rhythm and moved faster.

The track was well worn, and wide enough to take perhaps three or four men walking side by side. One of the *capitaos* was in the advanced guard, and behind him were half of the porters. The British were in the centre of the column, followed by the remaining porters under the second *capitao*. Inevitably, they walked at the pace of the slowest – the porters, each of them with a load of about fifty pounds. Surprisingly, the *machila* bearers were more sprightly and cheerful, being chosen for strength and fitness.

Alan was struck by the loud conversations that developed in the column. The African voices were strong and clear, and he could detect exchanges along its full length of perhaps a hundred yards. He could not understand what they were saying, despite early efforts to learn ChiNyanja, but thought that anecdotes and jokes were being bandied around, with much laughter. Not long after they started one of the porters started singing, and the chorus was picked up by the others, using natural harmonies.

The track wound up through the rocky hills, which were covered with trees, so there were few vistas. The trees were mostly species of *Brachystegia* and *Acacia*, strongly branched, with spreading canopies. The density of the shade beneath them inhibited growth of grasses, which tended to be sparse and straggling. It was past the middle of winter and had not rained for at least three months, so the vegetation was dry and dusty, with a high risk of bush fires.

Kennedy talked at length with his wife and daughter, whom he had not seen for three years. He walked beside their *machilas* as they chatted about friends and family so far away. Meanwhile, Alan struck up a conversation with one of the *capitaos*, who spoke quite good English and was happy to tell him the ChiNyanja names of common things along the route. Alan jotted the words in a notebook – renewing his effort to learn the language. This man, whose name was Joseph, had worked for Mandala for five years. He had earlier had some schooling at the Church of Scotland mission, and said he was a Christian, hence he was baptised with a biblical name.

They stopped every hour for about five minutes. This gave the *machila* bearers a chance to change positions, and the porters could ease their loads and relieve themselves. At most of these halts there was water to be found in a stream, or small river, where the water was clear and clean.

At midday they ate some food and rested for an hour. Before dusk they reached a small village with a clearing dedicated to transport columns. It was lined on one side with grass huts for the Europeans to sleep in, while the Africans slept on mats on the bare ground. The remaining daylight was used to collect wood and light fires, intended to provide warmth and scare off wild animals. They had climbed several hundred feet, and it was noticeably cooler.

Some of the porters prepared communal food – *nsima* – in large pots that were stored at the village. Jock Kennedy grilled a chicken, and they ate some *nsima* with it, serving themselves from the pot, as well as roast squashes he had brought from the farm. They were very tired, and conversation was sporadic. Alan went off to sleep as soon as he had eaten. He found his hut claustrophobic, so pulled his bedding roll into the open, near one of the fires. He built a frame of branches for his mosquito net and kept his rifle by his side.

her voice was hoarse, and her body was filthy; rivulets of sweat ran down from her breasts, washing away the dust on her skin.

"What will happen to us, brother?"

He tried to console her. "We will get away from them somehow. We must be patient and find a time."

"What do you think Mother and Mercy are doing?"

"They will be back in the village now. They will be alright. We must find a way to get back to them – to be with them again. Don't be afraid, Mary." He knew that his tone lacked conviction, but he did not know what else to say.

On the next day they started the long overland trek to the coast of the Indian Ocean. They had been joined by other captives from another stockade, so there were now about two hundred slaves. They were assembled into a long line by the *ruga-rugas*, a dozen of them now. To Goodwill they seemed frenzied, as if they had been smoking *ganja,* the hemp that was widely grown. They pranced and shouted, while one of them beat on a small drum. They wore their hair in dreadlocks, bound with red beads. Their white calico blouses and shorts were stained with sweat and dust. All of them, except the drummer, carried muzzle-loading flintlocks; belts with shot and powder hung from their shoulders.

The captive men and older boys were again yoked with *gorees*, while the women, girls and younger children were strung together by the neck with long ropes. Goodwill strained to catch a glimpse of his sister, but their numbers were too great, Elephant tusks were brought out of a guarded hut and given to the men to carry. Each tusk weighed from ten to fifty pounds, and had leather thongs attached to each end, to make them easier to carry. The women were made to carry pots of maize meal, for the midday food.

Each day they stopped at about noon for a couple of hours, to rest, and for the captives to relieve themselves. This procedure involved the whole line shuffling off the path. It was during these times that

Goodwill and Kawa started to work at the thongs that bound their wrists, using sharp edged stones, knowing that it would take a long while. But two days later the *rugas* made a routine inspection and discovered the frayed bindings. They beat the two young men furiously before tying them with a length of chain. Then they marched on.

On the third day the first laggard was killed. She was a woman of about thirty, who stumbled on the path and sprained her ankle; it soon swelled and she was unable to walk. The *rugas* gathered round and summoned Musa, who had been walking ahead of the long line of slaves. Goodwill and Kawa watched from a distance as Musa shook his head and pointed at a tree with his ebony cane. The guards tied the woman to the tree and swiftly slit her throat. A collective gasp of horror and dismay rose from the captives.

"Why did they kill her?" a woman cried.

One of the *rugas* was standing near Goodwill. He was older than his fellow guards, scrawnier, and quieter. "Musa has paid for her", he said. "Why should he let another take her for free? Besides, it shows you people what will happen if you cannot keep up."

Two days later a child was killed. She was a young girl of about twelve and had become sick. It happened at the further end of the line from where Goodwill and Kawa were bound, but the information was passed back in whispers. The girl was vomiting and had diarrhoea; she was unable to walk, even though her mother and others tried to help her. The *rugas* untied her and one of them smashed her skull with the butt of his flintlock. The women wailed, and the male captives growled in anger, but there was nothing they could do. The dead girl was left beside the path where the jackals and hyenas would eat her.

"What men are these," Goodwill asked, "who can kill a child?"

"They are evil – like the spirits that we were told about – when we were children."

"It could happen to us."

"Of course." Kawa growled.

"Can we overcome these *ruga-rugas*?"

"They are clever. They stay apart. Their guns are always ready."

— • —

Ten days into the journey they reached an area of open grassland, a huge *dambo*, where herds of kudu and waterbuck grazed. The *rugas* became excited and tried to shoot the antelopes, but with no success. Goodwill had heard at the mission school that it required much skill and training to shoot accurately with a musket or rifle.

Later on the same day the guards spotted a group of six elephants, and decided to hunt them. Leaving two of their number to watch over the captives, they approached the small herd, slowly moving upwind. Goodwill and Kawa watched as the tiny distant figures converged towards the massive grey beasts. Suddenly, puffs of smoke appeared and they heard the reports of the guns. The elephants rushed away, except for one that slowed, then stumbled. Faint cries of glee drifted across the *dambo*.

The *rugas* returned and led all the captives to the dead elephant. While two guards lit a bonfire the others started to carve up the huge grey animal. Using machetes they opened up the belly, from which spilled the entrails with massive gasps of gases. The intestines were dragged out like a long rope and taken to the fire to be cooked. Then all the elephant's flesh was cut into large chunks, each weighing a couple of pounds. The captives were allowed to hold the lumps on the ends of sticks, over the fire. They ate the half-cooked meat ravenously, having had barely enough food for ten days. By the end of an hour there was little left of the elephant – only the bloody skeleton and skull, draped with the empty hide. The tusks had been hacked out and added to the collection carried by the slaves.

Goodwill and Kawa whispered to each other in ChiNyanja when-ever they had an opportunity. Talking was forbidden by the guards, but they were often some distance away. Goodwill was growing to

37

appreciate Kawa's irrepressible good humour. He had not been to school, but he was bright and inquisitive. He seemed to know very little about the history of the region.

"You were an Angoni," said Kawa. "Why does your former tribe attack us people near the Lake?"

Goodwill said, "Hmm. You see, they are cattle owners. They do not grow much crops like maize and cassava, like the Lake people, or at least it is easier for them to come down from the hills in raiding parties."

"Why do they live in the hills?"

"Many years ago – maybe fifty years ago – my Angoni ancestors settled in the high country to the west of the Lake. A hundred years ago they were part of the great Zulu nation. But my tribe quarrelled with the big chief, Chaka, and moved north. They found the hills looking over the Lake were like their former country. Their cattle were healthy because there are no tsetse flies in the hills…"

"Why is that?"

"My teacher told me that the tsetse flies like to live in warmer places. Also, they like thick bush, where they can stay in the shade during the day. In the hills there are only a few trees, no thick forest like near the Lake."

"My people hate the Angoni," said Kawa; he was grinning disarmingly.

Goodwill smiled back. "I know, and I can understand why."

"My people keep their maize hidden in the reeds so that the raiders cannot find it. Also, they now grow more cassava, which the Angoni found too difficult to dig up and cook."

"That is wise. Maybe they will stop their raids, if they cannot find enough food to steal."

"But they steal women and children, too. Was not your mother stolen?"

"True. The tribe adopted her, but she was never treated as a true Angoni. That is why she fled when my father died."

They were walking along the path, at the rear of the long line. A forty pound elephant tusk was slung from the *goree*; it swung to and fro with the rhythm of their movements. They had learned to match their stride to reduce the rubbing of the *goree* on their necks. Except when they took the weight of the tusk, their hands were free during the march, and now and then they would pluck grass stalks and suck the moisture from the end.

"Have you seen the mission where I was at school?" asked Goodwill.

"I have not seen it, and I have not seen the school, or the church where you pray to your God. Who are the *azungu* – the white men – there?"

"They are missionaries. They came from Britain, which is a country far away from here."

"Why did they come here?"

"To teach us about God, and Jesus Christ…"

"Who are they?"

"Jesus was the son of God. He was sent by God to this world. He was a wise man and a teacher. A religion started after he was killed; it is called Christianity – after his name Jesus Christ."

"What is this religion?" Kawa sounded sceptical, but he always spoke lightly and with humour.

"Hmm. You see, if you are Christian, like me, you believe in one God and his son, Jesus Christ, and you follow their teachings, which are written in a book called the Bible."

"And what is the Muslim religion – that these Yaos follow?"

"They, too, have a God called Allah…"

"Is he a different God?"

Goodwill thought for a while. "I don't know, my friend. They had a different leader. His name was Mohammed, and he lived in a country far from here…"

"Further than Britain?"

39

"Not so far. Anyway, his followers wrote a book of his teachings called the Koran."

Kawa laughed. "It is very confusing. So the missionaries at your church taught you about a God and Christ?"

"Yes, but they also taught me to speak English, and to read and write the language."

"Is that good?"

"It is good. I can read the teachings and stories in the Bible…"

"Could I learn to read?"

"I'm sure you could – if you had a teacher, or if you could go to a school."

"You could teach me."

They were quiet for a while, when a guard walked past, then resumed their conversation. Goodwill said, "My religion forbids slavery. The missionaries want to stop it, but they lack the power. They have no soldiers or guns. All they can do is tell the chiefs and headmen that it is wrong to sell their own people. They tell the slavers that it is wrong to take people like us from their villages."

—•—

Three weeks passed. The caravan of captives averaged about eight or ten miles a day. They could have walked further on an open road, but the path was rough and winding. One or two captives died, or were killed, almost every day. Dysentery was rife, as was malaria, when they descended to lower altitudes.

One day the captives heard the *rugas* shouting that a fire was coming. They looked to the west, from where they had walked, and saw the plumes of smoke. A strong breeze blew towards them, and the grass and bushes were tinder dry. Gouts of vivid orange flames rolled up into the sky, lighting up the oily blue-grey smoke. The deadly crackling sound carried to them, interspersed with occasional explosions as whole trees convulsed in the blaze.

Goodwill heard Musa giving instructions; he appeared to be calm as he gave his orders. He told the *rugas* to light fires ahead of them, downwind. The fires soon caught and swept away from them, leaving the ground bare and smoking. The captives were herded forward, treading carefully to avoid stepping on red-hot embers. The big fire behind them was approaching fast. They could hear the roar and the crackle of burning trees. Clouds of smoke enveloped them and choked them as they pressed on. The heat was almost unbearable.

Wild animals rushed past them, fleeing the fire. A small herd of kudu ran amongst them, the male with his great spiral horns laid back, his eyes wild with fear. The *rugas* shouted and tried to fire their flintlocks, but the kudu had disappeared. Hares and jackals darted past, and birds swooped from the sky to catch the insects thrown up by the flames. They saw burnt animals on the ground – a tortoise with its shell split open, a chameleon roasted to a charred lump.

Some of the captives were terrified and screamed, which made the guards angry. They ran around cracking their whips and shouting at the slaves to be quiet. All this time Musa was calm and dignified, striding around, satisfied that all his slaves had survived.

The fire reached the place they had burnt themselves and having no fuel it died behind them. To their sides it swept past, terrifying in its speed and ferocity. It faded only when the wind changed direction leaving thousands of acres charred and smoking.

— • —

By the end of the first month Musa had lost some seventy captives, a third of the total. But the rate of attrition was declining. The weak among them had been culled, and they were becoming accustomed to their meagre diet and the rigours of the march. Each night they slept in a small village, where fires were lit to ward off marauding lions and hyenas.

A rumour was passed round one evening; it was said that a woman captive knew how to prepare poison, and she intended to put it in the food of the *rugas*. She was the mother of the young girl who had been killed by them early in the march, and she wanted revenge. The other captives told her that she would be caught and killed, but she said she did not care.

She collected the poison plants in an area where they had stopped at noon. It was a grove where the plants flourished, and she had placed the material in an empty food pot. All that was needed was to crush the roots and cook it with the *nsima* that would be given to the guards. The food was prepared by five young girls, one of whom was Mary. They were used as concubines by the *rugas*, who took them to their huts after the evening meal, for as long as they wished.

When Goodwill heard about the plan he was fearful that his sister would be incriminated, as one of the food preparers. He sought her out and begged her on his knees to have no part in it, but she was adamant.

"You cannot understand, my brother, what it is like for me – to lie with these filthy men every night. They tell me that I should get used to it, because it will be my life as a slave. But I cannot live such a life. If they kill me, so be it." She wept and he tried in vain to comfort her.

The guards' food was poisoned that evening. Nine out of thirteen ate from the pot and they were all violently ill. They rolled on the ground, clutching their bellies and howling with pain. Musa hurried up to see what was happening. He knew at once that the *rugas* had been poisoned and ordered the five servant girls to be brought to him. In front of all the captives he told them that they had to identify the source of the poison. They remained silent.

Musa turned to the surrounding captives and demanded angrily, "You must tell me who made the poison, otherwise these five girls will be killed."

Amidst the murmuring and wailing from the captives there came a scuffle and the culprit was pushed forward. She fell forward, her hair matted and dusty, her naked body streaked with sweat. The four *rugas* who had not eaten the food lashed her with their hide whips until Musa ordered them to stop. He told the woman to stand up and she struggled to her feet.

"Is it true?" he asked her. "Did you make the poison and give it to the girls?"

The woman nodded. She was bent over, swaying, and Musa asked her which girl had put the poison in the guards' food. She shook her head slowly.

"Well, you will be killed. You have caused me much trouble. You have delayed our journey to the coast, and you must pay for it."

Musa pondered about the method he should use to get rid of this woman. He decided to let the guards choose. The poisoned men were too ill to make a choice, but he called to the four *rugas* who had not eaten from the poisoned pot and asked them to select a method for killing the woman. Goodwill and Kawa were standing together and watched the men arguing in Swahili; they were shouting and gesticulating. They were saying that two of the poisoned guards had died. Finally, one of them went up to Musa and spoke to him.

The half-caste slaver approached the line of captives, gazing at them in his calm, contemplative way, but there was a glitter of fury in his eyes. "My men have chosen how this woman will die. It will be the crocodile!"

Gasps and cries rose from the captives, and the woman poisoner collapsed in a heap on the ground. The four healthy guards were prancing around her, one of them beating on his drum.

Musa continued, raising his voice. "She will be tied to a stake on the river bank, where a crocodile will come to take her." He raised his hand to silence the hubbub, and waved to the *rugas* to be quiet. "Two of my men have died from the poison, so I have decided that two of you slaves will be killed. This woman is one, and I will select one of the serving girls who put the poison in the food. If she will not admit responsibility, I must choose one."

43

He ordered the girls to be brought forward. The guards hauled and whipped them into a huddle in front of the line of captives. Goodwill felt faint as he watched Mary kneel down with the others. He knew that the victims would be tied to a strong stake on the river bank, so that the crocodile would not be able to drag them into the water, but would tear at their bodies. It would be a terrible wait and an agonising death.

Kawa put his arm around Goodwill's shoulder to steady him. "Let us hope he does not choose your sister."

Goodwill prayed that Musa would not choose Mary. He fell to his knees and put his hands together, bowing his head. Kawa, kneeling beside him, watched him and wondered if the prayers would have any effect.

Musa walked up to the girls and regarded them. He had slept with two of them, including Mary, before they had been given to the guards. He stretched out his arm and started to chant a rhyme to himself in Swahili. "Sun and moon, hot and cold, dry and wet, wind and rain, start again." As he chanted he pointed to the head of each slave girl.

— • —

5

"You might as well try to hunt an elephant with a pea-shooter!" Fred Moir sat back and shook with laughter. "What calibre do you have? Show it to me."

Alan handed over his rifle, diffidently. "It's a .357 magnum." He thought it was a really good piece of equipment. "High velocity – and very accurate."

More laughter from Moir. He had bushy dark hair and a huge spade-shaped beard that flowed down his chest. His eyes twinkled. "Wait until you're hot and sweating from chasing a herd of jumbos, and your heart is thumping when the bull turns towards you and trumpets and flaps his ears. What you need then, Spaight, is stopping power, not accuracy."

Alan was standing in front of the desk; he had not yet been invited to sit down. He decided to take a passive stance; after all, he was the new recruit. "What would you recommend, sir?"

"Nothing less that .450, and preferably .500."

"Could I buy one here?"

"I expect so. We can sell you a Snider – that's .577 calibre. It can stop a charging elephant in its tracks – presuming you can hit it – and if you don't have a misfire." He erupted into more laughter.

Surely I could hit an elephant, Alan thought. He was a very good shot; captain of his school VIII, and a champion at Sandhurst.

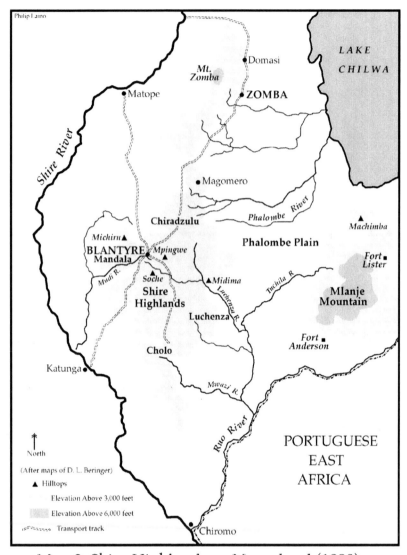

Map 3. Shire Highlands — Nyasaland (1890)

"Am I expected to hunt elephants?" He did not relish the prospect, having always regarded them as peaceful, intelligent animals.

"Depends. We make income from ivory. We have to give one tusk to the local chief. The other tusk we sell to raise funds for imports..."

"What happens to the chief's tusk?"

"Usually it's sold back to us." Moir snorted.

"For cloth and beads?"

"Precisely. You are not forced to hunt, Spaight, but if you're keen you can."

The door opened and Fred Moir's brother John came into the room. Alan knew they had been appointed 'founding' joint general managers of the Company soon after its formation in 1877. At the time they were in their mid-twenties and had spent some time in East Africa opening roads from the coast. Now, ten years later, they were 'old Africa hands', and seemed much older than him.

John Moir was clean-shaven except for fashionable drooping moustaches. Alan thought he looked rather studious. He wore spectacles – the famous ones that gave the Company its nickname – and like his younger brother spoke with a strong Scottish accent.

"Are you not going to let the young man sit down?" he remonstrated.

Fred waved to a chair and indicated that Alan should sit in it. "We were talking about elephant guns. Spaight has a .357."

John Moir sucked at his teeth. "Too light, Spaight. Better get something larger." He sat down in an armchair in the corner of the room. "Now, tell us about yourself."

He told them he was twenty-six years old, that his father was a Scottish lawyer, and his mother English. Because his father worked for a London firm the family lived in England, spending the summers in Scotland. He had been to Cheltenham College, a minor public school, and then to Sandhurst – the military academy.

"I was lucky to get a commission," he added. "in the Royal Berkshires. I was posted to the Sudan in '84, and then seconded to the 15th Ludhiana Sikhs. I went back to India with them and spent two years there; then I resigned my commission and returned to England."

"We know about your father," said John Moir, "And your uncle, Bentham Russell, spoke highly of you. Why did you leave the army?"

He shrugged, and tried to make it sound unimportant. "It wasn't the way of life I wanted – but the deciding factor was a run-in I had with my Colonel."

"We heard stories about that – what happened?"

He wondered how much he should tell them, suspecting they knew more than they were revealing. "He told me to order the flogging of one of my NCOs. I refused, because the man had not had any trial or hearing – it was just the word of another officer – who I did not trust. The Colonel told me to write out my resignation that day."

"I suppose he argued that orders must not be questioned? That's the way the army works." John Moir was frowning. "Was flogging common practice? What was the typical sentence?"

"The extent of flogging depended on the views of the senior officers. They were not all in favour. The typical sentence was forty to sixty lashes. But it wasn't the *type* of punishment I opposed – it was the lack of any hearing or trial. The Sikh NCO was accused of theft by a young British ensign who was fairly new to the regiment. The senior NCOs were convinced that the alleged culprit was not involved."

John Moir turned to his brother. "Shades of the missionaries in Blantyre," he said.

In response to Alan's questioning expression, Fred Moir said to his brother, "Perhaps we shouldn't go into that now."

John Moir said, "He'll hear about it sooner or later." To Alan he added, "I expect you know that the Church of Scotland started a mission here in '76. It was started by artisans, but was later headed by a minister named Duff Macdonald. In '79 the mission staff were punishing miscreants rather too severely. They had no proper system for trying suspects. A hundred lashes and time in the stocks was a typical sentence for theft. There were a couple of cases of sentenced men dying and one was executed."

"Was there no magisterial system?" Alan asked.

Fred Moir laughed. "Not then, nor now. It was argued by some that the suspects should have been sent to their chief for trial under local law, but such trials would probably have been bizarre and the punishments might have been more severe, even brutal."

"So an enquiry was held," continued John Moir. "The Church of Scotland appointed a Dr Rankin, and he was assisted by a lawyer named Pringle. They 'recalled' virtually the entire staff of the mission."

"Except for a couple of artisans," added Fred Moir. "One of them was John Buchanan, the gardener, who had moved to Zomba before the enquiry. He's now a coffee planter – I'm sure you'll meet him soon."

"You wouldn't take him for a flogger," mused John Moir. "But perhaps your Colonel was a strong silent type like him."

Fred went to a locked cupboard and took out a bottle of whisky and three glasses. He started pouring tots. "I want to hear what those fellows in London told you about the company." He looked at his brother. "We'll have a dram?"

Alan summoned up memories of meeting with officials of the African Lakes Company in London. "They told me that you were pioneering commercial trading in this region. They said that Dr Livingstone wanted to establish trading as a means to rid the country of slavery..."

"True," said John Moir, sipping from his glass tumbler. "The good doctor knew that there had to be an alternative to the trade in slaves. He also thought that legitimate trade in goods would bring Europeans here. Sadly, that will take too long. We need to stop the slaving as soon as we can. Trouble is, the company is not equipped to fight the slavers. It really isn't our job, either. Nor can the missionaries do it – it's even less their job."

"You see," interposed Fred Moir, "there's no authority here. This is not even a country – in the legal entity sense. We have no government, no law, no police force. The only Europeans are the missionaries and company officials such as ourselves..."

"...and a handful of hunters," added his brother. "Tell us about your journey?"

—•—

Alan had been recruited as a trader, starting on a low rung with the prospect of rising much higher. The Moir brothers were pleased during this first meeting. The young man seemed assured without being over-confident. He was cheerful but gave their opinions serious considera-tion. He had the right sort of background – service in the army and formal training in estate management, which included accounting and secretarial practice.

They regarded him shrewdly. "You look as if you need a good feed," said John Moir. "You'll find they have quite good food at the company mess. You must come to supper tomorrow; I'll ask my Mrs Moir to cook something special for you." He added: "I'll ask Dr McPhail to come. He has just returned from Karonga, at the north end of the Lake, so we can hear a first-hand account of conditions there. You see, you may be sent there soon – to assist Monteith Fothering-ham, the manager there."

"What exactly will be my duties, sirs?" He tried not to sound querulous.

Fred chortled. "Nothing is exact in this place, Spaight, as you'll soon find out..."

"Monteith has built us a trading store in Karonga," John interrupted. "It's a sort of lake port, but there's no proper harbour. There's a large African village there. He's planning some smaller stores in the district, but he has to negotiate with the local chiefs. Also he's working on extending the road into the interior. We plan to take it to Lake Tangany-ika. We call it the Stevenson Road, after the benefactor, who's a director of the company. You'll assist Fotheringham in all these activities."

"But you'll be faced with serious difficulties," said Fred Moir. "There's a slave-trader there, named Mlozi, who is disrupting the region by trading in slaves and ivory. He has a large militia that finds little opposition from the local natives. We fear that unless Mlozi is brought to book, the company will not be able to operate in the area much longer."

Alan cleared his throat; he wasn't sure whether he should ask a lot of questions. "Why is so little being done to stop the slavery – I mean by the government at home?"

John Moir raised his eyebrows. "You may well ask. You see, Spaight, we are not really equipped to tackle the slavers. When Livingstone and his fellow missionaries came here they were severely criticized for taking pre-emptive action to release slaves from their captors. Our task in the Company is to support the missionaries. We don't have the resources to fight the slavers."

"But," he started, "I've been reading Edward Young's book 'Nyassa', and he was quite clear that the British authorities ought to put a gunboat on the Lake. He said it would be effective in stopping the transport of slaves across the Lake. He even estimated the cost – I think it was ten thousand pounds, ten years ago – that doesn't seem a lot to me..."

"True," interrupted John Moir. "Young was a fine man, an excellent sailor – and foresighted".

"I mean you could put a gun on your boat, couldn't you – the *Ilala*, the one Young brought to the Lake?"

"Hold on, young man!" Fred expostulated, tugging on his beard. "You've been in this country for how long? Three days? You'll find out it's not so easy. If we started firing from the *Ilala* at the slavers' *dhows* it would be a declaration of war. Sooner or later we would have to fight on land and then we would be horribly outnumbered. That was the flaw in Young's thesis. You see, not all the slaves are transported across the Lake. Many of them are taken overland to the north of the

Lake, and others to the south – around Lake Chilwa. A gunboat would be valuable in a broader strategy, but would have to be supported by ground troops."

"And there is no likelihood of seeing any of them – not for the foreseeable future," added his brother gloomily.

—•—

Alan was given a room at the company mess in Blantyre, a four bed-room house made of sun-dried bricks, with a grass-thatched roof. It stood in a rectangle of cleared ground surrounded by natural bushveld, most of which had been thinned for firewood. Beyond, the forest stretched for hundreds of miles. The other three bedrooms were occupied by men who were younger; they worked for Mandala as storemen and clerks. Two of them had been recruited in England, the other in South Africa. They showed him to his room and talked to him as he unpacked.

"So you're going to have supper with the Moirs?" said the South African, whose name was Dirk. "We've all been there – once."

Hubert, the older of the two Englishmen, already portly, said to him, "Well you don't expect the bosses to have you to eat every night do you?"

Dirk's shrug was his only reply. He was tall and fair-haired, in-clined to be sullen.

"They've invited a Dr McPhail," Alan said. "He's just come back from Karonga, so he'll be able to give me news about conditions there."

"No doubt Mrs McPhail – the lovely Nora – will be there," said the younger Englishman wistfully. His name was Peter Moore; he looked under-nourished.

His companions laughed. "Poor Peter; we think he's fallen in love with her."

"There's precious few women here to fall in love with," said Dirk. "I heard today that there are only nine adult women in the country..."

"You mean white women," Alan said.

"Of course, man. The natives don't count, do they. Unless you're desperate, of course." The South African laughed. "You might feel like that in Karonga. There aren't any white women there – at all!"

Alan's room was crudely furnished with a bed, a small table, and a chair. They had been made out of packing cases used to ship materials from England. The floor was hard beaten earth and the walls were covered with skimmed mud. Hessian cloth had been used to make a rough ceiling, which would also catch any insects or other vermin that might fall from the thatched roof.

It was winter, and the nights in Blantyre were cold enough to warrant a fire. The four men sat in front of the crackling logs and talked about life in the settlement, about shooting and cricket, about their bosses, and about the lack of young women. Their supper was brought by an African servant and consisted of boiled guinea-fowl and rice, followed by fresh mangoes. After supper they returned to the fire and lit pipes.

"What do you think of Tweedledum and Tweedledee?" asked Hubert.

Alan laughed. "They seem decent enough. Do you like them?"

"They're as tough as old boots," snorted Hubert. "They are very superior about being old Africa hands, and dealing with natives – they think no one knows as much as they do?"

"But they have been here a long time," said Peter Moore. "Came here in '79, but they had worked in Dar-es-Salaam before that. My biggest criticism is the pittance they pay us, and the conditions we work in."

"Do you get out of Blantyre much?" Alan asked.

"Oh of course," answered Hubert, with a sarcastic tone. "We make regular trips down to Katunga and Matope – on the river, to supervise the unloading and loading of the ships. All the barter goods and other materials have to be carried overland through Blantyre. It's stored and recorded here before being dispatched to other places. It's our job to supervise all that."

"We've all been to the Lake," added Dirk, "but only once. We'll go again some time."

"So you've never been to Karonga?"

"No, and I'm not keen to go – sorry, Alan, but it's right out in the bush. The only white man there is Fotheringham, and he's a funny bloke. There's a couple of missionaries at Chirenje, a few miles inland from Karonga."

He asked about their social life in Blantyre. "There's the club," answered Peter. "Everything happens at the club. We have about twenty members..."

"Is that all?" Alan was surprised.

"Of course. There are only about fifty people in this part of Africa – white people, I mean. There's about twenty in Blantyre, and the rest are scattered around in mission stations, and men like Fotheringham – and a few hunters. Anyway, we have a good time at the club. We play cricket and soccer, and we have Scottish country dancing."

"Trouble is," said Hubert, "there aren't enough girls."

"There aren't any," grumbled Dirk. There's only married women and children. I don't think there's one single woman."

"There's Phyllis," said Peter, and they all burst into laughter.

"Who's Phyllis?" Alan asked, joining in their laughter.

"She's the sister of the storeman's wife. She's very plain – to be polite. Mind you, after a few more months here we might start to think she's good looking."

Alan decided not to tell them about Jess Kennedy, mostly because he did not want to hear her as the subject of any ribald comments.

Peter Moore said, "Well there are some nice looking wives..."

"Oh yes, and he's thinking of Nora McPhail", added Hubert knowingly.

"And there's Sarah Bruce," Peter retorted.

"That's about all the adult women there are," Hubert sighed. "We can only dream – and long for our leave."

Dirk threw another log on the fire. "I don't envy you going up to the north, Alan. Sounds as if it's all savages there – maybe even cannibals." He glanced at Hubert with a smirk.

"Seriously," said Hubert, "there'll just be you and the grumpy Mr Fotheringham among thousands of primitive tribesmen who are being stirred up by Arab slave traders. No, I don't envy you either."

Alan said nothing but was growing more concerned about his prospects. He had imagined something more easy-going and interesting, with opportunities for travel, sport and other recreation. He never imagined anything as hostile as the environment that seemed to await him.

— • —

Three days after he arrived in Blantyre some mail arrived at the mess. There was a letter from Alan's mother, with news of his brother and sister:

My dearest Alan,

Your father and I are missing you so much. We wonder all the time about where you are and whether you are safe. It seems to us as if you have disappeared into a void and we will be concerned until we hear from you.

Fiona has had her exam results and we think she will be accepted. She is very excited at the prospect of going to University at Oxford. It will be easier for her knowing that she has several friends who will start with her.

David has been messing around in boats all through the holidays and is itching to get back to Dartmouth. He envies you going on that long voyage – following Vasca da Gama, as he says. He is looking forward to reading your account of your journey – indeed, we all are.

We went to visit Uncle Bentham and Aunt Isobel last week-end. It was glorious summer weather and we were able to take tea in the garden. They had just heard from your cousin Martin that he, too, has resigned his commission. They told us that he was not satisfied with the Army way of life and is coming home soon. He has a place at Oxford, studying Natural Sciences – so he and Fiona will be undergraduates together.

The letter also gave him news of other family and friends. He folded it up and put it in his suitcase, from which he took a notecase which held writing paper, pen and ink, to write his reply.

—•—

6

Alan Spaight walked the two blocks to Mandala House at dusk. It was a cold evening and he wore his smartest clothes, a khaki cotton suit, white shirt and tie. The suit was a bit crumpled; there was no smoothing iron at the mess.

Mandala House was by far the largest structure in Blantyre. It was built of fired bricks with a corrugated iron roof, and had spacious verandahs on both floors. He went up the stairs and was greeted by John Moir and taken into the drawing room where he was introduced to Elizabeth Moir, a solidly built Scottish woman in her late thirties with rosy cheeks and a ready smile. Fred Moir and his wife Jane were there too. The ladies asked him about his family and his journey from England.

They were joined by David Robertson, a missionary with the Free Church of Scotland. He was tall and jovial, and soon engaged Alan in conversation about his roots in Scotland, and a mutual interest in fishing. Robertson had come to Blantyre not long after the mission started, and later moved to the branch at Domasi, north of Zomba, where he built a small church and a school.

A few minutes later the McPhails arrived. Alistair, the doctor, was thirty years old, of medium height and rather frail looking. His dark hair was very long and his beard unkempt; he explained that he had not had time to have it cut since his recent return from Karonga.

It was Nora McPhail who captured Alan's attention. She looked young enough to be a schoolgirl, though he discovered in conversation that she was twenty-three and had a year-old child. She was quite tall, with long brown hair plaited and coiled around her head. She had large brown eyes that regarded him seriously. She wore a long pinafore dress. He was surprised at the strength of her handshake; she spoke with a Highland Scottish accent.

Now that all the guests were present they were led into the dining room. Alan was seated between Elizabeth Moir and Alistair McPhail, and since the hostess was busy ensuring that the food was correctly served, he spoke mostly to the doctor. The Moir brothers had asked McPhail to tell them all about his trip.

"Poor Fotheringham," said the doctor, "he firmly believes that the slaver Mlozi wants to oust him and the Company from Karonga."

"Who is this Mlozi?" Alan asked.

McPhail nodded to Fred Moir to answer.

"He's a half-caste Mohammedan who came to the north end of the Lake about three years ago," said Moir. "He'd been around before that, perhaps going as far as the Luangwa Valley. He settled at a place called Mpata – a few miles inland from Karonga's village. The local people are WaNkonde, a peaceful agricultural tribe; they have no weapons other than bows and arrows. Mlozi wasted no time in subjugating them. He used his militia of men from the coast. They're armed – mostly with flintlocks. He started a lucrative trade in slaves and ivory, with the connivance of local chiefs."

"Has Mlozi threatened Mr Fotheringham?"

"Not yet," replied Dr McPhail, "but he has the potential to make trouble. I fear that Monteith is ill-equipped to offer any resistance. He has a dozen old rifles, but the natives using them are barely trained." The doctor turned to the Moir brothers. "Is there nothing we can do to help him? Can't we send him reinforcements?"

The brothers looked at each other; John answered. "We are thinking about it, McPhail. But our resources are stretched. We're sending young Spaight up there..."

"You have military training, Spaight?" asked the doctor.

As he spoke Alan was feeling more and more concerned about his future. What had seemed a straightforward job in Africa was now becoming a potential nightmare, peopled by aggressive savages, like the ones he'd escaped in the Sudan. He was relieved when the subject changed to more mundane matters – a forthcoming dance and a cricket match.

After the meal the men went out onto the verandah to smoke their pipes. An animated discussion started, about the cause of malaria.

"I had a letter from a friend who went to a meeting in Edinburgh," said Alistair McPhail. "They were talking about a fellow named Laveran who is said to have isolated a parasite that they think causes the fever."

"How can it do that?" asked John Moir.

"By infecting the blood cells."

"So how do we get the parasite? Could it be from mosquito bites?"

McPhail shrugged. "Perhaps. There's no proof that they carry the malaria."

"Besides," said Fred Moir, "they suck blood out of us. They don't put blood in."

"True," answered the doctor, "but it's possible that when the mosquito stings it pushes something through its proboscis into the skin, perhaps to stop the blood from clotting."

"That's a rum theory, Alistair," said Fred Moir. "If you're right, it would mean that all blood-sucking insects would do the same thing – for instance tsetse flies."

"Precisely. It may be that sleeping sickness is also caused by a blood parasite, and the tsetse fly may be the vector."

"What do you think of Livingstone's 'rousers'?" asked Robertson.

McPhail stroked his straggling beard. "I have some faith in them – if I can use that expression..."

"Could we make our own?" asked John Moir.

"Of course. I make and dispense them. I use eight grams of resin of jalap, eight grains of rhubarb liquor, three grains of calomel and three of quinine, and some tincture of cardamom that helps to make the pills. I give a man four pills and a woman half that number."

"What is jalap?" asked Robertson.

McPhail coughed. "It's a tuber, a member of the convolvulus family – you know, the 'morning glory'. I don't know how Livingstone got to include it in his prescription. I get my supply from India; it's grown in Ootacamund, in the hill country in the south."

Alan was trying to listen attentively, but his thoughts were drifting; his pipe had gone out. He looked back into the drawing room where Nora McPhail stood alone, looking at a book. Elizabeth Moir was evidently in the kitchen, and he knew that Jane Moir had gone home – she lived next door.

He went into the drawing room and Nora looked up and smiled.

"You are quite brave to go and live in Karonga," she said, moving towards him.

"Your husband has been up there..."

"Yes, but not to live. It's different if you are just visiting."

"I think you are brave – to come out here, to Africa – with all the hardships."

She laughed lightly. "It isn't so hard. The journey was quite trying – as you know – the heat and the mosquitoes. There were risks in having a baby here, but, as I always remind my friends back home, it's a natural process. If babies didn't survive, the human race would have become extinct." She laughed, and then added. "The climate in Blantyre is quite pleasant, don't you think?"

"Yes, it is. Surely you must be lonely when your husband is away?"

"A little. The Moirs keep an eye on me, and there are several couples who invite me for meals. I have my son to look after, and I have my horse to ride... Well, perhaps I'm more than a little lonely."

"A horse? I thought it wasn't possible to keep horses here."

"Oh, it is." She smiled indulgently. "The Moirs have three horses. There are no tsetse flies up here. There is horse sickness of course, but my mare Barushka is salted – she has had the disease and won't have it again – it's some kind of immunity."

"Surely to get her here you must have passed through tsetse fly country?"

Her brown eyes shone. "Of course. She came from South Africa. Her native groom covered her with a sort of poultice of aromatic leaves that kept the flies off her. Anyway, she's my delight." She put out her hand and touched his arm. "Do you ride, Alan?"

He nodded. "I used to ride a lot in Scotland. I've been out fox-hunting several times – in Oxfordshire, where my uncle lives."

She frowned. "I don't like hunting – it's so barbaric. I've never liked the types who do it. Don't mind me. Would you like to ride Barushka?" She touched his arm again.

"Oh yes." He was captivated, but reminded himself that this young woman was married. He supposed it would be quite proper to ride her horse.

"I have a jenny too – a female mule. They say mules are less prone the effects of tsetse fly bites. We could ride together."

"What is a mule like to ride?"

"Oh, she's not at all like the conventional image of a mule. She's docile and biddable; a pleasure to ride."

Elizabeth Moir came from the kitchen. She said, "I hope you'll come to the dance in our party, Alan. I think you'll enjoy it. I suspect you won't want to talk shop like John and Fred, so you can give us ladies a whirl round the floor."

—•—

A few days later he heard that Jess Kennedy had started working as a nurse at the hospital in Blantyre. Just as she had told him, she was living with the McPhails, and in exchange for her board and lodging helped to look after their baby son. The men at the mess were almost frantic with desire to meet her, and envious that Alan had already spent the best part of a week in her company. They hoped she would come to the dance, but he told them she would probably return to the farm at weekends.

The cricket match was on Saturday at the Blantyre Club. The African Lakes Company, Mandala, played 'The Others'; there were only seven players on each side, so fielders had to be shared. Alan was a competent medium-pace bowler and managed to take several wickets for Mandala. While fielding he searched the crowd for the Kennedys.

"Looking for someone?" Dirk came up beside him and sniggered.

—•—

The dance was held at the Blantyre Club which had an auditorium for meetings; it could seat up to fifty people and was large enough for dances. The band consisted of three men, a pianist, a violinist and Hubert on drums. Because most of those attending were Scottish, the dances were mostly of the country variety, interspersed with the occasional waltz; there were plenty of reels. Alan knew most of the dances well, having been brought up in an Anglo-Scottish family.

The Moir party sat at a round table and consisted of the brothers and their wives, the McPhails, and Alan. There was no partner designated for him, but, to his surprise, Dr McPhail seemed reluctant to dance, stepping onto the floor only when cajoled by his young wife.

Nora was much in demand; the young men gathered around, pleading with her to put their names on her programme. But she told them firmly that she would dance mostly with the members of her party. The Moir brothers were often engaged in conversations about business and

Alan was thus able to step onto the floor several times with Nora. It was during the waltzes that he learned more about her.

She had been a nurse in the hospital in Edinburgh where Alistair McPhail completed his medical studies. She was an only child, and her elderly parents had been quite obstructive about her studying nursing and taking a position with the hospital. They felt it was not really appropriate for a young girl just out of school to be exposed to the harsh reality of tending to patients in a ward. They were somewhat mollified when the newly qualified Alistair McPhail asked them for their daughter's hand in marriage. He was seven years her elder, but had good prospects. Then, to their dismay, he applied for a post with Mandala in Africa.

"Alistair's a great admirer of Dr Livingstone," she said. "He has read all his journals, and several books written about the great man. So it was natural that he should want to come out here. I encouraged him because I wanted to come too, despite my parents' objections."

"I can understand how they would be concerned." He was finding it difficult to concentrate on the waltz while listening to Nora; her physical proximity was disturbing and he suspected that she was being provocative.

"Well, they had the typical misconceptions of what life is like here. They thought it would be unbearably hot and steamy. But it's really quite pleasant, don't you think? They thought the place would be overrun with lions and other dangerous wild animals. Anyway, I like it, even though it can be a bit lonely when Alistair goes on *ulendo*."

When she laughed he could feel the vibration of her breasts against his chest, as she held him closer.

"Is it much different to what you expected?" she asked.

He swallowed, feeling his tongue dry and knotted. "I never expected to meet a young woman like you."

She giggled. "I do believe you are flirting with me, Mr Spaight."

"Oh no. Well..."

"Well?"

"You are very attractive, Nora, but I know you are bespoken."

"That's very quaint, but thank you for the compliment."

—•—

He spent his working days learning how Mandala operated. He was shown the warehouses, mostly large thatched huts, where the imported goods were stored, and was taught about the system for keeping the inventory. The company imported large quantities of cloth in bales, as well as beads and copper wire, all of which were used as quasi currency. At that time there was no proper currency, although some British banknotes were used amongst the expatriates. Certainly the Africans had never seen a note or coin.

Hubert, who was his guide said, "This calico is much in demand by the natives." It was plain woven cotton, undyed, and from low quality yarn. "We also import goods required by the European settlers, such as building materials, cooking utensils, clothing, and dry foods."

He showed Alan how Mandala kept its accounts, and how it transported goods to its stores in different locations around the country.

"Outside Blantyre," said Hubert, "there are stores in Katunga and Matope on the Shire River; Zomba; and Karonga on Lake Nyasa – where you're going. There are no roads to these stores, only sort of wide footpaths, so we use river and lake transport as much as possible."

He explained that Mandala had two screw-driven lake steamers: the *Ilala*, the first to ply the Lake, and the *Domira*, which had just arrived. The company also had the four paddle steamers on the Lower Shire.

Alan knew that the *Ilala was* named after the district where David Livingstone died, and had been built in England and brought out to the Lake via South Africa in 1875. She had been disassembled for the voyage and re-built at the mouth of the Zambezi, to steam up the Shire River to the Murchison Cataracts. She was then disassembled again and the parts carried to the Upper Shire, where she was re-built for the last time.

"What about the *Domira,*" he asked Hubert.

"She was built in Scotland – I think last year – she's larger than the *Ilala* – about 90 feet long and 15 feet wide. The Universities Mission has a steamer, named the *Charles Janson...*"

"That's the missionary who died of fever on the shore of the Lake?"

"That's right. She's a 65 foot single screw steamer, built a few years ago. Both the *Domira* and the *Charles Janson* were brought to the Lake in the same way as the *Ilala*."

In the evenings Alan would often walk to the club with his fellow residents from the mess. They ate supper on the verandah, and there was a bar that served whisky, gin and beer. The billiard table was greatly in demand. The Moir brothers seldom visited the club, though when they came they would buy a round of drinks for the young company employees. The McPhails never came to the club.

Five days after the dance he saw Nora riding along one of the wide streets. She sat astride her mare Barushka, wearing khaki trousers, with a solar topi perched on her head. She looked utterly delectable, as she steered the horse towards him.

"How are you, Alan?"

"I've missed you."

"I have exciting news. The Consul, Mr Hawes, has invited Alistair to start a new hospital in Zomba. He'll be leaving the company."

"So when will you move there?"

"As soon as we can."

"Surely there aren't enough people in Zomba to warrant a hospital." He was standing beside the horse, his hand on its neck, looking up at her.

"Your counting only Europeans, Alan." Her tone was mildly reproving. "This hospital is for both races – in separate buildings, of course.

Alistair will be the district medical officer, and I will be his nurse. He's not interested in titles, but he's excited about the new venture. Jess Kennedy will work for us as a nurse and my part-time nanny."

He had not yet been to Zomba; it was forty miles north of Blantyre, so a day's journey. By all accounts there were just a few houses clustered at the base of a mountain that rose to over four thousand feet. The place was reputed to be cooler and healthier than Blantyre.

"Would you like to come for a ride, Alan? Tomorrow? You can have Barushka, I'll ride Jenny – the mule."

He was ecstatic and could think of little else until the following day. He walked to the McPhail house after work and found Nora saddling the mule outside the stables, behind the house. She wore a white cotton shirt and khaki trousers as before, and looked cool and demure. She insisted that he ride Barushka. They followed a wide path into the hills above the town, riding side by side.

"What will it be like, living in Zomba?" he asked.

"We'll have a small house – we'll build it ourselves." She laughed. "I don't mean we'll lay the bricks, but we'll design it and supervise the builders. John Buchanan will help – he's a planter who lives near Zomba. He and his brothers know about building houses. They've been commissioned by Mr Hawes to build a Residency in Zomba. Our house will be near the new hospital. It will be an adventure. There are only a few Europeans there – we know some of the planters, like the Buchanans and the Kennedys. It will be a quiet life. I'll have my son Malcolm to look after, and I'll ride Barushka and Jenny. There's a track to ride up to the plateau at the top of Zomba Mountain. I've been there once – it's so beautiful – like a huge bowl, with a stream that flows out over the edge of the escarpment. It's the same stream from which we'll get the water for the new hospital." Her eyes were shining and he felt truly smitten.

On returning to the house they were met by a servant who came out with a note.

"Alistair's held up at the hospital – an emergency appendectomy. You can stay for tea, keep me company until he gets home."

She had a young groom waiting to look after the horse and mule, but dismissed him and did the work herself, with Alan helping. They removed saddles and bridles, rubbed down the coats of Barushka and Jenny, and gave them water and hay. It was growing dark and the only light in the stables came from a hurricane lamp near the door. A moment came when Nora passed him and she caught him and pulled him against her.

She kissed him vigorously and he could feel the movements of her breathing. She held his cheeks in her hands.

"You're on fire," she said.

"You're married."

She laughed. "I think I know that."

A moment later she added, "We have to go, Alan. Come." She led him by the hand to the house.

It had all happened so suddenly. He wondered if she was just flirting with him. Perhaps she did this with any new young man who appeared on her scene. Or was she genuinely lonely and wanting some deeper involvement?

The house servant was in the parlour and Nora gave him instructions in ChiNyanja, to make tea. She waved Alan to a seat. "You're a sweet boy, but..."

"Boy?"

She smiled. "I think of you as young, because you're younger than my husband. If you were not so sweet I would never have... We will see each other again. I don't want Alistair to become suspicious – and I don't want anyone else to find out what we're doing. I trust you not to say anything."

He wondered what they were doing. It almost sounded as if she was scheming, drawing him into her net. He did not want to become involved with a married woman, but he found her achingly attractive.

At that moment the servant came in with the tea. Nora quickly poured for them and brought Alan his cup. She went to fetch her son and came back with a dark-haired child. Malcolm was nearly a year old and able to totter around the room, squealing with high-pitched laughter, much to the entertainment of his mother.

"Where is Jess?" he asked.

"She's not well – stayed at home the last couple of days."

They were silent for a while, then she said, "You must leave now, Alan. It would be better if you were not here when Alistair gets back."

He nodded and stood up. She took his hand and squeezed it. "We'll ride again next week."

—•—

7

Towards the East Coast - September 1887

Musa let his hand drop onto the head of the girl kneeling beside Mary. She wailed with anguish, knowing the horror of her fate. A chorus of gasps swept through the captives gathered round. Mary fainted and was hurriedly pulled away by her companions. The *ruga-rugas* rushed forward and dragged the woman poisoner and the young girl towards the river.

The clearing on the bank was about a hundred yards from the village. The slave captives watched the guards tie the woman and the girl to stakes driven into the earth. The men then retreated into the scrub, so that the crocodiles would not see them.

A crocodile lay on the far bank of the stream; it slid quietly into the water while the victims were being tied. It drifted with only its nostrils and eyes protruding above the surface, and watched until there was no more movement. It could see the two females on the ground and recognized that they were potential prey when they moved their arms and legs.

This crocodile was about fourteen feet long and had survived for two decades by balancing caution with aggression. The victims were only a few feet from the bank, and there was a shallow gully where the villagers were accustomed to step down to fill their pots with water. The crocodile had watched this activity many times, but kept away because the people beat the water with sticks. However, this time there were no people – only the two writhing bodies.

With powerful sweeps of its tail the reptile glided towards the bank. It had made its decision. Keeping its body low to the ground it scrambled up the short gully and onto the flat ground. The victims were ten feet away. The crocodile paused to assess the scene, its amber eyes glittering with reflections of the camp fires. Goodwill and Kawa watched from the outskirts of the village, about a hundred yards away, as did most of the captives. A few of them, including Mary, turned away.

The crocodile dashed forward with amazing speed. It caught the young girl by one of her legs and her shriek rose to the onlookers, who gasped and muttered. The great reptile lunged back, attempting to wrench its prey loose and carry it back to the water. But it was thwarted by the bindings holding the girl to the stake. It tried again and another piercing scream came from the unfortunate victim.

This time the crocodile succeeded in breaking the ropes. It quickly dragged the girl into the water. The *rugas* shouted and danced to the beat of their drums. Musa stood to one side, watching impassively. The captives wondered how long it would be before another crocodile came for the woman poisoner.

Nearly an hour passed before a second crocodile emerged from the river; this one was a mere eight feet long. It, too, advanced up the bank in stages, pausing before each spurt. When it finally clamped its jaws on the victim it lacked the strength to break her remaining bonds. Finding itself undisturbed it wrenched the limbs off the unfortunate woman until her torso, with one arm still attached, was free of the ropes. It then dragged her into the stream.

Throughout the ordeal this woman had remained silent. The captives conjectured about the reason. Some thought she must be a witch, while others said she had fainted. The *rugas* emerged cautiously from the scrub and picked up the woman's legs and arm, throwing them into the river with shouts and laughter.

— • —

A few days after the crocodile execution Kawa started limping. Good-will, at the other end of the *goree* pole, noticed it at once. At the noon rest Kawa examined his left foot. The sole was like hardened leather, but the side of his instep was extremely painful. He asked Goodwill to look at it.

"I think you have a thorn in your foot," said Goodwill. "The pain is because the wound has become bad. It smells like rotten meat."

Kawa laughed. "You are not polite." Then he winced as his friend squeezed the place. A dribble of pale yellow pus emerged. "What shall I do? If I can't walk they will kill me."

Goodwill shook his head. "We must take out the thorn; then we must clean the wound." He found a twig and snapped a piece off it, to give a sharp point, which he sucked to wash off the dirt. Then he probed in the inflamed wound, feeling the thorn embedded there. Each time he touched the thorn Kawa jerked in pain. Goodwill wondered how he could pluck the thorn out. He fashioned another probing twig, this one with a broader point. Then he tried to pinch the thorn between the two twigs.

While he was doing this the *rugas* shouted to the captives to get ready to march. One of them came up to the two young men to see what they were doing. They called to Musa.

The half-caste strolled up to the group. "What are you doing?" he asked of Goodwill, who explained how he was trying to extract the thorn.

"How long will it take?"

"I think I can take it out in a few minutes," Goodwill replied. "Then I need to suck out the poison and wrap his foot in a cloth."

"Will he be able to walk?"

Goodwill looked into Musa's eyes, wondering if the slaver was calculating whether to dispose of Kawa so that the caravan could keep moving. "He should be able to walk, but it would be easier if he did not have to carry the tusk."

71

"Then you can carry the tusk yourself." Musa's voice was gentle and sinister.

"I will. But if my friend cannot walk I will need to carry him."

Two of the *rugas* who were standing nearby snorted in derision, but Musa merely smiled. "Let us see. Now, get on with your medicine."

He waved the guards away and watched as Goodwill poked the twigs into the wound. Within a couple of minutes he extracted the thorn. Kawa let out a deep sigh. Then Goodwill bent down and sucked the wound, periodically spitting out the pus. Since both men were naked, the only cloth they had to bind the wound was a folded piece of calico that Kawa had used to pad his shoulder when he was carrying the tusk. Goodwill tore a narrow strip off it, and used it to bind the remaining cloth round Kawa's foot.

"See if you can walk," said Musa quietly.

Kawa tried a few steps. It was agonising, but he knew his life depended on it.

"I could make him a crutch," said Goodwill.

Musa nodded and called to the guards. They hurried up to their master, who instructed them to cut the crutch from saplings growing nearby. The slaver told the guards to remove the *goree* from the captives' necks, and within minutes Kawa was swinging along the path. Goodwill followed with the tusk on his shoulder.

Emboldened by the slaver's apparent generosity, Goodwill said to him, "My sister knows plants that will heal my friend's wound."

"She can find some tonight," answered Musa and moved ahead.

— • —

It took another two months for the caravan to reach a place called Nacala, near the Mozambique coast. Musa was concerned about Portuguese soldiers. It was not that they would prevent him from continuing his trade, but they might extract extortionate bribes. So he moved the caravan away from the main track, onto smaller paths leading to the north.

Goodwill and Kawa were now carriers of Musa's *machila* – he had grown tired of walking. The canvas hammock was suspended from two stout bamboo poles. A man bore each end of the poles, four in total. Every hour they changed with another team of four, resting as they walked without any load.

The two young men preferred carrying the slaver. He was not a large man, weighing perhaps a hundred and fifty pounds. They were still chained together when carrying and resting. Musa came to know them by name and made sure that they were given sufficient food to maintain their strength. Goodwill tried to make contact with his sister, but the guards kept their serving girls away from the other captives.

In October they reached the coast. It was the first time they had seen the sea; they thought it was another great lake, but the *ruga rugas* explained in condescending terms that this was the real sea – the ocean – and it was limitless.

They came to a fishing village where two *dhows* were moored; the slaves were embarked and chained up below the deck. Rumours spread among them, and the consensus was that they would sail for Pemba, further north on the Mozambique coast, where there was a slave market. It was general knowledge, imparted by the *rugas*, that some of the males would be castrated before being sold.

Goodwill and Kawa often discussed the dreadful prospect. "I would rather die that lose my balls," said Kawa gloomily.

Goodwill said, "I heard a guard say that some men will escape the knife."

"We cannot risk that. We must escape before we reach Pemba. How long do we have?"

"They say three days, but the weather is bad, so it might take longer. They have to sail into the wind, and you know how difficult that is."

Kawa nodded. "Where is your sister?"

"I was told she is on the other ship. I'm worried about her, Kawa. They said she has fever. There's no way I can help her."

"I'm sorry, my friend."

The two young men were lying on the lower deck of the *dhow*, among the other male slaves. They were chained by their necks, and the chain was passed through a ring in the deck. Other slaves were merely roped together. There was scarcely room to move. They felt the *dhow* twist and heard it groan. Shouts rang out from the crew. The ship was leaving the small harbour. She heeled over and some of the slaves cried out in fear. Then the *dhow* started to roll rhythmically and seasickness overcame most of the captives. The stench was terrible, confined as it was to the overcrowded hold.

— • —

When they disembarked at Pemba the slaves were segregated, males from females, and Goodwill realised that he might never see his sister again. He thought he glimpsed her shuffling away, head bent, among a group of girls. The men were taken to a stockade where they spent the night knowing that on the following day the decision would be made about their castration.

The rains would soon come and the days were blisteringly hot. Huge thunderclouds gathered on the horizon and flickered with lightning like enormous lanterns. The coconut palm fronds lashed to and fro, and sand grains flew into the slaves' eyes.

Next day they were led out into a sunlit square, where Musa and a robed Arab examined each of the men in turn, exchanging remarks in Arabic that the captives could not understand. A guard carrying a slate made notes of their decisions while another with a brush and pot daubed white lime on the shoulder of those chosen for the operation.

Goodwill and Kawa were shaking with agitation, but were passed over, to their great relief. They were soon put in a team of strong men to hold each victim on a flat board, in a supine position. A guard would tie a tight ligature around the root of the scrotum, then slice open the sack and cut out the testicles. The procedure took less than a minute, but there was no anaesthetic. The victims thrashed and struggled, while Goodwill and some others who had been spared held them as best they could. Some fainted, others staggered away, blood dribbling down their legs.

—•—

A couple of days later the two friends were taken onto a *dhow* and the guards told them they were heading north for the Persian Gulf, where they would be sold in a slave market. As they were led onto the ship they saw Musa standing by.

"Goodwill! Kawa!" he called to them, "I might see you when we get to Doha".

The *dhow* was large enough to carry sixty captives; all of them were held below in the foetid hold where the only light and air came through cracks in the hatches. Goodwill and Kawa lay beside each other. As before, their neck chain passed through a ring bolted to the floor of the hold, but now their neck collars were fashioned from leather, not rope. Escape was impossible.

Kawa wriggled to try to get into a more comfortable position. He felt something sharp against his buttock and searching with his hands found a sharp piece of metal. He pulled it out of the decking. It was a short length of steel.

He nudged Goodwill and whispered. "Look at this."

"What is it?"

"It must have broken off something, perhaps when they were building the ship." He twisted round and said in Goodwill's ear. "Let us see if we can use it to free ourselves."

Kawa tried to saw the leather collar round his neck. It was too difficult and painful. There was no way that he could insert the steel between the collar and his neck. Instead, he decided to gouge out the ring holding their chain to the deck. He used the end of the steel piece to gouge out the wood around the bolt that held the ring to the deck. When he was tired Goodwill took over the task. They were careful to conceal everything from the guards.

It took them two days to release the bolt. Now, although they were still chained together, they were no longer attached to the deck.

"What now?" asked Goodwill.

"We wait."

—•—

8

When Alan returned to the mess he found a note from Fred Moir. It read: *"We've decided you should leave for Karonga on Monday. See me at the office tomorrow and we'll talk about plans."* It was signed *"F. Moir."*

Fred Moir was in buoyant mood next day. "You'll take the *Ilala* from Matope on Wednesday, so you'll have to leave here on Monday at noon, and camp for the night at Ntipe. You might be able to get to Matope on Tuesday evening; otherwise camp for a second night and get there early on Wednesday morning. Feel fit enough for that?"

"I think so. There are a few things I have to buy..."

"Of course. I've made a list for you." Moir pushed a sheet of paper across the desk. "I've given you Joseph, he's one of the Mandala *capitaos* who has been on *ulendo* with me several times. He'll look after you."

"How long will I be there – in Karonga?"

"Can't say, Alan. It depends somewhat on what Fotheringham wants to do. If he needs to take some leave for a few weeks you'll have to stay there to look after the store, so to speak. He wants you to supervise the work on the road to Chirenje – that's the one I was telling you about – the Stevenson Road. We must extend it further inland to Lake Tanganyika. It's not really a road, more of a track through the bush, so the work should go fast."

Alan imagined he was about to journey into a sort of void, where there were no means of communication. There would be no friends there, only natives, and the allegedly grumpy Mr Fotheringham.

—•—

They left Blantyre at noon on Monday and walked hard. Such journeys were known as 'going on *ulendo*'. It could be a casual affair, especially for the inexperienced, or for the impecunious hunter,. Alan had been on *ulendo* only once before, when he walked from Katunga to Blantyre, but now he had the benefit of the Moir brothers' years of experience. They offered him a mule to ride, but he preferred to walk and used the mule to carry his belongings.

The estimable Joseph, who had accompanied him on the journey from Katunga, was a jovial Nyanja. He organised the four bearers, known as *tenga-tengas* – the term came from the ChiNyanja word *tenga* – bring. They also had two Company guards carrying rifles, and Alan wondered how much use they would be if the little caravan was ambushed. The possibility of an attack from local natives, or a gang of Angoni tribesmen, was remote, but the Moirs assured him that an armed guard was a worthwhile deterrent.

Fortunately the trek was mostly downhill. There were few wild animals to be seen because much of the forest on both sides of the track had been cut down for firewood by travellers. The air was chilly and clear when they started, but the temperature rose sharply with the sun, and the views became hazy with wood smoke.

Joseph was a cheerful companion, and Alan found it easy to converse with him. He pointed out and named the birds and small antelopes that scattered when they approached. He explained that this track had been used many times, and camps had been made at frequent points along it. Trees had been cut down to build makeshift shelters and to fuel fires. Thus the forest had been opened, making it more difficult for marauding gangs to ambush a party such as theirs.

They halted an hour before dusk at a forest glade. Joseph instructed the porters to collect firewood and pitch tents. They lit the main fire in the centre of the clearing. Then they built four more fires at the perimeter, taking care not to start a bush fire. There had been no rain for almost five months and the grass was tinder dry.

A large iron pot for *nsima* was placed over the fire and Joseph grilled some chicken for Alan. Elizabeth Moir had packed a couple of bottles of beer – they were wrapped in a wet cloth napkin, so were quite cool. The Africans had *pombe*, their own beer. They gave him some to taste, and watched him drink with much laughter. He found it sweet and somewhat insipid.

It suddenly became dark while they were eating around the fire. The Africans talked in loud voices and laughed a great deal. They were tired, but enjoyed the convivial occasion. They were somewhat nervous of wild animals, and would now and then glance over their shoulders. Alan asked Joseph whether predators might come into the camp.

The *capitao* tried to be reassuring. "There are few lions here, because their prey have run away from this forest. Also, they dislike fires. They would come only if they were very hungry."

"What about leopards?"

"No, *bwana*, the *nyalugwe* would never come into a camp like this. It might come into a village, to catch a dog, or a goat."

"And hyenas?"

"Hmm. The *mfisi* do not live much in this hilly forest country. They also dislike fire, but we fear them most at times like this. They are bold animals, even when near humans. If we hear them, we will be alert."

The darkness was intense; there was no moon, and the trees seemed to crowd in on them. Numerous mosquitoes whined at their faces. Alan wiped citronella oil on his hands, face and neck to repel them. When the men finished their *pombe* they wrapped themselves in blankets and curled up with their backs to the fire. Alan crawled into his tent; he was so tired that he soon fell asleep.

— • —

Joseph called to Alan before dawn and he emerged to find the porters already cooking over the fire. He joined them eating *nsima*; it was coarse and gritty and he soon felt satisfied. He washed the porridge down with a mug of strong black tea that tasted of wood smoke.

They stopped at noon for a rest, near a small stream of clear water. Joseph lit a fire and boiled water for tea, then unpacked a small hamper with bread rolls provided by Elizabeth Moir. After eating Alan lay on his back and fell asleep, thinking that this was not an unpleasant way to travel.

They reached the Shire River at dusk on Tuesday, and there was the *Ilala,* moored on the east bank. The river at Matope was about a hundred yards wide and flowing strongly. The ship was of classic design for that period, with a vertical prow and a transom that projected well aft of the single screw. She was 48 feet long, with a steel plate hull and a three-foot draft. The single funnel was amidships and there were awnings on both the forward and aft decks. She could steam at eight knots with a single boiler. Knowing that she had come all the way from England made Alan feel proud of her.

He was greeted by Mr Howat, a former North Sea trawler man, who had applied in England for the job of skipper. He was short and stocky, wearing soiled khaki clothing, and Alan soon discovered that he had few words.

Joseph and his troop set off to return to Blantyre after they had carried Alan's possessions aboard. They would get there by the end of the next day.

"She's a good little craft," said Howat, as he showed Alan round. "A little on the small side, but seaworthy enough – or should I say, 'lake worthy'?" He pointed out a small cabin that was hot and stuffy.

"I prefer to sleep on deck," he said. "It's cooler, and when we're out on the open water there are no mosquitoes."

"I'd like to do the same." Alan had brought a mosquito net and rigged it on the foredeck, knowing that the skipper would sleep aft.

There were eight crew men, known as 'steamer boys' and a cook; they slept amidships. Alan shared a supper of boiled chicken and rice with Howat and soon after fell asleep, weary from the long walk.

When he woke next morning the steamer was under way, chugging up the river against the strong current. From both banks they were greeted by scattered groups of Africans who shouted and waved. They wore no clothes, only strings of beads, or small loin flaps of animal skin. Every few miles they passed a little village where grass huts huddled near the river bank and where larger groups of Africans gathered.

"They lead miserable lives," said Howat. He was sitting in a canvas chair at the helm, puffing on a pipe. "Poor beggars subsist on maize and fish. You should see them devour a hippo when we can shoot one. Worst thing is that they can be raided at any time – by the Angoni, or the Yao slavers."

It took two days to reach Lake Nyasa. They moored for the first night near Lake Malombe, the big Lake's little appendage, where the mosquitoes were worse than any Alan had experienced since leaving the Zambezi Valley. On the next day they passed Chief Mponda's large village, stretching for a mile along the river back. Howat told him that the old chief was an inveterate slaver, and seldom sober.

At dusk they moved into the Lake and moored at a small rocky island just west of the point where the Shire River flowed out. Alan was excited to at last reach Livingstone's Lake, the mighty expanse of deep sweet fresh water – an inland sea. It was too dark to see anything except the flicker of fires in local villages and the lights of fishermen.

He woke at dawn to see labourers carrying firewood on board. The *Ilala* consumed large quantities of wood, and the men were instructed to cut only certain species with high calorific value. They were paid by the 'cord', a stack that was eight feet long, four feet wide and four feet high. Each labourer was paid in calico for the cord, after it had been carried aboard and stowed.

They set off on a dead calm, heading north-west towards Kota Kota, half way up the Lake. A fine mist hung over the surface so the horizon was not visible. As this veil lifted he could see the mountains on the eastern and western shores. To the north the Lake stretched for three hundred and fifty miles. The width was forty to fifty miles, although there were some narrower parts.

Alan stood near the wheel, beside Howat. He was excited to be travelling to new territory, and glad to be in relative comfort. Yet he was apprehensive about the conditions that awaited him in Karonga. Everyone had said that it was extremely primitive, but he was more concerned about the conflict that had developed there. No one he had spoken to seemed to have a clear idea of what would happen.

Howat navigated partly by dead reckoning and partly by sightings on prominences on the western shore. The charts he had were primitive, and there was always a risk of running onto rocks. "I prefer to stay well off-shore," he said. "It makes navigation trickier, but the Lake is deeper – in fact, in the centre it's virtually bottomless. The problem is that when a storm blows up – and it can happen with little notice – we can't just throw an anchor out – it's too deep."

"I've been meaning to ask you about storms," Alan said. "I've been reading Edward Young's book about his circumnavigation ten years ago." He held the book up, and the skipper nodded. "He describes some horrible storms, as if the *Ilala* was lucky to survive them..."

"Aye. I think Young and the others who first encountered the Lake came in for a shock. Partly it was the suddenness of the storms, and partly their ferocity. Luckily we know a bit more what to expect."

"Listen to this," Alan said, reading from the book. *"At sunset the most furious storm broke on us from the south, with such rain as I shall never forget. We came to an anchor, and tried to ride it out with both anchors down, steaming at the same time gently ahead to take the stress off the cables. Unfortunately, we were so light that, with the heavy sea which got up, our screw was continually out of the water..."*

"Problem of a shallow draught," Howat interrupted with a grunt. "Ship design is a matter of compromises. They wanted this craft to have a shallow draft for the river work, but that makes her tender in a storm, and leads to the problem Young wrote about – the screw coming out of the water – especially if she's out of ballast."

Alan continued: *"The night, to make matter worse, was pitchy black, we were on a lee shore, and the waves by this time running mountains high. Our position was critical in the extreme, and I momentarily expected our little vessel would go ashore. At midnight the wind shifted, and what an immense relief it was! We had taken in a great deal of water, and it required all we knew to keep her free enough to prevent foundering, but the sea was past all conception; indeed, it is the peculiar nature of this lake to raise a sea that could only be found off the Agulhas Bank or in the Atlantic, and but for the build of the* Ilala *and her wonderful qualities as a sea boat we would never have weathered the storms we had on this trip."*

"This is a naval officer, Mr Howat," he said, "who I presume is not given to exaggeration."

The skipper laughed shortly. "It's a surprise to all of us – how high the waves get."

"What did he mean when he said 'her wonderful qualities as a sea boat'?"

Howat took off his cap and ran his hand through grizzled hair. "She has a balance about her, Spaight. You can feel it when you have the helm. It's something to do with her dimension – her length and beam, and her weight."

"But it would seem to me that she's vulnerable in a storm, because the jib wouldn't help much. That makes you dependant on steaming to keep her headed into the wind. If you can't use the anchors – and there are many parts where the Lake is too deep – you're totally dependant on steaming. What would happen if the boiler went out..."

"Or if you ran out of wood?" Howat laughed. "That nearly happened to Young."

"Yes. Here it is: *"A fresh anxiety now arose: we were almost out of wood, and the gale freshened every minute. Seldom have I seen a nearer thing than it was. Could we fetch the anchorage or not – that was the question? If the steam ran down, a pretty mess we would all be in. It was now pitch dark, and as dirty a night as one could see. The engineer reported the wood all but gone. Calling to a hand, I bade him stand by with an axe, and at the word, to rip up the Ilala's deck as fast as he could, and pass the planks into the stoke-hole."*

Howat laughed again. "Well, luckily he didn't have to rip up the deck. I vowed, when I read that passage, that I would never get caught in a storm without a good supply of wood."

—•—

Later, Alan sat on a chair under the awning on the foredeck. It was cooler here, with a breeze generated by the progress of the ship. The skipper had told him that cruising speed was seven knots, and he estimated that it would take about fifty hours to reach the northern end of the Lake, or roughly two days to reach Karonga, if they did not stop anywhere.

He had heard that the western shore, on the port side, was mostly populated by the Anyanja, Atonga, and WaNkonde tribes that survived by cultivating crops and fishing. They were subject to periodic attacks by the Angoni tribesmen who lived in the hills rising to the west. Livingstone in the 1860s, and Lt Young and Dr Laws in 1877, had found the lakeside plains littered with the skeletons of unfortunate victims of these raids.

To starboard, the eastern shore of the Lake was populated by Yao people, who were Muslims and had been in contact with Arab traders for several centuries. It was they who had developed, mainly in the last fifty years, the lucrative trade in slaves and ivory. They used dhows, locally built sailing boats, to ferry the slaves across the Lake. Other captives were taken overland.

— • —

In the late afternoon Alan spotted what looked like a cloud on the surface of the water. Then he thought it was a waterspout. He pointed it out to Howat.

"*Nkhungu* flies," said the skipper laconically. "The pupae float on the surface and they all emerge at the same time – millions and millions of them. That's a cloud of tiny flies – they can choke you. The natives eat them. They make cakes – patties – out of them. They're probably quite nutritious."

"Surely the pupae would be eaten by fish?"

"I dare say, but there are more than the fish can eat. Fine fish in the Lake, you know. The bream-like fish they call *chambo* is great eating. We'll grill some for you."

Near the shore they saw fish eagles roosting on lakeside trees. Now and then one of the birds would fly down and strike the water, then carry off a shining silver fish. These birds had a haunting cry that seemed to echo in Alan's mind.

— • —

They stopped at Bandawe, the mission station founded by Dr Robert Laws in 1880, after he moved from Cape Maclear; he had already lived in the country for ten years. He was a Glaswegian who had been educated at the University of Aberdeen and joined the London Missionary Society expedition led by Edward Young and accompanied him on his circumnavigation of the Lake.

"I understand you came out with Young in '77, sir," said Alan, as they sat having tea on the verandah of the missionary's house.

"That's right, Spaight..."

"And you don't have to call him 'sir'," added Mrs Laws kindly. "Robert will do."

"We brought the *Ilala* with us, and I think it must have fulfilled one of Dr Livingstone's dreams to have a steamer on the Lake. He was an amazingly foresighted man, and he knew that the accessibility of Lake Nyasa from the sea gave us a unique opportunity to penetrate the interior of Africa and thus spread the gospel. He foresaw the steamer as the logical mode of transport, to supply the missions. It's a pity that the Shire River is not navigable all the way from the Zambesi, but we must be thankful that there's only the fifty mile portage past the Murchison Cataracts to deal with."

"Was it difficult to bring the steamer up to the Lake?"

"Oh aye, it was difficult, but we had good men, led by Young. The ship was built on the Isle of Dogs, you know. Then she had trials on the Thames before she was taken apart. We brought her out on the *Walmer Castle* to Port Elizabeth, and then the bits were loaded onto a German schooner, the *Hara*, which brought us to the mouth of the Zambesi." He laughed, "We were lost for a while – the mouth of the great river has no landmarks or charts..."

Mrs Laws frowned at her husband. "Hurry along, Robert."

"Yes, dear. Well, we chose a spot on the bank of the Zambesi and started to assemble the ship. Then we found that all the nuts and bolts had become rusted in their storage barrel. Poor Young had the thankless task of cleaning every one of them. Anyway, we were able to launch the *Ilala* at the beginning of August and worked our way up the Zambesi and then the Shire – you must have come that way?"

Alan nodded, and Laws continued. "At Katunga we had a friendly reception from the Makalolo, which is just as well, because we needed plenty of labour for the portage. We disassembled the ship and divided everything into fifty pound loads – as far as we could. There were some bits that weighed more. The largest were the boilers, but Young had brought an axle-tree and two wheels, which helped. We used eight hundred labourers and we paid them as little as a yard of calico a day! We eventually reached the top of the rapids at the end of September and set about re-assembling the ship – it took us two weeks."

"It was the third time she was put together," said Mrs Laws, "counting when she was first built."

"That's right," added Laws. "We reached the Lake by mid-October, five months after we left England. We've been here ever since."

—•—

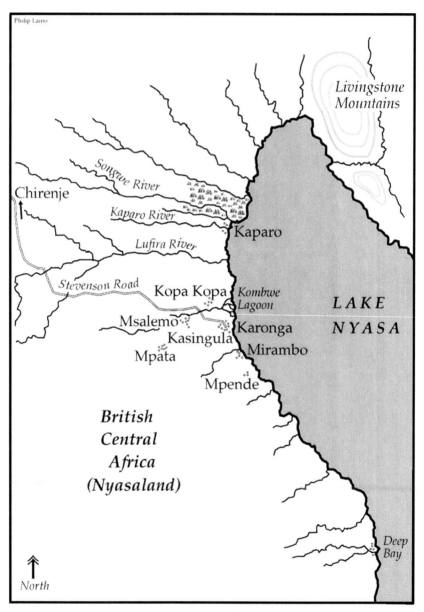

Philip Laino

Livingstone
Mountains

Songwe River

Chirenje

Kaparo River

Kaparo

Lufira River

Stevenson Road

Kopa Kopa   Kombwe
             Lagoon   LAKE

Msalemo   NYASA
         Karonga
      Kasingula
Mpata   Mirambo

         Mpende

British
Central
Africa
(Nyasaland)

North

Deep
Bay

**Map 4. Karonga & the 'North End'
of Lake Nyasa (1887-95)**

9

Karonga - October 1887

They reached Karonga on the second day after leaving Bandawe. Alan was surprised that there was no harbour at all, only a crude jetty made of logs. Because the Lake was calm, Howat was able to moor the ship long enough to unload his cargo. He then anchored about a hundred yards offshore and plied to and from the shore in the ship's dinghy.

Monteith Fotheringham strolled down to the jetty to meet them. He was tall and heavily built, an imposing figure, with a large spade-shaped red beard. He spoke with a strong Glaswegian accent as he greeted Alan and Howat.

"Gentlemen," he said, after the introductions, "we have a dire situation here. Mlozi, the Arab slave trader, has virtually declared war on the WaNkonde tribe. We ourselves are in a serious predicament. Did you bring my trading cloth, Howat."

The skipper shook his head slowly. "I'm sorry, Fotheringham. They told me at Matope to sail with empty holds, so that I could collect rations from Bandawe."

Fotheringham frowned. "That is a serious setback. It will make it much more difficult for me to negotiate with Mlozi."

He paused, seeming to realise that he had alarmed his visitors. "As you can see, Spaight, there are few amenities here." He waved towards the group of pole and thatch houses set back from the lake shore. The ground between had been cleared; the grass had been slashed, and paths scraped to the soil, with stone borders to delineate them. "We have an office and store rooms, and a few houses, one of which is yours."

They walked up from the jetty to the compound. Fotheringham showed Alan his house. It, too, was made of poles and mud, with a grass-thatched roof. The walls and floors were of smoothed mud. It reeked of wood smoke. Some of the furniture was made of wooden boxes that had formerly contained tins of kerosene or paraffin. The bed frame consisted of bush poles strung with ropes on which was laid a mattress filled with kapok; the pillows, too, were filled with kapok, known locally as 'tree-cotton'.

Later, they had lunch at Fotheringham's house, a simple meal of guinea fowl and cassava. The manager explained the situation that prevailed. "These are the forces assembling against us: Mlozi and his mercenaries in Mpata; and the *ruga-rugas*, who are unruly brigands – they have a sort of leader, a Baluchi Mohammedan named Ramathan. Mlozi has subverted the chiefs in two other villages: Kopa Kopa and Msalemo. So there are three large villages, not far from each other, that oppose us. They are well stockaded, and the occupants are armed, albeit with old muzzle-loaders."

"I have been negotiating with both Mlozi and Ramathan, trying to prevent them from destroying the local people. They are burning villages, taking able-bodied people into slavery, and killing those who are no use to them. They say they intend to replace the peaceful WaNkonde with another tribe, named the WaHenga."

"Can we get help?" Alan asked.

"I have sent runners to the mission at Chirenje, asking for Mr Bain – the missionary in charge – to come here. He has been in this region for several years and is well respected. I expect he will be careful not get into conflict with the slavers, but he could support me in negotiations. Unfortunately, my deputy John Nicoll has gone to

Lake Tanganyika, and he has most of my armed men, as his escort. All I have here are a dozen men with muzzle-loaders and very little ammunition."

"Do you think the slavers will attack Karonga?" asked Howat.

Fotheringham stroked his large beard as he considered his answer. "They might, but they know something of the power of Britain – at least Mlozi does. He's an educated man – albeit a villain. I think men like him have an innate respect for white men. They see our clothes and our weapons, they see ships like the *Ilala*. They see that we can bring trading goods into the country..."

"Yes, but they must know how vulnerable you are."

Fotheringham nodded and turned to Alan. "The company is making a road west from Karonga inland towards Lake Tanganyika. It was my intention that you would supervise the work of improving the road at least as far as Chirenje. Unfortunately, both the civil engineers who worked on the road, Stewart and McEwan, died of fever – they're buried here in Karonga, poor fellows."

"I know nothing about making roads," Alan said apprehensively.

"Neither did I when I came here, Spaight. You'll learn – I'll teach you. Besides, it's not a road like you would expect in Britain. It's a wide track that might one day take an ox-drawn wagon." He sighed and his shoulders slumped. "But first we have to deal with Mlozi and Ramathan. The Moir brothers must have told you about Mlozi. He's the archetypical slave trader – half Arab, half African – a cunning bastard. He buys ivory – in competition with me. He's been buying up the local chiefs, who supply him with slaves, who he sends to the coast. He sees the Company, and me in particular, as obstacles. I think he wants to frighten us away. Militarily he is much stronger than me. He can assemble perhaps a thousand men..."

"And you?"

"Not more than a couple of hundred. Also, about fifty of his men are armed with ancient flintlocks."

"What will you do?

The Scot shrugged. "Stick it out. I'm telling you all this Spaight, not to scare you, but to warn you."

— • —

Later, they sat outside Fotheringham's house looking out over the Lake, now shrouded in darkness. A fire glowed in a pit about ten yards in front of the verandah. To ward off the mosquitoes they wore long trousers tucked into boots, and long-sleeved shirts. They rubbed citronella oil onto any exposed skin, face, neck, hands. Even so, the whining sound of the insects was incessant.

"'Lake of Stars', Livingstone called it," said Fotheringham, musingly.

"Perhaps 'Lake of Slaves' would be a more appropriate name," Alan muttered.

He thought Fotheringham seemed a decent sort. He was a bit gruff, but kindly, and he spoke to the Africans in a respectful way. Alan had been led to believe that he was eccentric, but his first impression was a man coping well under difficult circumstances.

"I sent a message to Ramathan," said Fotheringham. "I told him that all the WaNkonde chiefs around Karonga are my friends and have done nothing to harm him. He sent a note back, saying that he will spare the local chiefs if they each pay a tribute of three cows to Mlozi. I then sent my messenger to Mlozi, and he replied asking me to send gunpowder, percussion caps and flints, as well as trade cloth. His demands are increasing in scale and I doubt if we can meet them – or should."

Later, Alan walked to the jetty with Howat; the Mandala manager had gone to bed. Howat climbed into the dinghy and set the oars. "You can come and sleep on board, if you like," he offered.

Alan wanted to, but could not. "Thanks, but I have to get used to living here. Good night."

He watched Howat row out to the *Ilala*, then turned to walk up to his little house, feeling a weight of gloom. His family and most of his friends were thousands of miles away. Nora was hundreds of miles away and might as well be on the other side of the moon. Did she think of him, or was it merely a little romantic episode for her, to reassure herself that she was attractive.

He wondered how he had come to be in this forsaken place. They had not told him about it when he was briefed in England; perhaps they did not know how bad the situation was. The menace from the slavers was almost palpable. At this very moment they might be planning an attack. They would come surging in, shouting and whooping, stabbing with their horrible spears. He remembered only too well the frenzied Dervishes at Tofrek – who had wielded swords as well as spears. It was easy to recapture the horror of their attack, and their excited shrieks.

How on earth could they defend themselves here? What if Fotheringham was imprisoned or killed by Mlozi? He would be in Karonga on his own.

—•—

Next morning, as the manager was showing Alan around the Company stores, there was a commotion and clapping – the traditional African greeting. Mr Bain had arrived from the mission at Chirenje. He was of medium height, clean-shaven except for a small moustache, and with his dark hair parted in the centre. Alan took a liking to him soon after they made their introductions.

Fotheringham said, "I hope you will come with me, Bain, for a meeting with Ramathan."

"Don't you think we should put up some kind of fortification?" Alan suggested, and when Fotheringham looked puzzled he added: "We could put up a *zariba*."

"They call it a *boma* here," said Bain, with a faint smile.

He nodded. "It would protect us from a charge, but not from gunfire. For that we would need a wall or thick stockade..."

"He served three years in the army," said Howat to the other two men. "He was in the calamitous Battle of Tofrek – in the Sudan – when the Dervishes overran the British square."

"Well, do the best you can," said Fotheringham, seemingly unimpressed by Alan's military credentials.

— • —

Fotheringham took Alan for a short tour of the countryside west of Karonga. They visited several villages, all devastated by the slavers. The manager pointed out clusters of neat huts, drawing attention to the woven grass walls and neatly thatched roofs. "So different to the usual rough dwellings." There were few inhabitants, and they were almost all elderly or children, naked, emaciated and unsmiling. Between the villages were groves of bananas, interspersed with small fields in which cassava, maize and millet had been grown.

Fotheringham could speak the local dialect and interviewed several villagers, conveying their answers to Alan. Their stories were invariably of raids by slaver militia who emptied their granaries, stole their bananas, and took away those people who they thought would be able to walk to the coast.

With tears in his eyes, Fotheringham said, "How dreadful that their peaceful productive lives should be so destroyed by these invaders. How shameful that we are doing nothing to stop it."

— • —

Fotheringham and Bain returned by early evening from their meeting with Ramathan. Over supper they explained to Howat and Alan how the leader of the *ruga-rugas,* had gone back on his word. He had made outrageous demands for sparing the local chiefs.

"I warned him I would report him to the British Consul in Zomba," said the manager, "but he scorned me. He said, 'Bring the Consul here and I will show him who is the Sultan of Nkonde'."

Fotheringham decided that he must go to see the top man, Mlozi. "It will be venturing into the lions den, but I can't wait here while he devastates the WaNkonde villages. Perhaps I can make him see reason."

"Perhaps he will imprison you, Monteith – or worse," said Bain gloomily.

"I can go with you," Alan volunteered, hoping his voice did not betray his nervousness.

Fotheringham shook his head. "Thank you, Spaight, but I need you to stay here with Bain and Howat – to fortify the compound."

—•—

10

East African coast - October 1887

At dawn on the third day of the voyage the slaves in the hold of the dhow heard shouting. Word came down from the deck that a British frigate had been sighted. The Arabs headed towards the coast; reaching across the wind was their fastest point of sail. The sailors shouted to each other in Swahili, and the captives below remained quiet, so that they could hear what was happening. There were squalls around that threatened to knock the ship over while she was carrying full sails, but they also hid her from the frigate.

An hour passed and then another, but the squalls escalated into a storm. It seemed that the shore must be near. The frigate had not been sighted for twenty minutes and the sailors thought they had given her the slip.

Suddenly, there was a fearful grinding noise. The torn timbers of the *dhow* shrieked. She shuddered and listed over. Within the confines of their bonds the slaves were tumbled into a heaps, screaming in terror.

"We must have hit a reef," Kawa shouted to Goodwill. "We're going to sink. We have to get out of here."

Water poured through rents in the sides of the ship, filling the hold. The captives wailed – most of them were still fastened to deck bolts, as Goodwill and Kawa had been. The others were still roped together. Most of them could not swim.

Kawa dragged his companion to his feet and lunged for the nearest hatch. He pulled Goodwill by the chain that joined them, and together they pushed the hatch open. There were a dozen sailors on the sloping deck, and as the two men emerged they saw half of them swept off by a wave.

"We must swim for the shore!" shouted Goodwill. "We must stay together."

Kawa laughed, deliriously. "Have you forgotten? We are chained together."

The next wave took them away, tumbling over and over, thumping into each other, the chain tugging and cutting, yanking at their necks. Goodwill felt surprisingly calm, even though he realised that if one of them drowned the other would be dragged down into the depths. But Kawa was a strong swimmer. They found the surface and pulled towards each other.

"Drift!" commanded Kawa. "Like a log. Save your strength."

It was a sickening journey that lasted over three hours. One moment they would be on the crest of a swell, the next they would swoop down into the trough. At times they could see the breakers on the coast, a phosphorescent line that came closer as the hours passed. Then they could hear the roar of the waves breaking on the shore. They were barely conscious when minutes later they were thrown onto a beach with a force that wrenched their necks and grazed the skin on their naked barely-conscious bodies.

—•—

It was a crab that woke Goodwill. He felt it scratching on his foot and shook it off. Kawa was lying nearby. Amazingly the chain had broken. He crawled over and shook his friend, for a moment thinking he was dead.

Then Kawa stirred and smiled. "We are free, my friend. Do you know that?" He had the collar on his neck, and a four foot length of chain attached to it, but he was free.

Goodwill looked around the deserted beach, grey-brown and soaked in the aftermath of the storm. It was two hours before sunset, they judged. The sky was dark grey and filled with low clouds swollen with rain. He looked out on the heaving sea but there was no sign of the ships. At the edge of the beach was a fringe of mangrove. There was no evidence of habitation.

"There is nothing to be gained by walking inland," said Kawa. "We have no water. Better to walk along the shore. Perhaps we can find some fishermen."

They walked north along the Mozambique coast, instinctively away from the horrors of Pemba. They soon found three bodies – two slaves and a sailor – all had drowned. They picked up fish thrown onto the beach by the storm, and cooked them over driftwood; both were adept at starting a fire. They slept on a huge log.

At noon on the second day they found the mangrove forest disappearing; it was replaced by jumbles of rocks covered with scrubby trees. The narrow beach changed to a succession of coves, and in one of these they came across a small stream. They were about to wallow in it and slake their thirst when they noticed a hut among the rocks. Sitting in front of it was an old woman. They approached her cautiously.

"You were slaves," she said, without emotion in her voice; she spoke ChiYao. She pointed to their leather collars and the lengths of chain that they carried.

She went into her hut. "I have two shifts, but this old one is too worn for me to use." She tore it in half and gave the pieces to them, ordering them to cover themselves. They wrapped the lengths of cloth like Indian *dhotis*, laughing until they found a way to knot the material so that it would not fall off.

She waited while they drank from the brackish stream. Then they told her about the shipwreck while she listened impassively. Afterwards, she explained that she had once been a slave, but had been released after many years by the half-caste who owned her. Now she lived alone, eating fish and crabs, and growing small patches of millet and yams that she watered from the stream.

"You cannot go far like that," she said. "You have to get those collars off, then let the sores heal. Otherwise, everyone will know that you are escaping slaves."

Removing the collars proved a daunting task. The old woman had an axe with a blade made from iron that was of quite good quality. They used the blade as a saw, but it took them several hours, each working in turn on the other's collar. When they finished they threw the two collars and the lengths of chain into the sea.

— • —

A dozen days passed. The woman fed them well, so they grew stronger. Only once did other people come by; a group of fishermen. Goodwill and Kawa hid in the scrub and watched as the fishermen greeted the old woman, whom they had known for a long time. They chatted with her for a while before continuing their journey along the beach.

They left the old woman a month after the wreck. She told them to follow the stream west and then head for the mountains. She advised them to walk only in the evenings. "That is the time when villagers are near their homes and less likely to see you. During the early morning and in daytime they might see you and capture you. Then they might sell you back to the slavers."

She gave them an old worn knife; it was merely a length of thin iron about four inches long, set into a wooden handle. She also gave them a leather bag, about nine inches deep, which she filled with some grains of maize and millet. "Your next meal. After that you have to fend for yourselves."

They thanked her with tears in their eyes and waved to her until she was out of sight.

— • —

11

Karonga - October 1887

Alan watched Fotheringham set off to meet Mlozi, taking with him six men from the Ilala, 'sailors' as he called them, who were armed with Snider breech-loading rifles. He said they would be of little use against Mlozi's militia, but he thought that the slavers might be impressed by the presence of men that were strangers, and might think that there had been some recruiting going on.

When Fotheringham returned he told Alan about his experience. Mlozi's village, Mpata, was ten miles inland from Karonga. It was surrounded by a stockade made of tall poles, with a single entrance leading into a narrow lane along which Fotheringham's party walked in single file. The end of the lane opened into a square surrounded by grass huts and a few pole and mud houses. The square was filled with several hundred *ruga-rugas* and militia, many of whom were dancing frenetically to the beat of a large drum. There was an air of menace as they bowed mockingly to the white man, waving their loaded muskets. The *rugas* were the most intimidating, with their braided hair covered with feathers and gaudy pieces of cloth, and necklaces of human teeth swinging as they gyrated.

The white man was led into a high-ceilinged room in a substantial house; there were no windows, the only light coming from the open door. He was greeted by Mlozi, who was above medium height, slender, with pale brown skin. His expression was benign, but his

101

eyes were cold. He wore a long white *kanzu,* and on his head was a small round Mohammedan cap. The slave trader greeted him cordially in Swahili; Fotheringham could understand him well enough.

Mlozi explained that some of the depredations by his men against the WaNkonde people had taken place without his knowledge.

"As for the killing of one of the chiefs," he said, "believe me, I knew nothing about it." He explained that the WaNkonde chiefs could return to their homes and would not be molested, but there were some chiefs who would remain his enemies because they had captured and killed some of his women.

Fotheringham implored Mlozi to do nothing until the British Consul, Mr Hawes, and Fred Moir, the Mandala manager, visited Karonga to discuss the matter. However, Mlozi would not agree to this proposition. Then the white man asked that Ramathan and his *rugas* be sent away. Mlozi agreed to this and wrote a letter to Ramathan.

The discussion then ended with a meal of curried chicken with rice, the participants eating from the communal bowl. The white man was given a spoon, but the Africans ate with their fingers.

—•—

On his return Fotheringham was pleased to see that Alan had made good progress with the fortification of the compound. Using as many labourers as he could find he had organised the construction of breastworks, about four feet high. This low stockade stretched down to the jetty, although anyone embarking to the steamer on the ship's dinghy would have little protection.

When the manager described his meeting with Mlozi he was convinced that he had achieved only a temporary respite. "I don't trust the rascal," he said. "I think he's playing for time, waiting while he gauges our strengths and weaknesses. He may strike when he has made his assessment."

That evening Alan had a long discussion with Mr Bain about the local tribes. "The WaNkonde are essentially peaceful and sedentary," said the missionary. "They led an idyllic existence until the slavers appeared on the scene and stirred up the WaHenga, and aberrant chiefs like Msalemo and Kopa Kopa. It's tragic what has happened."

"Can't the WaNkonde defend themselves?"

"They have only bows and arrows – and rather primitive ones, at that. I'm not talking of longbows. They use them for short-range hunting of small animals. You see, the slavers have their militia with muskets, and the WaNkonde are no match for them. As you saw, they've been devastated."

"Why doesn't the British government do something? They could send a military force."

"It was ever thus, Alan." Bain smiled. "Part of it is ignorance. The politicians at home don't really know about, nor understand, the situation here. Part of it is money – we are low on their list for spending – if we are on it all."

"What do you think is needed? My uncle is an MP. I could write to him."

Bain shrugged. "I'm not a military man, so your guess would be better than mine."

"Most of the military experience in Africa is defensive," said Alan. "The Boers defending themselves against the Zulus, the British squares holding out against the Dervishes in Sudan – although we attacked the Zulus after Isandlwhana."

"That was a huge expeditionary force – commanded by a general. Bain smiled wanly. "There's little prospect of them sending anything like that to Lake Nyasa."

—•—

A couple of days later the *Ilala* departed, taking a despatch from Fotheringham to Consul Hawes. On the following day some half-caste emissaries from Mlozi came to Karonga. Their message was that the WaNkonde chiefs should pay tributes to Mlozi, consisting of women, cows and goats. When Fotheringham refused to convey these demands the slaver emissaries told him that he should not be disrespectful to Mlozi because it was he who had prevented Ramathan from attacking the Company compound at Karonga.

While this discussion was going on Ramathan the Baluchi suddenly appeared, with about a hundred armed militia. They stood at the outskirts of the compound, menacing as they rattled their spears and brandished their guns.

"So much for Mlozi's undertaking to get him to leave the area," Alan muttered. "You were right Mr Fotheringham, you can't trust the man."

The Mandala manager invited Ramathan to join the meeting with Mlozi's emissaries and politely asked him to cease his attacks on the WaNkonde villages. Surprisingly, he agreed, and said he would head for Lake Tanganyika, taking his *ruga-rugas* with him.

It later transpired that the main WaNkonde chiefs were told that Fotheringham had been successful in his negotiations, and that Mlozi had invited them to come down from their refuge in the hills. Naturally, the chiefs and their followers were anxious to return to their villages. They came to Karonga to speak with Fotheringham, who was quick to warn them that they had been deceived. and that Mlozi's men were not to be trusted. He advised them to return to their villages and take precautions. Despite this warning large numbers of WaNkonde people camped around a lagoon, not far from the Mandala compound, hoping they would get support and protection.

On October 23, 1887, news came of a fight between slaver forces and WaNkonde people near the lagoon. Ramathan's *rugas* had come to steal crops and cattle and had been driven off by the WaNkonde.

"I fear that they will attack this compound," said Bain, while he sat with Alan and Fotheringham near the Lake shore.

Alan gazed across the grey water that had been whipped into choppy waves by a strong breeze. Although it was the warmest time of the year the breezes were pleasantly cool. He thought again about his predicament – the possibility that they might be overcome by a horde of uncontrollable natives, probably drunk on local beer.

He said, "Shouldn't we put pickets out, so that we get some warning?"

"The WaNkonde will warn us," replied Fotheringham gloomily, "if only to seek our help. You know, Bain, I've been wondering whether we should abandon this compound. We could take the trade goods with us, up to your mission in Chirenje."

"It's a plan worth considering," said Bain. "Certainly, I would like to return home."

"Surely they could attack us on the trek?" Alan volunteered. "It would be more difficult to defend ourselves on the road. At least here we have some protection."

"True," replied Fotheringham, "but if they see us departing they may leave us alone, knowing that we have given in to their pressures."

—•—

Three days later, while they were still deliberating, and continuing to fortify the *boma*, they heard the sound of gunfire from the direction of the lagoon. A Nkonde tribesman came running into the stockade and informed them that Mlozi was gathering his forces at Msalemo's village. An attack on Karonga seemed imminent.

They renewed efforts to fortify the Mandala compound, using any Africans they could find. At noon next day they heard firing, again from the lagoon area to the north. It later transpired that the slaver forces had surrounded the people sheltering there.

Many of the slavers were armed with flintlocks, while the WaNkonde tribesmen had only spears, bows and arrows. The slavers fired volleys into the reeds among which some of the defenders fled.

The main opportunity for escape for the terrified WaNkonde was to go towards the north, but the area was swampy and many of the victims became mired there, easily shot or speared. The frenzied *rugas* set fire to the reeds, forcing many people into the lagoon water and its swamp inlets, where they were attacked by the crocodiles that infested the area.

The victims' screams rose with the crackling of the burning reeds and the revolting grunting of voracious crocodiles. Orange flames danced into the evening air, lighting the billowing acrid smoke. The forest around the lagoon was lit like some macabre theatre. Mlozi and Ramathan were seen to climb nearby trees from which they could more easily view the massacre. The orgy of killing ended when darkness came. Those WaNkonde who survived fled north to the Songwe River, while the slavers returned with some captives to their stockades.

— • —

12

The defenders knew that it was just a matter of time before the slavers attacked the little enclosure at Karonga. Alan expected that the Arabs would be elated after their successful massacre at the lagoon, which had proceeded without interference from the white men. He felt disgusted and helpless as he heard accounts from a few survivors who stumbled into the *boma*.

A messenger came from Mlozi telling them to desist from further fortification. He was a truculent fellow with shifty eyes. They told him to go back to his master and tell him they were here to stay. Meanwhile, they heard that the *ruga-rugas* were attacking villagers in the neighbourhood.

One morning, as Alan was standing by the Lake shore contemplating the feasibility of escape by canoe or swimming, he saw the *Ilala* approaching in the misty distance. He called to Fotheringham and Bain and they stood together watching the little steamer manoeuvre towards the jetty. She stood off about fifty yards and her dinghy was lowered.

All four European passengers were strangers to Karonga. They were Henry O'Neill, who was Her Majesty's Consul at Mozambique, the Reverend Lawrence Scott, from Manchester, Dr Tomory of the London Missionary Society, and Alfred Sharpe, a British solicitor on an elephant hunting expedition.

O'Neill brought a packet of mail from Blantyre; he distributed the letters to Fotheringham and Alan, leaving a small pile for Nicoll. There were three letters for Alan, two from his mother and one in a handwriting he did not recognise. He opened it first and found it was from Nora.

Dear Alan,

I trust that you are keeping well. I have been told by Alistair that Karonga is not a healthy place, so you must take care that you do not contract fever. The Moir brothers told me that you might be up there for several months.

We are well here in Blantyre. And I'm making plans for the move to Zomba which should be some time next month. Alistair has built a temporary house near the new hospital. I went to see it last week and found it quite nice. I also went with the Buchanans for a walk up to the plateau. We took Baby Malcolm with us. It is a lovely place and I look forward to showing it to you. It would be nice to live there, but it would not be practical because of the distance from the hospital and the other (modest) amenities in Zomba.

I look forward to your return when your time in Karonga is over. It would be fun if you could ride with me again and perhaps we could do some more exploring.

Alistair joins me in wishing you all the best.

Your friend Nora

—•—

The visitors who arrived on the *Ilala* had heard about the increasing friction between the slavers and the local WaNkonde tribesmen. They were dismayed when they learnt about the massacre and the plight of the victims. Their expressions grew anxious when Monteith Fotheringham explained the gravity of the situation, although he was delighted to hear that the *Ilala* had brought the trading goods he needed to pay off Mlozi and Ramathan.

O'Neill decided to take command of the small force in the *boma*. He was, in theory, the senior British person in the yet un-named territory.

Although Consul in Mozambique, he also had responsibility for the inland areas of British interest. He had been an officer in the Royal Navy during their efforts to suppress the transport of slaves along the coast of East Africa. His stern florid face was surrounded by luxuriant mutton-chop whiskers. Alan had heard of a celebrated dispute O'Neill had had with Will Johnson, the missionary, about whether the Lujenda River rose from Lake Chilwa.

Alan sensed that Fotheringham was not pleased about O'Neill taking command. The Mandala manager had been 'the laird' for several years, and now he was a mere deputy, and adviser on local affairs. Alan noticed that little frowns appeared on Fotheringham's brow every time O'Neill gave an instruction, as if he felt it signified that his own management had been deficient.

The Consul ordered that a ditch be dug outside the *boma* wall, and clearing of vegetation from the field of fire. They had few labourers at their disposal, but enlisted small groups of refugees who came to seek protection, and were rewarded with permission to camp nearby.

John Nicoll joined the defenders three days later with his platoon of eighteen men armed with breech-loading rifles. Alan soon grew to like the young Scot. He was Fotheringham's deputy, and at first seemed rather subservient, but Alan admired his willingness to take on tasks, such as his *ulendo* to Lake Tanganyika, that were not without risk.

— • —

Several days passed, and more refugees trickled in to Karonga with news of threatening behaviour by the slavers; it was rumoured that they would attack next day. O'Neill called a meeting of the eight white men and made an inventory of the weapons. They had eleven Snider rifles, but only 600 rounds of ammunition. There were twenty other older guns, as well as thirty-two breech-loading muskets and a dozen muzzle-loading flintlocks. Sharpe had a heavy calibre elephant gun and two other hunting rifles, while Alan had his .357 magnum rifle.

"What weapons do you think the slavers have," O'Neill asked the Mandala manager.

After some thought Fotheringham replied. "At least a hundred guns, perhaps as many as two hundred – they are almost all old muskets. Of course they have hundreds of men armed with spears, and bows and arrows."

"How many men in total?"

"Perhaps a thousand."

O'Neill frowned; the numbers were daunting. Every white man in Southern Africa knew about the slaughter of the British regiment at Isandlwhana, and the subsequent heroic defence at Rorke's Drift, that happened eight years ago. They also knew that the Boers had defended their wagon *laagers* against hordes of Zulu and Matabele tribesmen at battles like Blood River and Vegkop.

"Well," said the Consul, "we must strengthen our defences. I propose we fill the ditch with thorn branches. We must make sure that the route from the *boma* to the Lake shore is secure. That is where we can flee if we have to."

"What about the sheds?" Alan asked. "Surely if the slavers attack they'll try to use the sheds for shelter – to hide behind while they shoot at us."

"Perhaps," replied O'Neill, "but we don't have the time or the labour resources to pull them down."

"We could burn them down," Alan retorted.

O'Neill looked at Fotheringham questioningly and the manager shook his head. "I think they are too far away from the *boma* to be much use to them. They are more likely to make frontal attacks."

Alan turned away in frustration and walked over to Sharpe, who was cleaning his rifle outside his tent. He looked up quizzically as Alan approached.

"Does our commander have a plan?"

Alan could not help laughing. He liked the quiet solicitor; he had grown sugarcane in Fiji before coming to Africa, and he seemed quite relaxed despite the dangers that loomed.

"They expect a frontal attack," Alan replied.

"I think they're right. I doubt if there's a tactician in their ranks. Look, Alan, you and I will have to do most of the shooting. You should have a second rifle – use a Snider – and I'll give you one of my Tonga men to load for you. Be careful, the Snider kicks like the devil – you'll have a bruised shoulder in no time."

—•—

A few days later the white men were sitting down to a breakfast of *nsima*, grilled goat mutton and tea. Half way through the meal they heard a volley of gunfire from the south side of the clearing and glimpsed white clothing through the trees, the *kanzus* worn by the Arab slavers. This sign of impending attack forced a decision by O'Neill to send John Nicoll to the north end of the Lake. It was hoped he could recruit Mwamba tribesmen, whose chief had offered assistance. It was a dangerous mission for Nicoll, since he would have to travel through an area controlled by the slavers. Yet he accepted his orders calmly, and without question.

Alan wished Nicoll good luck. "It seems as if you're setting off on a military mission, yet you are a civilian like me."

Nicoll smiled. "I know what you mean. We are civilians, and volunteers. We could refuse to take orders at any time – in effect we could resign and leave..." He laughed, "...subject to the availability of a steamer."

The young Scot slipped out of the *boma*, taking with him a two-man armed guard, the best of the dozen he had taken to Lake Tanganyika. He also took six Mwamba men as guides. Watching them leave Alan wondered if he would ever see Nicoll again.

—•—

111

Alan woke before dawn feeling stiff and feverish. It was noticeably warmer as he pulled on his breeches and boots before going out to stand by the embers of the fire. O'Neill was already sipping from a mug of coffee, and ordered his servant to get one for Alan.

"A rude introduction to Africa for you, Spaight?"

"This part of Africa." He explained how he had served in the Sudan. "At least I'm in the company of good men. I was a bit nervous when it was just me and Fotheringham – Bain was not taking part. I wished then that I had my regiment of Sikhs."

"Why did you leave the army?'

He explained without much detail and the Consul said, "You may have as much action here as you did when you were a military man."

At that moment, as if to justify O'Neill's words, they heard gunshots from the trees beyond the clearing, shortly followed by the heavy dull reports of the sentries' Snider rifles. They shouted to wake the other white men as they ran to the tents for weapons. Alan grabbed his rifles and bandoleers and hurried to the embankment, calling for his Tonga loader. The edge of the clearing around the *boma* was a hundred yards away. In the dawn light he could just make out dark moving figures.

The white men spread themselves evenly along the rampart, but were still within shouting distance of each other. "How many of them?" was the common question.

"Four hundred with guns?"

"Nearer five hundred – I'm guessing!"

"How many altogether?"

"A thousand?"

"Good luck, men," called O'Neill. "Fire only at definite targets. Conserve your ammunition."

— • —

13

Inland through Mozambique - November/December 1887

Goodwill and Kawa evolved a strategy of using the clearly defined paths taking them inland from the Mozambique coast towards the mountains in the far west. For the first several weeks the forest was dense and full of shade. There were few large animals, and therefore few predators such as lions and hyenas. Yet the forest was full of wildlife. Birds called and swooped through the trees, monkeys chattered, and wild pigs grunted in the undergrowth.

During the day the two young men lay in denser patches of vegetation, eating what little food they could find, and sleeping as much as they needed. They had an innate sense of conserving energy. In late afternoon they would take to the path, one walking ahead, the other a few paces behind. At the slightest sign of other people they melted into the undergrowth. They developed a way of warning each other – a sharp deep cluck was a minor warning; it sounded like an axe striking hollow wood. Two clucks in quick succession meant imminent danger.

When it grew too dark to see, or if the moonlight was not strong enough, they stopped and went into hiding. They were used to sleeping in the open after their three month walk to the coast, but it was an uncomfortable existence. It was the end of the dry season, and there was plenty of firewood and kindling, but they were cautious about lighting a fire, fearing that it would attract attention if there were villagers nearby.

They would whisper for a couple of hours, pausing frequently to listen to the forest sounds. Kawa told Goodwill about growing up in a fishing village near Lake Nyasa. It had been a precarious existence because they were subject to raids from the Angoni tribesmen, who came down from the hills and stole women and children, and their crops. They learned to live in a constant state of caution, sometimes living in huts built on stilts in marshy areas, where the Angoni were afraid to venture because of crocodiles.

"But weren't you afraid of them, too?" asked Goodwill.

"Oh yes. But we knew where they stayed, and we were very careful."

Goodwill told Kawa about his family's flight from the Angoni, and how they found the mission station at Domasi. He told his friend about lessons at the school and started teaching him the alphabet and basic arithmetic. Kawa was an apt pupil and made the lessons enjoyable with jokes and good humour.

Goodwill was an expert at trapping animals and spent many hours fashioning devices from wood and fibre strings. He set them in the little paths made by francolins, guinea fowl, mice and hares. Perhaps one night in three brought success and they would devour the bird or little animal half-cooked or raw.

They gathered thorny plants while it was still light enough to see, and used them to surround themselves, making a sort of nest to keep away inquisitive animals. On several occasions hyenas sniffed at the barrier, then backed away from the thorns.

Goodwill always carried an ember in a green-bark tube, as his uncle taught him. It was slung over his shoulder and kept alight by the draught as it swung by his side. He carried some kindling too, and he could use the ember to ignite it, if a predator came near.

Shortage of food was their main problem. The village field crops had been harvested, since this was now the last few weeks of the dry season, and the local people left little in their fields to glean. Sometimes they came across small fields of rice, irrigated from streams that ran into the Rovuma River, but these were usually guarded by children, tasked with keeping birds away. There was often a night guard near the field, to prevent wild pigs from rooting up the crop.

At times they were so desperately hungry that they would raid an outlying granary. Goodwill was very unhappy to do this. "Thou shalt not steal," he told Kawa, translating the commandment.

"Perhaps your God will allow us to steal if we are dying of hunger?"

Goodwill shook his head. "I don't think so. He would expect us to ask for food..."

"And risk being captured – and killed?"

"We don't know that, Kawa. These villagers might take pity on us."

Kawa snorted. "Not them. They live a hard life. They would try to make money by selling us."

—•—

Goodwill was especially adept at catching guinea fowl, a practice he had learnt from his uncle. The birds were plentiful around the settlements, where they gleaned grain from the fields – maize, sorghum and millet. Their habit was to run when disturbed, and they took flight only when in danger of being caught on the ground. He made nooses of wild hemp strands, which he fastened to sticks bowed into the earth on the pathways used by the birds. Then he would drive them gently towards the trap. An adult guinea fowl is heavy and surprisingly powerful, and Goodwill knew how strongly to make these traps. One of these birds would last them two days. They would cook it on a spit over a low fire that generated virtually no smoke. Every part was eaten, except the feathers and bones; even the claws and head were nibbled and sucked.

Every few days they heard a honey guide. The little grey-brown bird would lead them to a hive, usually high in the hollow trunk of a tree. Goodwill had robbed many such hives with his uncle. Their technique then was to light a fire at the base of the tree to drive the angry bees away. They would then cut the tree down and always took care to leave a honey comb – preferably one with grubs – for the honey guide.

But the fugitives current situation precluded them from using an axe – it would make too much noise. So Goodwill assessed whether the hole in the tree was large enough to take his hand. If so, he climbed up using bark fibres tying his ankles and looped round the trunk. He took a smoking brand with him and put his hand into the hole to pull out the combs. He was stung many times, but hunger overcame the pain. They made parcels from bark to carry the honeycombs, which sustained them for several days.

One evening as they walked cautiously along the path Goodwill double-clucked and melted into the undergrowth. Kawa was quick to follow and they crawled to a point about twenty yards from the path. Four men strolled past, returning to their village. They had a dog with them, a scrawny brindled cur with a tail that curled into a circle. It caught the scent of the fugitives and started barking. Goodwill and Kawa could see it looking in their direction, its hackles raised.

"What's the matter," growled one of the men to the dog. "What have you seen?"

"He's barking at shadows," said another man. "Let's keep going; it will be dark soon."

"Come on stupid!" commanded the dog's owner.

They moved on.

—•—

After nearly two months of walking they found the vegetation changing. The forest was more open, with patches of grassland among the trees. It became more difficult for the two men to hide. They had to drift from one patch of trees to another, but it also became easier to move without using the path, while keeping aware of its location. Fewer people lived here because the climate was drier, making cropping more risky. The villages were further apart, as were the fields that surrounded them.

The open savannah woodland held more game animals. They saw small herds of zebra, kudu, eland, and sable, and in lower areas bushbuck and puku. They attracted predators: lions, hyenas, jackals and wild dogs. Goodwill and Kawa debated the feasibility of hunting the larger antelopes, but decided they lacked adequate resources. They had no weapons, and Goodwill's attempts to make a bow and arrows failed; he could not find the types of tree wood that his uncle favoured. They considered digging a pit trap but thought it would take too long and might advertise their presence.

One day they came across the carcass of a zebra surrounded by jackals and vultures. It appeared that lions had eaten the choicest parts, leaving the remainder for the scavengers. The two men were able to drive the jackals and vultures away and took most of a back leg with some of the haunch. They cooked the flesh on a low fire; it was two days old and beginning to putrefy, but when grilled it tasted delicious.

"We have become like jackals," said Goodwill, as he gnawed at the femur hungrily.

"We are better, surely," replied Kawa, laughing. "We are wiser and stronger – we drove them off the kill."

— • —

They had been in the savannah for two weeks when they heard shouting ahead. Hiding at a nearby rocky knoll they watched a slave caravan approach, with nearly two hundred slaves and a dozen guards. The latter made a great deal of noise with their shouting and beating of drums. The slave trader was borne in a *machila*, and for a moment Goodwill thought it might be Musa, but this man was larger and darker.

The caravan stopped opposite the knoll where Goodwill and Kawa were hidden. They were about a hundred and fifty yards away. The slaves quickly dropped to sit or lie on the ground, while the *ruga-rugas* formed into a separate group and lit a fire. It was unusual for a caravan to stop in a location that had no water. The slaver got out of his *machila* and walked a few paces towards the knoll, to relieve himself.

After about thirty minutes the guards started shouting and hammering on their drums. The slaves stood up, too slowly, and the whips were brought into use. Some of the guards could be seen in discussion with the slaver; there was much gesticulating, and a chorus of wails from the slaves.

"What are they doing?" whispered Kawa.

"I think they have a problem slave – one who cannot walk. That is why they stopped here."

Two guards dragged a young boy out of the line and half lifted him into the grass at the side of the path. He was limp and helpless, and some slaves moved to help him but were beaten back by the guards.

"They are going to kill him," whispered Kawa.

"I fear they will," replied Goodwill.

Then the slaver came forward. He had a walking stick – a long carved wooden staff – which he pointed at the boy, who lay motionless on the ground. The slaver swept his staff and the guards cringed away. He shouted in a deep voice and climbed back into his *machila*. Loads were lifted and the *rugas* beat their drums in the marching rhythm. The caravan moved forward, leaving the boy behind.

— • —

He was dying. It was soon obvious when they crept up to the path twenty minutes later. The sounds of the caravan had faded to the east. The boy lay curled up in the foetal position.

Goodwill felt his brow. "He has fever. Perhaps that slaver decided it was not worth killing him because he was already dying."

"Is there anything we can do?"

"Let us carry him to the rocks."

They tried to make him drink a little water but he was unconscious and the precious liquid dribbled onto the ground. He woke an hour later, and in a faint voice he told them that his mother and father were in the caravan, and when he spoke of them his eyes filled with tears. He said that the *rugas* wanted to kill him, but the slaver, Ali Juma, told them to leave him beside the path because he was nearly dead.

His name was Chisiza; he was ten years old. He and his parents had been captured in their village, far to the west. There were other captives in the caravan from even further away. They were taken to Kota Kota, on the western shore of Lake Nyasa, where there was a large camp with many stockades. They were kept there for several weeks before being shipped across the Lake in *dhows*.

During the evening Chisiza became unconscious again. "We must keep him warm," said Goodwill, so they lit a fire behind a screen of thorn bushes that formed their little *boma*, fearful that it would be seen. They had nothing with which to cover the boy, but Kawa brought water from a stream, about one mile away, carrying it in the little leather bag that the seashore woman had given them. They lay on either side of him.

When they woke in the morning Kawa's first words were, "Is he alive?"

"I fear not," replied Goodwill, touching Chisiza's brow – it was cold.

Then he saw the boy's eyes open. "Dear God, he's alive!"

Kawa was in tears. "Will he stay alive?"

"Only if we feed him." Goodwill was surprised at the emotion of his companion.

At that moment they saw three men walking towards them from the path. All carried spears, and two had bows and quivers. A black dog trotted behind them.

— • —

14

On November 24, 1887, the slavers attacked the little boma at Karonga and its small group of defenders. With its adjoining rough stockade it also contained over a thousand helpless refugees. The attackers had about five hundred men armed with ancient guns, many of them muzzle-loaders. Perhaps a thousand others carried spears, and bows. They advanced in haphazard fashion, making a tremendous noise, shouting and calling to each other. A few of them yelled abuse.

The defenders opened fire, and Alan got two quick shots off, then heard the deep bark of Sharpe's elephant gun. He saw some men fall, while the others faltered. Then all the attackers turned and retreated. They sheltered in the trees about a hundred yards away from the *boma* and started to fire in a desultory fashion.

The six white men cheered and shook each other by the hand. O'Neill said, "You were right, Spaight, we should have destroyed the houses and sheds. Those bastards are using them as shelters. We have to do something about them."

They held a prolonged discussion over mugs of tea, as they sat hunched behind the breastworks, taking it in turns to keep a lookout. Bullets whizzed and whined into the *boma*, spattering the earth and sending splinters of wood flying. The African refugees were terrified, lying on the ground, moaning and wailing, while the servants and *askaris* tried to reassure them, instructing them to keep down and out of the field of fire.

The Consul and Alfred Sharpe, accompanied by half a dozen armed Africans, bravely made a sortie from the *boma* to set fire to the company houses. Alan watched with mixed feelings as his own house went up in flames. At least he knew that his personal possessions were in the *boma*. The posse were unable to burn the company store because its thick grass roof was too wet from rain. It was destined to become a major problem.

By dusk it was evident that the attackers were besieging the *boma;* they seemed afraid to make another frontal attack. The defenders, under O'Neill's directions, arranged a guard system with at least two white men awake for two-hour shifts.

Alan shared his guard duty with Alfred Sharpe, and asked about his pastime of hunting elephants.

"It's exciting," said Sharpe, "because there's plenty of danger in it. It's not just the elephants, but there's the other animals that can emerge from nowhere. You have to be very wary of buffaloes."

"Do you make much from the ivory?"

"Not really." Sharpe sucked on his pipe. "It pays my expenses, but not much more. You see, you have to give one tusk to the local chief – as a sort of tribute. Then there's so much of it on the market; the price has come down a lot. These Arab slavers have opened up a huge trade in elephant tusks. Now every villager is getting into the business. The slaughter of jumbos is dreadful. They're being driven further and further into remote places. Of course there are still plenty of them, but I think they're becoming much more wary of us humans."

"With good reason."

"True." Sharpe pointed the stem of his pipe at him. "So I hear you were in the army in India."

"I was, but I resigned my commission last year."

He looked at Alan sharply. "Why did you do that?

Alan wondered how much to tell him. He seemed shrewd – very much a lawyer. "It was not really the life I wanted. I liked the men – I was with a Sikh regiment – but there was too much dull routine. Then I had a run-in with my CO."

"Not that it's any of my business, but what was that about?"

He told him what had happened, and Sharpe said, "I suppose your adjutant was right. The army can only function properly if officers and men obey their orders. Mind you, I sympathise; there are too many floggers in the forces."

—•—

At dawn the defenders in the Karonga *boma* could see some of the slaver militia moving into the abandoned Mandala store, about eighty yards above the *boma*. They were making a hole in the roof, and then used bush poles to construct a platform inside that allowed them to stand in the roof and fire down into the *boma*. They also made platforms in a large *Brachystegia* tree from which they started to snipe. Another group started building a stockade near the beach.

Sharpe did his best to disrupt their activities by firing back at them, while the other defenders conserved their ammunition. Meanwhile, O'Neill put Alan in charge of raising the height of the *boma* walls with bales of cloth and boxes of trade goods; Fotheringham complained bitterly, muttering about 'company property'. Alan instructed the small labour force to dig trenches and pits inside the stockade, in which the refugees could shelter from the intermittent bullets. Evidence of the intensity of the incoming gunfire could be seen in the tents inside the *boma* that were now riddled with holes.

When another attack seemed imminent Alan stayed alongside Sharpe. They both used their hunting rifles to pick off any of the slaver militia who showed themselves, but they were constantly concerned about lack of ammunition. Sharpe had only about a hundred rounds, while Alan had even fewer.

Sharpe and Alan took several armed Africans in another sortie to the Mandala store with the intention of dislodging the snipers in the roof. It was a risky affair, because there was virtually no cover. Sharpe was able to fire his elephant gun at the front door, which blasted it half open, terrifying the occupants at ground level, who fled. Alan took his hunting rifle, but after firing several shots at the slaver militia on the platform, it jammed. The snipers on the platform remained in action and the posse had to retreat back to the *boma*.

When night fell Fotheringham persuaded two of his senior African staff to creep out of the *boma*; carrying glowing embers to start fires. They crawled round to the rear of the store and tried to set fire to the edges of the grass-thatched roof. The grass was wet and did not immediately ignite, so when the men returned it was thought that their mission was a failure. But an hour later, to everyone's surprise, the store erupted into flames. The snipers in the roof scrambled down and fled, followed by ringing cheers from the defenders.

The siege continued for five days with desultory fire from both sides, constrained by shortage of ammunition. On the fifth day the defenders heard a commotion in the enemy stockades, accompanied by blaring horns and rattling drums. They feared that a major charge was about to be launched, and vowed to sell their lives dearly.

Alan stood at the breastworks, rifle in hand, a bandoleer with his remaining three dozen rounds slung over his shoulder. Behind him stood one of Sharpe's Tonga servants holding a Snider-Enfield .577 rifle, a box of cartridges at his feet. Sharpe was ten yards away, smoking his pipe, his elephant gun propped against the barricade. He, too, had a loader with a Snider rifle behind him.

Silence followed and it eventually became apparent that the enemy had gone. The defenders cautiously emerged from the *boma* and approached the enemy stockades, finding them empty.

Soon after, John Nicoll arrived with about five thousand Mwamba men. He was greeted with hearty thanks. It had been a brave sortie by the young Scot, and his return had effectively raised the siege.

The Mwamba men, warriors of a sort, were anxious to get into a scrap with the slavers and to capture some booty. It was now obvious that the approach of this 'army', superior in numbers, had caused the slaver force to disperse. Meanwhile, it was deemed safe for the half-starved refugees in the *boma* to venture out to forage for food in the surrounding countryside.

— • —

That evening the eight white men held a council of war, sitting around a blazing fire, having made sure there were no Africans within earshot. They could hear rumbles of thunder and distant tall clouds flickered with lightning like enormous lanterns. The rainy season was about to start.

"We have two options," said O'Neill. "We can remain as defenders in the *boma*, or we can attack. We cannot expect outside assistance in the short term, and we will always be short of food if we stay cooped up here."

"I think we should attack," said Sharpe, in his languid deliberate way, stroking his long nose. "Now that we have Nicoll's Mwamba men we can show the blighters we mean business. What do you think, Alan; you've been an army officer."

Alan was embarrassed, suspecting that Fotheringham would want his opinion sought first. "I agree, Alfred. Besides, I think if we cower inside the *boma* it will be seen by them as a sign of weakness."

It was eventually agreed they would attack a small village that was the nearest slaver stronghold, and the home of the Baluchi, Ramathan. Setting off at dawn they discovered the village abandoned. To their dismay, Nicoll's Mwamba men then decided to return home to the north end of the Lake, although they promised to return if needed. Nicoll tried in vain to persuade them to stay. Meanwhile, the local WaNkonde people were reluctant to return to the *boma*, fearful that they might become trapped there if the slavers attacked again. They preferred to hide in the bush near their villages.

The white men held another camp fire council on the following night. Consul O'Neill led the opinion that Karonga had to be abandoned. "It makes sense to move north of the Songwe River, to the Mwamba country, where there are no active slavers, and where we would have plenty of support from the local tribesmen."

"I cannot abandon the company's goods," said Fotheringham gloomily

"Of course not," reassured O'Neill. "We'll take your stuff north with us."

So they used the Mwamba 'army' as carriers. O'Neill, Scott, Bain, Tomory, Sharpe and Alan went with them. Fotheringham and Nicoll stayed behind for a few hours to load some canoes with more company trade goods, then followed on the Lake, keeping close to the shore.

At this time Dr Kerr Cross arrived from Chirenje; Alan had not met him before. He was dapper in khaki jacket and breeches, with long canvas leggings above his boots. He had a neat small beard and a large solar *topi* that seemed too large for his head.

Eventually, they all camped near a swamp that Sharpe named the Elephant Marsh. Plagued by mosquitoes and the foetid air they built grass huts in native style, but later moved into the local chief's thatched cow shed, where they could be together. Now all they could do was to wait for the *Ilala*.

—•—

When the little steamer arrived it brought Hawes, the Consul for Nyasaland territory, John Moir, John Howat, and a Hollander named Moolman. The visitors were greeted warmly, but there was disappointment that they had brought only a few guns with them. It was also soon evident that having two consuls together was a potential source of friction. It was not clear to anyone who of the Consuls was the senior.

Sharpe muttered to Alan, "That's why an outgoing ambassador always leaves before his successor arrives."

Yet another council of war was held that evening around a fire. They agreed that increased firepower, supported by the Mwamba tribesmen, justified an attack on Mlozi as soon as possible. Meanwhile, Dr Kerr Cross was asked to go south in the *Ilala* to the mission station at Bandawe to collect more guns and ammunition.

The meeting was interrupted by a heavy rain storm, accompanied by extravagant thunder and lightning. Alan stood at the entrance of the cow shed and watched the night sky light up. The trees and shrubs around the perimeter of the camp thrashed to and fro in fierce gusts. Heavy raindrops lashed the ground which was soon covered with a sheet of muddy water. He hoped that Howat and the *Ilala* were safe, riding out the storm.

The following morning he woke shivering. His clothes were soaked with sweat, and he nearly fell over when he stood up and tottered out to the long grass to relieve himself. Thinking he might have caught fever he went to see Dr Cross, who was washing himself, using a tin mug propped on a tree stump.

"What's the matter? You look a bit groggy." He checked Alan's pulse and temperature, then said, "I suspect you have malaria fever. Not surprising when you think how long you've been living in these unhealthy parts. It comes to all of us sooner or later."

"Do you have any quinine?"

"I have a little." He gave some of the evil tasting powder to Alan, who promptly retched, thus wasting the dose.

His temperature rose during the day and by that night he was delirious. He vaguely remembered Dr Cross tending him, swabbing him with wet cloths. He took more quinine, which the doctor mixed with bush honey to disguise the dreadful taste. The honey had been brought into the fort by one of Sharpe's men who had followed a honey guide; it had a sharp tang of wood smoke.

—•—

He made a gradual recovery during the next few days, but it left him weak and thin. To his great disappointment, he was judged unfit to accompany the expedition to attack Mlozi's stockade. It was led by Hawes, who was accompanied by John Moir, Fotheringham and Alfred Sharpe. The missionaries, Bain and Tomory, went as non-combatants to assist the wounded and to interpret. Dr Cross stayed with Alan, O'Neill and Nicoll, all recovering from bouts of fever.

Fotheringham organised the attack column, since he had the best command of the local dialects. He divided the Africans into three tribal 'battalions', each commanded by a headman, or minor chief. Those Africans with no affiliations to local tribes, such as the Mandala employees, formed a central company with the white men. The attack column first had to cross the Lufira River, then march for eight miles in pouring rain until they reached the Rukuru River, on the far side of which stood Mlozi's stockade.

Using an encircling formation the column charged, their progress hampered by numerous pits that the local people had dug to extract clay for bricks and pottery, and were now filled with rainwater. Fotheringham and Sharpe reached the stockade first, in the face of a hail of fire from Mlozi's men. The rest of the attacking force was close behind. They tore down the stockade and the defenders fled into the surrounding banana groves. Although Fotheringham urged his forces to follow the fugitives they were more interested in looting the huts inside the stockade, where they found ivory, gunpowder and bales of cloth, all valuable for barter. They were the equivalent of fat wads of banknotes, though not as wieldy.

Taking stock of their injuries they found that none of the attackers had been killed, though several had been badly wounded. Among the white men, John Moir received a bullet in the muscle of his thigh, and Alfred Sharpe was wounded by a spent bullet in one of his heels.

It was too wet to burn the huts within the stockade, so the attackers returned to base in high spirits. The wounded Moir and Sharpe were carried in *machilas*. That evening they recounted the story of their triumph, while Dr Cross attended to the wounded men.

Although Alan did not say so openly, he mentioned to Sharpe that the victory at Mlozi's was likely to be short-lived. A stockade could be re-built in days, and the defeated slavers would soon seek to replenish their stocks of ivory.

—•—

The *Ilala* returned from Bandawe four days later bringing John Lindsay, a Mandala employee, and a Mr Gossip from the Free Church Mission. They all celebrated Christmas is subdued style, far from the cold and snow they associated with the festival. It was hot and humid, with spells when it rained every day. Damp pervaded, and it was difficult to keep clothes and blankets dry. They had no gifts to exchange, so they drank toasts around a large fire and talked about Christmases they had enjoyed in the past, and that they hoped to celebrate in the future.

Hawes, Consul for Mozambique and the interior, and O'Neill, Consul for the Lake Nyasa territory, were the senior British men present, and called a meeting to debate what further action should be taken. Hawes wanted to withdraw the British presence in the whole of the north end of the Lake, excepting Bain's mission at Chirenje. He argued that they should return later with a larger force. Fotheringham was vehemently opposed to abandoning the local tribesmen and leaving them at the mercy of the slavers. He was supported by Nicoll and Dr Cross. It was finally agreed that these three would go to the mission station at Chirenje, where they would be relatively safe from the depredations of the slavers, and could gather intelligence about their activities.

"When I get back to Blantyre," announced John Moir, "I'll recruit a force of at least fifteen white men, with guns and ammunition. We'll return by the end of April."

The *Ilala* steamed south on January 5, 1888, taking all the remaining white men, except Bain and Moolman, who decided that the little ship too crowded and elected to walk to the Chirenje mission. Alan was ordered by John Moir to go south on the *Ilala*; he was deemed too weakened by fever to be of much use to Fotheringham.

—•—

15

East of Lake Nyasa - February 1888

Goodwill and Kawa had a quick discussion about running away. The three villagers were striding towards their hiding place, gripping their spears. The dog's hackles were raised. The two friends knew that they had been discovered, yet they could not flee without leaving the boy behind.

As the men approached one of them called in ChiYao, "Who are you?"

"We are travellers," replied Goodwill, trying to sound confident.

"Travelling where?"

"To the Lake."

The three men muttered to themselves. Then the spokesman said. "We saw your fire last night. Did you escape from the slave caravan?" He approached closer. "We can tell you are fugitives."

Goodwill decided it would be best to tell the truth. When the three men came closer he told them everything. They listened without interrupting, but the black dog snarled. Its name was Kuda, and every now and then the spokesman would command the dog to be quiet. Finally, he said, "We should take the sick boy to our village. You can come too. We will give you food." He explained that he was the village headman, and had determined to find out why a fire had been lit during the night.

Goodwill could hardly contain his relief, but he remained suspicious. He and Kawa took it in turns to carry the boy the two miles to the village. There were a dozen grass huts in a clearing near a small stream. On the slope above the village were empty fields. There was an atmosphere of desolation in the place.

A trickle of villagers came out of their huts to greet the headman and to watch the strangers he brought with him. Goodwill noticed that they were mostly older men and women, thin, even emaciated, with anxious expressions. The headman addressed them; there were about two dozen. He explained that the fugitives would be staying at the village until the young boy recovered to the point that they could continue their journey west. *Nsima* and beans were brought, and water from a dug well. Goodwill and Kawa ate the first proper meal they'd had since their capture six months earlier. They watched as the village women brought a warm cloth to wrap around Chisiza, who was then taken to a hut where he was washed and given water to drink.

The headman was about forty years old, quietly authoritarian. He said that his village was a regular stopping place for slave caravans. They typically captured able men, women and children, and commandeered any available food. The villagers tried to scout for approaching caravans, but the *ruga-rugas* went ahead to make sure that potential slaves and food were not hidden. Even so, they kept stockpiles of grain in clay pots amongst the rocks, that the slavers never found.

Goodwill and Kawa slept in the sun, then shared an evening meal with the headman and his wife before retiring to the hut where Chisiza had been sleeping. They helped the women to coax him into eating *nsima*, and more important, drinking. The poor boy bewailed the loss of his parents, and they tried their best to comfort him.

—•—

They stayed in the village for three weeks. They grew stronger and watched Chisiza recover from his fever and put on weight. They tried to repay the villagers by helping them repair huts and fences. Goodwill put his hunting skills to good use. He found suitable saplings to make a bow and arrows, and was able to bring in small game and guinea fowl to augment the village diet.

The time came for them to leave, and the villagers gave them an axe, the small one-handed type, with a four inch blade. They filled the leather bag with maize grain. They gave Chisiza a shirt and he was overcome with gratitude, weeping copiously in the arms of the village women.

Enormous thunder clouds gathered in the east as they walked away from the village. They heard from the headman that it would take them at least another month to reach the escarpment from which they would walk downhill to the Lake. They were feeling strong and hopeful.

By midday they felt heavy raindrops on their shoulders and looked for shelter. A hillock not far from the path was crowned with a pile of rocks, and they used the little axe that the villagers had given them to cut brush and place it in crude roof spanning two boulders. By this time it was raining in earnest. Any potential fire materials were soaking wet. They huddled under their shelter.

"Why did those villagers help us?" asked Kawa rhetorically.

"They know what the slavers are like," said Goodwill.

"Yes, but they have so little."

"They behaved as Christians are supposed to."

"But they are Muslims."

"Not strict Muslims. You saw that they pray only twice, not five times. They know little of the Koran."

"So is it better to be a Muslim or a Christian?"

Goodwill pondered. "My teacher told me that Jesus Christ explained how we humans should behave to each other. He was so clear and right that his preachings became the foundation of a religion. I have never read the Koran, but my teacher has, and he told me that it contains both good things and bad, and is not so clear as Christ's teaching."

Chisiza wondered about the two young men who had become his protectors. Would they be able to return him to his village? They told him that he would have to be patient and perhaps wait in the safety of a mission station until he was old enough to make the journey himself. He often asked them what would happen to his parents, and whether he would see them again. They tried to reassure him, telling him that his mother and father would probably become the servants of some rich people and Chisiza could visit them when he grew up and made his fortune. The little boy would watch them with solemn eyes, brimming with tears.

In moments when Chisiza was overcome with sadness the two young men would try to distract him. Goodwill told him about the wild animals and their habits, while Kawa would sometimes imitate these creatures in pantomime, making their strange noises. He would put his arm to his face to make an elephant's trunk, and then he would give the brassy trumpeting sound of the enraged bull. He would drop to all fours and grin like a hyena, uttering its strange haunting cry. Chisiza would smile and often break into laughter as he enjoyed Kawa's antics. His favourite was the klipspringer, with Kawa skipping about on the tips of his toes, turning his head from side to side.

— • —

The rainy season was in full force. It had started with isolated thunderstorms, but now the rain was more sustained, often falling in the afternoon and at night. At the first sign of a storm they would seek a shelter, such as an overhanging tree or rock. They hurriedly gathered thorn branches and firewood. They always carried a small parcel of dry moss and kindling to start the fire, together with a twirling stick to create the friction. Despite all their precautions there were times when everything became soaked and they would huddle together, waiting for the storm to abate.

Wild animals were both a potential source of food and a menace. Lions and leopards were more common in the savannah country, since their prey was more abundant. The grassland was scattered with small herds of roan and sable antelope, kudu, eland, waterbuck, and zebra. Generally the feline predators kept away from the three human travellers, but they could be heard hunting at night.

One night some lions came to their shelter and walked around, attracted by their scent. They knew that lions killed humans and ate them, but usually only when they could not find their natural prey. The thorn bushes protected them, because lions instinctively fear thorns and their potential to cause septic wounds. The huge cats grunted and purred as they nosed around. Chisiza was paralysed with fear. Goodwill hastily lit a flaming brand and they could see its reflection in the lions' eyes. After a few minutes they moved on and the night returned to normality – the whine of mosquitoes, the chatter of crickets, and the occasional hoot of an owl.

The three travellers kept away from human habitation. They seldom saw other people, and then only in the distance. The path rose higher and higher, reaching altitudes of three to four thousand feet. The nights were cooler and the dawns heavy with dew. Frequent rain made the path slippery and the ground beside it soggy. Firewood became more and more difficult to find. Progress was slowed by Chisiza, who, though he had recovered from the fever, was thin and frail on a meagre diet of grass seeds, roots, grubs, and the occasional small animal.

One morning, Goodwill, who was walking ahead, as always cautious, crested the brow of a hill. In awe he gazed at a great view spread before him. The slope fell for over two thousand feet to the great Lake which lay like a huge ingot of molten metal, striated silvery grey, textured by shifting winds. He could see the distant far shore and the hills beyond, and to his left and right the Lake stretched into the distant haze.

He turned and beckoned to Kawa and Chisiza who walked up to join him.

"How long will it take us to reach the Lake?" asked Chisiza.

Goodwill replied, "Perhaps twenty days. It is easier to walk downhill, except that it may be slippery. We must be careful, too, when we are nearer the Lake, because there are friends of the slave traders living there."

"How will we cross the Lake?"

"We will not cross. We have no boat. We must walk to the south end – then to Lake Malombe. It will be dangerous there, too, because there are more people – headmen and chiefs who deal with the slavers. We must avoid them as if they are dangerous animals."

The little boy gazed up at him. "Where will you end your journey?"

"I must go to the Christian mission at Domasi, near Zomba. The people there will protect us. Later, we can go back to our villages."

—•—

It took them over three weeks to reach the Lake littoral, but they stayed well away from the shore itself, where there were many small fishing villages. A gentle slope receded from the shore, covered with scrub vegetation that several generations had cut and burned for cultivation. Higher up, perhaps a mile or two from the shore, spread a network of paths used by hunters and gatherers of firewood. It was along these paths that they wended their way slowly south.

There was more food here, mice and rats that fed on the crops, birds that provided eggs or nestlings. They reverted to their earlier tactic of walking in late evening or on moonlit nights. A month of this ponderous travel brought them to the southern end of the Lake, where the Shire River flowed out.

Goodwill and Kawa debated whether to cut across the river to the western side, where the people would be friendlier. There were large villages here, with several hundred people living in them. But the chiefs were Yaos who were deeply involved in the slave trade. They had militia, some armed with guns, others with spears, and bows and arrows. It was a dangerous area.

The alternative, which they chose, was to continue on the eastern side of the Shire and Lake Malombe. They then skirted along the eastern shore of Lake Chilwa. More people lived here than in the highlands, but the village populations had been decimated by the trafficking in slaves.

On clear days they could see Mount Mlanje and Mount Zomba. Goodwill knew that he was nearing his home, but danger lurked everywhere. If they were captured by villagers they would be handed over to a Yao chief. Also, lions abounded and were known to kill humans if there was a shortage of bush pigs, their customary prey in this region.

One evening, as they settled down inside their thorn *boma*, huddled around a tiny fire, they heard voices. Kawa threw dirt onto the fire to extinguish it. The voices came closer and they saw a group of men carrying lighted brands made from reeds; they were armed with spears and bows. The men quickly surrounded the little *boma*.

"Who are you?" demanded one of the men; he spoke ChiNyanja.

"We are travellers," replied Goodwill nervously.

"Why are you travelling here?"

They had rehearsed an answer. "We were fishing on Lake Chilwa and a storm took us to the east shore. Since then we are lost."

The silence that followed suggested that the men did not believe them. "You must come with us."

The men started to pull away the thorn bushes. Goodwill, Kawa and Chisiza stood up; they were soon surrounded by an impenetrable ring of spear points.

"Do not give us trouble or try to run away." admonished the leader of their captors. His voice was deep and menacing.

They moved off in line, following paths that the men seemed to know well. They made plenty of noise to frighten animals away. Goodwill gathered from their conversation that they were returning late from hunting and had seen the light of the fire.

A half hour later they came to a village and went straight to the headman's hut. An old man appeared, gathering a cotton cloak around his thin shoulders. His spine was bent, and his hair and beard were grizzled.

"Who are you?" demanded the headman; he was a Nyanja. "Tell me the truth – it will be good for you."

Goodwill told him the truth. The headman and their captors listened in silence. Then the headman spoke.

"I am sorry. I have to take you to our chief. If he heard that we had freed you he would kill us."

"But your chief is a Yao, and you are Nyanja," said Kawa.

"True, young man. But he is the great chief. I am sorry; there is nothing I can do." The headman turned to his men. "Give them food and water. Put them in that empty hut near the anthill. After that you must feed yourselves."

Goodwill almost wept in his despair. After all those miles and all those days and nights, to be taken back into slavery was too much to bear.

— • —

16

Shire Highlands - January/February 1888

Alan felt much better by the time the *Ilala* reached its destination at Matope. The voyage down the Lake proved a tonic, even though the little steamer was heavily crowded. During the daytime he sat in a canvas chair, and at night he slept on deck, cooled by the Lake breezes. When the ship ran into occasional showers he took shelter under the canvas awnings.

His fellow passengers were good company, especially the wounded men, John Moir and Alfred Sharpe. They exchanged anecdotes from their past. John Moir told how he and his brother had worked in Tanganyika building a road from Dar-es-Salaam into the interior. They had suffered badly from the lowland fevers, and were glad to have a chance to work in the healthier climate of the Shire Highlands, and to bring their wives out from Scotland.

Alfred Sharpe described his life as a sugar cane planter in Fiji, and the wonders of the Pacific islands. He was a restless spirit, but seemed to have found a region that he found both attractive and exciting. Despite his wound he was eager to continue the campaign and to hunt elephants whenever he had the opportunity.

Alan told them about his short campaign in the Sudan and the horrors of the Dervish attack on the British square at Tofrek. He described his experiences in India, and they asked him about his conflict with the new Colonel of the regiment.

"Didn't any of your fellow officers support you?" they asked.

"They sympathised, but they were not prepared to jeopardise their careers in the army."

—•—

Moir and Sharpe were not well enough to walk from Matope to Blantyre, and much to their chagrin had to be carried in *machilas*. Alan was able to walk part of the way, though when tired he climbed reluctantly into his own *machila*.

John Moir insisted that he stay in Mandala House when they arrived in Blantyre . "It's a reward for looking after me," he said.

Elizabeth Moir fussed around them. "It's only a flesh wound," she said, while examining her husband. "At least it hasn't become septic." She sighed. "I don't know what you men were up to – playing soldiers up there."

She realised that Alan had suffered from a really bad bout of fever and needed good meals, which she was adept at providing. Meanwhile, he relaxed on the screened verandah reading books, and at night luxuriated in a comfortable dry bed, secure within his mosquito net.

He heard from the Moirs that Nora had moved to Zomba and was now living in a small house near the hospital. When he told Elizabeth that he had never been to Zomba she immediately suggested that he go there for a weekend.

"Remember that Jock and Marge Kennedy want you to stay with them. Every time I see them Jess pesters me for news about you."

Zomba was forty miles from Blantyre, so a long day's ride on horseback. The Moirs lent him one of their tough Basuto geldings and he set off on a Friday afternoon, planning to spend that night at the Bruce plantation near Magomero, half way to Zomba.

He arrived at dusk and was greeted by Andrew Bruce, one of the pioneers of a large family that had settled in the area and were starting to grow coffee and raise cattle. During supper he and his young wife

Sarah questioned Alan about his experiences at the north end of the Lake.

"Is it worth the trouble, feuding with the slavers?" asked Sarah.

"O'Neill and Hawes, the two Consuls, seem to think so," he answered. "They say that if we don't clear them out the Germans will do it, and then it'll become their territory."

"And is that area really worth keeping British?" asked Andrew.

He pondered. "I suppose so. There's fertile land between the Lake and the mountains – in the area west of Karonga. But it's normally heavily populated, so there's not much room for European settlers. We didn't see much of the area at the northern tip of the Lake. One of the main issues is that the Consuls and the Company want to keep control of the route from Lake Nyasa to Lake Tanganyika – that's why the Stevenson Road is being built."

"You see, it would be part of the great Cape to Cairo route that's being talked about. We British would control the territories along the route, and thus the trade. The two lakes would give us about seven hundred miles of easy water transport. Then there's Lake Victoria, and from there the Nile to Cairo – of course we have to get rid of the Dervishes in the Sudan."

— • —

He left next morning on his stocky gelding. The track was barely wide enough for an ox cart, but was being improved at the stream crossings. It was becoming a thoroughfare for Africans on foot. Women walked along it with bundles on their heads, with young children trotting beside them. Horses were a novelty in the country, and some of these Africans had never seen one before. Their eyes widened and they clucked in wonder at the strange beast with a man sitting on its back.

The Zomba massif loomed ahead, hazy purple, and fascinating to him because Nora wanted to live up on the plateau. As he rode closer he questioned local Africans for directions to the Kennedy estate. The few Europeans were well known and had their nicknames – Jock was known as *Wafira*, because of his red hair.

He saw their house at last; it stood on a knoll, with broad verandahs and a thatched roof. Two ridgeback dogs bounded out to greet him. The Kennedys were having tea on the verandah and Jess ran down the steps to give him a hug, blushing as she did so. He could not have had a warmer welcome.

During supper and later, over nightcaps of whisky, they caught up on their news; they had not seen each other for five months. The Kennedys were avid for news about the fights with the slavers. Only basic news had filtered back to them, and they were not aware of the strength of the opposition, and its obstinacy.

They told Alan about the farm and the progress of the coffee plants. All was going according to plan, although Jock was concerned about the lack of labour, and interference from local chiefs.

"We may have to bargain with them," he said. "They have a tight control over the villagers who are our source of labour."

"And without labour we can do nothing," added Marge.

He asked after the McPhails, and said that he hoped to see them next day.

Marge and Jock went to bed, but Jess stayed up talking, although Alan was growing sleepy and having difficulty keeping his eyes open. She told him how she enjoyed working with Alistair McPhail, and had become his operating theatre nurse, while Nora spent more time in the wards and dealing with outpatients.

"He's such a kind man," she enthused, and he felt strong twinges of guilt.

"What do you think of Nora?"

"Och, she's a dear too. But between ourselves, I think she does not value Alistair as much as she should."

It was obvious that Jess was deeply fond of the child Malcolm. She often stayed overnight with the McPhails, because it would have been too dangerous to ride back to the farm in the dark.

— • —

He got up early next morning and toured the estate with Jock on horseback. Jess joined them a short while later. They rode around the fields while Jock described how he'd cleared the bush and planted the coffee seedlings.

"Not with my own fair hands," he laughed. "I had about a hundred labourers, though I've cut down to half that number now."

Alan admired the glossy dark green leaves of the plants – they all looked healthy and free of weeds. Some of the fields had irrigation channels, so that Jock could provide the plants with water if the rains failed.

"How often does that happen?" he asked.

"There's no knowing. You can have several perfect seasons, and then a drought, which might be followed by another one. Too much rain can be a problem, too – more insects and diseases. As you know, Alan, the downpours can be tremendous, and damaging. But the shade trees help."

Some of the larger indigenous trees had been left to provide shade for the coffee plants, and Jock had started to plant silver oaks (*Grevillea robusta*) in formation.

They returned to the farm house for a hearty breakfast and Alan then took his leave, promising to return that night.

— • —

Alan saw the first sign of European settlement as he approached Zomba Mountain. The new Consulate was being built by the Buchanan brothers, local Scottish planters who had been contracted by Consul Hawes to put up a substantial building that would serve as his residence and offices. While in Karonga, Hawes told Alan his reasons for making Zomba the administrative centre for the country.

"I'm not popular with the Blantyre people," he said, "including the Moirs. I think the Government should be apart from the missionaries and the merchants. Besides, Zomba has a better climate, and it's closer to the Upper Shire and the Lake, so slightly more central. The plateau above the town provides a good supply of clean water that can be distributed by gravity."

John Buchanan was standing outside the half-built Residency; they knew each other from playing cricket on opposing sides, but this was their first conversation. Alan knew that Buchanan had been trained in horticulture at Drummond Castle in Perthshire, where his father was a gardener. He then came to Blantyre to work at the mission, before moving to Zomba before the results of the enquiry into unjustified flogging of African so-called miscreants.

Alan found the tall bearded Scot to be rather dour, but he became more talkative when the subject turned to the campaign against the slavers. He listened to Alan's news about the activities at the north end of the Lake.

"We need to make a more serious campaign. Otherwise, from what you describe, we're never going to achieve an outright victory and clear the slavers away."

"I agree, but I don't know how we can mount such a campaign without support from the British Government."

"It may be a while before that happens." Buchanan, pondered, then pointed to the mountain. "So you're heading for the plateau?"

"I probably won't have time on this trip, but I thought I would camp up there one day."

Buchanan stroked his beard and shook his head slowly. "It gets very cold at night up there. It's over four thousand feet up. But I guess you're used to camping out – after your experiences at Karonga."

The hospital was being built about half a mile north of the Residency. When Alan got there he found some workmen laying kiln-fired bricks, using mud as mortar. Nearby, an African carpenter was sawing roof trusses. He asked for the doctor and was told that he had gone to Lake Chilwa, but the *Dona*, Mrs McPhail, was at the house. The carpenter pointed to a modest wattle and daub house up the slope; it had a thatched roof, and curls of blue smoke rose from its chimney.

Nora was at the front giving orders to a young African who was digging a flower bed. She smiled when she saw him, and he hugged her self-consciously.

"I heard you had a bad go of fever," she said, releasing herself, her cheeks flushed. "You look quite healthy." She invited him into the house.

It was furnished simply. A woven reed mat covered most of the mud floor, and there were mosquito nets covering the windows, inside the curtains. The furniture was roughly made – by local carpenters, she told him, as she brought a glass of lemon juice.

She said, wryly, "Alistair puts all the money into furnishing the hospital. We get what's left over."

She went to fetch her son Malcolm, and dandled the toddler on her knee. "Alistair is at Lake Chilwa for the day; he's back this evening. Please ride up to the plateau with me? Barushka would love the exercise, and I see you have a strong pony. My servant girl will look after Malcolm."

He was afraid of being drawn in too close to her, but she was so urgent in her request. He wondered about her motives and concluded that it might only be loneliness.

—•—

On the ride up the mountain she wanted to be told about the fights against the slavers. The track climbed steadily, with some bends and a few flat stretches. It was wide enough to ride side by side most of the time. The vegetation was luxuriant, creepers grew thickly on the trees, which, higher up the mountain were bearded with lichen. They heard the occasional bark of a baboon.

On reaching the rim of the plateau Nora pointed out the features of the gigantic bowl. The highest point of the rim was four thousand seven hundred feet in altitude. At the base of the bowl was a stream that flowed out at the lowest part of the rim and cascaded down the mountainside near the Residency.

They rode down into the bowl, along a narrow path, and Nora explained that African farmers from the far side of the mountain sometimes carried produce along this path to sell in the embryonic market in Zomba.

"No Africans live on the plateau; it's too cold and misty – and its lack of human habitation is one of its attractions for me."

The horses were anxious about the slippery track. After a mile they came to the stream; it reminded Alan of trout streams he had fished in Scotland. It flowed over granite slabs and through still pools, often in the open sunshine, sometimes in the deep shade of overhanging ferns and trees. There was strange stillness, broken occasionally by the cry of a hawk.

They dismounted and led the horses alongside the cascading water. There was no track so it was slow going. After a while they came into an area of open downland where Nora stopped and tied her reins to a stunted tree, then walked to the stream. Alan did likewise and followed her.

"It's so peaceful here," she said. "I would like to live here – I mean on the plateau."

"Isn't it too cold and wet?"

"No more than the Highlands of Scotland. I would have log fires. It's usually sunny in the daytime – like this, even more so in the dry season."

She moved closer and took him in her arms. She kissed him with an urgency that he found disconcerting, so he broke away. She lay down on the flat rock and he sat beside her, wanting to touch her but trying to avoid it. The rock was warm from the sun. Her cheeks that were flushed. She caught his hand.

"Did you miss me?" She laughed and put his hand on her heart.

—•—

17

The three captives were led away in deep despond. Goodwill could not believe that after all these months they had returned, almost to his home, only to be captured again. Yet the headman had seemed a kindly man, and there was something strange about the way the headman had spoken.

They were given cold *nsima* to eat and a pot of water. Then they were led to a hut on the very edge of the village. In the moonlight Goodwill could see a huge anthill behind the hut, the one the headman had mentioned. Beyond, a path led from the village towards the south.

They were pushed into the grass hut and the door was shut and tied. When his eyes adjusted to the sudden complete darkness Goodwill searched the hut; it had probably been used as a storeroom and was now empty. He soon found that the walls were very flimsy, and at one point, near the back, he could thrust his arm through.

It took only ten minutes for them to open a hole large enough to wriggle through, but they waited for an hour. The moonlight was disconcertingly bright as they emerged from the darkness of the hut. Goodwill led them round to the path. The village was quiet; all the inhabitants had retired for the night. They set off down the path and after about a hundred yards Goodwill saw a glint ahead. It was their axe, confiscated when they were captured.

"They left it here," he explained to the others. "It is a sign that they meant us to escape."

Later, it started to rain. It was too wet to light a fire and too dark to collect thorn bushes. Finally, they found a tree to climb and wedged themselves into the crooks where branches joined the trunk. They slept fitfully until dawn and then pressed on.

— • —

Before noon they saw Lake Chilwa ahead, with its distinctive island near the far western shore. They found a lone fisherman, approached cautiously, and asked him to take them across the lake; they offered to help him mend nets. He agreed and gave them two paddles, while he used a pole in the shallow areas. The surface of the lake was calm, reflecting the grey rain clouds above. At that point it was ten miles across and it took them four hours to reach the western shore, where they meandered through patches of reeds. The mosquitoes were insatiable, and to fend them off they wiped their arms and legs with oil that the fisherman kept in a clay pot.

They had nothing with which to pay the fisherman so they mended his nets on the following day. He let them sleep on clear ground near his hut and helped them to light fires. His wife gave them *nsima* and fish to eat while her four pot-bellied children watched silently.

They spent a second night with the fisherman's family after mending his nets, and next day set off for Zomba along a well-defined path. It was too far for Chisiza to walk in one day, but they stopped at an Nyanja village. They felt safe there, and were given a hut in which to sleep.

When they reached Zomba they went to the thriving market but they had nothing with which to barter for food. They offered their services for food without success, so they collected scraps from the market sellers – a rotten banana, some stale *nsima*, and bones from a goat that had been slaughtered in the morning. They slept in a drain at the side of the market.

—•—

At the Domasi mission, ten miles north of Zomba, the Reverend David Robertson saw two tall young men approaching; they had a young boy trailing behind them. Robertson was walking from the little brick church to his house, thinking about the sermon he would give on Sunday. He wiped the sweat off his brow and looked again at the trio coming towards him. There was something familiar about one of them.

"Goodwill? Is it you?"

The tall young man fell at Robertson's feet, kneeling and holding the minister's ankles. He was sobbing, the months of hardship and stress leaking away in the presence of his former mentor.

"What happened to you my boy?" Robertson bent down and lifted Goodwill up. "Who are your friends?"

Brushing away his tears Goodwill introduced Kawa and Chisiza. The minister led them to the mission dining hall, a large open-sided thatched building, where the workers in the kitchen rustled up a meal of *nsima* laced with an *ndiwo* – relish – of beef and green beans. As they wolfed down the food they told Robertson about their experiences while he listened gravely.

"I was afraid I would never see you and Mary again. It's tragic – what's happened to Mary. I've spoken to your mother every Sunday, trying to console her. You must go to her straight away."

The missionary offered to look after Kawa and Chisiza while Goodwill went to his village.

—•—

Nsofe was sweeping outside her hut as her son walked into the village. She straightened her back, a tall woman, and squinted into the bright sun. Then she fainted.

Goodwill rushed up, as did his younger sister Mercy and some of the village women. Nsofe soon recovered and there was much weeping and laughter as the inhabitants of the little village gathered round. Goodwill was the first person they had heard of who had escaped from a slave caravan and returned to his home.

— • —

Goodwill walked back to Domasi after three days at his home village. He explained to Mr Robertson that he wanted to stay within the relative safety of the mission and asked if there was any work he could do.

"As a matter of fact, I told my friends in Blantyre and Zomba about you," said Robertson. "There's a man named Alan Spaight who might take you on as a clerk. He works in Blantyre as an assistant to Mr Moir of the African Lakes Company. If you like, I can arrange an interview."

Goodwill asked about his friend Kawa. "I think he should work with *azungu*. I have taught him a little English and he would like to learn more."

"I like Kawa – he seems to be a good man. Does he have any special skills?'

"He has lived all his life by the Lake. He is a good boatman and can swim well. Do you think he could work on one of the mission ships on the Lake, like the *Ilala*?"

Robertson pondered. "Perhaps. I will make enquiries."

— • —

18

Shire Highlands – February 1888

Alan spent the night with the Kennedys, where Jess engaged him in conversation after supper. She was such a cheerful girl that it was difficult not to find her attractive. He found himself wondering why he was so entangled with a married woman, who was not overly friendly, almost aloof. Yet here was an attractive young girl who was unattached, and, as far as he could see, was well disposed towards him.

When they went out onto the verandah it seemed a natural progression to take her into his arms. She kissed enthusiastically, but then drew away from him.

She sighed heavily. "You're in love with Nora, aren't you?"

"No, Jess."

"I believe she fancies you – some things she's said to me."

He told himself that he should have had nothing to do with Nora, who was probably using him to bolster her self esteem. Meanwhile, here was Jess, cheerful and affectionate, likely to be a willing partner.

"I have to go." She slipped away.

—•—

He left before breakfast, wishing to stop at Magomero church to hand over a letter from John Buchanan. He arrived soon after the morning service; Andrew Robertson, David's brother, had taken the service, and Alan found the missionary saying farewell to the last members of his congregation.

"I'm sorry you missed our service, Alan," he said, as they shook hands. He was dark and angular, slightly stooped.

"So am I, but I might not have come here at all, except to give you this – from Buchanan." He handed over the letter.

"There's a young African man I would like you to meet. He was taken from his village by slavers but escaped. He's bright and well-schooled – at Domasi Mission. He's doing some teaching here. My brother David thought you might be able to find a place for him in Mandala."

Robertson sent one of his African clerks to find the man. Meanwhile, he took Alan to his house where they sat on the verandah, while Mrs Robertson brought lime juice.

"I have to return to Karonga," he said. "They say I should wait until I'm fully recovered from my fever, but I feel perfectly well now. Perhaps I will go with Buchanan. He will be the Acting Consul when Hawes goes on leave. He told me he needs to go to the north of the Lake, not having been there before."

"Buchanan's a good choice as Acting Consul," said Robertson. "Knows this country as well as any of us. He seems to have put the Blantyre scandal behind him."

"Yes, I heard something about it. What happened?"

Robertson explained what had happened – essentially what the Moirs had told him. "John says he was only carrying out instructions, but he could have refused."

"Didn't you leave the army in India because you would not condone flogging?" asked Mrs Robertson.

Alan laughed. "I wonder where you heard that. Well, it's true." He told them the story.

"I think you did the right thing," said Mrs Robertson. "Ah, here's Goodwill."

—•—

19

Shire Highlands – February 1888

Alan saw a tall young African walk up the path to the house and then wait deferentially at the foot of the steps. He wore a khaki shirt and long grey trousers, but his feet were bare. His expression was diffident, as if he did not care if he stayed or went.

Andrew Robertson went down to greet him and invited him up to the verandah, whereupon he shook Mrs Robertson's hand, and then Alan's. He used the formal way, holding his right forearm with his left hand.

"This is Goodwill," said Robertson, "the young man I was telling you about, who was taught by my brother David at Domasi."

Alan liked the smile and demeanour of the young man, who said, "How do you do" in a rather formal way.

"Mr Spaight works for Mandala," said Robertson. "I asked if he could find you some work in the company." He indicated that Goodwill should sit down. The African seemed reluctant as he lowered himself slowly into a cane chair.

Alan said, "Tell me about yourself."

The Robertsons excused themselves, and Goodwill shifted in his chair, as if it was uncomfortable. He had never sat with white people before. He then told how he had been educated at the mission school for five years before he was captured as a slave. Alan did not interrupt and was fascinated by the account of escape and return to the Zomba area. He was astonished at the quality of Goodwill's English and his clear way of speaking.

When he had finished the story Alan asked, "Where are Kawa and Chisiza now?"

"Chisiza is at the school at Domasi," replied Goodwill, beginning to relax. "When he has finished school he may return to his people in the Luangwa Valley. Mr David Robertson found a job for Kawa, working on the steamer *Domira*. He is very happy with his job."

Alan said, "Your command of English is exceptional."

"Thank you, sir. I was taught well by the mission staff."

"I would like to see how well you can write, because the work at the Company would entail copying records and letters. I do not have a writing kit with me – travelling light – but I'll ask Mr Robertson if I can borrow pen and paper."

Alan went into the house and found Robertson working at his desk. He provided a sheet of paper and pen and ink, as well as a document that Goodwill could copy.

"He speaks English amazingly well," Alan said.

Roberson leaned back and smiled. "Most of the mission boys learn well. Goodwill was one of the best. I wish I could employ him as a teacher, but our budget is over-stretched."

Goodwill copied the document in a steady confident way. When Alan saw the finished version he was impressed with the even, characterful handwriting, and the accuracy of the transcription.

"Excellent. I would like to offer you a job as my clerk in Mandala. It will have to be confirmed by the managers." He explained the terms of employment, and asked him to come to Blantyre by the end of the week following.

—•—

He stopped for lunch with Andrew and Sarah Bruce. They peppered him with questions about Zomba and the plateau, not having been up there themselves.

"I'm beginning to think I would like to live there," said Alan. It's really like a magical fragment of Scotland. Yet it's only an hour's ride, or a couple of hours' walk, from Zomba. Wherever I work in this territory I could go there as a holiday retreat."

They talked about the practicality of building a log cabin on the mountain, and improving the track that led up to the plateau.

Andrew Bruce seemed distracted and then said in a serious tone, "Do you think I should volunteer to go up to the Lake to fight the slavers?"

Alan replied, "I go there because I'm a Mandala employee, and Karonga is my station. Everyone who's there has a reason – except Alfred Sharpe, and he has left. He was a true volunteer."

"It seems unfair that you and the other Mandala people should risk your lives while we sit here in comparative safety."

"'T'was ever thus," added Sarah. "You just stay here, my sweet."

They talked about the future for coffee farming. Andrew was enthusiastic. "It's such an ideal crop for us, with its high value to weight ratio. The London merchants seem to like the quality. But we need more production. Have you thought about buying some land and growing coffee?"

"I'm under contract to Mandala for another year. After that I might consider it."

"Perhaps you should start planning now. It can be a slow process finding the land and getting the title. You could hand them your notice and then start looking for a property. We'll help you to choose good land."

That night, in his room at the mess in Blantyre, he thought hard about Andrew's suggestion. He had been with the Company for only six months of his two-year contract and imagined that the Moir's would not be pleased if he resigned so soon. But he now saw that the way of life of a planter was more attractive than the trader employee, who had also become an accidental soldier. He guessed they might

157

release him from his contract early, so he decided he would look for some land. He liked Africa and felt certain there was a great future for coffee.

— • —

Four days later Goodwill came to the Mandala office in Blantyre, dressed in his best white shirt and khaki trousers. A messenger told Alan that there was a young man asking to see him and Goodwill was shown in.

"I may have to go to Karonga next month," Alan told him. "Although you are to be my clerk you don't have to come up there. There's no housing and conditions are terrible and it can be dangerous – attacks from the slavers..."

Goodwill breathed deeply. "Sir, no conditions could be worse than when I was a slave. As for fights with the slavers, it would be a privilege to help."

— • —

Alan spoke with the Moir brothers on the next occasion when he found them together. "I'm thinking of taking up coffee growing when my contract is completed."

The brothers looked at each other glumly. Fred spoke first. "I was expecting this. If it's the posting in Karonga that's the problem we could keep you in Blantyre. John and I were hoping you would stay with the company and eventually have a management role."

"It's nothing to do with Karonga. I've been talking to planters – Jock Kennedy, John Buchanan and Andrew Bruce – and I like their way of life. They seem to have all the many advantages of living in Africa, as well as the huge one of being one's own boss."

"True," said John. "It's much better than being an employee. It's not so bad for Fred and me because we have so much autonomy – our Board is so far away."

"Coffee planting is not without its risks," Fred added with a serious expression. "You never know when there's going to be a drought, or a flood. You know, it isn't ideal coffee country – not enough reliable year-round rainfall – compared with Jamaica and Colombia. Besides, some awful pest or disease might emerge to decimate your crop. The market might collapse."

He laughed. "You seem to be doing your best to dissuade me."

"Only because we don't want you to leave."

—•—

20

Karonga - March 1888

In March 1888 the Mandala doctor, Thompson, deemed Alan fit enough to return to duties in Karonga. His departure was delayed because Monteith Fotheringham was still at the Chirenje mission. Meanwhile, the Company's station at Karonga had been effectively abandoned, but the Moirs wanted to bring it back into service, if they could drive the slavers away.

Fred Moir decided to travel up the Lake on the *Ilala* to N'sessi, north of Karonga; he instructed Alan and Goodwill to follow him. The Moirs were appreciating more and more the usefulness of Goodwill as an interpretor and scribe. Meanwhile, Alan was becoming increasingly concerned that his bosses would deprive him of his assistant.

As soon as Moir arrived at N'sessi he arranged for the six white men there to return to Karonga to re-occupy the *boma*. He brought with him sixty Mandala African employees and a hundred rifles. They were a sort of private army, and were deemed a sufficient force to re-occupy the *boma* there. Fotheringham came down from Chirenje, and the whole party went south to Karonga in mid-March, some walking along the coastal track, and the others voyaging on the *Ilala*.

They found the little *boma* pulled to pieces. The few brick walls had been broken down and most of the woodwork burnt to ashes. The houses and storerooms, which were mostly destroyed during the siege, and had been abandoned for several months, were now overgrown with weeds and long grass. From what they could see, the whole Nkonde plain was desolate, with no sign of the villagers, who had fled into the hills.

Because the rains were still in force Moir organised his men to build new grass huts inside the perimeter of the former *boma*. He also ensured that the barricade was repaired and that sentries were posted on the paths leading into the settlement. The white men took it in turns to check on the sentries.

Alan travelled up to Karonga a few days later on the steamer *Charles Janson*. With him was Acting Consul John Buchanan; Goodwill came too, as his assistant. Alan got to know Buchanan a little better during the voyage. They were very different in temperament and perhaps that was a reason they enjoyed each other's company. The rather dour Scot seemed to enjoy answering Alan's insatiable enquiries about the early settlement of the territory, while the younger man's good humour was a foil for Buchanan's tendency to be rather serious.

The new arrivals were welcomed into the *boma*. Hands were shaken all round and they broached a bottle of whisky at dusk as they sat round a bonfire near the Lake shore.

"I must have a meeting with Mlozi, Kopa Kopa and Msalemo," Buchanan announced in grave tones. "I believe it's my duty as Acting Consul to try to make them sign a treaty. If they refuse, or if they breach an agreement, we will carry the fight to them."

Alan thought they were brave words, but he doubted whether the slavers would ever make a genuine agreement or treaty without being forced into acceptance. He urged Buchanan not to be taken in by the blandishments of the slavers, who had proved in the past to be untrustworthy.

He was dismayed to see how the fortifications had deteriorated. In Africa it needs only a few weeks of neglect for nature to take over. His former house was a pile of sodden ashes, in which numerous enterprising weeds were flourishing. Goodwill organised some of the Mandala men to build for the British men a low grass hut with a roof thick enough to keep out the heavy rain. Alan wanted his assistant to build a shelter for himself, but was assured that he would share one with the other Africans.

—•—

Two days later Buchanan, Moir, and Fotheringham, set off to meet the slavers; they invited Alan and Goodwill to go with them. They walked along local paths to a spot half way to Mlozi's village. After messengers were sent to and fro they at last met the infamous Mlozi and the two main local chiefs who supported him. They wore clean white *kanzus* and traditional Muslim caps. It was the first time Alan had met Mlozi, and he was impressed by the half-caste's quiet, serious demeanour. He was obviously deferred to by the African chiefs, Msalemo and Kopa Kopa.

To everyone's surprise they admitted that their attack on Karonga had been unprovoked, and agreed to pull down their village stockades. Mlozi even agreed to leave the area within two months.

"It's too good to be true," said Moir later. "I seriously doubt they'll abide by the agreement."

"If that's the case, we pursue the campaign against them," replied Buchanan, reluctant to admit that his efforts might have been in vain.

A further meeting was arranged to sign a treaty but this time the slavers did not turn up. Mlozi sent a message to say that he had decided against leaving the area: '*If you want me out of the country you must put me out*', he wrote in a note, delivered by a truculent messenger.

Buchanan sent a formal message to Mlozi and the two chiefs, written in Arabic, requesting that they destroy their stockades and leave the area within two months. He then left on the *Charles Janson* to return to Matope and thence to Zomba.

Alan was convinced that this last attempt to persuade the slavers into withdrawal was unlikely to work. Although some skirmishes had been successful the British men certainly had not established superiority. It struck him as an uneasy stalemate that could easily erupt if the slavers thought they had the upper hand.

Fred Moir was now in charge of the *boma*. He organised further strengthening of the defences and improvements to the living quarters. He also started experimenting with fire darts that could be fired from muzzle-loading guns, thinking that he could use them to ignite the huts within the slaver stockades. Meanwhile, a number of sorties were made, led by Monteith Fotheringham, in the course of which he discovered some items that had been looted from the *boma* at Karonga when it was abandoned.

Moir and Fotheringham also reconnoitred the villages of Msalemo and Kopa Kopa; sometimes Alan went with them. They found the stockades to be well constructed, with double rows of vertical poles. Each stockade had an inner wall – a sort of thick earth embankment. The outer wall had loopholes at intervals so that the defenders could fire out, while presenting a very small target. Msalemo's stockade had a tower inside it, from which sharp-shooters could fire, although, as Moir pointed out, these snipers were vulnerable. He was now confident that the darts he had invented would set fire to the grass huts within the stockades.

John Nicoll and Dr Cross arrived from Chirenje bringing with them two hundred African tribesmen. This raised the total force in the *boma* to about 500 men, with 270 guns. Food supplies had to be augmented from N'sessi, at the north end of the Lake, because the fields around Karonga had been so devastated by the slavers.

Moir delegated the task of strengthening the defences to Alan, who in turn used Goodwill to help give instructions to the local tribesmen. Alan's knowledge of ChiNyanja was fast improving, and Goodwill was able to fill in the gaps. He was respected by the local people for a number of reasons, particularly his association with the white men.

Also, his height and demeanour were unusual, and it soon became known that he had been brought up in the feared Angoni tribe.

—•—

"We are ready to attack Msalemo's," announced Moir, one evening at the camp fire. "We can muster eight white men and a modest army of *askaris*. I reckon it will be the strongest force to attack the slavers so far."

After much careful planning they advanced west. About half a mile short of Msalemo's they stopped at a large tree and christened it 'The Doctor's Tree' because Dr Cross decided to base himself there, to treat the expected wounded. Mr Bell, who was an engineer by training, stayed with him, to assist and to be in charge of the ammunition.

Fred Moir fired three revolver shots to signal the attack, and they advanced at a brisk pace. Alan stopped now and them to snipe at the tower inside the stockade. The other white men fired at the loopholes in the wall, but it was like trying to hit a bullseye at a distance of over a hundred yards.

Moir fired some of his darts into the stockade and the huts inside were soon in flames. The attackers were elated by this success, and congratulated Moir, but suddenly a number of slaver militia came running out of the stockade and rushed towards them. Alan saw that the African *askaris* were falling back as they realised they were being fired on from the side. He did not blame them; after all, they were amateur soldiers.

Moments later Goodwill pointed out that Fred Moir had been hit. He was sitting on the ground clutching his elbow. They ran up to him and saw blood seeping between his fingers.

"Damn, damn," Moir gasped, obviously in severe pain. "Of all the blasted bad luck."

Alan said, "We'll get you back to Dr Cross." To his surprise he felt calm, almost detached from the chaotic surroundings.

Some of the retreating men carried Moir in a makeshift *machila*. He groaned as it lurched along the path, but they had to get him back to the safety of the Doctor's Tree. Dr Cross bound up the wound, and Alan could see from his expression that he regarded it as very serious. He leaned over to say to Moir, "I think we should all withdraw."

Moir nodded. He was gritting his teeth against the pain. "Take charge, Alan."

He passed the orders around for an organised withdrawal, then arranged for a section of *askaris* to protect their rear, in case there was another sortie of militia from the village.

"It was a victory," he said to Moir, who smiled weakly.

— • —

The bullet had damaged Moir's elbow joint and Cross pondered long and hard about whether he should amputate the arm. The decision was ultimately made by the patient, who was adamant that he wanted to keep it.

For the next two weeks the little force in the Karonga *boma* made sorties against the slavers and their supporters, most of them led by Fotheringham. Meanwhile, Moir's wound was being tended by Dr Cross, and Alan helped as much as he could, with Goodwill invaluable as Cross's assistant. Without having to be asked, he fetched and carried for the doctor and his patient. Meanwhile, the *Ilala* was ferrying food supplies from the north end of the Lake, and making trips south to Bandawe for medical supplies and ammunition.

At the end of April news dribbled in that Mlozi was gathering support from tribes to the west, including his favoured WaHenga. The defenders realised that the situation in Karonga was becoming dangerous. Dr Cross insisted that Moir should return to Blantyre, and then to England, to have his wounded elbow attended to, and eventually Moir decided to go. He left on the *Ilala* with Cross attending him.

— • —

21

Karonga - May 1888

A month passed before the *Ilala* returned to Karonga. To the surprise and delight of the defenders she carried a large group of British men. Accompanying John Moir was Captain Frederick Lugard, DSO, of the 9th Norfolk Regiment, who was on leave from the British Army; he had volunteered to help with the fight against the slavers. With them were five employees of Mandala and nine mercenaries from Natal. They were augmented by Howat and Wilson from the *Ilala*. The newcomers brought several Martini-Henry and Snider rifles and a good supply of ammunition.

Fotheringham was elated. He claimed that it was the largest ever assemblage of armed white men in Central Africa, and no one could deny him. Not until the Pioneer Column entered Mashonaland in 1890 was there a larger group in the region.

As the man with the greatest military seniority and experience, Captain Lugard was made commander. He had a slight build and large drooping moustaches that gave him a solemn expression – the Natal men nicknamed him 'Lugubrious Lugard'. His large eyes were both sad and fierce, as if he'd suffered but did not want to discuss it. He was friendly to Alan, particularly when he discovered that they'd both served in the Sudan.

Lugard at once set about reorganising the *boma*. He moved most of the refugee African population, who had drifted back to Karonga, into a compound outside the stockade. At the same time he made sure they had adequate shelter in the form of grass huts. Thus he effectively segregated the Africans from the British men. The only Africans allowed in the British section of the fort were personal servants, and Goodwill, although even they slept in the African quarters. Lugard's rationale for the segregation was partly hygiene, and partly security.

"We must be certain that members of the slaver force cannot infiltrate the stockade."

Lugard divided the armed Africans into companies based on tribal affiliations, each commanded by a headman. Goodwill helped him in the laborious process. When they were sorted out, the companies were trained in attack and defence formations, and in using rifles. Lugard delegated the training to Alan, who organised drills to make sure that the *askaris* understood basic orders. He also held rifle practices on a makeshift range, using a large anthill as the butts.

Alfred Sharpe arrived a few days later, having marched from Bandawe with a force of Atonga tribesmen. He reported skirmishing with one of Mlozi's slave caravans near Deep Bay, the northern harbour from which *dhows* crossed the Lake. He had been able to release some slaves.

The force in the *boma* was also augmented by Mwambe tribesmen from the north end of the Lake. The defenders suspected they were again hoping to find booty. Even so, they were welcomed, as they brought the total number of armed men to about three hundred and fifty in seven companies, each with about fifty men and each headed by two white men. Captain Lugard was in overall command, with Alfred Sharpe as an unofficial deputy, and Alan as their ADC.

They marched on Kopa Kopa's a week later, and attacked at dawn. The slavers knew they were coming and their fire intensified as the column approached the stockade. Bullets fizzed around, whacking into trees and swishing through their leaves. Now and then a man was hit and cried out.

The loopholes in the stockade presented very small targets. Their efforts to snipe at them as they advanced seemed fruitless, and it was not possible to see whether the holes had been hit.

The command group was first to reach the stockade wall, in a hail of bullets, but had no clear plan about how to proceed. Alan realised that it was imperative to avoid the loopholes through which the defenders were firing. He was contemplating climbing up the stockade wall when he saw Lugard knocked sideways by a blast at point-blank range from one of the loopholes, leaving him choking from the gunpowder smoke.

Alan ran to his side and he seemed to recover quickly. They discussed climbing the wall and decided that it might surprise the occupants of the stockade. Also, they might encourage the *askaris* to follow them.

Alan was looking up at the daunting ten foot high stockade wall when Lugard suddenly fell to the ground.

"Are you alright?" he shouted above the din.

"I've got it," Lugard replied in a faint voice. He was sitting with his arms limp beside him. "Right through the stomach."

Alan crawled over to him, and Lugard said, "I think both my arms are paralysed."

Sharpe joined them, his beard dripping sweat, and his felt hat sitting askew on his head. He looked at Alan questioningly. The noise of the battle was deafening – gunfire from both sides and the cries of wounded men. Terrified cattle within the stockade thundered about, lowing plaintively. The air was thick with dust and smoke.

"Sharpe, you take over command of the attack," Lugard said insistently, his voice barely audible.

Sharpe asked Alan to take the wounded man back to another 'Doctor's Tree'. Alan looked around for Goodwill in the confusing melee of attackers. Then he saw him hunched against the stockade wall. At first he thought Goodwill had been hit, but then he saw he was grinning, his face covered with dust. Alan called to him to bring some Atonga men as stretcher bearers. After a while they were able to assemble six of them, but Lugard insisted that he could walk and set off, stumbling, accompanied by his servant, his arms limp by his side.

Alan followed, to make sure that Lugard got out of range, then turned and went back to the stockade. He could see that several of the attacking Africans had been killed. Moir and Fotheringham both told him that their solar helmets had been knocked off by bullets. Word was passed around that one of the Natal men, Rolfe, was wounded in the head, as was his compatriot Jones. Goodwill, who had followed Alan, told him that the defenders were shouting to each other to concentrate their fire on the white men.

Sharpe ordered a general withdrawal. He came up to Alan and muttered that the attack was unlikely to make any impact on the heavily defended stockade, so they started back towards the Doctor's Tree, the agreed assembly point. The slavers' bullets followed them, whining past them and knocking twigs and leaves off the trees. Looking over their shoulders they saw several of the stockade defenders come out to jeer at the retreating force.

"Watch our rear, Alan," called Sharpe. "Take a few of my Tongas and make sure those Arabs don't follow us."

With Goodwill's help he gathered about a dozen armed Atonga men and formed them into a line, ordering them to turn round to their rear every fifty yards, checking that the column was not being followed. They were about a third of the way to the Doctor's Tree, and Alan was looking back towards the slaver stockade, when he was thrown backwards by a blow on his left shoulder. It was as if a huge invisible hand had struck him. He stumbled and fell onto his back. A wave of fierce pain swept through his chest and back as he collapsed.

—•—

22

Karonga – May/June 1888

"What's the matter?" Sharpe came hurrying to Alan's side and tried to help him up. "Have you been hit?"

He felt dizzy as Sharpe pulled open his shirt and started to prod his shoulder. He yelped as the intense pain spread out again.

"It's alright," Sharpe said. "I think it's too high to have done much damage." He helped Alan to stand up and walk groggily, propping him up on his right side. Goodwill came up on his other side with an anxious expression, but he could do little more than hold Alan's arm.

They reached the Doctor's Tree where Cross was attending to the wounded while Bell supervised their transfer onto makeshift stretchers. Rolfe and Jones, from the Natal volunteers, were lying supine on the ground, waiting to be carried back to Karonga, as were five badly wounded Africans.

"Where's Lugard?" asked Sharpe, looking around the group.

Cross looked at him blankly.

"Have a look at Spaight, Doc. He's caught one in the shoulder."

Sharpe looked at the tired men around him, "We'd better get back to Karonga." To Fotheringham he said, "Take my Tonga men and guard our rear. I don't want those bloody slavers chasing us."

Dr Cross examined Alan's wound, apologising for the pain he was causing. "It seems the slug failed to come out. I think it's lodged behind the scapula. It'll need an operation to get it out." He stood back.

"You'll do better to walk back. A stretcher will be mighty uncomfortable."

Alan opted to walk. He felt as unsteady as if he'd had a beer too many. Looking back he saw that Fotheringham had formed the Atonga men into a rough line about a hundred yards wide, just as he had done earlier. They were retreating slowly, turning at intervals to check that they were not being followed.

It transpired that Lugard was meanwhile stumbling through the bush with his servant. He had missed the Doctor's Tree and was virtually lost. He was losing blood and suffering from thirst. To his surprise his legs were quite strong, though his arms were useless and he was unable to brush the long grass and branches aside to protect his face. Hearing the firing behind him he regretted leaving the action prematurely.

It was a seven mile walk back to Karonga, and about half way there Lugard and his servant stumbled onto a track. He told Alan later that he had lost his hat and was feeling the effects of the blazing sun, but he was able to buy a hat from a passing African. Dizzy and weak from loss of blood he was greeted about a mile from Karonga by a search group and was soon placed on a stretcher and carried into the *boma*. It was then three o'clock in the afternoon.

Waiting his turn at Karonga Alan watched as Dr Cross instructed two of the Natal men to put Lugard onto a wooden table so that he could examine the wounded man.

"I'll give you a whiff of chloroform, Lugard," said the doctor, holding a cloth near the Captain's nose. "Tell me if you feel yourself losing consciousness."

Lugard nodded and a moment later said, "Enough." his head drooped.

Cross started probing, and Alan moved closer to watch. Goodwill was standing patiently to one side, in case he was needed. The doctor muttered as he worked. "The bullet entered here, at the right elbow – it must have been fired close up – see these pieces of wadding. Thank heavens it missed this artery. It then hit his chest – look here, it went under the skin – must have glanced off a rib. Then it came out here at his breast – it must have hit his left wrist next. Good Lord! Look here – pieces of paper – must have come from his breast pocket. It's done a lot of damage to his ulna here, but it might be possible to save it. Hmm, all I can do now is to clean up the wounds."

"What about the paralysis?" Alan asked in a low voice.

"Shock, I would think. I can't see any damage to major nerve routes. I'll have a closer look tomorrow."

When it was his own turn Alan was lifted onto the table so that he was prone, allowing the doctor to probe his shoulder. Bell gave him a whiff of sickly sweet chloroform which made him feel drowsy.

"As I thought," said Cross. "The slug hasn't emerged." He sounded exhausted.

He made Bell and Goodwill turn the patient over. "I'm going to see if I can pick it out from the front, but it may be too deep. Sometimes it's better to leave these things alone until you can get to a hospital." A few moments later he said, "I can just touch it – against the scapula. I'll let it be for now. Sit him up and I'll put a sling on the arm."

Alan suddenly felt a wave of nausea and started retching. Bell and Goodwill supported him on a wobbly walk to the hut he shared with Sharpe and Nicoll. They put him in a canvas chair, and he remained there for the rest of the night, sipping from mugs of tea brought by his companions.

——•——

Next morning he tottered out of the hut, pleased that he was able to walk unaided. He found Alfred Sharpe sitting outside smoking a pipe as he cleaned his rifle, pulling a cord through the barrel.

"I cleaned yours," he said. "How do you feel?"

"Thanks, Alfred. I feel strange. My whole shoulder feels numb."

"Just as well it's not worse."

"How's Lugard?"

"Not good, but he's a tough nut."

"What about Jones and Rolfe?"

"Jones has a bullet in his brain," replied Sharpe. "Doc thinks he's unlikely to recover, poor fellow. Rolfe was hit here," he pointed to his head above the right eye. "The bullet seems to have broken off some of the skull bone. Strange thing – it's given the man an insatiable appetite. He's been stuffing himself with food ever since we got back here."

Alan tried to light his pipe, but had to let Sharpe do it for him. "What do you think, Alfred? Was the attack a failure?"

Sharpe looked at him, frowning. "Don't quote me, Alan. Yes, it was a failure – at least in terms of what little we achieved. You have to weigh up the dead and injured on our side. Fotheringham told me we had five natives killed and several not likely to live, plus Lugard, you, Rolfe and Jones wounded. He thinks there were lots of casualties inside the stockade, but we have no way of knowing."

——•——

Later, Alan walked slowly over to Lugard's hut and found him sitting in a rough bush chair. His clothes had been removed and he had a blanket round his shoulders. His arms were still limp and he was too weak from loss of blood to stand. He was slightly delirious, muttering about being a burden and leaving the attack prematurely. Two of the Natal men were looking after him. Binns rubbed citronella on him and tried to sooth him, while Kaufmann spooned some chicken soup into his mouth. These two men had formerly shared the hut with Lugard, but moved out so that he could have it to himself. The nearby kitchen, that generated much noise and smoke, was re-located.

Thus Lugard sat in his chair day and night, relieving himself into a makeshift bedpan with the assistance of Binns, and becoming seriously depressed. Alan spent as much time with him as he could. He liked telling about his campaign in Burma, and he urged Alan to recount in great detail the story of the Battle of Tofrek. He was fascinated by an account of one of Alan's cousin's exploits in Egypt and the Sudan, especially his experience of the shelling of Alexandria by the Royal Navy. He tried to persuade Alan to re-enter the army, arguing that he was well suited for a military career.

"I can tell that you're a leader, Spaight – and you have courage. Those are the most important qualities of an army officer."

—•—

Two days later Lugard felt well enough to call a meeting. The men gathered around his chair while he addressed them, his voice faint, but still full of authority. "You all did extremely well. In fact, I cannot imagine how you could have done any better. The only reason we failed was because it was impossible for us to breach the slavers' stockade."

"We nearly succeeded," said John Nicoll. "There was a major fire inside the stockade."

"Well, I'm sorry if my wounding caused a premature withdrawal. Now, I recommend that you do your utmost to strengthen our fort – you never know when the slavers might attack." Lugard paused to recover his strength. For a moment Alan was afraid he might faint, but he continued.

"I believe it would be fruitless to make further attacks on the slaver stockades without a heavy cannon. With such a weapon we could breach the stockade wall – like Wellington in the Napoleonic Wars. Fred Moir has told me that he can get one sent out from England, and one of the Natal men knows of one in South Africa that he might be able to purchase – though it may be difficult to bring it past the Portuguese authorities."

They further agreed that, in the meantime, the Karonga anti-slaving force would restrict itself to a guerilla campaign of occasional sorties, led by Fotheringham, with the object of gaining information about the disposition of the slavers.

—•—

For six weeks – the latter half of May and the whole of June – they waited for one of the steamers to come from the south. Alan found life in the stockade stifling. His shoulder was always painful, especially if he inadvertently moved his arm. He was afraid of lead poisoning after one of the men warned him about it. Some of the time Dr Cross was stricken with fever and unable to dress his wound, so it was left to Bell to do it. Alan reminded himself that he had been much more fortunate than Lugard, Rolfe and Jones.

It was a sombre day when Jones died. They buried him with as much military honours as they could muster, including a volley from rifles. His grave was dug under a large baobab tree, beside the two engineers who died of malaria while building the Stevenson road. Fotheringham recited the burial service, and Lugard added a few well-chosen words.

Alan was disappointed when his friend Sharpe left on a hunting expedition – he said he found the inactivity in the *boma* irksome. Alan knew that the hunter had no pecuniary interest in his pursuit; he merely wanted to get back to the thrill of tracking and shooting elephants. He invited Alan to go with him, but he said his wound would make him a nuisance. Besides, he was still an employee of Mandala.

Fotheringham was often away from the fort; he seemed to keep the sorties to himself, though he sometimes took one or two of the other Mandala men. Alan tried to occupy himself with the task of strengthening the stockade. He could not do any physical work himself, but supervised the work of dozens of African tribesmen. This allowed him to practice his ChiNyanja and to improve his understanding of the native culture. The men working under him were cheerful and willing, but were often distracted by events outside the *boma*. They were far from home and concerned about the welfare of their families and friends, particularly if they suspected that the slavers were nearby.

—•—

When at last the *Ilala* arrived there was a common desire among the British men to abandon Karonga and head south. However, Captain Lugard insisted on remaining. He argued that if they left the fort its defences would disintegrate. He feared that the Natal men would refuse to take orders from Fotheringham.

The wounded men were told to go to Blantyre for proper medical attention. Moir felt that he should leave to make arrangements for getting a cannon. All the remaining Natal contingent wanted to go, and when they were told that there was no space for them on the steamer they started muttering about building a raft. It took all of Lugard's persuasive powers to make them stay in Karonga.

Lugard approached Alan to ask if Goodwill could remain with him. "He would be invaluable to me, Alan. I know it's a lot to ask."

Alan asked Goodwill what he wanted to do. He was clearly uncertain, and eventually said. "I would like to go back with you, sir, but I think Captain Lugard needs me more."

—•—

They sailed from Karonga towing a steel barge full of Africans, some sick and wounded, and others intended for the defence of Deep Bay, further south down the Lake. Wilson and Kaufmann were the only white men on board the barge.

Alan watched Karonga receding as he stood on the foredeck of the *Ilala*, glad that he was back on his favourite ship in the company of good friends. They had barely got under away when he heard an explosion from the rear. He hurried aft and saw the barge drifting; the tow rope had been cut.

"What happened?" he asked Howat.

"They have a fire on board. Moir thinks they can put it out and paddle back to shore."

It later transpired that sparks from the steamer had ignited some gunpowder carried by the men on the barge. Many of the men on the steel boat leapt into the water and swam for the shore, but others could not swim or were too sick.

To Alan's consternation the *Ilala* sailed straight on. He never discovered who made the decision or why. He supposed that Moir and the skipper were afraid that the fire might spread to the steamer, and perhaps they did not realise that there had been so much damage on the barge. Alan had been near the prow of the *Ilala*, and by the time he'd moved back to see what had happened the steel boat was floundering far behind.

He heard later that when the barge reached the Karonga shore they found that sixteen of the men were severely burned; several died soon after. Wilson and Kaufmann were furious at being abandoned by the *Ilala*, though thankful to be alive.

—•—

23

Blantyre/Zomba - August 1888

B y the time the *Ilala* reached Bandawe mission station an infection had set into Alan's wounded shoulder. His temperature was soaring, and his clothes were saturated with sweat, attracting flies by day and myriads of mosquitoes at night. He and Rolfe were seen by Dr Laws, who dressed their wounds, assisted by his wife. When Alan was put on the the operating table he repeated what Dr Cross had said, about the bullet being lodged behind the scapula.

"Aye, I agree with Kerr. In fact, I can feel a place where I think the bullet has fractured the scapula and pushed out a bump. The question is: how do we get it out? There are two options – go in from your back and cut a hole in your scapula to bring the bullet through, or we could go under the scapula and pull it out from the inside – that's the way I'd do it."

"Or you could leave it be," he offered weakly.

"Not a good idea for the long term. It would be a bother and a constant source of infection. Besides, you'd be poisoned by the lead." Dr Laws sighed. "I won't do it myself, Alan. I'll leave it for Thompson in Blantyre, or McPhail – I've heard he's moved to Zomba."

He started to imagine what Alistair McPhail might do to to him, a helpless invalid, if he suspected his feelings for Nora.

"Do you know them?" asked Mrs Laws, dabbing potassium of permanganate on the wound.

"I've met Dr Thompson playing cricket," he replied. "I met Dr McPhail and his wife at the Moirs last year, and I saw them once when I went to Zomba."

"She's a pretty thing," said Mrs Laws, almost to herself. "They say half the men in Blantyre were in love with her when she lived there."

He said nothing and shivered; his fever was rampant. Mrs Laws wiped his head and torso with a wet cloth.

"What can we do for him?" she asked her husband.

"Keep his temperature down, dear – the way you're doing. Give him lots of broth. Tomorrow I'll probe into the wound to see if I can clear any sepsis."

Alan asked about Rolfe, and Dr Laws replied, "Doing well, considering his wound. He'd best go back to South Africa to get a metal plate put in his head. By the way, tell me about Lugard's wound."

Alan recounted Dr Cross's diagnosis of Captain Lugard's wound, watching Laws's expression growing grave.

"He ought to have come home with you and Rolfe."

"He has a strong sense of duty. He was afraid that if he left Karonga, the men there would quarrel and the *boma* would become untenable. For him that meant the slave traders would gain the upper hand."

——•——

Two days later Alan's fever had abated, leaving him weak and sore but able to continue the journey. So the *Ilala* continued her voyage south with the two patients as passengers lying on the deck. They were cooled by the Lake breezes, while John Moir did his best to care for them, although Rolfe's condition was serious. At Matope they were put in *machilas* for the trek to Blantyre. Alan found the swaying and bumping of the hammock exceedingly painful and uncomfortable and was glad to get to Mandala House, where he received a fond welcome from the ladies. They were shocked at his condition – his shoulder was inflamed, his temperature simmering, and his body emaciated.

Dr Thompson was ill with hepatitis, so it was decreed that Alan would be taken to Zomba for treatment by Dr McPhail. "And you'll be looked after by Nora," added Mrs Moir. "You'll like that."

He blushed and hoped they would not notice. He was put in a *machila* the following morning, carried by one of Mandala's best teams. There were eight men, two teams of four, taking it in turns. They covered the forty miles in one day, reaching Zomba at sunset. Despite the long journey they were laughing and singing when they arrived.

He directed them to the hospital, where he was carried in and placed on a bed, propped up in a sitting position. McPhail came in, looking tired and wan. He smiled a little and sighed. Then he felt his patient's brow with a cool hand.

"So, Alan, what have they done to you?"

"I feel like hell, Alistair." He laughed weakly.

"Not surprising. You have malaria as well as your bullet wound – the long journey has not helped." He pulled off Alan's shirt to expose the entry wound in his upper chest. "There's no inflammation – that's a good sign – just the remains of the bruising." He moved round to the back and probed gently around the scapula. "The priority is to reduce your fever; then I can operate. We'll give you more quinine. Let's hope you can keep it down."

McPhail sent a messenger to his house and Nora arrived soon after, looking concerned. Even when she was alone with Alan she said nothing, though he was hoping for a few words of endearment. He supposed that he looked and smelled particularly unappetising.

After dosing Alan with quinine she was joined by her husband. They stood by his bed and asked him about the fights against the slavers and how he got his wound. He soon grew sleepy but before he dozed off Jess Kennedy come into the room. She wore her dark hair in a plait that hung down her back. Her white uniform came down to below her knees, and a small white cotton cap perched on her head. She was brisk but cheerful as she supervised an African orderly, who removed his sodden clothing and replaced it with a pair of dry cotton pyjamas.

"How are you, Jess?" His voice was hoarse as he tried to keep his eyes open.

"I'm well. I'm so sorry about your wound. Thank heavens it's not more serious." She sounded too polite, not as friendly as he would have expected.

He asked after her parents and she said they were well and wanted to come to see him. He then asked her how she liked living in Africa – after a year.

She turned the corners of her mouth down. "I'm not sure that I'm the pioneering type." Then she laughed. "But I'm glad to have this work. I enjoy helping to care for little Malcolm too."

—•—

Alistair McPhail operated two days later. He anaesthetised Alan with chloroform; Nora and Jess assisted. They told him later that McPhail sliced through the flesh below the scapula and then cut upwards, trying to avoid the main muscles. It did not take him long to locate the lead bullet and he picked it out with his forceps. Then he poured carbolic acid disinfectant into the wound before stitching it up.

In less than an hour Alan was back in bed and gaining consciousness. He vomited for about half an hour with Jess holding a dish and wiping his face. The nausea from the chloroform gradually receded and he was able to sit, with the pressure taken off his shoulder by carefully positioned pillows.

Nora was brisk and had no inhibitions about removing all of his clothing and swabbing him with a wet flannel. However, Jess was hesitant and blushed deeply, though she remained cheerful and tried to keep up a conversation to distract him from the pain.

He spent a week in the hospital. When he was discharged he thanked Alistair McPhail and Nora, and the other hospital staff and rode Nora's mule slowly down to the Kennedy's farm, and the Mandala *machila* team walked with them, ready to carry Alan if he felt too weak to ride. Jess rode beside him; she was constantly concerned about him, making him stop now and then to check his pulse and temperature. It took about an hour to reach the farm, where Jock and Marge helped him into their guest room. Seeing that he was well enough, they asked for a full account of the fighting at Karonga.

He was able to walk to the dining room for supper that evening. Later, Jess put him to bed like a little boy, then sat beside his bed.

"I am your captive," he said, trying to sound amusing.

"So you are, but your thoughts are elsewhere."

He denied it.

"It's none of my business, I suppose," she said. "It just seems a pity you are fixated on a married woman, when I am..."

"Nora?"

"Of course, who else?"

"But I mean nothing to her, nor she to me."

"I wish I could believe that." She left without saying goodnight.

—•—

He stayed with the Kennedys for a week, and wondered if he could buy land to grow coffee in the Zomba area instead of Cholo, where the rainfall was known to be more reliable. He knew that most of the planters believed rainfed coffee to be of better quality than the irrigated crop, but Zomba had several attractions.

Jock had told him how John Buchanan had arranged with the curator of the Edinburgh botanical gardens for some coffee plants to be sent out. Three plants were brought to Blantyre by Jonathan Duncan of the Church of Scotland Mission; two of them died but one survived and bore fruit that became the source of seeds and seedlings for the development of the coffee plantations. The variety was *Caffea arabica*, which had the advantage of fetching a higher price than Robusta coffee.

"Coffee originated in the forests of Ethiopia," Jock told him instructively. "It likes to be in semi-shade with cool, but not cold, temperatures, and with year-round moist, but not wet, soil conditions. Somehow irrigation does not give the ideal conditions that natural rainfall provides."

"But you grow it here."

He nodded. "Aye, I'm settled here now. This place may not be ideal for coffee, but it's good for other crops. Anyway, I like the Zomba area – I never liked Blantyre or Cholo much."

Alan was much influenced by the attractions of the Zomba area. He was determined that one day he would build a log cabin on the plateau. He tried to tell himself that it was nothing to do with being near Nora, but he was thinking of her, even though his prospects of an affair with her were slight. He recognised that his judgement was clouded by her physical attractions.

Later, he discussed with Jock the prospects for using the Likengala River for irrigation. The Mulungusi was the stream that flowed off the bowl of the plateau and supplied the embryonic town with drinking water. It then entered the Likengala River which flowed across the Phalombe plain and into Lake Chilwa. Jock thought that a gravity scheme could be devised a couple of miles east of Zomba. He offered to search for about a five hundred acres of arable land.

Soon after his return to Blantyre Alan told the Moir brothers that he had decided to leave the Company at the end of his two year contract. At first they assumed that his decision was due to the conflicts in Karonga and his lucky escape there. But when he told them that he wanted to buy land to grow coffee they offered to release him from his contract.

"We don't want to hold you with us against your will," said John. "We know that your mind will be directed towards your farming venture. Go for it. Just give us one or two months to wind down your work and find a replacement."

He thanked them and arranged to ride back to the Kennedys the next weekend.

—•—

24

When he arrived at the Kennedys Alan told them he had resigned from Mandala to start a coffee plantation. He had a lot to learn. Jock was enthusiastic about his plans, but also cautioned about the risks entailed.

"The first thing you'll have to do is find suitable land. The soils are quite fertile around Zomba, but water is most important. Every few years there's a drought and then the coffee plants would suffer badly or even die. I suggest you buy land that has a permanent stream from which you could draw water – in fact use it for irrigation."

"I presume you mean by gravity?"

"Yes. It would be too laborious and expensive to cart water. I know some places along the Likengala River, east of Zomba. The best land has been taken by Buchanan, but there's more available – next to me."

"Is the land not used?"

"It was used, but the native population now is very sparse. The poor blighters were wiped out by the slave traders; and if it's not them it's raids by the Angoni. Most of this area was purchased by Consul Hawes, for future settlement by people like you. He bought it from Chief Chibisa."

He took Alan to the point where the Mulungusi stream joined the Likengala River; they dismounted from their horses and walked along the bank. Because it was the dry season the water flow was limited – about two or three cubic feet per second, he estimated. They soon reached the Kennedy farm, where Jock had established coffee plants the previous year. They then walked on further downstream, looking for his eastern boundary, where there was a cairn of rocks. A couple of hundred yards further the river passed through a series of rock out-crops, dropping fifteen feet in the process.

"This would be a good place to take off water," said Jock. "It's like a natural weir. You could dig a small canal here, to divert some water. Then you could make a network of smaller canals to take water to the fields and the individual coffee plants."

"It sounds like a lot of work." Alan was bemused.

"Aye, it is; but labour is cheap. You could use oxen and scoops for the canal excavation, but it could all be done by hand."

Jock led him into the sparse bushveld beside the stream. It had been cultivated in the past by local Africans, though there was no sign of them now. Their former fields were now overgrown with grass and small trees. Some scattered large trees remained, usually in rocky areas – mainly wild figs and acacias. There were flocks of doves and green pigeons feeding in the fig trees. Jock warned him to watch out for buffalo beans, which had rufous velvety pods; the hairs on the pods caused horrendous itching.

Jock explained that land levels could be very deceptive, and ad-vised Alan to borrow an engineer's level to survey the canals.

"Much of this land would be commanded by a canal coming off the river at those rock outcrops. Once you've confirmed that with a survey you could go to the land agent in Blantyre with a sketch plan of the area you want to buy."

They rode back to the Kennedy farm, about a mile away. After see-ing that the horses were rubbed down and fed, they walked from the stables to the house. Alan again admired the style of the planter's house, raised above the ground on a brick foundation, with wide cool verandahs and a broad neatly thatched roof. He determined to build something similar.

"How much would I have to pay for the land?" he asked.

"About five shillings an acre."

"And how many acres should I aim for?"

"If you can afford it, a thousand acres. So that would be 250 pounds. But remember that you need to clear the land for the coffee – and the homestead – which takes a lot of labour. Also, you need to build fermentation tanks for the coffee cherries, and storage sheds. Then you have to wait for three years before you get any produce. As a rough rule of thumb I reckon you should budget to spend about ten pounds for every acre of coffee you grow. So, if you aim for two hundred acres, your costs to reach full production would be about two thousand pounds."

"And how much could I earn from that?"

Kennedy laughed. "An important question. Let's have something to drink."

Chairs were arranged on the verandah and a servant brought fresh lime juice.

"We must slake our thirst first, Alan. The beer will follow. I'm brewing my own now. I've brought the dried hops from South Africa. I'll be interested to hear what you think of it."

"You were going to tell me how much I can earn from the coffee."

"Firstly, I suggest you budget for two hundred acres of coffee. You ought to be able to get about 300 pounds of beans an acre, so that would give you 60,000 pounds at full production, say 500 hundred-weight..."

"And the price?"

"For good quality you should get a hundred shillings a hundred-weight, but because the Zomba climate is not ideal, you should budget for eighty shillings. So that would give you a gross income of ...forty thousand shillings, so...two thousand pounds."

"Phew! That's a good income..."

His host laughed. "Remember, that's gross income, Alan. You have to pay for labour, lots of it."

"How much do you pay them?"

"The general rate is three shillings a month, but you have to add the cost of food rations – *posho*. Some of the planters give their labour calico in lieu of *posho*, but I think it's better to give them some food; they work better. *Posho* costs about five shillings a month. You can budget ten shillings a month for each of your labourers, including their wages. You'll need at least a hundred men to start – to clear the land, dig the canals, and plant the coffee. Later, you could manage with half that number, for weeding and harvesting. Remember, their work rate is not what you would get at home!"

"So the labour cost would be about fifty pounds a month?"

"About that. It's your main cost. We have continual problems with labourers leaving work, or being driven away. The local chiefs ought to cooperate, but in practice they're obstructive. They want to be bribed for allowing their villagers to work on the estates. I think, sooner or later the dominance of the chiefs will diminish. But we also have the problem of the Angoni intrusions – as soon as they appear our labourers vanish. You see, there's no force of law to control the Angoni and send them packing. We planters are so few in numbers that we have to be very conciliatory."

Jock brought two bottles of cool beer and opened them, then watched Alan's expression. The beer was well brewed and he praised it. Then he said, "Your in a bind similar to Mandala in Karonga. Not enough resources to combat the local brigands. If only we had a police or military unit here, that could be used to keep them under control."

—•—

Three months later Alan had title to his farm and was released from his contract with Mandala. He named the farm *Khundalila* – dove's cooing – after the sounds of the many mourning doves that inhabited the farm; they were numerous around the rocks. He moved into the Kennedy's guest cottage while he rode every day to the new farm. A week later he moved into a temporary house he built with poles and mud. It had a roughly thatched roof and open windows covered with mosquito netting. Jock loaned him a *capitao*, or labour master, to recruit and manage his expanding labour force.

His growing command of ChiNyanja helped him to explain the work to the men. There was a team that built the first house; they then moved on to make kiln-fired bricks for the main house. The bricks were formed with anthill mud, then allowed to dry before they were stacked in a kiln, fired with bush wood for five or six days.

Another team was employed digging the irrigation canal. A surveyor, moonlighting from Mandala, pegged the line from the Likengala River, at a gradient of one foot drop in two hundred. A small quantity of water was released down the canal to test the gradient and to soften the soil for digging the next section.

The main labour force was employed clearing land for the coffee. Alan decided to give each worker a quarter of an acre to clear at a contract price, which varied according the the number and size of the trees on the plot. Each tree had to be 'stumped': that is, dug out. Most of the trees had a deep tap root that had to be cut at least two feet below ground level, and the larger lateral roots had to be removed. The trunk and branches were cut into lengths and stacked in 'cords' at the margins of the fields; they would be used later as firewood.

He aimed to plant a hundred acres of coffee in his first season and contracted with John Buchanan and Jock Kennedy to buy half the required seedlings from each of them. With advice from these two neighbours, and by careful management of the labour force, he was able to plant the seedlings in the latter half of November, while the rainy season was starting.

Meanwhile, building work on the main house started. The foundations were being laid when Nora came to visit. She was riding Barushka, wearing a white shirt and khaki trousers; a solar topi was perched on her head. Alan stopped working with the builders and went to greet her, taking hold of Barushka's bridle while she dismounted.

"I was bored. Alistair has gone to Blantyre – a big operation. Malcolm's with the Kennedys – Jess loves looking after him – so I thought I would come to see how you're getting on." She waved to the expanse of cleared land. "I'm impressed. You've done so much in just four months."

"I couldn't have done it without Buchanan and Jock."

He showed her the plans for the house. He was building it on a knoll overlooking the Likengala. Some shade would be provided by a huge fig tree on one side, and a spreading acacia on the other. He was afraid that the rocks on the knoll would give off too much heat, so carted in soil to fill the spaces between the outcrops, creating a series of small flat areas that would be planted with lawn grass.

The water for the house and garden came from a hydraulic ram that took surplus water channelled from the main canal, dropping it to the river. The water was pumped up to a metal storage tank at the highest point of the knoll, where he planned to build a larger brick reservoir.

He invited Nora to his temporary house for a drink and something to eat. Because it was in the shade of a *mbawa* tree, and caught the breeze, it was quite cool inside. His house servant was not there, and he found some fruit juice and cake from a gauze storage box that had damp muslin around it to keep it cool. Nora had tethered her horse and looked around the house.

"You keep it very tidy," she said approvingly.

"Not many possessions to keep in order."

She accepted a glass of lime juice and looked at him over the rim as she drank. Then she put the tumbler down and walked over to him, putting her arms round his neck. "I've been looking forward to coming here." She kissed him.

"I need to see how your wound has healed," she said, removing his shirt.

———•———

Two hours later Nora said she must leave. He watched as she dressed, recalling how he had responded greedily like a starved man, scarcely believing that he could be so fortunate. She patted his head and walked to the door. Then she turned and said, "I'll need to check that wound again – perhaps next week."

He got up and stood at the door, watching her ride away.

She came back a week later, then two more times after fortnight intervals. Each time she left her child with Jess Kennedy. The fourth time she came he was in the fields, supervising the planting of the coffee seedlings. Buchanan was with him, advising about the correct methods of setting the plants; he left after about ten minutes of conversation.

When they were alone, Nora suddenly said, "I'm expecting – a baby. It's yours."

———•———

25

Zomba - Christmas 1888

He felt his insides knot. "How can you know?

"I know. I'm a woman – and a nurse; remember?" She was standing beside him, holding Barushka on a long rein. The mare was picking at grass stalks. Then she prepared to ride. "It has to be kept secret. I'm sorry. Alistair must never find out. Do you promise?"

He nodded.

"I can't come again – not on my own."

"When is it due – the child?"

"In July." She rode off with a wave.

—•—

The Kennedys invited him to their Christmas party. It was the main social event for Zomba and he knew the McPhails would be there. It was a lunch party, allowing guests to ride home before dark. He rode over at eleven and was greeted by Jock, Marge and Jess. It was strange to celebrate in the heat and humidity of an African summer. He remembered his last Christmas, in Karonga, with whisky and brandy drunk maudlin round the camp fire.

Nora seemed to avoid him deliberately. He spoke with her husband for a while, mostly about his work on nutrition and parasites. Alistair McPhail enthused whenever on the subject of medicine in Africa. To

Alan he seemed less interested in the fights against the slavers, and the precarious conditions of the settlers.

After lunch Alan lit up a pipe and stood near the railing of the verandah. To his left the Zomba massif loomed, blue-grey and mysterious, its rock scarps wet and glistening. Much further, to his right, Mlanje mountain rose precipitously from the plain; he thought to himself that he would climb to the summit one day – nearly ten thousand feet.

Jess came up beside him. She looked cool and demure in a pinafore dress. "What are you dreaming about?"

"Climbing Mlanje."

"I'll do it with you."

He laughed. "I believe you would. You're a brave girl."

"Talking of bravery – will you be going back to Karonga?"

"I don't want to – and I don't have to – but I feel I have a duty. Do you think I should?"

She did not hesitate in her reply. "I think you've done enough. You've campaigned as long as anyone – and you've been wounded – and suffered from fever. Surely there are others who could take your place?"

"Who, Jess? There are only Mandala employees, and a few volunteers like Alfred Sharpe..."

"Then you should wait until the British Government sends troops here."

He sighed. "That might take years. In the meantime the slavers and the chiefs that deal with them, will get the upper hand. Who knows what might happen then. It might become impossible for us to farm if our labour is kept away."

"I suspect, Alan, that you enjoy soldiering. Remember, it was what you wanted, when you went to Sandhurst. You were proud to receive your commission and to travel on active service. Then it all ended, with the incident in India. But now you have a chance to be the warrior again." She ended with a questioning expression, afraid she'd said too much.

"Perhaps you're right, Jess. But this is a different sort of soldiering..."

"I suppose so, but I hate to see you go away."

He took her hand. "Do you care?"

She laughed ruefully. "Yes, but I always ask myself why I do."

"You're still blaming me because of Nora. Although I admit I'm at fault, I promise you I never pursued her."

"I wish I could be sure of that."

—•—

26

Early in the New Year Alan received a message from the Moir brothers, asking him to come to Blantyre for a meeting about the anti-slavery campaign; they invited him to stay in the guest room at Mandala House. He arrived at dusk and handed over his horse to Fred Moir's stable boy, then went inside, where he was greeted by both the Moir brothers and their wives, and was shown to his room. After he had a bath he walked with them to the Blantyre Club. The meeting was attended by about forty people, mostly settlers and a few Mandala employees, and was chaired by John Moir.

"We need to carry the fight to Mlozi," Moir said, trying to sound encouraging. "The seven-pounder mountain gun has arrived. It should ensure our success. We ought be able to blast away the wall of his stockade. Now, we need volunteers to go up there."

A grizzled settler stood up; he had a bottle of beer in his hand. "It's all very well for you, Moir – to ask for volunteers. But it's your fight – it's your trading station up there. You are the company that's building the road to Lake Tanganyika. Why should we do your fighting for you?"

Moir shook his head. "Firstly, Macready, it's not just the Company's fight. Surely we all want to rid this territory of the slavers. They are the people who steal your labourers and are blighting the economy."

Another man stood up, tall and sunburnt, and shouted in a strong Glaswegian brogue. "Tell that to the British Government, Moir. Tell them to send us some soldiers to do the fighting."

"I have told them," retorted Moir. "They will help us – in time. But we don't have time – we need to act now."

While listening to these exchanges Alan decided that he had to make a gesture. He held up his hand. "I'll go, John, but I'll need help on my farm."

Jock Kennedy jumped up. "I'll keep an eye on it for you. I'm sure Buchanan will, too."

John Moir hoped that others would follow Alan's lead, but there were no other volunteers. Among the small group of Europeans who had fought at Karonga there had been one death and several seriously wounded. Besides, some people thought the prospects of contracting malaria were an even greater risk.

They trooped back to Mandala House, where Elizabeth and Jane had supper waiting. They asked Alan about life in Zomba. He told them about the small cohesive and sociable group there, and enthused about the beauty of the plateau.

"We hear that Nora McPhail is having another baby," said Elizabeth.

"Really?" Alan pretended he had not heard the news, marvelling at the way these tid bits got around the settler community.

"She's fortunate to have Jess Kennedy to help her with the children," added Jane. "What do you think of the young lass, Alan? You're neighbours, aren't you?"

He laughed, relieved that attention was no longer focussed on Nora. "Is that a loaded question? Oh, she's a sweet girl – and very cheerful. It must be quite hard for her, being in a strange country, with very little company..."

"Well, she has Nora and Alistair, and she has you – perhaps John Buchanan will think of her as a wife, if you don't."

Of course the idea of marrying Jess had occurred to him, but he'd pushed it aside because he was so busy and financially vulnerable. He felt a distinct pang of jealousy, while realising that he had no right to it. Of course Jess was eminently eligible in the territory of few women. Miscegenation was out of the question, although it was rumoured that a few planters had African concubines. So a bright young girl like Jess would be most desirable.

—•—

Alan arrived at Karonga in mid-January, on the *Ilala*. He was growing fond of the little steamer, and the breezy voyages up the Lake. They seemed to remove him far from the cares of farming and the risks of fighting. Here it was the steady buffeting of the waves, the throbbing of the engine, and the hiss of the boiler steam. The Lake had many moods, from dead calm to ferocious storms, although he had not yet experienced the latter. Its colours, reflecting the sky, ranged from metallic grey to the deepest indigo. At dawn and sunset the surface flamed with orange and scarlet, as if they were on some vast cauldron of molten iron. The mountains that embraced the north end of the Lake were distant and mysterious. The men talked about the Nyika Plateau which rose to misty heights of nearly nine thousand feet and was the home of a rare antelope.

He was not happy to be back in Karonga. His thoughts were centred on his farm and the coffee crop. He had seen Nora several times after her fateful announcement, but she was always in company with other people. They had not spoken privately again, and he was frustrated because he knew so little about her feelings about him and the expected child she said was his. He also thought a lot about Jess, and wondered if he should forget about Nora and throw his cap at her instead. She had been a friend at first, but she was undeniably attractive. If he was going to settle down and raise a family in Africa he should make a move, or someone else would.

He was pleased to see his former colleagues again. The first to greet him was Goodwill, who helped with the unloading of his baggage. The tall young African wore a rare smile as he hefted a leather case. "How is your wound, sir," he asked.

Alan told him about the operation, then explained how he had resigned from Mandala and started a coffee farm. "You can remain with the company if you wish, Goodwill. But I would like you to work for me on the new coffee estate. I need someone like you to help me with the records and accounts – a sort of assistant manager. I could pay you a little more than you're getting now. Think about it. We can discuss it later."

He was pleased to see Frederick Lugard walking slowly down to the jetty, but shocked at his gaunt appearance. He felt guilty for leaving him in this remote and inhospitable place.

"We have your gun, Fred," he said. "An Armstrong seven-pounder – a breech-loader, with a rifled barrel. The Moirs think it will make mince-meat of Mlozi's stockade."

Lugard shook his hand cautiously, and Alan could see that at least his damaged arms had made good progress. They exchanged news about their wounds.

"Your man Goodwill has been a boon to me, Alan. But, much as I welcome your return, I regret that I'll lose his services."

"You must use him as you need, Fred, while we're here. Your need is more important. Even so, I've invited him to come and work for me." He then told Lugard how he had resigned from Mandala to grow coffee.

The Captain was generous in his good wishes. "I admire your enterprise. Better to be your own master." As they walked up to the houses, he added, "It's good of you to come back here, Alan. It must have been difficult for you to leave your new farm – a real sacrifice."

Alan found Dr Kerr Cross tending to Monteith Fotheringham, who was recovering in bed from a bad bout of fever. "I thought I was resistant," said his former boss wryly. "Cross tells me that there's no such thing as resistance to malaria."

"Except that the natives are generally more resistant than we Europeans are," said Dr Cross. He demanded a detailed account of Alan's operation and recuperation. "It sounds as if you were fortunate to have the services of Alistair McPhail."

—•—

Next day they assembled the gun and set it on its carriage and wheels. Alan thought it looked rather small and insignificant for it's important task. The prospects of using it were receding because Lugard was negotiating with Mlozi using an Arab envoy.

This was an urgent task because some of the white men, and most of the Atonga warrior contingent, were restless and talking about leaving Karonga; they wanted to go back to their homes and families. Another complication was a disease that was afflicting the Mambwe men, which they thought was caused by witchcraft. Lugard discussed the problem at length with Alan and Goodwill.

"Sir, you could find out the cause of death by an operation," suggested Goodwill.

"A post-mortem?" Lugard eyed him sharply.

"Yes, sir. Dr Cross could cut the dead man open. The Mwambe men could see that there is no 'spirit' inside."

"I see," said Lugard, nodding. "You mean they could watch the post-mortem."

It was performed the next day, with a dozen of the senior Mwambe warriors watching wide-eyed. Dr Cross found that the dead man had a severely inflamed lower bowel, which he was able to demonstrate to the onlookers. "We need to find out what caused this. Something in his food or drink, I have no doubt."

The dead man was buried with much ceremony, and the Mwambe men seemed to accept that he had died of natural causes.

Shortly afterwards Alan was delighted when his friend Alfred Sharpe arrived at the *boma*; he had been hunting at the north end of the Lake. They talked late into the night over the embers of a fire.

"What do you think of our prospects now we have the gun?" Sharpe asked.

Alan lit a new pipe, taking his time before replying. "We still lack the numbers to defeat Mlozi. We may be able to knock down their stockade, but they will merely re-group somewhere else. I think we have to root out the leaders and perhaps exile or execute them. Surely there's enough evidence to convict them."

"Perhaps. I think we need at least a company of regular soldiers, but where will we find them?"

Alan was gazing into the fire as he thought. "The nearest soldiers are in South Africa. We could recruit there."

Sharpe laughed. "Yes, Alan, but who will pay for them? You're talking about thousands of pounds."

"It would have to be the British Government."

"Of course. O'Neill has been sending dispatches to London, asking them to send a force, but so far to no avail."

———•———

Next day Lugard called a meeting of the Europeans to discuss strategies for attacking the stockade of Msalemo, Mlozi's henchman. Opinions were equally divided between those favouring a determined invasive attack, and those wanting to merely test the effectiveness of the gun. Lugard cast the deciding vote in favour of testing the gun.

It was near the end of February when they set off to a pre-selected vantage point about two hundred yards from the stockade, advancing cautiously, fearing that the slaver militia might charge out and capture the new weapon.

When they fired on the stockade they were full of confidence that the gun would destroy it. But it took three hours to fire twenty-three shells, and there seemed to be little evidence of damage. They withdrew the column to Karonga and held a post-mortem discussion. The disappointing conclusion was that the seven-pounder was not the ideal weapon to break down a stockade made of poles, with walls of thickly packed mud. The shells seemed to have passed through the walls causing little damage to them. Some may have exploded inside, but they had no way of knowing. There may also have been a psychological effect on those defenders in the stockade, but the main objective of making a breach had not been achieved.

There followed a period of nearly four weeks during which Lugard continued negotiating with Mlozi. The Captain was convinced that the arrival of the gun had strengthened his hand, but time had run out and the *Ilala* was waiting to take him south.

They held a farewell party for Lugard. Speeches were made and toasts drunk in whisky and brandy. With the possible exception of Fotheringham, whose leadership Lugard had usurped, the men were sorry to see him go. He had been an inspiration with his courage and stoicism.

There was one more action under Lugard's command. The column once more attacked the stockades of Mlozi's subservient chiefs, Msalemo and Kopa Kopa. Again, the walls remained largely undamaged because the high velocity shells merely penetrated and exploded inside. The attackers thought there would have been considerable casualties inside the stockades, but again had no way of knowing.

The *Ilala* had stood off Karonga during these hostilities and now came to the jetty to pick up seven British men, including Lugard, Sharpe, and Alan, who brought Goodwill with him. Left behind were Dr Kerr Cross, Monteith Fotheringham, and John Nicoll. Though he tried to remain cheerful, Alan could not help feeling guilty about leaving the little group behind. The gun had not been the expected boon, and the hostile atmosphere in Karonga was almost palpable.

The *Ilala* stopped at Bandawe, where Dr and Mrs Laws greeted everyone with their usual enthusiasm, and the kindly doctor checked Lugard's wounds.

They eventually arrived in Blantyre at the end of March, and soon after discussions were held among the senior Europeans about the merits of continuing the war in the north. John Moir was in favour of continuing the fight and planned to recruit men to help. Lugard, supported by Sharpe, argued that it was essential to have a military contingent of some kind, with properly trained soldiers in support of the European volunteers. Alan suggested that a contingent of Indian soldiers could be recruited, but no one could think of a way of financing such a strategy.

—•—

27

Zomba - March-June 1889

Alan reached his farm *Khundalila* at the end of March 1889. He had been away for over two months and was now in his twenty-ninth year. As he rode along the track leading through the fields he was astonished to see how quickly the coffee plants had grown. Their leaves were glossy and free of blemishes; only a few had failed to survive the trauma of transplanting. Their places had been re-filled with new seedlings; though they remained smaller than their companions. There was scarcely a weed in sight. He felt a great surge of gratitude for the friends who had protected his investment.

John Buchanan was at the new house, supervising the bricklaying. He greeted Alan with his usual diffident handshake, and said laconically. "I hear the mountain gun didn't make the difference."

"We'd have done better with an old Napoleonic muzzle-loading cannon, or one of that type we used in the Indian Mutiny to break down the walls round Lucknow and Delhi." He gestured to the field of coffee. "I'm so grateful to you, John..."

"Well, it wasn't just me."

"No, I know you were helped by your brothers, and by Jock."

"Jock's not well, Alan."

"What's the matter?"

"We don't know." He explained that Kennedy had been having abdominal pains that were debilitating, and wearing him down. "We've been going over to his estate to help, because Marge and Jess can't cope on their own."

Alan said he would go over there as soon as he could. They walked around the house while Buchanan explained how the building work had progressed. The walls were about breast high, and the timber trusses and grass for thatching had been prepared for the roofing and were stacked in piles around the site. The rains were effectively over now.

—•—

One day Alan rode over the to the Kennedy estate. Jock was sitting on the verandah and waved as he approached, then called for a stable boy to take the horse.

"I hear you haven't been well, Jock."

"Och, it's nothing. Probably just indigestion..."

"Have you seen Alistair McPhail?"

"Aye, I have. He's puzzled...Let us not talk about it. I want to hear about Karonga."

Alan told him about the campaign and thanked him for taking care of his estate.

"I did little – it was mostly the Buchanans who went there. Look, we're grateful to men like you who go off to fight with those bloody slavers. I'm only sorry that it wasn't more successful."

"We'll never get rid of them, Jock. Not until we have a proper military force."

"Hmm. I think you're right, but I don't know when that will happen."

Marge came out onto the verandah. "I thought I heard your voice." She went to fetch some lime juice, saying, "I'll tell Jess you're here."

When Jess came out onto the verandah she greeted him with a hug and a broad smile, her brown eyes shining. She and her mother listened as he repeated what he had told Jock about the campaign in the north.

Later Jess walked him around to the side of the verandah, where she could talk to him privately. "How is your bullet wound?" she asked. "May I see?" She smiled. "I'm a nurse – it's only professional interest."

He removed his shirt and said, "It hasn't troubled me. I'm just a bit stiff." He couldn't help laughing. "I don't know if it will affect my cricket."

Jess prodded the shoulder and touched the scar without saying anything. He put his arm around her and kissed her. She responded eagerly, but when they drew apart she said, "Where is Nora in your mind?"

"I never wanted her, Jess. Not just because she's married. I suspect she's lonely and needed some sort of re-assurance."

"But you didn't turn her away."

"I never sought her out, but I ought to have said 'no'." Trying to change the subject, he said. "I'm concerned about your father."

"Yes." She frowned and looked away. "Alistair doesn't know what's the matter. He's considering an exploratory operation – in case there's a growth – a tumour, or something like that. Nora thinks he should see a specialist. We've even considered taking him to South Africa, but he won't hear of it. By the way, Nora's baby's due soon. It'll be easier for her, being her second, and having a doctor as her husband. She still rides." She looked at him with what he thought was an arch expression.

—•—

The next morning Goodwill told Alan that a leopard had been killing goats in his home village, about five miles from *Khundalila*.

"Could you go there and shoot it? It would greatly help the people there."

"I can try. As you know, they are elusive creatures and difficult to shoot."

A few days later they walked to the village together. They were greeted by Goodwill's mother, Nsofe, and Alan was introduced to the headman, an elderly man, who had lost two goats to the leopard. He showed Alan the enclosure where the small flock was kept at night; it was like a flimsy hut, with a thin roof of grass. The leopard had leapt through the roof and Alan guessed it must have swiped around, killing two goats and injuring two others. It had then jumped out, carrying one of its victims.

"Has anyone seen where the goat was taken?" he asked.

Goodwill replied, "They are not sure where it sleeps."

"Surely you can follow the trail?"

"Perhaps, sir. We can take the headman's dogs."

They set off, the dogs unhappy about Alan's presence and strange scent. He carried his twelve-bore shotgun on his shoulder, loaded with SSG cartridges, safety catch on. Goodwill traced the path of the leopard's pug marks and spots of blood from the goat. It was slow work and took them two hours to reach a small knoll of rocks on which grew a large fig tree. As they drew closer the dogs became excited and foraged ahead.

Alan was admiring the green pigeons feeding on the wild figs when he noticed that the dogs had vanished into the long grass at the foot of the knoll. He was ahead, and behind him were the headman, who carried a small axe, and Goodwill who was un-armed.

He heard a sharp yelp and saw the two dogs race out of the long grass; they spotted the three men and headed straight for them. Behind the dogs bounded a leopard, its tail almost vertical; it gave two short coughing sounds. Then it saw the men.

Alan brought his shotgun off his shoulder and pushed the safety catch off with his thumb. He was raising the gun when he saw the leopard veer away, just as the dogs rushed to shelter behind their owner. He swung the gun to follow the racing leopard, but did not fire. The chances of wounding it were too high, and a wounded leopard is a fearsome creature.

They walked back to the village, discussing the incident. The dogs had been lucky. Was that the leopard's home, or was it there to eat the goat? What could they do now?

Alan promised to return. He had an idea, based on discussions with fellow officers when he served in India, and with his godfather, an experienced *shikari*. He explained his plan to the Kennedys. He would build a *machan*, a platform, in a tree overlooking the headman's goat enclosure, then tether a young goat below the tree, as bait for the leopard.

"Will the goat be killed?" asked Jess.

"I regret, yes. With the spread of pellets from the shotgun it would be difficult to hit the leopard and not the goat."

Jock asked, "Why not use a rifle?"

"There'll be hardly any light. The shotgun will give a better chance of hitting the target. That became the collective wisdom in India."

He then told them how his godfather sat up in a tree for a man-eating leopard in India, whose half-eaten victim was below. "He had an Indian *shikari*, a hunter, sitting above him. My godfather fell asleep and was woken by the *shikari*. He looked up and saw the leopard at the end of his shotgun. It was coming for him and he had just enough time to pull the triggers. The animal's head was blown to pieces and it's hair singed – I saw the pelt in his office."

"Will you have someone with you," asked Jess. "I'll come."

He thanked her and explained that Goodwill had volunteered and had acute senses for the sights and sounds that would tell him that the leopard was near.

——•——

He rode into Zomba on the Saturday to play cricket; his horse boy went ahead on foot. There were nine men in the Blantyre team, but only six playing for Zomba, so fielders were added from the opposing team, and five men from the home team were allowed to bat twice. When he came in after his innings, he was surprised to see Nora talking to Jess. He walked up to the two women and Nora reached out her hand – it was almost as if she was distancing herself from him.

"I'm relieved that you're back unharmed. Alistair said he didn't want to dig any more bullets out of you." She laughed, and Jess walked away. He asked about the baby she was expecting.

"I feel very well," she said, then frowned slightly. "There's a slight problem – don't ever mention it. It's a breech presentation; do you know what that is?"

"The baby's facing the wrong way."

"Precisely. Alistair's trying to manipulate it, to turn it, but it's being obstinate – just like Malcolm was."

She seemed more frail than ever, despite the bulge of her belly. Glancing over her shoulder she replied. "This place is a hotbed of gossip. The settlers have nothing else to talk about..." She stopped speaking abruptly as her husband approached.

After exchanging handshakes, he said to McPhail, "I was about to ask Nora about Jock Kennedy. He looked poorly when I saw him a couple of days ago."

"Doctor-patient privacy, Alan," replied McPhail primly. "I expect the Kennedys would welcome some help with their coffee crop."

He assured them he was already doing that. Then they heard John Buchanan calling everyone's attention.

"We're here to decide whether we should build a clubhouse. I propose we put up a simple building with a meeting room and a verandah – changing rooms and bathrooms, of course. If we each chip in about twenty pounds I would be glad to do the building..."

"You're always doing the work," said Marge Kennedy. "We should all help you."

Buchanan said. "Any help will be welcome. Now shall we have three volunteers to draw up some plans?"

Alan was co-opted onto the planning committee, along with Alfred Sharpe. He rode home before dusk, his thoughts drifting back to brief times spent with Nora. He still did not know why she had sought the relationship. She preferred not to talk about it, in fact she spoke little at any time, seeming to want to keep her thoughts to herself. She would question him about his earlier life and the campaign in the north, but would never ask about his emotions.

—•—

He woke early with the *simbi* clanging, and was watching Goodwill take the roll call of labourers when a messenger came up with a letter from Jess. It read: *"Nora fell off her horse. Alistair thinks she's broken her pelvis – doing an emergency C."*

He rode over to the Kennedy farm at once. Jock was on the verandah in irritable mood, shifting in his chair and grumbling. He said he had heard that an Angoni *impi* was approaching, and many of his labourers had disappeared in terror.

"*Impi* isn't the right word for them." Jock growled. "They're not like Chaka's warriors, more a ragtag bunch of brigands." He said that Marge and Jess were assisting with the operation. "Nora was foolish to ride so late in her pregnancy. Alistair should have stopped her. Something spooked her horse on the way back from the meeting, and she was thrown off."

A servant brought toast and cold chicken, and a mango purée. They ate on the verandah because Jock was loathe to move into the house. Alan was about to ride into Zomba when Marge drove up in the donkey cart. She looked haggard as she told them, "We were up all night. You know, Alistair's a good general surgeon, but he's not a specialist. Jess did a great job helping him, but it's not easy operating on your own wife. Anyway, Nora seems to have come through it, despite losing a lot of blood. The baby's fine – a boy."

They talked for half an hour before Marge urged Jock to have a nap, saying she would join him. Alan set off for Zomba, then changed his mind and went back to *Khundalila*, afraid to betray his concern for Nora and fearing that he would not be welcome.

—•—

Next morning he decided to ride into town to congratulate Alistair McPhail. When he rode up to the hospital he was surprised to see Marge on the steps, talking to Dr Thompson, who had come over from Blantyre. They nodded to him, and he waited for them to finish their conversation. When Thompson went inside Marge came down the steps.

"She's got a fever – Nora, that is. Tommy thinks it might be puerperal fever."

"What's that? Is it serious?"

"Very serious. It used to be call childbed fever. It's an infection from germs getting into the womb and causing sepsis." She sighed. "We were very careful. There's not much we can do except to keep her hydrated and as cool as possible."

Feeling helpless he asked if there was anything he could do.

She shook her head. "Jess is looking after the new baby, and Malcolm. We're trying to find a native wet-nurse. You could best help me by keeping Jock company. Jess and I will stay here until Nora gets better."

He rode back to the Kennedy farm and helped Jock by checking on his labour. He rode around the farm looking for problems in the coffee – there were none. Later, Jock was in expansive mood and talked at length about the delights of living in Africa and being one's own boss.

As evening approached there was no sign of Marge and Jess, so they had supper and smoked pipes on the verandah, watching the light fade, and listening to the crickets chirping. By nine o'clock there was still no sign of the women, who had presumably spent the night in Zomba. Jock persuaded Alan to sleep in the spare room.

He rode in to the hospital next morning, but could find only an African orderly.

"Where is the doctor?" he asked, in ChiNyanja.

The man pointed up to the house.

"And *Dona* Nora?"

"She died, *bwana*."

———•———

28

Zomba - June 1889

For a moment he felt as if a great hollow had opened in his chest. He walked slowly up to the McPhail house, leading his horse. A group of about a dozen Europeans had gathered outside, among them Marge Kennedy, John Buchanan, the Bruces, Alfred Sharpe and David Robertson.

Alfred came up to him. "You've heard?"

"The orderly at the hospital said Nora died."

"At four this morning. Poor girl. Alistair's bearing up well, but he doesn't want to see people yet. He asked Buchanan to arrange the funeral. She's to be buried on the mountain tomorrow morning."

Buchanan joined them, stroking his long moustaches, looking like an undertaker. "My carpenter is making a coffin. We've decided to carry her up tomorrow, four men at a time. I'm counting you in, Alan – is your shoulder up to it?"

He nodded glumly, then saw Jess come out of the house carrying the baby boy. She walked towards the men and showed off the swaddled child. It had wisps of white blonde hair and blue-grey eyes the same colour as Alan's; they were squinted against the bright light. He remembered his mother saying that new born babies look like their grandparents and then saw the likeness.

Jess was watching him. Her eyes were shadowed with fatigue but retained traces of their familiar sparkle. She said, "I'm staying here for the time being, to help Alistair with the boys. Mama will go back to the farm to look after Pa." Then she turned away.

Buchanan said, "Alan, come up the mountain with me now. Help me choose a spot for the grave."

—•—

They carried Nora's body in procession up the mountain path. The coffin was surprisingly light and Alan guessed she must have wasted during the operation and the fever. Alistair McPhail walked ahead carrying the baby in a sling; he had named it Andrew, after his father. Jess and Marge were alongside him, with little Malcolm toddling at their skirts; they picked him up when he tired.

It took an hour to reach the rim of the plateau. The freshly dug grave was among rocks near the cliff. The view across the plain to Mlanje was blurred in haze, but looking back into the bowl Alan could see the glint of the stream and the pools where he had walked with Nora. It was a superb location for any act, including the final one.

David Robertson read the funeral service – Presbyterian, short and simple. Marge said a few words in tribute to the young wife and mother who's life had been cut short. They threw handfuls of earth on the coffin before the men filled the grave and piled stones on it. A wooden cross was driven into the head of the grave; it would later be replaced with a carved stone.

Alan glanced occasionally at Alistair McPhail and once caught his eye – he smiled weakly and nodded silent thanks. They spoke briefly on the walk down to Zomba, when Alan took a turn at carrying the sleeping Andrew. Looking at the baby he wondered if it was really his child. Had Nora told the truth? If not, why should she have invented his paternity? But she had done many strange things. This little Andrew would never be known as his son, but no matter.

Jess walked at his side for the last half mile. They dropped back from the others, and she said, "I'm glad you didn't show undue emotion at the house – or at the service."

He looked at her sharply, and she added, "I know she was seeing you. Perhaps there was more. She hinted to me how she felt about you." She was trying to smile. "I'm glad that Alistair wasn't hurt. Now there's no reason for him to know. It would be devastating for him..."

"It's over now."

"No it isn't." She laughed in a way that he had not heard from her before, with a trace of bitterness. "Typical male statement. I just hope the memories don't get in the way of the next woman."

He saw sadness in her expression. "How long will you stay with Alistair?"

"As long as he needs me. But Pa needs me too. I'm very worried about him."

"He's tough..."

"Yes, but perhaps not tough enough." She sighed. "He enjoys your company, Alan. Please come over as often as you can." After a pause she added. "I would like to see you too."

—•—

In the days that followed Alan tried to distract himself. He kept himself busy on the farm, and with Goodwill he built the *machan*, using lengths of wood cut by the villagers, who were somewhat mystified by the *mzungu*'s activities. The platform had two levels, with Goodwill's seat higher and behind Alan's. It was about fifteen feet above the ground, with a clear view of the stake where the goat would be tied.

An hour before dusk the two men climbed up a ladder, which the headman took away. Alan wore a jacket with large pockets in which he had spare cartridges for his double-barrelled twelve bore shotgun, as well as sandwiches and a canteen of cold tea. Thirty minutes before sunset the headman brought out a young goat and tethered it to the stake. Thinking it was alone, the goat started bleating plaintively, dismayed at separation from the rest of the flock, now penned in their enclosure. Alan hoped that the cries would be heard by the leopard and would bring it to the bait.

The villagers were all in their huts. The birds in the forest beyond the clearing made their roosting calls as darkness enclosed them. Far away a dog barked and another answered. Alan wondered if the leopard was on the move.

Soon after dusk a half moon rose, bringing a cold colourless light. Another village dog barked, nearer this time, perhaps a mile away. The goat was still bleating at intervals. If the leopard was within a mile it would certainly hear the sound. The shadows seemed to move, although there was no wind, as if there were wraiths in the clearing.

Alan noticed that the goat stopped bleating. The silence was scary. He sensed Goodwill bend forward and heard him whisper.

"*Akubwera* – it's coming."

How does he know? thought Alan. Even with his deep knowledge of the bush, can he be certain? He could hear nothing, and knew that the leopard would not make a sound. Intently he watched the faint figure of the goat.

There was a sudden scuffle and a grunt; a higher-pitched gasp from the goat. It must be there. He raised the shotgun and could just make out the leopard's sinuous length. He fired, then re-adjusted his aim and fired the second barrel. The sounds were magnified, and he heard voices from the headman's hut.

"*Wakufa*, it's dead," muttered Goodwill.

"Maybe I should fire again." He was re-loading.

"It's not moving. We can get down." Goodwill called to the headman, and told him to bring the ladder. "Be careful, throw a stone at its body."

The headman came out of his hut, carrying a lantern. He held it up to illuminate the clearing. The leopard and the little goat lay side by side, as if friends sleeping. He threw a stone which thudded into the leopard's side.

"*Nyalugwe wakufa*," he called. "The leopard's dead." He brought the ladder to the tree.

Alan and Goodwill climbed down. They were joined by the headman's family and then other villagers, who stood in a circle looking at the two animal bodies. Remarks were made about the *mzungu*'s skill at shooting, and who might share in the goat meat. Alan decided to walk home and borrowed the headman's lantern. He asked Goodwill to arrange for the villagers to bring the leopard's body to *Khundalila* next morning, explaining how they could sling it under a pole.

—•—

He woke early from habit and was drinking tea on the verandah when the villagers arrived. The leopard was swinging under the pole, tethered by its paws, its tail almost reaching the ground. They laid it down, and he saw it was a full-grown male. The slugs from the shotgun had penetrated the skin around the neck and shoulder. Death would have been immediate.

Under Goodwill's instructions two of Alan's men skinned the leopard, taking care that they did not cut the pelt. Jess arrived on horseback, and Alan had to hold the nervous horse's bridle while she dismounted.

She wrinkled her nose. "The body looks so small without its skin – like a cat that's got wet."

"It's a good-sized male. Six foot nine inches from nose to tip of tail."

"Are you proud?" She looked at him.

"No. You know I don't like shooting animals, except for necessity. I'm glad I didn't wound it."

"What will you do with the skin?"
"Tan it, then give it to Jock."
She laughed. "He would like it."

—•—

29

Kota Kota and Karonga - September/October 1889

In September 1889 a thirty-two year old Englishman came to the Lake Nyasa territory. He would be instrumental in formalising the boundaries of the country that became British Central Africa and later Nyasaland. It was he who organised and pursued the fight against the slavers. His name was Harry Hamilton Johnston, and he had somewhat accidentally become a consular official. A talented artist, who had exhibited at the Royal Academy, he was also an enthusiastic biologist and explorer. He was a linguist, able to make conversation in French, German, Italian, Spanish, and Portuguese. He was fascinated with the relationship between Bantu languages, and learnt to speak Swahili. He had been an honorary Vice-Consul in Tunisia and Consul in Nigeria, then travelled to the Upper Congo where he met Henry Morton Stanley.

In 1889 the Foreign Office sent him as Consul to Portuguese East Africa, to succeed Henry O'Neill. He had an additional remit to deal with Portuguese ambitions in the region around Lake Nyasa. He travelled by ship up the Zambezi and then the Shire River, where he encountered the expedition of the Portuguese Colonel Serpa Pinto and persuaded him to abandon territorial ambitions in the region south of the Lake, saying that this would provoke conflict between Britain and Portugal.

As soon as he arrived in Blantyre, Johnston called a meeting of Europeans at the club. He asked John Buchanan, then Acting Consul, to be chairman, and he was duly introduced to the assemblage of about sixty settlers, missionaries and African Lakes Company personnel. Alan sat beside Jock Kennedy, with the Bruces on his other side. Jock had insisted on making the journey, despite his debilitated condition.

"Mr Johnston is the most senior British official to have visited us. He has the ear of the British Government, sending and receiving regular despatches to the Foreign Office. We must give him every assistance. We must inform him as best we can about the major issues that we face. We must tell him what we need, but also what we can do to help him."

When Johnston stood up to speak the audience was surprised at his short stature and youthful looks. He was only five foot three inches tall, and appeared somewhat like a schoolboy dressed for church. His light brown hair was neatly brushed back and he wore a short soft beard and moustache. His eyes were expressive and his movements suggested pent up energy.

"Ladies and Gentlemen! Thank you for attending this meeting." Johnston turned to Buchanan. "And thank you, Mr Buchanan, for introducing me."

There followed a ripple of applause before Johnston continued. His diction was clear and his tone authoritative. "I have a very broad and flexible remit from Her Majesty's Government. It is my intention to listen to you, to hear about your ambitions and your problems." He paused to sip from a glass of water.

"But you must know that I have my own agenda. I need to ensure that British interests are protected in the region. You may have heard of the tension with our neighbours the Portuguese..." there was an outbreak of laughter, and Johnston smiled, nodding. "Negotiations are going on between the British and Portuguese governments about the boundaries that will define the territories. In the north, we want to ensure that there is a continuous British presence through to Lake Tanganyika, and thence to Lake Victoria and the Nile. By the way, I had the honour of leading an expedition to Mount Kilimanjaro, so I know something of the Tanganyika country."

He paused to sip water again. "I hardly need to tell you that the Lake Nyasa country has been devastated for many years by predatory Arab slavers, and also the marauding raids of the Angoni tribe. I intend to make sure that these activities are stopped. I will start by negotiating treaties, but my longer term objective is to establish a military presence here." Johnston was interrupted by vigorous applause.

Alan leaned towards Jock Kennedy and said, "This is what we need, but does he have the power to make it happen?"

"Aye, we'll see."

Johnston invited questions, and several hands shot up. John Moir stood up and said, "The problem with treaties – with these people – is that they are honoured more in the breach than the observance. In fact, I doubt they are worth the paper they're written on."

Johnston nodded, and said, "Obviously we will not tolerate breaches of treaties..."

Moir continued: "I'm sure the British Government wants the settlers in this territory to succeed, but we depend on local native labour. The chiefs are obstructive, and the slavers buy or steal our labourers from their villages. Also, the Angoni raid this area and cause mayhem. We desperately need a police force, or some kind of military presence, to enforce a rule of law." His final words were drowned in applause.

Johnston said. "We have to formalise the very existence of this territory. That is a pre-requisite for a number of important actions. You see, Her Majesty's Government is reluctant to spend its funds without some security for its investment, and perhaps some return. If we can establish an administration we can raise revenue – initially through customs duties, and later by taxation."

There followed a concerted groan, but Johnston raised his hand. "It stands to reason that you cannot have the protection of the

Crown without contributing something. If we are to have a local
police force and a judiciary, we have to pay for them. I don't mean
only the settlers – the Africans must contribute too."

"Not much hope of that!" someone shouted.

Johnston smiled indulgently. "We have precedents in India and the
west coast of Africa. A time will come, I am certain, when we will be
able to levy some simple tax on the native people."

"Who is going to stop the slavers?" came another shout. "We've
made precious little progress."

Johnston nodded vigorously. "I intend to negotiate treaties with the
principal chiefs. I have the authority to do this, and to offer incentives.
In time, we will bring in some kind of trained military force, which
will be supported by local police. I urge you to be patient. It will take
time, but I'm determined that we will prevail."

When the formal meeting broke up Johnston was taken round to
meet members of the audience. John Buchanan made brief introductions. Buchanan explained that Alan was a former Mandala employee,
now a coffee planter, and that he had held a commission in the British
Army. "He has been to Karonga several times and participated in the
fights there."

Johnston shook his hand. "I'm holding a meeting tomorrow – Buchanan has already recommended that you join us. Will you attend?
We need to hear from you men who have experience fighting at the
north end of the Lake."

—•—

The meeting was held in the Moirs' office in the Mandala office in
Blantyre; in addition to John and Fred Moir, it was attended by Buchanan, Alfred Sharpe, John Nicoll, and Alan Spaight.

"I wish to visit Chief Mponda first," Johnston told them. "I plan
to strike a treaty with him. I hope that Bishop Smythies will loan me
the steamer *Charles Janson*, so that I can then proceed up the Lake to

Kota Kota, where I will deal with Chief Jumbe. After that, we will go north to Karonga, to negotiate with Mlozi. I need to proceed from there to Lake Tanganyika, but will return to finish any outstanding work here."

"Now, I need some help from you gentlemen. I realise that you all have your jobs and your estates, so I am seeking your voluntary services. Mr Spaight, I would have liked you to come with me to Karonga, but I've heard that you have already given more than your fair share of time. You need more time to attend to your estate, and I will wait for another opportunity to use your services." He paused. "However, I need an African assistant to complement Ali Kiongwe, who is my Swahili interpretor. I'm told that your man, Goodwill, would be ideal for my purposes."

It was Sharpe who had made the suggestion. "Sorry, Alan," he said, "but Consul Johnston ought to have the best services we can provide."

Alan agreed, somewhat reluctantly, and Johnston said, "Thank you. Please send your man to me."

—•—

Goodwill walked to Blantyre where he found Consul Harry Johnston in his temporary office at Mandala House. He handed over Alan's letter to a peon, and was then invited to enter the office. He studied Johnston as he read the letter, noting the intelligent face that was almost effeminate in its soft texture of skin and hair.

The letter from Alan introduced Goodwill and hoped that he might be useful to the Consul for his forthcoming journey to the north, particularly because the young Nyanja man had first hand experience of slavers.

When he had finished reading the letter Johnston put it down on the desk and asked Goodwill to tell him about his captivity and escape. He did not interrupt, and at the end of the account he asked Goodwill if he would work for him temporarily, and perhaps accompany him in a journey to the north.

They set off two weeks later on the steamer *Charles Janson.* They first stopped at Likoma Island where Johnston conferred with Bishop Smythies, and then he continued to Bandawe, on the west coast of the Lake. There Johnston met with Bishop Laws, who had by now been in the country for twelve years. On one occasion they invited Goodwill into their discussion, and he noticed that the Consul seemed to have much respect the Scottish missionary's views about the country and the slave trade.

"Now, Goodwill," said Dr Laws, "you were brought up as an Angoni. Why do you think they are so warlike and prey on weaker tribes like the Atonga?"

After a pause to consider his answer, Goodwill replied, "I think, sir, it is because they have a long tradition of fighting other tribes to gain control of grazing lands and water. My ancestors came from Zululand – a very few of them broke away from the Zulu tribe. They became a great tribe themselves because they conquered weaker people and took the women and children to become Angonis. It is their way of life, their custom – the way they have survived and prospered."

Dr Laws nodded. "I suppose you're right, but it's brutal and disruptive. If you had remained as an Angoni you would be like that now."

"I suppose so," replied Goodwill, smiling slightly. "I would not have known anything different."

—•—

After three days the Consul's group left Bandawe and set off in the *Charles Janson* for Kota Kota, to visit the chief, Tawakali Sudi. He was commonly known as the Jumbe, and claimed to have met Dr Livingstone. Johnston made a camp near the town and sent his Swahili servant Ali Kiongwe to visit the Jumbe. He returned two days later to say that the Chief would receive them.

It took them half a day to walk to the large village. When they arrived they were greeted by the old Chief, who was an Arab-African half caste. He was genial and offered them the use of a large thatched mud house in which to sleep.

During this time Goodwill had long conversations with Ali Kiongwe, hampered slightly by his lack of fluency in Swahili. He asked, "Why do you work for the *mzungu*, so far from your home?"

Ali shrugged. "He is a powerful man – an official of the British Government. You must know that is the strongest government in the world. Mr Johnston may be small in size, but he has the power to deal with chiefs, such as this man Jumbe. I like to watch how this power is used. A small part of it comes to me when I act as the interpretor."

—•—

Goodwill went with Johnston and Ali to several meetings with Chief Jumbe. When they spoke in Arabic he understood not a word, but they soon changed to Swahili, and then Goodwill could understand more. He heard Johnston describe to the Chief how the great powers – Britain, Germany and Portugal – were vying with each other to control this part of Africa. None of them would tolerate the trading of slaves and they would use their powers to stop it. So, it was just a matter of time before the Arab and Yao slavers were defeated and punished. The Consul produced a draft treaty that defined Jumbe's territory and insisted on the cessation of slavery. He offered the Chief an annual subvention of two hundred pounds, so long as he abided by the treaty. It was a small fortune for an African in his situation, and Jumbe duly signed.

There followed a wait of five weeks before the *Charles Janson* returned to fetch them from Kota Kota. Goodwill could see that the young Consul was beside himself with boredom. Although Johnston often kept to himself, reading, and writing his diary, he would sometimes invite Goodwill and Ali to join him, talking to them while he sketched, and trying to improve his knowledge of ChiNyanja.

Having seen how the other white men camped in the bush, Goodwill was intrigued to see the comparative luxury with which Johnston surrounded himself. He had a folding camp bed, with a bedding roll of sheets and blanket. A mosquito net could be hung over the bed. The Consul used a folding table and chair for his meals, with a linen table cloth, china plates and silver-plated cutlery. His travelling boxes contained glass tumblers and a whisky decanter, besides all manner of condiments. Goodwill noticed that he always washed before his evening meal, and changed his clothes. His servant, instructed by Ali Kiongwe, brought the meal with some ceremony.

Archdeacon Smythies arrived on the *Ilala* and he explained that the *Charles Janson* had broken down; hence the long delay in coming to fetch them. They voyaged to Karonga in the north, where they discovered that John Nicoll had already negotiated a truce with the Arab slaver, Mlozi. They then continued round the northern end of the Lake, which was now German territory, and finally viewed the spectacular Livingstone Mountains, rising to nearly ten thousand feet.

On returning to Karonga the Consul decided to meet with Mlozi and the other Arab slavers to formalise the treaty. He took with him Nicoll and Fotheringham, while Ali Kiongwe and Goodwill went as interpretors. Johnston read out the terms of the treaty in Swahili, sometimes clarified by Ali, and the Arabs duly signed. They ceremoniously slaughtered a bull, and the Union flag was hoisted.

While Johnston went on the Lake Tanganyika he sent Goodwill back to Zomba, where he was glad to return to work on Alan Spaight's farm.

—•—

30

Alan planted the remainder of his coffee crop in the early part of the rainy season, at the end of November 1889. His days were full from dawn to dusk, supervising the labour force as they planted and weeded the coffee fields. He also sowed a hundred acres of maize for labour rations. There was a long dry spell in December, but the river continued to flow. They worked hard to bring water along the main canals. Each coffee plant was given a drink of water, using syphon tubes made of canvas. The maize could not be irrigated, but a shower came just in time to save the young plants.

He rode to the Kennedy farm at least once a week. First he would bathe and change his clothes, then ride the mile and a half to reach his neighbours at dusk. They gave him supper and he would then chat to them for about an hour before riding home by moonlight. If there were lions around he stayed overnight.

Jock's condition deteriorated in December. Dr McPhail recommended an exploratory operation. "It's probable that there's something in there," he said. "I don't know what, or whether I can deal with the problem. Also, there's some risk in the operation, from sepsis."

"Go ahead, Doc," growled Jock. "I'd rather die under your knife than exist like this."

The Kennedys decided not to delay the operation for Christmas, and Alan offered to look after their farm for as long as needed. On

December 20 Jess assisted McPhail at the Zomba Hospital. It was soon evident that her father had a cancerous tumour in his lower intestine.

"I have to cut it out," said McPhail. "If I take out a few feet of intestine he should be none the worse. Ask Marge if she agrees."

Jess went out, realising too late that her gown was alarmingly bloodstained. Marge merely frowned and said that McPhail should go ahead. Two hours later the operation was over and Jock was in the recovery room.

"So far, so good," said McPhail. "But we don't know whether there has been any metastasis. Only time will tell."

—•—

Consul Harry Johnston left Nyasaland in January 1890, travelling via Mozambique Island to Zanzibar. In May he went by steamer to Port Elizabeth in the Cape, and thence by coach to Kimberley, where he stayed with the mining magnate Cecil Rhodes, who had made his fortune from diamonds. He discovered to his surprise that John Moir was in town, expressly to discuss with Rhodes the possibility of incorporating the African Lakes Company into the British South Africa Company. He also met James Rochfort Maguire, an Oxford friend of Rhodes.

Johnston had wide-ranging discussions with Rhodes about regional matters. He raised the issue of fighting the slavers around Lake Nyasa, and the need for a small, but efficient military unit.

"The local natives have little in the way of military background, except for the Angoni tribe, who are a diluted shadow of the their parent tribe that fought so well against the Boers, and against us British at Isandlwhana."

Maguire, who was sitting in on the discussion, said, "Why not bring a regiment of troops from India? They would be more able to cope with the climate than British troops."

Rhodes nodded. "Why not? It would be far less expensive than bringing troops from England."

"I've raised this matter before, at Whitehall," said Johnston. "They seem reluctant to commit the funds."

Rhodes grunted, as if to indicate his disapproval of bureaucracy. "Perhaps I can make a contribution. You two make an estimate for me." He pointed his cigar at Maguire. "Why not see if your brother Cecil could raise a unit of Indian soldiers? You told me he wanted to see Africa."

Johnston and Maguire travelled together to Cape Town, and were passengers on the same ship to England. During the voyage they had several discussions about the feasibility of importing a contingent of Indian soldiers to Nyasaland. Maguire volunteered to write to his brother seeking his advice, and asking him whether he would be interested in participating.

—•—

Alan now had two horses: the Basuto gelding named Rascal that the Moirs gave him as a parting gift, and a half-Arab he bought from the estate of a planter who died of fever. He also had three cows and a bull, all bought from nearby villages. They were very small by European standards, but were well adapted to local conditions. The cows were docile and easy to milk, but they produced hardly any surplus after their calves had been fed.

Time seemed to pass quickly for Alan; he thought it was because he was so busy with his farm. He had now been in the country for three years and could speak ChiNyanja fluently. Goodwill tutored him on the finer points of the language, as well as local customs. Maintaining a sufficient labour force was his main difficulty. The local chiefs and headmen could be obstructive, demanding gifts that were barely concealed bribes, to allow their villagers to work on the coffee estates. When he questioned his workers he was convinced that most of them wanted to keep their jobs, but they were too timid to disobey the local chiefs if instructed to stay away from work.

It was a frequent task for him to ride out to a chief and bargain for his support. These chiefs were hereditary, and not all of them were old. They had the support of clan elders, who were also anxious to participate in any contributions that this *mzungu* could make.

Alan took Goodwill with him on these trips, and was amused at the consternation when the villagers saw one of their own kind riding a horse, a *carvallo*. It was their common belief that only the white men could ride horses, and could shoot rifles with accuracy.

On arrival at the village Goodwill would first approach the chief, moving forward with his knees bent, clapping his hands softly. When he was about ten feet in front of the chief he would prostrate himself until commanded to rise and speak.

Alan would sit with the chief and his elders, with Goodwill behind him. They would start with rambling exchanges about the weather and the state of the crops before he politely broached the subject of the chief restraining his villagers from working on the estate. Of course, the chief would deny that he had done such a thing, and would counter, at great length, about the need for his men to cultivate their own crops and tend their own animals.

Both parties knew that these tasks were not demanding and were usually performed by the women and children. Meanwhile, *pombe*, the local beer was served from a large calabash, and they would drink with gourd cups. Sometimes, *nsima* was brought, perhaps with an *ndiwo* of pieces of goat meat.

As the discussion progressed the issue of presents for the chief would be discussed. Lengths of calico were mentioned, as well as copper wire and utensils, such as metal pots. The planters had an unwritten agreement that they would not offer excessive amounts, but the chiefs knew that they had the upper hand because a planter without labour would soon be bankrupt.

The planters would often discuss options for preventing the chiefs from being obstructive. At one such meeting the more belligerent members wanted to use force to coerce them into submission, but it was pointed out that they could assemble a posse of only about a dozen armed men, which would probably be insufficient.

"Imagine if you were faced with a mob of several hundred villagers," Jock said, "even though they might have only a few flintlocks and bows."

"How about a formal agreement – a subvention – a bribe of so much a year. Then, if the chief broke the agreement he could be made subject to some sort of retribution..."

"We don't have the power to enforce any sort of retribution."

"If only we had a police force we could drag the blighters into a jail."

—•—

Jess was now a regular visitor to *Khundalila*. She would ride over at any time of the day, and Alan looked forward to her visits and her cheerful presence. When he felt weighed down with worry about his crops she would distract him with news from the community outside, and with her infectious laughter. She was intensely interested in the farming activities, but even more in the wildlife. They would walk through the woodland areas of the farm while he pointed out the animals: a pair of otters in the *dambo*, sleek and furtive; a group of ground hornbills, hooting as they fossicked for grubs. He showed her the pugmarks of a leopard that had walked on a dusty path only a few hours ago.

The Kennedy's Ridgeback bitch had a litter of six puppies, and Alan was given first choice of two of them. He chose two dogs and named them Ranter and Bellman. He gave them the best food: milk, meat, and wholegrain meal. They grew fast and became his constant companions. They scared the Africans on the farm, but they grew fond of Goodwill. Rabies was a serious risk, and Alan had to shoot any dog that strayed in from the villages showing strange behaviour. Likewise, jackals and hyenas were shot on sight.

He often thought about proposing to Jess, but his financial position was precarious until the coffee plants started to produce. He was so preoccupied with his farm, and the dogs and horses, that he seemed to lose track of time.

—•—

By September Alan felt assured that the coffee crop would be successful. The trees were growing well, the irrigation system was functioning, and prospects looked good. He decided to propose to Jess.

He chose a day when he knew the Kennedys would be together – they had invited him for lunch. He intended to ask Jock and Marge for their daughter's hand, and he prepared a little speech that he would give to Jess.

When he arrived at the farm the family were standing on the verandah drinking shandies. With rising spirits he took his horse to the stables and then joined them.

"We have some news for you," said Jock and paused dramatically. Alan looked at Marge and she was smiling archly. Jess looked subdued.

"Jess and Alistair McPhail are to be married."

—•—

31

Alan supposed that if he were a girl he would have fainted. In a daze he gave Jess and Marge hugs, and shook Jock's hand. They must have noticed his shock – it was glaringly obvious. What made matters worse was that he was uncharacteristically speechless.

He cursed himself for being so unaware. It was such a logical union to make. She had been a proxy mother to the two boys and Alistair McPhail's helpmate for three years. Yet he was certain she did not love the man. Why had she said nothing to him? He tried to recall conversations in which the doctor had figured. His name had been mentioned only in connection with the boys. Alistair had seldom been out to the Kennedy farm, and then only to deliver the boys, or to fetch them, when Jess was looking after them.

Alan knew that Jess had never stayed overnight at the doctor's house since Nora died. He ground his teeth in frustration, wondering what physical relationship they might have had. Although he'd seen them together on several occasions since Nora died, there had been no hint of physical attraction.

The meal passed in stilted conversation about wedding plans, and about how wonderful it would be for the boys to have a mother. When it was over, Marge and Jock went for their nap, and Alan walked with Jess to the stables.

He could not contain myself. "You're not in love with him, are you, Jess?"

She looked at him sorrowfully. "No, but I do love him. He's a dear, kind man. He needs me; the boys need me."

"But that's not a proper basis for a marriage, is it?"

She shrugged. "We get on well together. We've worked together for three years. I've lived in his house – while Nora was alive – for weeks – months."

"Have you..."

"Please don't ask me things like that, Alan. You are a true friend, and I love you too. You had every opportunity to ask me to marry you – almost from the moment we first met. But you fell for Nora instead. I try not to blame you – except that it was unfair to Alistair."

He knew he was at risk of behaving like a child who sees his favourite toy given to a friend. He wanted to stamp his foot and shout. He wanted to say, 'Do you know that I was going to propose to you today', but he closed his mouth and said nothing.

She started to weep. They were in the stables now, and she turned away, sobbing. "It's too late, Alan. You had so many chances to say something. Now I've made up my mind. Alistair and I have waited until a year passed since Nora died."

—•—

The marriage was in November 1890, at the little red brick mission church at Domasi, performed by David Robertson. Dr Thompson was Alistair McPhail's best man. Jess had Malcolm as a page boy, and Fiona Bruce as her matron of honour; she was given away by her father. As she walked up the aisle on Jock's arm Alan clenched his teeth and imagined that it might have been him waiting for her at the altar.

Jock's health had improved and he was an affable host at the reception in the Kennedy home. A very large proportion of the Europeans in the Protectorate attended the wedding, including many planters and Mandala officials. Alan proposed the toast and gave a short speech of congratulation to the bride and groom. Alistair McPhail replied with thanks to Jock and Marge, then eulogised Jess. He shyly extolled her virtues and thanked her for all she had done for him and his sons.

They did not go away on honeymoon. John had a list of operations to perform on his African patients.

—•—

In early 1891 the settlers heard that Harry Johnston, still in England, had been asked by Her Majesty's Government to organise the administration of the 'territories of British influence in Central Africa', including the Nyasaland Protectorate and the area north of the Zambesi River.

News gradually filtered through to Zomba that Consul Johnston had proposed that all the territories now under British influence should be designated as 'British Central Africa'. A few months later the Anglo-German Convention was signed, which defined the borders between the British territory and German East Africa. In particular, it defined the boundary at the north end of Lake Nyasa as the Songwe River.

John Buchanan was made a Companion of the Order of St Michael and St George, and Harry Johnston was made a Companion of the Order of the Bath. Alfred Sharpe was commissioned as a Vice-Consul under Buchanan, who was then Acting Consul. A party was held at the Zomba Club, at which these honours were announced. Alan sat at a table with the Buchanan brothers and the Kennedys; Alfred Sharpe was away on a hunting trip. When he congratulated Buchanan, he replied, "It's ironic, Alan, that Her Majesty's official representatives are just a humble farmer and an elephant hunter."

"Your CMG is well-deserved, John," he said. "If anyone should know it's me."

—•—

239

Harry Johnston was appointed Commissioner of the new Protectorate, and Consul-General for the British territories. The area north of the Zambesi River had been ceded to Rhodes's British South Africa Company, the Chartered Company, which in turn has chosen him to be the Administrator – it was an unpaid post that he was to hold for five years.

The link between the Nyasaland Protectorate and the Chartered Company was crucial. Rhodes pledged to spend £17,500 a year in the region, with an additional £10,000 for a campaign against the slave traders. The funds were intended for some sort of para-military police force.

A post of Military Commandant was created for Captain Cecil Maguire, Rochfort's brother, who would command a contingent of Indian troops. Rumour had it that he jumped at the opportunity to come to Africa, and the appointment was endorsed by Lord Roberts, then Commander in Chief in India.

All the news was greeted with enthusiasm by the Europeans in the region. The slave trade was as active as ever at the north end of the Lake, with Mlozi as the main protagonist despite the treaties. In the south it was Chief Mponda, and Chief Makanjira to the east, who were the main villains. Only in the centre of the Lake shore, where the treaty had been signed with the Jumbe, was the slave trade dormant.

—•—

32

Shire Highlands – April-June 1891

Alan Spaight stood on the bank of the Lower Shire River at Katunga, watching the little paddle steamer approach the jetty. It had three barges in tow, and the skipper was manoeuvring the whole convoy carefully forwards against the current. Alan could see him at the helm, a small swarthy man with a blue peaked cap. Beside him in the foc'sle was a tall young man wearing a khaki uniform, and he guessed this must be Captain Cecil Maguire. The barges were full of Indian sepoys, three companies of them – two of Mazbi Sikhs and one of Hyderabad Lancers. The small force was seconded from the Indian Army to fight the slavers in Nyasaland. With them were ten Swahili policemen recruited by Harry Johnston in Quelimane. The troops were armed with Snider rifles. They had three mountain guns – a nine-pounder and two seven-pounders – as well as a Maxim gun, an early form of machine gun, with a rate of fire equivalent to about a hundred rifles.

Alan knew that Harry Johnston had been detained by administrative duties in Chiromo, down river. The Commissioner had sent a message asking him to meet Maguire and escort him to Zomba. When the steamer and barges has been moored he walked down to the jetty and introduced himself.

As they walked together off the jetty, Alan explained. "It'll take us two or three days to march to Blantyre. It's hard going – all uphill."

241

Maguire smiled. "That's good. We need some exercise. We've been cooped up in boats for three weeks."

One of the subadars, the most senior of the Sikh soldiers, came up to Maguire and saluted. He was a tall man with a full dark beard streaked with grey that was swept up and tucked into his large turban. He had luxuriant eyebrows and glittering brown eyes that turned towards Alan, regarding him carefully.

"*Namaste,*" Alan said.

The subadar continued looking into his eyes for a moment, then turned to Maguire. "Excuse me, *sahib*," he said in English. "Was the other *sahib*.." he nodded towards Alan, "...with a Sikh regiment?"

Maguire frowned and turned to Alan. "Were you?"

"I was with the 15th Ludhianas," Alan replied, grinning. "I was seconded to them in the Sudan, after Tofrek. Then I went back to India with them for two years. My Punjabi is very rusty – I haven't spoken it for a while."

"Well I'm damned!" said Maguire and started to laugh.

"You see, *sahib*," the subadar cut in. "We have a *naik* here, Shazar Singh, who recognised this *sahib;* he served with him in Sudan. He said that, back at base, the *sahib* tried to prevent his brother from being flogged..."

"Hold on, Gulab," Maguire interrupted. "Bring Shazar here."

The subadar saluted and went off.

Alan said, "He's referring to an incident a couple of years ago that caused me to resign my commission." He told Maguire the story briefly before the young *naik* came up to them and saluted extravagantly.

"I confess I don't remember him," Alan said, and asked. "Do you speak English?"

Shazar Singh nodded. "Yes, *sahib*. My brother and I were sepoys at the Battle of Tofrek. It was my brother who was accused of theft and flogged – you asked the Colonel to have a hearing."

"What happened to him – your brother?"

"He resigned, *sahib*. He works for our father, as a tailor. He was not a thief."

"I thought he was not." Alan laughed. "Well, perhaps it was a better outcome for both of us."

—•—

Maguire ordered his three subadars to fall the men in, pointing to the shade on the edge of the clearing. The subadars in turn shouted orders, and in a short time the three companies were lined up in ranks of three. Then Maguire strolled to a position in front of the assembled men. He stood them at ease, and addressed them in Hindustani.

"Well done, men. We have come to the end of our journey in boats, and I'm sure you're glad about that!" Quiet laughter came from the ranks. "You are now in the Nyasaland Protectorate and our real work will start. It is called a Protectorate because the British Government wishes to protect the local people from the Arab slavers. As I have told you before, for many years the Arabs have been buying slaves in this part of Africa and have taken them to sell at the coast. Our job is to put a stop to this evil trade. We may have to fight the slavers – to teach them a lesson – and I know you will do that well."

"First, we march to a town called Blantyre. This *sahib*, Mr Spaight" – he pointed to Alan – "tells me that it will take two or three days. He will be our guide. By the way, Spaight *sahib* served with the 15th Ludhianas. You must be prepared at all times for action. The slavers may have heard that we are coming and they might attack us."

"Before we start, we must fill our water bottles – not from the river, where the water is dirty, but from the big pots." He pointed to some large cauldrons that had been taken off the steamer, under which fires were being lit.

Maguire told the subadars to take over and turned to Alan. "We'll be ready to leave in about half an hour. Where will we spend the night?"

Alan explained that he had arranged for them to stay in a village about ten miles along their route. "We ought to cover greater distances on the following days, but I thought we shouldn't be too ambitious on the first day. Also, food might be a problem – you might not always be able to find rice. It's not as easy to procure as maize and millet."

Maguire laughed. "You know my chaps – they will eat anything, within reason. Remember that they have their religious restrictions. The Lancers won't eat pig meat – they're Muslims."

When they started the march Maguire and Alan were near the front of the column. It was the same track that Alan had walked four years earlier. It was still mere beaten earth, barely wide enough for two or three men to walk abreast. It had not been widened because there were no wheeled vehicles in the territory. It wound up into the hills, occasionally crossing small streams. They were surrounded by dense woodland, with an undergrowth of small shrubs and straggling grass. The sounds the column of soldiers created – their talking and laughter – frightened any wild animals away.

Maguire walked easily, with an athletic stride. He was twenty-eight years old, and had achieved his Captaincy in the Madras Staff Corps earlier that year. He had been seconded for a three-year tour to Africa. His dark drooping moustache contrasted with his sallow complexion. On his head he wore a large pith helmet with his regimental colours in the binding. He admired Alan's broad-brimmed felt hat, remarking that it must be much lighter to wear.

"Have you ever travelled by *machila*?" Maguire asked.

"I had to once, when I was wounded. I don't like the idea of being carried by other men. Besides, it's very uncomfortable – you know, it swings around, and you can be dropped!"

"I must say I agree with you. I'm sure I'd never use one."

Alan explained that some of the settlers had volunteered their services in the long campaign against the slavers. "It's in our interests. The slavers deplete the villages of able-bodied men, who are our source of labour. They just disrupt everything. We've had no police or military force to control them. That's why we're all so pleased to see you – and we want to do all we can to help."

Maguire asked for his opinion of Harry Johnston, and Alan was cautious in my reply. "He's very competent in his administration. He seems to have a clear idea – a commitment – about dealing with slavery. He believes that only force will convince the slave traders to stop. You may know that Livingstone and others thought that commercial trade would eventually replace the trafficking of slaves and ivory. Johnston thinks that we must act now, not wait for some long-term economic development. We know who the slavers are, and we know which local chiefs and headmen are selling slaves to them."

—•—

The first day of the march was uneventful. They spent the night at a village, where they erected a *boma* of thorn bushes to surround the encampment. The sepoys were talking nervously about wild animals; they were concerned about lions, having heard that they could take human victims from villages at night. Maguire addressed the men and told them they would be safe as long as they kept their fires burning.

On the second day they covered twenty miles, and, by making an early start, reached Blantyre at dusk. Maguire and his men seemed impressed by the change in environment. They reached an altitude of three thousand feet, and it was noticeably cooler. The small settlement was surrounded by hills covered with thick vegetation. The buildings were mostly single-storey, made of red brick or sun-dried Kimberley bricks, many were grass-thatched, though some were roofed with corrugated iron. Some houses were made of wattle and daub. The dominant building was the church; the tower was the tallest structure in the town. Of the European inhabitants of the Protectorate, about two-fifths lived in Blantyre; most of them were Scottish.

Alan led the column to the Blantyre Club where a nearby field had been commissioned for the sepoys to camp. Some tents had been set up for them, but most of the men preferred to sleep in the open; mosquitoes were less prevalent here. The clubhouse had three rooms for guests, and two of these were taken by Maguire and Alan. They had a convivial supper with leading members of the European community, before retiring early after their long hike.

The column set off for Zomba soon after dawn next morning. There were more local people here, and some of them came to the path to watch the sepoys pass. They were silent, gaping at the soldiers and wide-eyed at the sight of their weapons and strange clothing.

After twenty miles they reached the old mission station at Magomero. Alan explained to his companion that this was the first site of permanent settlement of white people in the Protectorate, where missionaries led by Bishop Mackenzie established a church and school thirty years ago. The column continued a mile further, to Frank Bruce's coffee estate, where they were greeted by the owner. After ensuring that his men were fed and bedded in a safe compound, Maguire came into their host's house, where the two men would spend the night.

They sat with Frank Bruce and Fiona and their two young children to a supper of roast guinea fowl. Frank described how he had come to the country three years earlier and had purchased large tracts of land from the local chief, some parts of which he had sold, and other parts he had leased out.

"Coffee's an ideal crop for us," he said. He was a tall man who was inclined to bluster. "It's not perishable, and it has a high value related to its weight, so that it can be exported profitably. Tea would be a good crop for us too, and the climate is suitable, but we need better transport to get the factory parts shipped in. You see, coffee can be processed quite simply by fermenting the cherries in water tanks, whereas tea requires machinery and higher investment."

"It's a very primitive country," Fiona Bruce chipped in; she too was tall, and her Highland Scottish accent was strong. "As you know, there are no roads and no vehicles, except for a few ox wagons and carts. There's no telegraph, so the only means of communication is by letter carried by hand. The people here have no written language, and they have no currency. There are no police, and no soldiers – until you came, Captain Maguire."

"The rule of law hardly exists," interjected Frank Bruce, "and the natives sometimes take advantage of it."

"As do the settlers," said his wife with a wry smile.

"Are the local people friendly towards you?" asked Maguire.

"Our local chief seemed quite happy to have us," said Bruce. "I think he expected us to support him against any incursions from the Arabs and Angonis. But we're not really able to do that. As a consequence he's making contrary noises – as if he's changed his mind."

"The chiefs generally are making trouble for us settlers," added his wife. "They try to prevent our labourers from coming to work. We hope you can put a stop to the trouble."

"Perhaps we can. We'll see what the Commissioner wants us to do." Maguire thus made it clear that he would take no initiative himself.

Next morning Maguire asked Alan what he thought of the local African people. After considering for a while he laughed. "It may sound rather patronising, but they are really quite primitive in their government and culture, compared with the Indians."

"You said 'government' – what do you mean?"

"Well, they have village headmen, who are both hereditary and chosen, and they have chiefs above the headmen, but the way they govern is through customary law, permeated by superstition and corruption. I'm sure it was like that in Britain hundreds of years ago. It's as if we've gone back in time to the dark ages. The life of typical villagers in the hinterland is precarious in the extreme. They often struggle to find enough to eat, there are diseases like malaria and blackwater fever, and there are dangerous wild animals – lions, buffaloes, hippos, crocodiles, snakes and scorpions. To cap it all they have raids from slavers and Angoni warriors."

Maguire asked. "What do you think we handful of foreigners can do?"

"We can establish the rule of law. Whether it's our law or theirs, or a combination of both. But to do that we have to have the resources to enforce the laws. That's where men like you come in. We need a military force of some kind. Initially it's to rid the country of the slavers and the chiefs who trade with them, but later it could be a police force – perhaps a para-military force."

Maguire frowned. "Who's to pay for it – in the long run. Rhodes is funding my lot, but do you suppose the British Government will take it over. Where's the quid pro quo? Or do you think they'll do it for altruistic reasons?"

"We should ask Johnston that question."

—•—

They reached Zomba by late afternoon the following day. The mountain loomed as they approached, dominating their view. Maguire said it seemed like some ancient volcano, its rim dipping and rising, its sides covered with sinister dark rocks that glistened in the sunlight. At its highest point the rim rose to four thousand seven hundred feet. To the right, to the east, was the Phalombe Plain and the shining disk of Lake Chilwa, which, Alan explained, was very shallow and full of fish. It had the strange high island on its western side, like some strange primeval monster heaving itself from the water.

They stopped on open ground that Alan had prepared for the troops, not far from the broad track that passed through the embryonic town. There was a stream nearby that flowed from the mountain, where the column could draw its water. The sepoys soon set up a makeshift kitchen for their evening meal.

Maguire and Alan walked on for another mile until they reached the small settlement of Zomba. At the foot of the mountain was a huddle of huts and a market; higher up were a few brick bungalows occupied by Europeans, and higher still was the Residency, now the home of the Commissioner, Harry Johnston.

Alan took Maguire to a guest bungalow, not far from the Residency. It had been built with fired bricks, a rectangle with a tin roof. It contained two bedrooms and a living room; the kitchen was in a lean-to at the back. There was a bathroom between the two bedrooms. The furniture was made out of wooden boxes that had been used to crate four-gallon tins of kerosene. They provided modular units from which tables and storage chests could be assembled. The beds and chairs were made of sawn timber roughly nailed together. In the bathroom was an oval tin tub and a table with a tin wash basin. The toilet was a wooden box in the corner and a flush pipe to a deep hole in the garden.

—•—

A week later Alan visited Maguire at his temporary quarters. They were sitting on the verandah when a uniformed servant arrived from the Residency with a note inviting them to supper. Johnston had arrived in Zomba the day before.

"We'll get good fare there," Alan said.

"What dress is expected?"

"The best you have. I suppose you have a mess uniform?"

"I do, but it's very creased."

"Don't worry, Cecil. He knows you've had a long journey. Besides, all I have is khaki trousers, and a clean shirt and tie."

They walked the short distance to the imposing wooden gate, where a sentry was on duty. He wore a khaki uniform, but was actually a household servant. They were shown a fine guest book which they duly signed, and then took a short walk up to the port cochere. The Residency had two floors; the roof was corrugated iron painted red. It had been built by the Buchanan brothers and was the largest building in Zomba.

The Residency's sole inhabitant was Harry Hamilton Johnston. Alan was again struck by the force of the little man's personality and the intelligence in his expression as he welcomed his guests. Somehow, he had brought a few bottles of wine into the country and ceremoniously opened one of them to toast Maguire's arrival.

"Have you ever thought of growing grape vines?" he asked Alan.

They discussed the climatic issues, agreeing that it might be worth trying some varieties. Supper was served in some style by a uniformed African servant and the topic of conversation turned to the problems facing the settlers near Mlanje, where Chief Chikumbu was becoming intransigent.

"I've heard," said Johnston, "that he's restricting their access to labour. It's nothing short of extortion, since they've already paid him large sums to ensure his cooperation. He's also well known as a slave trader. I think we need to teach him a lesson."

"A particularly aggravating incident," Alan added, "was the flogging of a British man named Pidder. He could not afford to pay Chikumbu the bribe for his release and he was put in stocks."

"What happened?" asked Maguire.

"Well, Fred Moir gathered a group of settlers to obtain Pidder's release, but Chikumbu threatened to cut off his head, so they withdrew. Eventually, Pidder escaped – he was helped by some friendly locals."

Johnston stroked his small beard thoughtfully. "I wonder if we can expect any support from local chiefs? What about the Chewa chief, Chipoka? He asked me for protection from Chikumbu." He stood up and started to pace around the room. "We must take action," he announced. "I propose that you, Maguire, take immediate steps against the recalcitrant chief. The aim must be to make him cooperate with the authorities. Please draw up a plan. What do you need from me?"

"I will take a strike force," replied Maguire. "I'll take about forty of my fittest Sikhs – and the Maxim. No sense in trying to take the mountain guns on village tracks." He paused. "I need a guide and an interpretor – and I need provisions..."

"Alan will ensure that you get your provisions. I believe we have the right man to be your interpretor." Johnston turned to Alan with a wicked grin and he knew at once who the Commissioner had in mind. "What do you say, Alan?"

He laughed wryly. "I suppose I have to agree." He knew that Goodwill would want to go. He was always eager to help in the campaigns.

The Commissioner stood up. "Very well, gentlemen. That chief will rue the day that he challenged the authority of the Crown."

—•—

It took a long time, but Alan was beginning to get inured to the fact of Jess's marriage to Alistair McPhail. He saw them regularly at supper parties, and picnics on the plateau. The couple seemed to get on well enough – Alan never saw them quarrel – but he could detect no passion in their relationship. Jess was always involved with the two boys and seemed to revel in motherhood. He dreaded the day she would announce her own pregnancy.

He talked many times with Alistair McPhail, who was a dedicated doctor; the only times that he became animated were when discussing medical issues. He seemed genuinely concerned for the lot of his African patients and their suffering from tropical diseases.

—•—

33

Phalombe Plain - July 1891

Alan introduced Goodwill to Captain Maguire in the garden of *Khundalila*, where the British officer had come for lunch.

"He's only in his mid twenties," he said, "but he's already had a searing experience of slavery. Tell Captain Maguire what happened, Goodwill."

Goodwill gave a short account of his capture and escape, and the long journey home. Alan could tell that Maguire was impressed with the young man's command of English, and his lucid descriptions.

"He also spent time at Karonga," Alan explained, "helping me and Fred Lugard."

Maguire questioned Goodwill about his knowledge of the languages, and of the area where they were about to campaign.

"I know the area quite well, sir," replied Goodwill politely, "but I do not know all the paths and streams. It would be better if you had a guide with local knowledge of these places. The people in the area are Nyanjas like me, but they have been conquered by Yaos. I can speak both of those languages."

"Have you had any experience of warfare?"

"Very little, sir. I was raised an Angoni, and know something about their methods. I first fired a gun during the fight against Mlozi in the Karonga area. Mr Spaight has taught me how to use a rifle."

Maguire said, "Your main task will be to help me negotiate with the local people. I need to have complete trust that you will convey my meaning properly, and I think you can do this because your English is so good."

—•—

The column assembled two days later on the new parade ground, on the outskirts of Zomba. The Sikhs were formed up in the pattern they would use for the march; the Lancers would remain in Zomba. There was an advance guard of four men, one to look ahead, two to look to each side, and the fourth to run back to the main force if they encountered opposition. The main group of infantry, numbering forty men, would follow about thirty paces behind, and behind them a rearguard of a dozen men. They took two mules, one carrying the Maxim gun, the other loaded with flour and spices. Those Sikhs who would be left behind in Zomba, and the Hyderabad Lancers, watched silently as the column was assembled.

A settler named McDonald, stocky and red-haired, had volunteered to accompany them as a guide. He had been in the posse that went to rescue Pidder and claimed to know the way to Chikumbu's village.

"So who is this *kaffir*?" asked McDonald, nodding towards Goodwill.

"He has been lent to me as an interpretor," replied Maguire, "by Alan Spaight."

McDonald grunted. "How do you know he will translate truly? Why don't you use me instead."

Maguire laughed. "If you speak the language so well, you can tell me if he fails."

Goodwill was puzzled by the Scotsman's use of the word *kaffir*. He sensed that it was used in pejorative way, but he knew it as the Swahili word for 'infidel'. Later, he asked Maguire why McDonald had called him an infidel, and the Captain explained that many white men in Southern Africa used the term for Africans.

They set off across the Phalombe plain. Maguire was at the head of the main column, with McDonald beside him. Goodwill followed a few paces behind. Now and then Maguire would call orders to the advance guard, and sometimes he would walk back to check the positions of the men behind. Every hour they stopped and the men drank from their water bottles and relieved themselves in the bush.

Goodwill was intrigued by the Sikhs; he asked Maguire about them. "Sikhism is a religion in India." the Captain explained. "It started about five hundred years ago. They believe in one God, unlike the Hindus, who have many gods. The British in India fought them in a series of wars and learned to respect their warrior qualities. Now there are Sikh regiments in the British Army in India. These men volunteered to come to Africa."

"Do they have their own officers?" Goodwill asked.

"They have a sort of junior officer, called a 'Subadar', and then they have a 'Havildar' – like a sergeant, and a 'Naik' – like a corporal." Maguire watched with interest how Goodwill nodded as he seemed to absorb the information.

"What language do they speak?"

"They speak Punjabi. I cannot speak it well, so I give my orders to the subadars and havildars in English or Hindustani."

Maguire went on to explain that the Sikhs did not cut their hair, nor did they drink alcohol nor smoke. "You will have to ask the subadar for more information about their customs."

They walked about fifteen miles on the first day. They passed several villages where the inhabitants watched them impassively, or perhaps a little fearfully. They had never seen men like the Sikhs, who had dark skin yet with European features and wore strange clothing, not least the turbans wrapped round their heads.

Goodwill tried to engage the subadar, whose name was Gulab Singh, in conversation, but the Sikh said he was too busy supervising his soldiers. He directed the African to a naik named Shazar Singh, who spoke good English. He was perhaps a couple of years younger than Goodwill, with a wispy new beard, the strands of which were gathered towards the top of his head. Goodwill asked him about Sikh customs and heard about the five sacred objects. Shazar in turn asked Goodwill about the way of life of these villagers, and about the depredations of the slavers. He was captivated by the story of Goodwill's escape and long walk back from the coast.

The column spent the night in a small village. Maguire and his subadar organised pickets to guard the sleeping soldiers, and a ring of fires to frighten away foraging jackals and hyenas. They used the flour they had brought on the mules to make *chapattis*, and boiled water from a nearby stream to use for drinking. McDonald slept in a vacant hut, but Maguire chose to sleep in the open with his men. They used citronella oil, which they had brought from India, to ward off mosquitoes.

Next morning, after a breakfast of tea, *chapattis* and local bananas, they set off towards the Mlanje massif. The plain had been cultivated for many years and the villages were not far apart, but they were sparsely occupied. When he questioned the inhabitants about the scarcity of people Goodwill was always give the same explanation: that the slavers had taken the able-bodied villagers.

It was nearly noon when they were suddenly attacked by villagers throwing stones and small rocks. It happened without any warning, and three of the soldiers were hit and injured. Captain Maguire gave the order for his men to fire at the assailants, but only if they were seen in the act of throwing missiles. The sepoys fired into the bush and the hail of stones and rocks ceased.

About an hour later, when McDonald judged that they were nearing Chikumbu's village, the column received incoming musket fire. The sepoys were trained to fall to the ground and seek cover. They then started to shoot at any Africans they could see. Goodwill spotted about a dozen men armed with muskets retreating in the direction of

Mlanje Mountain. The column then advanced for about a mile and came upon a large village, with a hundred or more huts, surrounded by a patchwork of cultivated fields.

"That is Chikumbu's place," announced McDonald, pointing.

Maguire ordered the Maxim crew to assemble their weapon, while his men formed an arc in readiness to attack. At first there was no sign of anyone in the village, but after a few minutes they saw knots of men emerging from behind the huts. Some carried muskets, but most were armed with bows and arrows.

"Tell them to lay down their weapons," said Maguire to Goodwill, who shouted the order in ChiNyanja and ChiYao.

The villagers seemed to pay no attention and advanced cautiously. Among them was a man in a white *kanzu* who was calling out orders.

"What is he saying?" asked Maguire.

Goodwill shook his head. "I cannot hear clearly." He shouted to them again, ordering them to lay down their arms.

The man in the white *kanzu* shook his fist in their direction and appeared to be urging his men to attack. They were evidently reluctant, but shuffled forward. Then their leader grabbed a musket and fired it towards the Maguire column.

"Very well," muttered the Captain. He ordered the Maxim crew to open fire.

Goodwill could see spurts of dust on the ground in front of the villagers and then they started to fall like ninepins. Some of them turned and fled, so Maguire ordered the Maxim men to stop firing and waved his sepoys forward. He ran with them and Goodwill followed.

About thirty villagers were lying on the ground, some bleeding from their wounds, others abject in their surrender, begging for mercy. Maguire's main concern was to find the man in the white *kanzu*. He stayed with Goodwill who was questioning the captives about the man.

"The man in the *kanzu* is the Chief," said Goodwill. "His name is Chikumbu."

257

"Where the hell is he?" growled Maguire.

"He has run away, sir," said Goodwill. "This man here says that the Chief was hit by a bullet in his belly, but some of his men helped him."

Maguire ordered the formation of a defensive perimeter. Through Goodwill he explained to the captive villagers that they would not be harmed if they ceased their past activities of slaving, and stopped harassing the European settlers. He announced that if they failed to keep this promise he would return with more men and guns and would execute them and burn their villages. The captives listened in evident fear and nodded their agreement.

McDonald was disgusted. "You should shoot the lot of them! Line them up and execute them, man. They attacked you."

Maguire ignored him and ordered his men to provide basic assistance to the wounded. He instructed Goodwill to find out how many villagers had been killed. He went around the captives questioning them and found that five had been killed here and another three in the bush when they were throwing rocks. Another dozen were wounded, two of them seriously.

An hour later the column turned back and spent the night at the same small village as before. The following day they returned to Zomba, reaching the town in the late evening.

—•—

34

Johnston was ecstatic when he heard the news of Chikumbu's defeat. He asked Maguire to parade the Sikhs and addressed them formally, praising them for their actions. Then he visited the injured sepoys and offered encouragement. He invited Maguire, Buchanan, Sharpe and Alan to dinner at the Residency to devise a strategy for further action.

"I want to crush the Yao chiefs in the Upper Shire," said Johnston. "They are the standard bearers of slave trading. Makanjira is the worst of them; he has attacked the mission ships on the Lake, and it was he who subjected you, Buchanan to that indignity a couple of years ago." To Maguire he added, "I recently demanded a fine of ivory – because he insulted Her Majesty's Vice-Consul – but he has not paid up."

"Who are the others?" asked the Captain.

"There's Mponda – he has a large village about three miles south of where the Shire River flows out of Lake Nyasa. I made a treaty with him two years ago, but he's been making a nuisance of himself, demanding toll fees from the steamers belonging to the missionaries and Mandala. More important, he's disregarding the treaty and is currently an active slave trader. There's another Yao chief a few miles to the north-west, who seems to be quarrelling with Mponda – he sent me a message asking me to mediate. Frankly, Maguire, I consider all of them to be villains. Do you think we have enough men to deal with them?"

Maguire pondered. "It depends how organised they are. Chikumbu's men were a rabble, but these other chiefs may have proper militia."

"I doubt they are well drilled," said Johnston, "but they might have superior numbers. Of course we have the Maxim, and the mountain guns."

"True, but my greatest concern is being overwhelmed by their sheer weight of numbers. You know how the Boers evolved their *laager* strategy for defending themselves against large numbers of natives. The *laager* can't be set up when our force is on the march, because we don't have wagons for protection. Alan knows well – from his experience in Sudan – what can happen when a column is attacked before they can put up their defences. I think we should build small forts at strategic locations, where we can keep supplies – ammunition and food – and reserve troops. Then, if we encounter extra large numbers of the enemy, we can retreat into the forts and defend ourselves."

"How would you construct these forts?"

"Each one would be a stockade, with an outer ditch, possibly filled with thorn bushes. We would have to use a lot of local labour to cut the timber and do the digging."

"Sounds like a good idea," said Sharpe. "The slavers' stockades we encountered at the north end of the Lake were pretty effective. We were the attackers, and we didn't have much success, even with a mountain gun."

At the end of the meeting Johnston asked Sharpe and Alan if they could help in the campaign. Sharpe explained that he was leaving for South Africa, but would return later in the year. Alan agreed to help, but his reluctance must have been evident.

Johnston said to him, "I know it's difficult for you to leave your coffee plantation, Alan, but your military training, and your experience at Karonga, will be invaluable – don't you think so, Maguire?"

Captain Maguire agreed, with a sympathetic smile.

"And we would like you to bring your man Goodwill," added Johnston. "He's proving to be an effective member of our campaign."

———•———

They set off from Zomba at the end of September 1891. Alan had now been in Nyasaland for four years. More Europeans were coming to the territory, most of them to farm, but others to trade and to augment the mission stations. That meant that he was no longer a newcomer. Besides, he had put down deep roots by purchasing a farm.

The column was organised in much the same way as for the attack on Chikumbu's village. However, they now had about a hundred bearers to carry food and ammunition, and several mules that carried the Maxim and the three mountain guns. They were joined by the ten Swahili men that Johnston had recruited in Mozambique to act as policemen.

Maguire's contingent had been joined by Dr Boyce, a Parsee army surgeon who had been recruited by Harry Johnston. Alan had several long conversations with him, finding him an engaging character. He had already encountered Parsees when he was in India, but this was the first time he had spoken with one at length. He introduced Goodwill and explained his background, then said to Boyce, "He wants to know something about Parsees."

Dr Boyce laughed. "Then I will tell him. We are descendants of Persians who came to India about a thousand years ago. Our religion is Zoroastrian, and we were being persecuted in Persia by the Muslims. You see, Parsee means 'Persian' – like the language 'Farsi'. We are followers of the prophet Zoroaster. We now live mostly around Bombay and Bangalore..."

"So are you pure Persians?" Alan asked.

Boyce laughed again. "Oh no. I believe that there was quite a lot of mixed marrying during the early years when our ancestors were in Gujarat. Nowadays, we tend to marry within our own communities. We have higher incomes and better education than other sects in India – that was because we benefited from early contact with the British settlers in Bombay."

Goodwill said, "I find it quite confusing that there are so many religions in India."

"Quite so," said Boyce. "It is confusing. It may be a reflection of religious tolerance, but, you know, there are underlying tensions, particularly between the Hindus and the Muslims. We Parsees are so small in numbers that we are not a threat to any of them. We keep to ourselves."

"I remember seeing the Towers of Silence when I was in Bombay," Alan said. "They struck me as rather macabre." He turned to Goodwill. "The Parsees place their dead in an open tower – the corpse is eaten by vultures."

Goodwill was visibly shocked. Boyce smiled. "I understand your reaction. You see, we regard the dead body as unclean. The Tower is simply a way of disposing of the body. After all, you bury your dead in the ground, for much the same reason."

So they wiled away some of the long march along the Shire. It was very hot and the tsetse flies stung them viciously. They were not as numerous as the mosquitoes that plagued them at night, but they were much larger and seemed oblivious of the repellent oil. The men were covered in dust – the column moved in a cloud of it.

—•—

On the second day the column reached Chief Liwonde's village, stretching for about a mile along the bank of the river. The land around had been cleared for cultivation, and to reduce the encroachment of grass fires. The chief was known to be a drunkard who had been subjugated by the stronger Yao chiefs.

It was evident that the local headmen in Liwonde's area resented the incursion of the column. They knew the objective was to disrupt the slave trade and feared they would suffer economic losses. Those most concerned were the Arabs and half-castes, who were directly involved in slave trading; they watched the column sullenly but did not threaten to attack.

Johnston and Maguire decided to continue without engaging Chief Liwonde in any conversation. The column marched up the east bank of the Shire River and camped for the night opposite Mponda's village, which was much larger than Liwonde's. On the column's side of the river was the village of minor Chief Chikusi. He had asked the Commissioner for protection against Mponda, who had ordered the beheading of fourteen of his villagers.

The column spent the night on an uninhabited stretch of river bank, camping well away from the water to avoid crocodiles and hippos. Alan arranged for fires to be lit in a large cordon around the camp, and Maguire posted pickets at strategic intervals. Tents were put up for the white men, and Johnston's cook prepared the evening meal of grilled guinea fowl. It was served in some style, with a table cloth, napkins and proper cutlery brought from the Residency. The Commissioner made no excuses for following the rituals of the evening meal, with a toast to the Queen, port and cigars.

—•—

Next morning, they cautiously passed Mponda's village on the opposite bank. The Maxim gun and its wheels were taken off the mules and carried at the ready, well guarded to prevent capture. Mponda's had several hundred grass huts spread for about two miles along the west bank of the Shire. In the centre of the village stood a stockade, and they soon saw the grisly evidence of the recent beheading. Spiked on the upright logs of the stockade were the heads of the recently decapitated villagers, beside many skulls from previous executions.

"This has to be stopped," muttered Johnston. He ordered the column to continue towards the Lake, a distance of about three miles.

Maguire chose a place to construct a fort. It was near the bank of the river, which would provide protection on one side. To the north was flat open ground stretching towards the Lake. He had sketched a plan for the fort during the evenings of the march, and discussed it with Alan. Meanwhile, Ali Kiongwe and Goodwill were instructed to recruit local people to work on the construction. The labourers were joined by about fifty of the sepoys who were not engaged in guarding the camp.

The fort took a week to build, and Maguire named it Fort Johnston. It was thirty yards in diameter, circled by a wall of vertical logs and bamboo stakes, about eight feet high. The inside of the stockade had a rampart of packed earth that would allow the defenders to have an overview of attackers. The column's three mountain guns were placed on this rampart. In the centre of the fort was a house with accommodation for the British men and Dr Boyce; the Sikhs and Africans had thatched barracks on the west side of the circle. The magazine, where the ammunition was stored, was on the river side of the circle, partially underground.

It was Goodwill who first heard news of a slave caravan that was in Mponda's village and would soon head out for Kilwa on the Indian Ocean coast. In the meantime the Arabs were purchasing more slaves from local villages to augment their numbers.

The Commissioner decided to send letters to Mponda and to a nearby Yao chief ordering them to cease their slaving activities immediately. He sent some of his Swahili men as messengers, thinking they would be well received as fellow Muslims. They did not return, so he assumed they had been taken prisoner: he determined to take action.

The Yao chief's large village was about ten miles to the north-west of Fort Johnston. Maguire took a strong force of his Sikhs to free the messengers, and Goodwill went with him as an interpretor. The chief and his militia fled, leaving the village deserted, except for the Swahilis, who were unharmed. As retribution Maguire set fire to the larger huts, that appeared to belong to the chief.

The sortie force returned to Fort Johnston and heard that Mponda's militia were coming up the Shire River; the Commissioner assumed their intention was to attack the fort. His concerns grew as their numbers increased to well over a thousand. However, they headed straight for the Yao chief's village.

Goodwill volunteered to go out of the back of the fort and mingle with some of Mponda's people. He soon discovered that they were intent on capturing women and children who had been left defenceless after Maguire's attack. Their plan was to bring them back to Mponda's where they would be sold to the slave traders.

On his way back to the fort Goodwill heard that Chief Mponda himself was coming up the river, so he informed the Commissioner and a deputation was organised, consisting of Ali, Goodwill and ten Sikh soldiers under a havildar. Their orders were to bring Chief Mponda to Fort Johnston.

They found the chief surrounded by a ragtag militia of Yao men armed with flintlocks, who regarded the Sikhs truculently, eyeing their Snider rifles with interest. Ali spoke to the chief in Swahili; he nodded, indicating that he understood. He eventually agreed to meet with Johnston outside the fort, and within twenty minutes the two men were in conversation.

Mponda explained that his men were impossible to control since they were drunk with *pombe,* the local beer. The Commissioner insisted that all the captives from the surrounding villages must be returned. Mponda then asked for three days grace to get his men back and to release his captives.

—•—

The British waited impatiently while the three days elapsed, and kept the occupants of the fort busy by improving the defences. They drilled the sepoys and held shooting practices. When there was no sign of Chief Mponda, nor the captives, Johnston decided it was time to act. He dictated a letter that Ali Kiongwe wrote in Arabic; the Commissioner thought that one of the Arab slavers would be able to read it. He was given until sunset to indicate his surrender, otherwise his town would be bombarded.

The messenger returned without an answer. The occupants of the fort searched in vain for signs from Mponda, but saw nothing. They wondered if he had fled or was planning a confrontation – or was so drunk he could not do either.

"Why not drop an incendiary on them?" Alan suggested. He was standing with Johnston and Maguire on the rampart of the fort, looking across the river in the twilight.

Johnston shook his head. "We'll give them until midnight."

Still no surrender message came, so Maguire fired the first incendiary shell from a mountain gun, followed a few minutes later by a second. Within minutes flames started to erupt from the grass huts flanking the river shore and villagers started flocking to the banks, shouting and waving their arms.

"What are they saying?" asked Johnston of Goodwill, who was standing behind him.

"They are begging you to stop, sir," replied Goodwill.

They could see some people getting into a canoe to come over, and Johnston ordered Maguire to suspend the bombardment. Sure enough, there were two half-castes in the canoe with a message from Chief Mponda. He agreed to the Commissioner's surrender terms and asked for a few hours grace.

The British men retired to their beds, but at dawn there was no sign of Mponda, nor any messenger. Johnston convened a council of war. He wanted to cross the river to the town, but Maguire feared a trap. Alan urged caution, arguing that the slavers were prone to be devious. Eventually they agreed to venture over in canoes, taking a platoon of Sikhs as guards.

They found Mponda's village deserted. All the men, women and children had fled, leaving empty huts, some of them charred ruins from the incendiary attack. Ali and Goodwill were sent with sepoys to reconnoitre the hills behind the town, where they found some fugitives and gave them a message that Chief Mponda should return and negotiate. Meanwhile, the village stockade was destroyed and the skulls buried.

Two days later Chief Mponda and his retinue returned and crossed the river to the fort. He brought the captives, who were ceremoniously released. Three days later, after protracted negotiations, a treaty was signed requiring Mponda to cease slave trading. Fort Johnston and the land around it became British property. The Commissioner had the right to control all caravans moving through the southern end of Lake Nyasa, and to examine them for any signs of slaving.

It seemed like total capitulation, but Alan was convinced that Mponda would return to his former ways. When he told the Commissioner of his misgivings Johnston shrugged and argued that he had at least bought some time.

—•—

Maguire and his column of Sikhs set off in pursuit of the slave traders who had fled Mponda's. He took Alan and Goodwill with him, and by questioning local people they were able to discover the route of the Kilwa slavers who were now heading east with over a hundred slaves. They were using the same route that Musa had taken when Goodwill and Kawa were captives four years before.

Goodwill remembered the track well, and they worked out a way to get ahead of the slave caravan and ambush them. By forced marches over three days they reached a low hill and camped behind it. The caravan could be seen winding towards them, the *ruga rugas* conspicuous with their red adornments, the crack of their whips carried faintly across the bush.

The slavers camped for the night about half a mile from the hill. Goodwill said to Alan, "I think the caravan may belong to Musa, the man who took me as a slave." He was obviously eager for some kind of revenge against his former captor.

Maguire attacked at dawn. He sent half a platoon around the the rear of the slave caravan and effectively trapped them. The well-trained Sikhs killed and wounded several *rugas*, and the slavers soon capitulated. One hundred and sixty-five slaves were released to find their own way home; most of them had been taken from the region around the southern end of Lake Nyasa, but others were from as far as the Luangwa Valley. To Goodwill's great disappointment Musa was not among the slavers.

Captain Maguire insisted on locking *gorees* onto the necks of the slavers, and they were marched back to Fort Johnston in disgrace.

—•—

Soon after the Maguire column returned to Fort Johnston the Commissioner received news that Chief Makanjira, whose large village was at the south-eastern end of the Lake, was threatening to attack Chief Mponda, unless he abrogated the anti-slaving treaty made with the British. Johnston decided that Makanjira had to be subjugated. He and Maguire agreed to attack from the Lake, and Goodwill was sent with a message to the Mandala depot at Cape Maclear, asking for the services of their steamer *Domira*.

Goodwill was delighted to see his friend Kawa, now working as a member of the ship's crew. They greeted each other in the traditional way.

"*Muribwanje?*" How are you?

"*Ndiribueno, zikomo; kaya enu?*" I am well, thank you; how about you?

"*Ndiribueno, zikomo.*" I am well, thank you.

Then they asked formally after the health of their respective families, while shaking hands, palm to palm, thumbs gripped, then palm to palm again.

Kawa told Goodwill amidst much laughter about his work on the steamer. When he first joined the crew he was a stoker, feeding logs into the furnace. He had since been promoted to serve on deck, and was evidently a favourite of the skipper, who was helping him to improve his English.

—•—

35

Alan was in Zomba one afternoon, after playing tennis on a rudimentary clay court with friends. He was chatting to Marge and Jock, who were also guests, when a messenger appeared with a note from Jess. Marge read it, then passed it to her husband. She said to Alan, "Alistair has a bad fever. Jess has asked me to look after the boys while she nurses him."

Alan rode beside the Kennedys, who had their donkey cart, to the McPhail's house. They were greeted by Jess, who looked worn out, as she described the severity of Alistair's fever; everyone had noticed that he'd seemed frail and exhausted. Marge then decided to stay with her, while Jock and Alan took the boys to *Namikango*. It was always an adventure for them to ride in the bumpy cart along the dusty road, with Jock singing Scottish songs to them.

The men had their rifles ready beside them. There was little risk from wild animals, but bands of African brigands were known to prey on travellers throughout the region. Some were splintered from Angoni *impis*, others were *ruga-rugas* from disintegrated slave caravans. Generally they would shun two British men, knowing they would have rifles and could shoot fast and accurately.

Jock gave the children supper and put them to bed, then the men had their own sparse meal before going out to the verandah for a smoke. Jock handed Alan a glass of whisky, and they talked about the campaigns for a while before Jock sighed.

271

"I'm not well, Alan" It was uncharacteristic for him to speak of himself. "I fear the old problem with my guts has come back."

"What does McPhail think?"

"I haven't troubled him yet. Jess says he's awful busy – she scarcely sees him." Jock paused to pour tots of whisky. "I must be honest with you. I wish she'd married you instead of the little doctor. He may be a Scot, and you half a Sassenach, but...Oh well, that's the way women are. Y'canna fathom them."

After a while Jock went on. "I want you to promise me something. When I die, I want you to look after Marge and Jess. You're a good man, and I trust you. I don't know what they'll do – whether they'll stay here, or go home – to Scotland. They won't discuss it with me. But they'll need help."

"I wish you wouldn't be so maudlin, Jock – but of course I'll look after them. Surely Jess would stay here – with Alistair – and Marge would stay with them?"

Jock shook his head. "I'm not so sure."

—•—

Alan slept in Jess's room because Jock was afraid he would not hear the boys if they woke up in the night. Hearing a commotion at dawn he came out of the bedroom rubbing his eyes. Jock was rewarding a messenger and handed Alan a note. He said, "I'll get you a mug of tea."

The note was from Marge: *Alistair died at 2 a.m. Must have been a really bad kind of malaria. He seemed to have little strength to fight it. Gave Jess a draught – she's sleeping. When she wakes we'll come back to the farm. Please bring the donkey cart for us. If Alan's still with you he can take care of the boys.*

Jock insisted on eating a breakfast of scrambled eggs and bacon before setting off for Zomba. However, he seemed not to want to talk, muttering occasionally, words like, "Poor bugger; first he loses his wife, then he goes and dies himself." And, "Those poor wee bairns, left without a father."

The four mile journey into Zomba would take him about an hour. The boys were waking up and Alan went to their room. Malcolm was four, and Andrew – his son – was two. They looked so different, one dark and the other as fair as could be. People often commented on it, though no one ever doubted their parentage. He helped them to get dressed; he was Uncle Alan to them. What would become of them? Would they belong to Jess? Would she take them back to Scotland? Nora's parents had died, as had Alistair's mother, but his father, a retired teacher, was still alive. It would make perfect sense for Jess to remain their mother.

Now he could marry Jess. He would not let her go to another man. Somehow he had to make that clear to her, without being crass in her time of bereavement.

He gave the boys breakfast before taking them for a walk. His mind was churning with thoughts about Jess. Although he knew it was hugely inappropriate, he could not stop thinking that she was now free to marry him. Even so, he could not assume that she would. Or it might take her years to get over her loss. There were plenty of precedents of widows who devoted themselves to their children while excluding another marriage.

They walked down to the river and the boys played with sticks they raced down the small current. Malcolm spotted a large water monitor, and Alan explained to them that it was a type of lizard, a giant version of the geckos on the farmhouse walls. He had brought a water bottle, but as it grew hotter they soon drank the contents, so decided to walk home. They were approaching the farmhouse when the boys spotted the donkey cart and ran ahead, shouting, "Mummy! Mummy!"

Jess looked drained, her skin pallid and her hair stringy with per-spiration. She hugged Alan as he helped her from the cart, and thanked him for looking after the boys. Then Marge hurried her into the house, with the boys tagging behind.

Alan smoked a pipe with Jock, who said, "It's a rum thing. She'll be better off with you." He looked at Alan sharply. "I'm assuming you'll marry her."

"I want to, of course." Alan couldn't help laughing at Jock's expression.

"I want to see it – if I can last that long. Don't tarry my boy."

Marge came out to the verandah. "Poor girl, she's worn out. Such a dreadful shock. He was right as rain yesterday morning. It's frightening how a man can be taken away, just like that. I've told the boys, but thank heavens they're too young to understand – they'll soon be over it."

—•—

36

Johnston and Maguire embarked on the *Domira* and set off for Chief Makanjira's village, taking with them a contingent of fifty Sikhs. They put one of the seven-pounder mountain guns aboard and secured it to the deck with blocks so that it pointed over the bow. They towed a barge that could be used to transport troops from ship to shore.

The shape of Lake Nyasa is like a left arm pointing south. The palm of the hand is at Cape Maclear, and the tip of the index finger is at the point where Lake water flows out into the Shire River – the only outflow from the Lake. Below the finger tip, like a ball suspended, is Lake Malombe. At the wrist of the arm, the narrowest point of the Lake, was Makanjira's village, on the east shore.

Chief Makanjira's village was a straggling collection of grass huts, with a scattering of better houses occupied by slavers and traders. It stretched for several miles along the Lake shore, with a population of about six thousand Africans. As they approached the *Domira* was fired on by the Chief's militia. They could see the tiny puffs of smoke, followed by the 'pop' of the musket discharges. Then there were two cannon booms in quick succession.

"What were they?" asked Johnston, more out of interest than alarm.

"They must have at least two field guns," answered Maguire, "to have fired in such quick succession. But where did the shots fall?" The surface of the Lake was broken by wavelets, and he guessed that they could easily have missed seeing the splashes.

Maguire trained his seven-pounder on the village and fired several incendiary shells that started fires at the eastern end. Meanwhile, Johnston clambered into the barge with thirty-four sepoys, and set off for the other end of the village.

Maguire landed at dusk with the remainder of the sepoys and made a rapid sortie in the direction of Chief Makanjira's guns, which he captured after a sharp skirmish. He also set fire to several *dhows* before returning to the steamer, where Johnston had also returned to pass the night. Next day Maguire returned the town and set it on fire.

When the expedition returned to Fort Johnston the Commissioner and Maguire were elated with their success. The British men sat round a fire that evening as they recounted the campaign. They discussed the concept of attack from the water, using the steamers. The ships were too small to carry more than about a dozen soldiers, but were strong enough to haul barges with additional men.

—•—

Johnston and Maguire returned to Zomba and continued planning their campaign to subjugate the remaining minor chiefs. They called Alan to some of their meetings at the Residency, where much whisky and many cigars were consumed. He admired more than ever the energy of the Commissioner and the quiet determination of his military commander.

A few days later they heard that Chief Makanjira was planning to make an attack on Fort Johnston. It was evident that its very existence aggravated him.

Maguire said, "I believe that Gulab Singh can easily hold off Makanjira. We may have fewer rifles, but we are much better shots.

We have an excellent defensive fort, and we have the three mountain guns and the Maxim. Even so, I must go back."

They were sitting on the verandah of the Residency, sipping tots of whisky. Alan said, "I can go with you, and I'm sure Goodwill would want to go."

—•—

In the end Maguire declined Alan's offer, but asked for the services of Goodwill, who was eager to go. When Alan spoke to him about the risks he replied in his quiet way, "They are bad men. We have to deal with them. If some of us are killed, so be it."

Maguire hurried back to Fort Johnston with the intention of trying to negotiate with Chief Makanjira. When he reached the fort he heard that a friendly minor chief named Kazembe had intercepted a slave caravan, and was anxious to hand it over to the British.

The messenger who brought the news squatted by the fire in the fort compound. He was drinking from a gourd of *pombe* provided by Goodwill. Now and then he would glance furtively around, as if overawed by the dimensions of the fort. Maguire stood nearby, impatiently waiting for Goodwill to pass on information.

"Tell us about the caravan," said Goodwill, coaxing the messenger, speaking ChiYao.

The man looked up at him, trying to assess his position in the hierarchy of fort occupants. "It belongs to Saidi."

"And who is he?"

"He is a Swahili, from Kilwa."

"How is it that your Chief Kazembe has detained him?"

The messenger sipped from the gourd, then looked up at Maguire. He was terrified of the *mzungu*, who seemed to be angry. "The slaver, Saidi, lost some of his *ruga-rugas*. Chief Kazembe knows that the British will reward him if he delivers this caravan – but you must hurry. Chief Makanjira is very angry. He will send his army to attack my chief."

277

"How do you know this?"

The messenger shrugged his thin shoulders and muttered. "It is known."

Maguire intervened and asked Goodwill to tell him what had transpired so far. When Goodwill had finished Maguire said, "Ask him how Makanjira will attack?"

After listening to Goodwill's question, the messenger answered. "Chief Makanjira has two large *dhows* on the Lake shore. He will use them to carry his army."

"Do you know where the *dhows* are?"

The messenger nodded. "Yes. That is why my chief sent me. So that I can guide you to the *dhows*."

"So, where are they?"

"In a cove, about a half day march from Chief Makanjira's village – to the north."

—•—

Maguire decided that he must act quickly, using the Lake to attack the *dhows*. He had no alternative to using the *Domira*, which was again borrowed from Mandala and brought to Fort Johnston. There Goodwill met Kawa again.

"Where are we going, my friend?" asked Kawa after the ritual greetings.

"To Makanjira's again. This time we plan to destroy his ships."

Kawa grinned. "He will be unhappy about that. Maybe there will be a big fight?"

"I think so." Goodwill frowned. "When I asked for this job for you, my friend, I did not think you would become involved in the fighting..."

Kawa laughed. "It is not your fault. It is nothing. In any case, the sailors are safer than you land men."

In truth, both Goodwill and Kawa wanted to join the fights, if only to avenge the capture of their relatives; Goodwill had heard nothing about his sister.

—•—

Maguire could not afford to take all his men; a strong force had to be left to defend the fort in case he was unable to intercept Makanjira. Eventually, he took the *Domira* and a barge, with thirty sepoys and six of Johnston's Swahili policemen. He took Dr Boyce, the Parsee doctor, to deal with expected casualties. He also took Goodwill, in case there were any negotiations requiring an interpretor.

Chief Kazembe's messenger took them to a point about ten miles north of the large Makanjira village they had burned down in October. It was dusk, and in fading light they could see a narrow channel snaking through rocks and sandbanks, leading to the cove where the *dhows* were hidden. It was too difficult for the *Domira* to negotiate this passage, particularly because a strong wind was blowing up waves.

Maguire held a discussion with the *Domira*'s skipper, Keiller, and his two engineers, MacEwan and Urquhart.

"What do you think, Keiller? Can we get your ship through the channel?"

"Aye, Captain, but at considerable risk. The wind's at a fair clip now, but it could get stronger, and it could change direction."

"So?" Maguire looked at him piercingly.

"My advice would be to anchor the *Domira* here and use the barge to take your men the rest of the way. It has a very shallow draft, and you can manhandle it – if you have to."

Maguire nodded. "Very well. That's what we'll do. I'll take all thirty sepoys and leave the Swahilis on board."

—•—

After waiting for darkness Maguire clambered into the barge with his men. They paddled up the channel for about a hundred yards, but soon after the wind became so strong that it forced the barge onto a sandbank. There was no alternative: they had to climb out and drag it up the channel towards the sheltering *dhows*.

Suddenly they were fired upon by Chief Makanjira's militia who were hiding in the scrub along the channel. Fortunately their fire was inaccurate, but the bullets from flintlocks and muskets were flying amongst the sepoys.

At last they reached the cove where the *dhows* were lying. They left the barge on a sandbank, crossed the beach, set fire to one of the dhows and disabled the other. Now Maguire could see, in the light from the burning *dhow*, that Makanjira's men were gathering in numbers and starting to advance. He ordered his sepoys back to the barge, only to find that it had been driven off the sandbank by the wind and had smashed on some rocks. He signalled to the *Domira* to launch the dinghy.

The fire from Makanjira's militia was intensifying and three sepoys were killed. At last the dinghy arrived, after being swamped several times by the waves. In a hail of bullets from the shore Maguire loaded some of his men into the boat and sent it back to the *Domira*, while he and the remainder of his men waded after them. They had almost reached the steamer when they came to deeper water and had to swim. The ship's engineer, MacEwan, tried to throw a rope to Maguire.

At that moment a bullet struck Maguire on the head and he was killed instantly. His body floated away despite attempts from the crew of the *Domira* to reach it. Meanwhile, the rising waves had torn the steamer from its moorings; it started to drift towards a sandbank. While Keiller was trying to steer into open water the rope that had been thrown to Maguire became entangled in the ship's single propeller and the steam engine stalled.

The *Domira* drifted helplessly around in shallow water, unable to draw away from the merciless fire from the nearby shore. The Sikh sepoys built barricades around the deck using whatever materials they could find, including bundles of trade cloth from the hold.

Goodwill squatted beside Kawa, who was in the wheelhouse; he had been given the helm in case the screw freed. Keiller was supervising the barricading and firing.

"We are in big trouble, my friend," said Goodwill, ducking his head instinctively as a bullet thudded into the woodwork.

"I have been thinking," said Kawa; "I could dive under the ship and cut the rope off the propeller."

"Could you do that?"

"Perhaps. Tell Captain Keiller – you are better at speaking to him."

Goodwill crawled out of the wheelhouse to where Keiller was firing a rifle from behind a low wall of cloth bales. He told the skipper what Kawa proposed.

Keiller stroked his chin while gazing out towards the bank. "Tell Kawa I thank him, but it's too risky now. We seem to be drifting further from those evil bastards. Perhaps he can try it in the morning."

—•—

37

Lake Nyasa – October 1891

As the next day dawned the *Domira* still drifted under sporadic fire. The skipper, Keiller, was wounded in the head. Several of the sepoys were also wounded. They were treated by Dr Boyce on deck, in whatever shelter could be found. They could now see the bodies of Maguire and three sepoys washed up on a sandbank.

Goodwill said to Keiller. "I could swim to the Captain's body and tie a rope to it, and we could haul it in."

Keiller was adamant. "No. I need you as an interpretor. Besides, what would we do with his body? You're a Christian, Goodwill. You know that the body is a mere shell when the soul has departed." He was also adamant that Kawa should wait until they were in shallower water before trying to free the rope from the screw.

On the third day the two Scottish engineers, MacEwan and Urquhart, were both wounded, the first in the thigh, the second in the face. They joined Keiller in the makeshift ward on the after deck, where Dr Boyce laboured in intense heat. Kawa at last had his own way; he and one of the other seamen made repeated attempts to free the *Domira*'s propeller. Goodwill alternated between assisting Dr Boyce and holding a rope for Kawa and his colleague as they dove under the ship.

By the fourth day the wind had abated. The attackers on shore waved a white flag and shouted an offer that they would stop firing if they were given sixty lengths of calico.

A small group of the militia came by canoe to discuss the terms. Goodwill interpreted for MacEwan, who could not conceal his disgust at the visitors. They were a rag-tag group, furtive and wide-eyed, chattering to each other in ChiYao about the strange ship, and the fact that there was only one *mzungu* on deck; Keiller and Urquhart stayed below, so as not to show that they had been wounded.

Makanjira's men offered to help haul the *Domira* into clear water. A condition was that two of the *azungu* should come ashore to negotiate the cease fire agreement. While the negotiators waited in their canoe, Keiller called a meeting of the three Europeans and Dr Boyce.

"You are in charge of the ship, Mr Keiller," said Dr Boyce, "but I am now the senior member of the military force. I volunteer, because I want to get Captain Maguire's body before the crocodiles tear it to pieces."

Keiller laughed, though he grimaced with the pain from his wound. "You of all people, Boyce. You leave your dead to the vultures. I hope they will accept you as a European."

Boyce laughed. "I doubt if they know the difference."

MacEwan insisted that he should be the other negotiator, arguing that Keiller and Urquhart were too badly injured. The two volunteers decided to take with them three of the Swahili policemen and three of the steamer's crew, including Kawa, as interpretor. They also took Maguire's Muslim orderly.

As soon as he heard about the composition of the negotiating team, Goodwill went to Keiller. "Sir, I would like to go as interpretor. I have a better command of English than my friend Kawa."

Keiller insisted that he remain on the ship, so Goodwill added: "Sir, please do not trust these Makanjira people. They may be setting a trap. You should keep some of them on this ship as hostages."

Keiller was not convinced; he ordered the *Domira*'s negotiators to set off. They were taken in the canoe by Makanjira's men, and walked to a pole and mud house, about two miles away; they understood it was to be the site for the negotiations. They were given water to drink, and the militia men said they would go to Chief Makanjira to tell him that the deputation was ready to negotiate. Meanwhile, Maguire's orderly was taken aside on the pretext of showing him his master's body.

"How long will it take?" MacEwan asked of Kawa.

"I don't know, *bwana*. They said it would take twenty minutes to find the Chief. Who knows if he will come at once."

—•—

Kawa sat with his back to the flimsy grass wall of the house. He felt deeply uneasy. He was suspicious of any Yao chief, and Makanjira had a dreadful reputation. He was nervously wondering if he should get out of the house when the front door burst open and bullets flew across the room. He saw MacEwan fall to the ground, obviously hit. Kawa turned with the swiftness of a wild animal, kicked a gap in the grass wall, and started burrowing backwards, using all his strength to squirm out. He thought to himself that he was just like a warthog, retreating backwards to safety.

He looked up for a moment and saw Dr Boyce being stabbed with spears; the two other steamer boys had already been felled. It seemed to him that the Swahili policemen had been pushed aside. Then the murderers came rushing towards him. He was stabbed several times and felt sharp jolts of pain and cried out even as he wriggled backwards.

Suddenly he was free. He scuttled away to hide behind a nearby hut, blood streaming down his chest from wounds in his neck and upper torso. His shirt had been ripped off in the struggle to escape, and he decided to take off his sailor's breeches, thinking they would make him conspicuous. Villagers ran in all directions, excited by the sound of gunfire and the shouts of the assassins. They paid no attention to Kawa, who was covered in dust; the blood on his body looked like sweat.

He took stock of his situation. The *Domira* was two miles away. In daylight he might be recognised as an escaper; he must wait until dark. For two hours he huddled behind the hut, his thirst raging. He used shreds of his shirt to stem the flow of blood from the worst of his stab wounds. He felt weak from loss of blood.

As soon as dusk came he walked slowly out of the village. He had to sidle into the bush to avoid a scattering of Makanjira's militia coming back from the banks of the Lake; they were whooping and shouting, and he suspected they were drunk on *pombe*.

It took him nearly three hours to reach the point where he could see the *Domira* in the moonlight. She was about a hundred yards away, and he felt a wave of relief that she was still there. But how was he to get to her? He doubted if he could swim because of his severe wounds, and he felt so weak he feared he would faint. He burrowed through the *Phragmites* reeds on the bank until he came to open water, fearful that at any moment a crocodile might take him. The water was waist deep, the bottom sandy. He sank down till only his head was above the surface.

There were no lights on the *Domira*, but he could see the faint glow of her furnace. He knew that the sailors would keep it alight because they might float free at any time. Most of the firing had stopped, though occasional volleys came from the far bank. He could see someone swimming near the ship and guessed that the ship's crew were still trying to dig her off the sandbank. He wanted to shout to them, but he was afraid that there might be militia nearby.

He waded slowly towards the ship, partly floating, afraid he might faint and drown. When he was thirty yards away he cupped his hands and called softly for Goodwill. He guessed that his friend would be on deck and probably helping with whatever activities were going on. At first there was no answer and he waded closer, still fearful of crocodiles.

He called again, and this time he heard: "Who is that?"

"Kawa."

"Kawa? Where are you?" He recognised Goodwill's voice; the figure at the side of the *Domira* was barely distinguishable.

He waved. "Here – I'm wounded. I can't swim."

"I'll help you."

Goodwill dove into the water. He was soon beside Kawa and heard about his wounds. They waded together to the side of the ship. Then Goodwill lifted his friend up to two of the steamer boys who pulled him up to the deck, while he groaned in agony. They threw down the rope ladder for Goodwill to climb up.

The Lake water had washed the dirt off Kawa's spear wounds. They were gaping, and still bleeding slightly. The injured man sat on the deck, overcome with exhaustion and emotion, but grinning widely.

Keiller and Urquhart came up to the group. "My God, it's Kawa!" said Urquhart. "We'd better get some carbolic into those wounds. If only Boyce were here to stitch him up. Where are they, Kawa?"

"The doctor is dead," said Kawa.

The two Scots were stunned. While Goodwill poured carbolic into Kawa's wounds, bandaging them as best he could, Kawa told them the story of the murders. He spoke in ChiNyanja, and Goodwill relayed the news in English. The white men were horrified; Urquhart was distraught when he heard what had happened to his friend MacEwan.

—•—

It was Urquhart who galvanised them into action in the morning. At first light he had a team of sepoys in the water, scooping sand away from the ship's screw and the rear part of the hull. The remainder of the small force shot at the banks, returning the sniping fire from Makanjira's men. The density of the incoming fire was only about a couple of bullets each minute, but they could not afford to be careless. The team in the water were relatively safe, since only their heads were exposed, and then only when they came up to breathe. Two sailors were given the sole task of watching for crocodiles.

Every hour Urquhart changed the teams. In the third hour they were able to free the rope from the screw. By the end of the day they had cleared enough sand to try turning the screw. When night came they stopped the work, because they could no longer see any crocodiles that might come near. However, guards were posted to watch out for any assailants.

On the following morning Urquhart built up a head of steam and tried to pull the *Domira* back off the sandbank. Goodwill was in the water near the screw and reported that is was sucking sand back, but had not filled the cavity where the screw was operating. He thought that the washed out sand was mostly coming from below the hull. Sure enough, within half an hour the ship floated free. Goodwill and the others scrambled aboard and they all cheered as Keiller pulled the *Domira* back into the channel, away from the bank.

No sooner was the ship free than the Makanjira militia started firing again as fast as they could re-load. But the distance was growing and it was only the occasional spent bullet that hit the ship. The firing diminished as the slavers realised that the *Domira* was moving out of range, and stopped when they rounded a headland.

As they steamed past the headland they saw a lone male figure waving frantically. At first they thought nothing of him, since waving spectators were a common sight. Then one of the sepoys recognised him as Maguire's orderly. Keiller turned towards the headland and when he was about ten yards from the shore the orderly leaped into the water and swam towards them. They hauled him on board and headed rapidly back to open water.

Goodwill could tell immediately that something was seriously the matter with the orderly. He started a rambling story about how Makanjira's men had taken him away from the others, so that he could retrieve Captain Maguire's body, but instead they had thrown him into a hut. They had given him food and water and asked him questions about how many soldiers there were on the boat. Then they had freed him and told him that he could leave the village or stay with them. He was increasingly incoherent as he told his story and Goodwill realised that he must have had some kind of emotional breakdown. He was taken away by his fellow sepoys.

As soon as they were in open water the Sikh subadar approached Keiller and Urquhart. Anxious for revenge he asked permission to shell the slaver village where the negotiators had been murdered. Keiller turned the *Domira* and steadied her into the light breeze. The sepoy gunners loaded an incendiary shell and trained the seven-pounder on the village, about two hundred yards away. They fired three shells; all of them hit the village and started fires.

"We will return," shouted Keiller, waving a clenched fist.

—•—

"They must have spared Maguire's orderly and my Swahilis because they are Muslims," said Johnston. He had invited Keiller, Urquhart and Alan to lunch at the Residency.

"Little doubt, sir," said Keiller.

"Well, it's a terrible business," said Johnston, shaking his head. "I fear it will give them confidence to make further attacks." He turned to Keiller and Urquhart. "You did well. I will mention your good services in my despatch to the Foreign Office, and I will send you my official commendation."

He looked at Alan. "We have lost our trusted military commander. I ask you, Alan, to take his position until I can get a replacement. I have already spoken to Subadar Gulab Singh, and he is very happy to have you in command. Will you do it?"

What could he say? He nodded, but knew that Johnston sensed his reluctance. He stayed on after Keiller and Urquhart left, and walked with Johnston round the garden, which had become a splendid calm oasis.

"When do you think we should attack Chief Makanjira?" he asked.

"Not now." Johnston was adamant. "Frankly, Alan, we don't have enough men. I regret to say that I think we should restrict ourselves to campaigns against the lesser rogues." He gave Alan a cigar and lit his own. "I would not admit this in public, but we must accept that the Makanjira episode was a debacle – two Europeans and Boyce killed, three sepoys and three steamer boys killed, and a dozen other men wounded. Most important – we have lost our brave commander."

—•—

38

Southern Nyasaland – December 1891-August 1892

Alan rode with Harry Johnston from Zomba to Blantyre on Christmas Day 1891 to confer with the senior Europeans about what action should be taken. The sad news of Maguire's death and the retreat of the *Domira* was foremost in everyone's minds. They sat on the verandah of the club, drinking beer and whisky and smoking pipes and cigars.

"The issue," said Johnston, "is whether we have sufficient resources to carry the fight to Chief Makanjira. We have lost our military leader, as well as several of the Sikh soldiers. The survivors are no doubt dispirited. I have appointed Spaight as temporary commander, because he has held a military commission, and has served in a Sikh regiment."

"Surely we should at least make sure we hold Fort Johnston," said Buchanan. "I've heard that Chief Zarafi may attack it."

Johnston nodded. "I propose to go up there to reconnoitre and strengthen the forces in the fort. Alan will come with me. I would be grateful for volunteers."

———•———

They set off for the Upper Shire, taking a couple of other British men, and soon discovered that a minor chief, just south of Mponda's, had sided with the renegade Chief Zarafi, and was rumoured to be planning an attack on Fort Johnston. However, news filtered back from the fort to say that only a few random shots had been fired.

Meanwhile, the British party was joined by John King, who had journeyed up from Port Herald, in the far south of the country. Using Goodwill to collect information they established that, to everyone's surprise, Chief Mponda remained loyal to the British.

The small column plodded north along the river bank, apprehensive that they might be attacked at any moment. They felt an immediate sense of confidence on entering the fort. They were greeted by the remaining Sikh soldiers who listened patiently as Johnston addressed them and tried to raise their spirits.

That evening the Commissioner held a meeting at which it was decided that Alan Spaight would lead a sortie of the fittest Sikhs to apprehend the recalcitrant minor chief. He took his sepoys out of the fort on the following day. Using Goodwill to question local Africans he was able to locate the village ten miles from the fort. Alan sent some of the soldiers to block the escape route and the Sikhs attacked the village. After only a scattering of return gunfire the chief surrendered with two of his headmen. They were bound with ropes and marched back to Fort Johnston.

The Commissioner interrogated the minor chief using Goodwill as an interpretor, while Alan stood by. It became apparent that Chief Zarafi was heavily involved in the insurrection, but he had retreated to his stronghold in the hills.

Next morning it was discovered that the minor chief had died in his prison cell. Johnston conducted an ad hoc enquiry, concluding that the man had poisoned himself. However, it was clear that he had been assisted by the two headmen, who said that the chief had been certain he would be hanged.

"The irony," said the Commissioner, "is that he would not have been executed. The worst that would have happened would have been exile to Mozambique."

—•—

A column led by two British volunteers returned three days later and announced that they had cleared out any remaining Zarafi supporters. Furthermore, they had located the probable stronghold where Chief Zarafi had fled; they proposed an attack. Meanwhile, several hundred Angoni warriors appeared and offered to fight for the British. They were interrogated by Harry Johnston, using Goodwill, who was still fluent in ChiNgoni.

"They are not real warriors," said Goodwill scornfully. "They have come to loot the conquered villages, like a flock of vultures. My father would not have done that."

"We should use whatever help we can get," said Johnston. He told the Angoni chief, Chifisi, that his men would be rewarded if they helped to overcome Zarafi's forces.

—•—

Not long afterwards an emissary came from Chief Zarafi to say that he would desist from any attacks on Fort Johnston. The Commissioner was relieved to hear this news, despite reservations about its sincerity. He and Alan returned to Zomba.

On February 24, 1892, Johnston sent a message to Alan asking him to hurry to the Residency, where Commander Keane of the Royal Navy was also staying. The naval officer commanded three small gunboats that had been brought up to Lake Nyasa.

"Look at this," said Johnston, passing a letter to Alan.

It said that several hundred Angoni warriors had come back to the fort, eager to fight Chief Zarafi, whose supporters had been giving trouble in the area for several weeks. John King, the volunteer who was in temporary command at Fort Johnston, had therefore decided to attack Zarafi. He was supported by another volunteer, Dr Watson and Petty Officer Henry Inge, from one of the naval gunboats, who knew how to operate the seven-pounder mountain gun, which they took with them.

I regret to inform you, Dr Watson's letter stated, *that we were re-pulsed. King was shot through the lungs, and is in a bad way. Six Sikh soldiers were killed, and three of your Swahilis. Fourteen of the Indian soldiers are missing. Inge used the mountain gun until he ran out of ammunition, but we had to abandon the gun. We are now in the fort, tending the wounded (myself included).*

"The news could hardly be worse," said Johnston. "I fear that this set back, coming on top of the debacle in October when Maguire was killed, will give the slavers new confidence." He turned to Alan. "I hate to ask this of you. Would you go with Commander Keane up to the fort. He will have overall command, but you can help him, and those Sikhs worship you."

—•—

Commander Keane and Alan met the wounded British men at Matope, where they had been brought down the Upper Shire by the *Domira*. They were on their way to the hospital in Blantyre. King had been shot through both lungs but he was in good spirits. He was being looked after by Dr Watson, whose flesh wound was not serious.

On arrival at Fort Johnston Keane brought in one of his gunboats and positioned it on the river, to support the defence, leaving the other two on Lake Nyasa. Alan was deeply relieved to find that all except one of the fourteen Sikh soldiers who had gone missing in the battle had returned to the fort – the fourteenth man arrived a week later, emaciated but in good spirits.

—•—

Alan remained at the fort until mid-June, when, on a brisk winter morning he was called by a sentry who said that a *sahib* was approach-ing. It was Captain Charles Edward Johnson of the 36th Sikhs, who brought with him fifty sepoys. He had been a fellow officer six years before, in India, and they greeted each other heartily.

"I was delighted when the Commissioner told me you were coming," Alan said.

"Well, I never expected to take over from you, of all people," said Johnson. "I hear you've done a great job with our men."

"Oh, I've enjoyed working with them. They're fine fellows."

Alan briefed the new officer before leaving to return to Zomba. He told Johnson about the disposition of the chiefs and their affiliations, with particular emphasis on Chief Zarafi. Also, he explained how the Yao chiefs all around the Shire Highlands were indulging in 'highway' robberies and could not be allowed to continue. Johnson would have to balance his command between the fort and these other areas.

—•—

Goodwill, who had stayed behind at *Khundalila*, was now very much an assistant manager, helping Alan with all matters to do with farm labour. They had many discussions about starting a farm school to take African children from the age of four, until they were old enough to go to the mission school at about ten. It went without debate that Goodwill would be the teacher, and he became much involved in the design and construction of the building.

The news that Alan was introducing a farm school soon reached the other settlers with varied reactions. Some, like the Kennedys, thought it was a sensible idea and would help the owner to retain his labour. Others were antagonistic – they felt that teaching should be left to the missionaries.

One day Goodwill told Alan that he was going to marry a girl in his former village. When Alan congratulated him, he said, "I would like to invite you to the wedding, but... You see, if you come, your presence will overcome the normal proceedings."

Alan laughed. "You mean that all the guests will be looking at me instead of the the bride and groom."

Goodwill smiled. "Exactly. It is a pity, because I would like you to be there."

"It doesn't matter. I would like to help you, Goodwill. What is the bride-price you have to pay?"

Goodwill whistled. "Oh, sir, it is a lot. The father wants three cows. He will accept goats, but I must give him at least one cow. You see, he knows that I work for a *mzungu*. He thinks I'm a rich man!"

"Let me help you to find the bride price."

Alan decided that he would purchase and collect the animals. He knew that Goodwill would have many other expenses. Although Alan had built a house for his assistant, using sun-dried bricks, Goodwill had to buy some basic furnishings.

—•—

About four months after Alistair McPhail died Alan chose a moment when Jess was in a cheerful mood to say, "I hope you won't re-marry without considering me."

As he spoke he realised it was a crass thing to say, but she was not upset. She laughed, and replied, "I promise, Alan – no surprises like last time."

A couple of weeks later he invited her to go to Lake Chilwa to see the bird flights at dawn. They rode to a camp near the Likengala River's outlet into the lake. They took six trusted men, including Goodwill, to help make the camp, and to guard them and the horses.

Jess's eyes were shining with excitement; she was like a little girl before Christmas. They had two tents, one for each of them, in a clearing; the Africans slept in rough grass shelters nearby. They built a huge fire in the centre of the clearing, that provided plenty of light and would scare away wild animals. They also lit three smaller fires on the outer perimeter of the clearing.

Jess had brought a chicken and sausages, and a loaf of bread, but she ate hardly anything herself. Alan guessed she was rather nervous being alone with him. As they sat by the fire they listened to the night sounds and when they could not identify a call they would consult Goodwill. In the far distance a lion grunted, and it send shivers through Jess. The horses snorted, and she wanted to hold Alan's hand for reassurance. The strange cries of hyenas echoed hauntingly across the plain; they knew that hungry hyenas could penetrate a camp in their desperate search for food. A jackal called, hideously cackling.

Before they retired Jess had to relieve herself in the bushes, and Alan stood guard. She had lived in Africa for six years, but she was still nervous of snakes and 'creepy-crawlies', as she called them. The mosquitoes were busy and searched for any skin left exposed. They had citronella oil smeared over their faces and hands, and marvelled that the Africans could cope with scarcely any clothing.

Alan slept soundly until five o'clock, when Goodwill woke him. He let Jess sleep a few minutes longer before waking her. They walked the last mile along a dirt track to the lake shore, where there was a pungent smell of rotting vegetation. Beyond the lake the sky was lightening. The strange high island loomed, and Alan told Jess it was reputedly the home of huge pythons.

When they reached the lake there was a small fishing village at the shore; half a dozen small huts, and a dying fire. At the water's edge were three dugout canoes and Goodwill arranged to hire one of them for a couple of hours. It was large enough to carry Alan and Jess, as well as two paddlers. They clambered in and the paddlers pushed off.

The lake surface was mirror-calm, scattered with patches of tall reeds. In the clearings were flocks of ducks and teal; they were waking up to the dawn light. The chorus of quacks, whistles and clucks grew in volume, and then they started to fly, swooping and circling, searching for feeding areas, then splashing down in their dozens and hundreds. There were whistling ducks, knob-nosed ducks, teals, Egyptian geese and spurwing geese. Sometimes the flights were so dense that the sky darkened.

After an hour the sounds and the movements diminished as it seemed that the birds had settled at their feeding places. Alan instructed the paddlers to take them back to the village. The sun was warm on their backs, and Jess broke her silence to enthuse about her experience.

During the fifteen mile ride back to the farms Alan realised with certainty that Jess was someone he would like to spend his life with. She was so happy and animated, and he sensed that she enjoyed his company. He recognised that she would always be a good friend as well as a wife. Nora had never been a friend; their meetings had been furtive and hurried, spasms of passion with no underpinning of comradeship.

In the weeks that followed their friendship deepened and a physical relationship started. Jess seemed inhibited at first, perhaps because of her suspicions about his affair. He knew she was reluctant to speak about it, he supposed because she did not want to hear about Nora. As the days passed she seemed to overcome her reservations, and became more passionate.

—•—

Alan proposed to Jess a year after Alistair McPhail died. They had skirted around the topic before, treading cautiously, probing each others feelings.

She was enthusiastic in response, but added, "I suppose we're both damaged goods, in a manner of speaking."

"I won't think of you that way, and I wish you wouldn't blame me too much for Nora."

She nodded. "It's not easy, when little Andrew is always there to remind me."

It was the first time she had mentioned it, and when she saw Alan's surprise, she went on, "I knew all along, my sweet. We women know about these things. Remember, I was with Alistair and Nora most days, and I knew when Alistair was away. I knew you were the father, and it was confirmed when Andrew was born – he looks even more like you now."

"Did Alistair suspect anything?"

"He never mentioned it." She took his hand and looked at him with an uncharacteristic serious expression. "Are you sure you want to take on two sons?"

"Certain. One I've known since he was a baby, the second is mine anyway."

She hugged him. "I'm glad. If I'd been in any doubt I would not have agreed to marry you."

—•—

They were married in August 1892, at the mission church at Domasi. It was five years since they arrived in the territory. Alan was thirty-one, and Jess was in the best of health, her hair lustrous and her eyes clear and sparkling.

Marge thought it would not be appropriate for Jess to wear white, but the bride opted for a plain white dress with tartan trimmings. It occurred to Alan that it was the same ceremony as two years before, with the difference that he was the groom. Also, Malcolm and Andrew were old enough to be page boys, and revelled in the process.

It was a large wedding, by Nyasaland standards; they said it had more guests than any wedding yet celebrated in the country, though there were only about a hundred people present. The Kennedys and Alan knew most of the farming community and the missionaries, and both sides knew many of the Mandala staff. The only other Europeans in the country were too far away to come. Goodwill was present as a supervisor of the African servants.

Jess was given away by her father. Alan's best man was Alfred Sharpe, At the reception at *Namikango* the languid solicitor toasted the bride and groom. Then he turned to Alan and said. "I have known Alan

Spaight for five years. We have been through some difficult times together. For me, he is the sort of man who makes a country, by serving unstintingly. He has always been ready to take up the cause of fighting the slavers and the villain chiefs. Of course, he has not been alone – John Buchanan, John and Fred Moir, Monteith Fotheringham – to name some, have been his companions in arms. It gives me great pleasure, as I'm sure it does for you, to see Alan marry this fine young woman."

Alan's speech was short, thanking Jock and Marge. Then Commissioner Johnston spoke. To no one's surprise he spoke eloquently, praising Jess for her stalwart nursing, and described her as the epitome of the pioneer young woman, who raises a family while serving the community.

There was enthusiastic applause before Johnston went on. "The fight is not yet over. We still have some slavers to bring to book. Though I hate to do it, I must ask men like Alan to continue to serve. I feel confident that within a year or two we will prevail. Then you should be able to live in this fine country in peace."

—•—

39

Upper Shire River - February 1893

In February 1893 Alan was on one of his regular visits to the Residency to see Commissioner Harry Johnston, when John Buchanan rode up. They sat on the verandah smoking cigars, while a servant served coffee.

"This is good stuff, John," said the Consul, waving his cup. "as I've told you before. I have no doubt that it will sell well in the overseas markets."

Buchanan nodded. "Yes, it is good quality." He frowned. "The reason I came to see you is that some of my labourers have been stolen by Chief Liwonde – seems he's in cahoots with an Arab trader named Abu Bakr..."

"Abu Bakr? I don't think I've heard of him."

"He's a true Arab – from Muscat," said Buchanan. "He and Liwonde have started slaving, and they took my boys. What are we going to do about it?"

"Hm." The Commissioner pondered. "I could send Captain Johnson. Most of his Sikhs are at Fort Johnston, but he has some Makua *askaris* that he could take with him."

"We must be careful that there are no more upsets, Commissioner. If those bastards think they've got the upper hand they'll start their nonsense all over again. Your treaties won't mean a damn to them."

"I agree, John, but you know as well as I do that we have limited resources. Also, they have the advantage of 'playing at home'. They know their ground and they can count on support from the local villagers."

—•—

Captain Johnson led a sortie that attacked Abu Bakr's caravan and rescued Buchanan's labourers. He also released a number of captives, but the traders escaped. A couple of days later the Commissioner was riding with Alan at the farm when a messenger came running up. He handed a letter to Johnston, who groaned in disgust.

"We have a problem on the river. Our men have been attacked by Chief Liwonde's people. It seems that all the locals have come out in support of him. We have to get up there – fast. Can you come with us, Alan?"

They arranged to meet at the Residency for breakfast – Alfred Sharpe, Gilbert Stevenson and Alan were there, all volunteers. Alan had to explain patiently to Jess that he felt obliged to join the column, but would leave Goodwill to help her manage the farm.

"I can't stay on the farm," he said, "and leave the fighting to the others. We all have to do our share."

"You've done more than your share!"

"It's not something you can measure, or apportion. You know that, sweetheart."

The column set off on the road to Domasi with their personal servants and a handful of Sikhs who were stationed in Zomba. News filtered back that a Mandala boat had been attacked and one of its crew murdered by Chief Liwonde's men. Furthermore, the *Domira*, coming to the rescue, had stuck on a sandbank opposite Liwonde's village and was under fire. Alan was beginning to think the steamer was ill-fated.

The little column hurried along the track beside the Shire River and soon heard the dull reports of flintlocks, presumably firing at the

Domira. As they came closer it was evident that several hundred of Chief Liwonde's men had gathered.

The Commissioner, on Alan's advice, decided to build a makeshift *boma* on the river bank, as close as they could get to the *Domira*. Inevitably it was a crude affair, made by felling nearby trees and hurriedly pulling them into a rough circle. At least it provided some protection from the bullets coming from higher ground.

Gilbert Stevenson, who was a strong swimmer, volunteered to swim to the *Domira*, to organise the efforts to get her off the sandbank. He had just reached the ship when he was severely wounded by a bullet that passed through his abdomen.

Meanwhile, communications with Zomba and Blantyre were cut off by Liwonde's men, who had circled behind the stockade. The British column was in a serious predicament, surrounded by hundreds of yelling spear-waving Africans, and running out of ammunition.

At dawn on the next day Alfred Sharpe suggested to Alan that they take some Atonga *askaris* out of the *boma* to a vantage point near the riverside track. "We'll be close enough to snipe at their leaders."

"I'll bring my .357 magnum," Alan replied, but he was dismayed at the prospect of again having to use his hunting rifle against human targets.

The two British men crawled out of the enclosure and slowly through the grass, followed by six *askaris*. They headed for a large acacia tree that had fallen not long ago. It provided good shelter for them, and their rear was covered by the men in the *boma*. Alan arranged the *askaris* in a line along the trunk of the fallen tree. He could see some of Liwonde's men who were encouraging the attack. They were within a couple of hundred yards and therefore not difficult to hit. He suspected that the *askaris*' fire was not very accurate, but it was good experience for them.

"Good shooting, Alan," called Sharpe. "They're pulling back."

"I wish I had more ammunition. It always seems a problem."

"Better to be conservative, rather than blaze away."

They went back to the *boma*, but kept up a regular accurate fire, preserving their ammunition. However, they were effectively in a stalemate.

On the third day Alan was relieved to see a party of men coming down river from the Lake. It was led by a German, Mr von Eltz, who had a German NCO and about twenty Sudanese *askaris* with him. They had a Hotchkiss gun which they used to good effect to disperse Liwonde's militia. This allowed Alan and his companions to dig the *Domira* off the sandbank. One of their helpers was Kawa, now something of a celebrity after his exploits just over a year ago.

They sent the steamer to Matope with the wounded Stevenson, and she returned with reinforcements. On the following day the force was augmented by Lt Commander Carr, commander of the gunboat *Mosquito*, who had a doctor with him, as well as a dozen sailors. The Commissioner now felt that his force has sufficient strength to attack Liwonde's village. They advanced on both sides of the river arresting anyone who had participated in the fighting. Chief Liwonde managed to escape, but was eventually captured and exiled to the Port Herald area, in the far south of the country. Two forts were later built on the Shire River near Liwonde's, one of them named Fort Sharpe.

——•——

Harry Johnston went to South Africa in April 1893, after appointing Alfred Sharpe as Acting Consul. John Buchanan had formerly been given this position, but Johnston argued that Sharpe had no estates to manage, and besides had a legal training. Lieutenant Edwards arrived from India with a hundred Jat Sikh soldiers, and later that year another hundred arrived under the command of Lieutenant W. H. Manning. This force was augmented with *askaris* from the Makua and Tonga tribes.

Meanwhile, Chief Makanjira had encouraged a Yao headman named Chiwaura to rebel against old Chief Jumbe in the Kota Kota area, half way up the Lake, who had stuck by the anti-slavery treaty. Chiwaura had built a stockade about five miles inland from Kota Kota. On his return to Nyasaland, Johnston arranged for the *Domira* and the *Ilala* to transport the new Sikh troops to the area to support Jumbe. They were accompanied by the naval gunboats.

Surrender terms were sent to Chiwaura, who rejected them and retreated into his stockade. The British force then started to shell his village with a seven-pounder mountain gun and soon set it aflame. Chiwaura's people retreated into a sort of citadel within the stockade, made of mud and poles, then asked for a truce by waving a white flag. However, when a party of Sikh soldiers went forward to parley they were fired on and made a hasty retreat.

Meanwhile Chief Jumbe had brought up several thousand of his own men. They were commanded by a man dressed in a scarlet cloak, hung about with charms and rattles. To the amusement of the British officers, Jumbe's men made advances towards the citadel, but each time hastily retreated as soon as shots were fired. By late afternoon it was evident that a stalemate had been reached.

"We ought to attack," said Captain Johnson to the Commissioner, "while there's still enough light."

"Yes, go ahead," replied Johnston. "We don't want them to think we're afraid."

Captain Johnson led the charge, in front of about seventy of his Sikhs and thirty Makua *askaris*. They ran through the burnt huts of the outer village towards the citadel wall. One of the Sikhs scrambled up to the top and started to pull his compatriots up. A moment later he was shot and toppled over.

In a few minutes the British forces were swarming over the walls. Captain Johnson ordered his men to cease fire, but this allowed most of Chiwaura's militia to escape. The Chief himself scrambled over the wall and fell into the marsh behind the citadel, where his corpse was found later.

Hundreds of women were found in the citadel, many of them wearing slave *gorees*. They were all released and sent to Kota Kota. Several of them, who were heavily pregnant, were said to have given birth during their terrified flight and abandoned their babies, who were collected by the Sikh soldiers and returned to their mothers.

After spending two days destroying the walls of the citadel the British force set off to the south end of the Lake. At Leopard Bay they encountered Kuluunda, a woman chief, related to Chief Makanjira. She and her militia, together with some of Makanjira's men, made a stand at a hill overlooking the bay. They were joined by a caravan with several hundred captives, commanded by four Arab slavers. There followed a siege that lasted for three days before Kuluunda and the Arabs surrendered.

Commissioner Johnston, Captain Johnson, Lieutenant Edwards, and Alfred Sharpe left the siege and went by ship to Makanjira's main town on the south-east shore of the Lake, stopping at Monkey Bay on the way. When they reached Makanjira's village the gunboats started shelling it, starting several fires. Meanwhile, the main force landed on a promontory near the town, taking a seven-pounder gun, which Sharpe used to shell the village.

Chief Makanjira's followers fled after about five hours. The British force destroyed the larger houses, thought to have belonged to the chief and the slave traders, including the house where Boyce, McEwan and their party were murdered a year and a half before.

The Commissioner decided that a fort should be built to prevent the return of Makanjira. He instructed Lieutenant Edwards to build what was named Fort Maguire, and to remain there with a force of Sikhs. This fort was attacked by Makanjira in early 1894, but he was heavily defeated.

—•—

40

Southern Nyasaland - 1893-1895

In early December of 1893 Jess gave birth to her first child; they named her Amanda. She had pale blonde hair and blue-grey eyes, like her father and her brother Andrew. She became the delight of her parents, and her grandparents, Jock and Marge. She spent much of her time with them, while her brothers were increasingly at their lessons or on escapades around the two farms.

Now that the southern end of Lake Nyasa was secure, Commissioner Johnston was able to turn his attention in 1895 to Chief Zarafi, who had been a constant source of trouble. He was now the dominant chief in the area to the east of the Upper Shire River and had continued to collect slaves and take them to the East Coast. He was known to have a stronghold in Mangoche Mountain, whence he had retreated in the earlier campaign.

Johnston called a meeting in Zomba of Major Edwards, Major Bradshaw, Captain Cavendish and Alan Spaight.

"Gentlemen," he started. "I'm determined to root out Zarafi. We cannot claim to have defeated the slavers as long as he is active – nor Mlozi in the north. Let us plan our campaign. I have invited Spaight to join us because he knows the country and has a military background. He will be my ADC, and I have asked him to bring his estimable Goodwill – as interpretor."

The mountain that was their destination lay about eighty miles north-east of Zomba. The column would have to march for two of its four days through hostile territory, where Chief Zarafi and his head-men held sway. It was agreed that Major Edwards would lead a force of sixty or seventy of his Sikhs, supported by a couple of hundred *askaris*, mostly Atongas. Alan was given the task of recruiting three hundred porters from the friendly chiefs to the south-east of Zomba and around Mlanje Mountain. He knew several of these chiefs from his previous campaigns, and from negotiations about estate labour.

The column set off in mid-October 1895 and reached Mangoche Mountain after a few minor skirmishes with hostile villagers. The mountain was essentially a long ridge stretching for twelve miles in an east-west direction, about a mile wide. It was 3,000 feet above the surrounding plain, heavily wooded, with huge boulders and deep ravines that echoed with the bark of baboons, presenting formidable problems for the advance of the column. Two guides led them into a deep gorge on the south-east side of the mountain.

The ambush was sudden. Scattered fire came from the forest ahead. Alan was walking with the Commissioner and he hurried forward to find Major Edwards crouching behind a rock.

"I'm going to send Bradshaw and Cavendish with some Atongas to clear them out," announced Edwards. "To be frank, I don't want to waste any of my Sikhs in this situation."

Alan agreed. "The Atongas know this sort of country. Let them make as much noise as they can – it helps to keep their spirits up. Besides, it will make the slavers think there are more of us."

He returned to Johnston, who was sitting on a rock smoking a cigar. They listened to the counter attack, which lasted for half an hour before Cavendish came back and told them that the enemy had fled. There were no casualties among the attackers.

They continued up the steep path and found a 'castle' of boulders that provided an ideal command post to cover the advance. Fortunately it was unoccupied, and they guessed that Zarafi's main force must have been expecting them from another direction. The officers posted sentries, and the porters shed their loads to rest. Not long after they saw some men advancing and opened fire on them.

Edwards moved his troops forward, leaving the porters to rest. The path continued up to the summit for a couple more miles, but it was commanded on both sides by steep forested slopes with massive boulders that gave the enemy ample cover. The bullets soon started to fly, but the enemy were poor shots and there were only a few casualties in the column. The Sikhs were effective with their return fire, using Snider rifles, and Edwards, Bradshaw and Cavendish used their Lee-Enfields to devastating effect.

At dusk, essentially unscathed, they reached a prominence near the summit. The porters carrying the gun parts had caught up and they assembled the seven-pounder. It was fired at any place where tell-tale smoke showed the presence of snipers. The slaver militia maintained their firing, and both the Commissioner and Major Edwards were lucky to escape injury when bullets struck near them.

They settled down for the night in the lee of the summit and advanced before dawn. On reaching the top of the ridge they advanced rapidly on Chief Zarafi's village, but he had escaped with all his supporters. He had evidently sent his valuable possessions, such as ivory and cattle, into Portuguese territory.

"Look at this!" shouted Cavendish. It was the seven-pounder mountain gun that Inge had used in '92 before it was captured by the slavers.

Johnston beckoned to Alan. "Look at these views. That must be the Lujenda River, flowing to the coast. And look there! You can see the Upper Shire and Lake Malombe, and that must be Lake Nyasa and Cape Maclear. What an amazing view."

It was stupendous, and Alan thought this would be a special place to have a settlement. The altitude meant that mosquitoes were less prevalent. No doubt there would be springs or pools that could supply drinking water, and there was sufficient arable land to grow crops.

Goodwill came up to them and waited patiently as the Commissioner showed him the views. Then he said, "Sir, these people are mostly Nyanjas. They were conquered by Chief Zarafi and the Yaos, but now they wish to live here in peace."

"So they shall," said Johnston. "We must ensure that Zarafi never returns. We will build a fort here." He called to Major Edwards. "We should leave Lieutenant Alston here, to build a fort."

"We can do that. I have sad news for you, sir. Prabjhat Singh has died of his wound."

"I'm so sorry," said the Commissioner flatly. "Our only loss, I think."

Havildar Prabjhat Singh had been struck by a sniper's bullet in the advance on Zarafi's village. His body was cremated that evening. On the following day the column set off to return to Zomba, leaving Lieutenant Alston and his contingent to build the fort.

—•—

41

Zomba - November 1895

On a hot October morning Jess told Alan she was pregnant with her second child. She was elated and could hardly contain herself. They went over the the Kennedys for Sunday lunch to break the news to them. Alan drove the donkey cart, while Jess sat in the back with Amanda and the boys; they took one of the horses on a long lead.

Marge and Jock were delighted with the news and toasts were made. After lunch, Jock produced a letter that had come for Jess, from Scotland. Alan saw her blanche as she read it. She handed it to him and ran from the room, her hand to her mouth.

He spread the sheet of paper – it was from Andrew McPhail, Alistair's father.

My dear Jessica,

After much deliberation I have decided that I should take my two grandsons to live in Scotland. While I realise that you have grown fond of Malcolm and Andrew, and have looked after them well, I believe they deserve to grow up in the safety and civilisation of their father's home country. I can afford to send them to the best schools ....

Alan gave the letter to Marge and followed Jess, who was in the spare bedroom sobbing.

"How can he even think of taking them away from us? How cruel and heartless to split our family!"

He tried to soothe her. "He can't do it, sweetheart."

She turned her tear-stained face to him. "He has a legal right. They are not my sons. They are his grandsons."

"Not Andrew. He's not related to him."

"No, but we can't prove it."

"I think we could. We must talk to Alfred – he's a solicitor."

"Oh, if only I had adopted them."

———•———

They invited Alfred Sharpe to lunch next day, knowing that he enjoyed visiting the farm. Jess's parents were invited too. Sitting on the verandah they sipped shandies, and Jess wasted no time before introducing the subject.

"Alistair's father, Andrew McPhail, is coming here from Scotland. He intends to take the boys back with him."

Alan watched his friend carefully. Sharpe's sardonic expression hardly changed, but one eyebrow twitched.

"That's most unfortunate, my dear." He tweaked his moustache while they waited. "It might be a wasted journey. His request would have to go before the Chief Magistrate, Peter Shand."

"Does he have any legal right – to take the boys?" Jess was trying to be calm, but Alan could tell that she was almost frantic.

"I don't know. He is the closest relative – you told me that Nora's parents had died. You are their de facto mother, by reason of your marriage – but only their step mother. If you had adopted them..."

"And it's not possible now?"

"I'm afraid not. It would have to have been done while Alistair was alive."

"What about the cruelty of taking Malcolm and Andrew from their adoptive family?" asked Marge, her tone pugnacious.

Sharpe nodded slowly. "It would be cruel, but the law is more concerned with rights than feelings..."

"I have something to say," Jess interjected. Alan raised his hand, anticipating what she was going to say, and wanting to prevent her. "Andrew is not Alistair's child."

"What do you mean, Jess?" Sharpe regarded her with benevolence.

"Andrew is Alan's son."

A silence descended on them, as if dense air had fallen from above. Alan looked at Marge; her expression had not changed. She must have guessed, and was probably dismayed because her daughter had revealed the fact. Then he glanced at Jock, whose mouth had dropped open.

Sharpe stood up and walked to the rail of the verandah, then he turned and faced the others. "Can you prove it Alan?"

"Nora told me."

Marge spoke up. "For heavens sake, Alfred, you only have to see the child to know that he's Alan's son. I've thought it all along."

"I can give evidence, too," added Jess. "Nora told me."

Sharpe smiled and said kindly. "That's what we call hearsay."

For the first time Jock entered the discussion. "So how can you prove paternity – when the parents have died?"

"There is no certain proof," Sharpe replied. "The judge – or magistrate – has to reach a decision based on whatever evidence is available." He turned his gaze to Alan. "I presume there is no evidence that you had an affair with Nora."

He shook his head. "Obviously we tried to keep it secret. There was not even anyone who could have seen her enter my house."

Sharpe said, "I dare say that one of your servants or employees could testify to Nora's visits, but a court might to give much weight to that evidence." After a pause, he added, "I fear that you would not be successful in a court. Alistair and Nora registered the child as theirs, and they gave no one an opinion that he was otherwise, and you made no objection. The fact that young Andrew looks like Alan would not be given much credence by a judge, nor your hearsay evidence, Jess – which could be construed as biased."

He started to pace up and down a short stretch of the verandah, turning at each end with a swift movement. Then he stopped abruptly. "I think you should keep Andrew's paternity to yourselves – and I will say nothing. It's my opinion that you should appeal to Mr McPhail's humanity. Alan, if you say you had an affair with Nora, he will be less inclined to favour you."

—•—

42

Karonga – November/December 1895

A letter came from Andrew McPhail to say that he was on his way from Scotland. Alan wondered if he ought to go down to Katunga to meet him and escort him to Zomba. Then there was the question of where he should stay.

Jess said, "He should stay with us. Surely it would be more difficult for him to break up our family if he experienced living with us."

Marge suggested that this arrangement would also persuade McPhail that the boys were well cared for. "He probably thinks they are getting no education, so we must be sure that he sees them being schooled."

Alan had a fixed image of a dour Presbyterian man with mutton chop whiskers and a permanent scowl. The thought of handing the boys over to him was more than he could bear. Their cries echoed in his mind.

—•—

Commissioner Harry Johnston invited Alan to dinner at the Residency. It was for men only, and, as usual, Jess raised her eyebrows and said. "Another expedition being planned?"

Her husband laughed. "I think it will be his last, my sweet. He knows that Mlozi has to be brought down before he can report the end of the slave trade."

She dandled the baby Amanda on her knee. "Is it really necessary for you to go, darling? It's so far away. Can't Harry be content with the peace we have here?"

"His view is that the other chiefs will renew their slaving as long as they know that Mlozi is getting away with it. I rather agree with him. They all need to be shown that we're determined to put an end to it – and that we are better able to do it than when we started – eight years ago."

"Very well. But do you need to go? He has professional soldiers like Edwards and Manning now, why can't he leave you in peace?"

Alan laughed again. "I'm not sure that he does want me."

—•—

They sat around the dinner table at the Residency. Harry Johnston presided at the head, dressed in a dinner jacket and black tie, his eyes twinkling as he prepared to light a cigar. The Queen had been toasted and port passed round. Those present, besides Alan were Majors Edwards and Bradshaw, and Lieutenants Coape-Smith, Alston and Herries-Smith.

"Gentlemen," announced the Commissioner. "It's time we talked about the expedition to the north. As you all know, I went to Karonga in July, to try to make Chief Mlozi stick to the treaty he signed with me six years ago. I regret that he refused to see me. He sent me a letter saying that he would close the Stevenson road to Tanganyika. Now, I've spoken to most of you already, so we need to make firm plans. I have it in mind to take our 'ever victorious army' to Karonga. I trust I will have your support."

All the others nodded, though they said nothing. Johnston continued: "I've asked Alan to join us because he knows the area, from the previous campaigns. Alan, we are grateful that you will join us. We have a hundred Sikhs, and three times that number of *askaris*. With that well-trained force we ought to have the measure of Mlozi."

"It's a lot of men to transport," said Edwards. "The three gunboats can take less than fifty. The *Domira* can take a hundred..."

"True," cut in Johnston. "I've spoken to Captain Berndt, and he has agreed to make the *Hermann von Wissman* available. I have to pay him, of course, but he has been generous in his terms. Also, I've sworn him to secrecy."

"That's important," Alan said. "We should catch Mlozi by surprise, otherwise he may slip away, and we would have wasted our opportunity."

"What would you propose?" asked Major Edwards.

"He is most likely to flee west," Alan answered. "He knows the country well – the tracks and hiding places. I suggest we position a strong force to cut off this route. The trick will be to do this without Mlozi finding out. It must be done at night – and that's not easy. If we could time the attack when there's some moonlight, it would be easier to position the cut-off troops."

———•———

The expedition left Fort Johnston on November 24, 1895, the officers sailing on the *Domira*. Alan took Goodwill, at the request of the Commissioner. Goodwill was delighted to see Kawa again. His friend had also married and started to raise a family. They joked about the delights of having wives and raising children.

Much of the three day voyage was taken up with detailed planning, using maps drawn up by Dr Kerr Cross. The military commander, Major Edwards, developed a severe fever and was incapacitated by the time they reached Karonga. However, the dispositions went ahead smoothly. Lt Coape-Smith placed the cut-off units during the night of December 1, and then met the HQ Force at Karonga early the following morning. This force was strengthened by a Naval unit under Commander Cullen with the mountain guns.

Msalemo's and Kopa Kopa's villages were shelled at daylight, and the opposing forces driven out. Goodwill and Alan interrogated the

317

prisoners and learnt that some of the militia had departed during the previous night to join Mlozi, having heard rumours about the landing at Karonga.

The attack on Mlozi's stockade began at midday. Commander Cullen's shelling started several fires, but they were soon extinguished by heavy rain. The attackers took shelter in huts located several hundred yards from the stockade. Meanwhile, Mlozi's force returned fire, but it was poorly aimed.

Mlozi's stockade consisted of a high double fence packed with clay, and covered with a thatched roof. The wall had two rows of loopholes, from which the defenders fired with their flintlock muskets. At the outside base of the stockade wall was a ditch, partly filled with rainwater. There were several entrances into the stockade that were closed with heavy wooden gates.

The shelling continued all afternoon and into the night. An attempted escape was repulsed by the Nordenfelt gun operated by Cullen's sailors. At seven o'clock on the morning of December 3, the defenders raised a flag of truce. Mlozi emerged from the main gate, wearing his habitual white *kanzu*, and accompanied by a small retinue. Commissioner Harry Johnston walked forward to meet him, with Ali Kiongwe, his Swahili aide, and Goodwill, beside him.

"Beware!" hissed Ali. "They're telling Mlozi to stab you!"

Johnston stopped and called out, "You must surrender, Mlozi. Put down your guns and release all the slaves in your *boma*. The lives of your men will be spared."

Mlozi called back, in Swahili, "I will consult with the other chiefs. These men can be your hostages while you wait."

The atmosphere was tense, since Johnston's party were within easy range of the flintlocks in the stockade. Ali questioned the two hostages, but they were sullen and unwilling to speak. After about ten minutes a shout came from the gateway that there would be no surrender, and requesting the return of the hostages.

The Commissioner sent the hostages back and returned to the huts, but firing broke out before the flag of truce was lowered. Lt Alston received a bullet through his helmet, that fortunately caused no injury.

Goodwill found some of the *askaris* gathered round a local man. On enquiring, he discovered that it was a WaHenga headman, who had slipped out of the gate during the parley. Goodwill asked him how much he knew about the layout of the stockade, and the man claimed to know it intimately.

"Do you know Mlozi's house?" asked Goodwill.

"Of course. See that taller roof? That's it."

Goodwill took the headman to the Commissioner and pointed out the roof. Commander Cullen was then instructed to shell the house, achieving several direct hits.

Not long after this, several of the stockade gates opened and defenders started to flood out. Although it appeared that they were fleeing, they were armed and occasionally firing. So the attackers returned fire in concentrated fashion, moving forward at the same time, until they were soon at the stockade.

Some Sikh sepoys scaled the wall and pulled up the young officers. They jumped down inside, and almost immediately Lt Herries-Smith was wounded in the arm. They were followed by Majors Edwards and Bradshaw, while Commander Cullen organised his sailors to break down the main wooden gate, using axes.

Alan was among the attackers who flooded into the stockade, where the occupants surrendered and a search for Mlozi was started. Rumours flew around that he had been wounded, but no trace of him could be found. Eventually, the attacking force withdrew to their temporary camp, disconsolate that they had lost the main target.

Goodwill came to Alan and said, "Sir, I would like to go into the stockade to find information about Mlozi. I can question the people who have been living there. They may know where he is, or where he has gone."

Alan was concerned for Goodwill's safety, but he was wearing the army's makeshift uniform of khaki shirt and breeches, that would distinguish him from the rabble of Mlozi supporters. Besides, he was determined to go.

—•—

43

Karonga – December 1895

Goodwill walked slowly into the stockade, careful to avoid any of Mlozi's supporters who might remain there. The village was in ruins, the huts burnt to the ground or smouldering. The air was acrid with the smoke from the grass thatch and the wall timbers. Dead and dying villagers lay on the ground outside the huts. Sikh soldiers and Atonga *askaris* went from one to the other, covering the dead and carrying the wounded out of the stockade, where they would be treated.

Mlozi's houses were prominent in the centre of the village and Goodwill worked his way towards them. One was a two-story building, the only one in the village. It was made of sun-dried bricks, and one corner had been knocked askew by a cannon shell. He peered inside, then walked in.

The furnishings were simple, but of a much higher standard than anything in a villager's hut. The floors were scattered with antelope karrosses, and the tables and chairs had been made from hardwood by skilled carpenters. Against a wall was one rack with several flintlock guns and another with some spears.

He walked through to an inner room, lit only from high windows. Gulab Singh, with one of his naiks, was probing the wall hangings and piles of tusks in the corners.

"Have you found anything?" Goodwill asked.

The Sikh turned and glared, then grinned when he recognised him. "Nothing. What about you?"

Goodwill shook his head. "I thought I would try to find out where Mlozi has gone." They spoke in English.

"Good idea. It would be a pity if we lost the villain. I expect he has fled with his bodyguard." Gulab Singh threw down a spear in disgust. "We're wasting our time here. Come on!" He signalled to his naik to follow him, and Goodwill trooped out after them, into the courtyard.

Goodwill found an old man sitting on the ground with his back to the wall of Mlozi's house. He seemed to be unharmed, though his eyes were glazed.

"Are you wounded?" asked Goodwill.

The old man shook his head; his neck was so thin that Goodwill wondered how it could support the head.

"Are you a supporter of Mlozi?"

"Not me." The old man's voice was faint. "I worked for him, as a sweeper."

"Where is he?"

"Who knows." The old man lifted a frail arm and moved it in an arc. "I suppose he has run away."

"Where was he during the fighting?"

The old man seemed to make a great effort to remember. His eyes wandered as he thought. "I stayed here – fool that I am – not knowing that the *azungu* could target the Chief's house. Mlozi was at the *boma* wall, but he came back. I saw him go in." He pointed to the doorway.

"Did you see him come out?"

The old fellow shook his head. "Perhaps I did not see him. There was so much dust and confusion. My head is ringing with the sound of the explosions."

Goodwill went back into the house. He was fascinated by the trappings of relative wealth. This was not the house of a *mzungu*, like Spaight's or Kennedy's. This was an African's house, albeit a half-caste.

He walked slowly through to the large room where he had met the two Sikh soldiers. He stood in contemplation in the centre of the room.

Suddenly he heard the sound of muffled voices. Where were they coming from? He walked slowly and carefully around the room. In an eerie way the sounds seemed to be coming from a wooden bed in the corner. He bent down and looked under the bed, his heart thumping. There was nothing.

He lay on the ground beside the bed and heard the voices again. They were coming from under the ground. His skin prickled with fear and he started to sweat. Carefully crawling under the bed he found a wooden trapdoor. He then realised there was an underground chamber hidden below.

"Who's there?" came a muffled voice in Swahili.

"It is I, master," replied Goodwill, pretending to be a Swahili servant.

"Move the bed and come down." The voice was indistinct.

Goodwill got up and pulled the bed aside. Then he lifted the trapdoor to reveal a dark rectangular hole. There were two men squatting inside. They stood up. One was slight, with Arab features, dressed in a muddy blood-soaked *kanzu*. The other was shorter and carried a spear, which he pushed forward threateningly.

Goodwill was unarmed, but he feinted to one side and grabbed the spear. He had learned the movement many times when he was with the Angoni. He twisted the spear from the guard's hands and stood back.

"Are you Chief Mlozi?" he asked the man in the *kanzu*, who nodded. Goodwill could see that he was wounded; there was a large stain of blood on the shoulder of his *kanzu*.

"You are my prisoners," he said. "You must come with me."

—•—

Commissioner Johnston decided to put Mlozi on immediate trial. It was discovered that he had ordered many hostages to be killed during the bombardment. Johnston thought this was a sufficient crime to try him for murder. They assembled five WaNkonde chiefs and headmen, who would be the jury. Mlozi was led out, his hands tied behind his back. Because he had been wounded he was allowed to sit on the ground.

Johnston, using Goodwill as his interpretor, listed the evidence against Mlozi, and asked him if he had anything to say in his defence.

"What is the point?" he said. "You people have decided to kill me. My hour has come."

Johnston then pronounced the sentence, that he would be hanged. This would be done in Karonga, in the presence of the chiefs, head-men, and as many people as could be gathered.

However, shortly after, they heard that some of Mlozi's men had overcome their Atonga guards and run away. News also came that pro-Mlozi forces were coming to rescue him. Johnston decided that there was a distinct risk of an attack on the way back to Karonga. Not wish-ing to offer any chance to rescue Mlozi, he decided that the execution should be carried out then and there.

A large acacia tree with an overhanging branch was chosen. One of the Sikh soldiers tied the noose around Mlozi's neck and he was lifted onto a makeshift platform. As many people as possible were gathered to witness the execution.

Johnston read a statement in English, that Ali translated into Swa-hili and Goodwill rendered in ChiNyanja. It said that Mlozi had been convicted for murder after a fair trial, and that he deserved to die for other crimes against the WaNkonde people. At a hand signal from the Commissioner, the Sikh soldier then pushed Mlozi off the platform.

—•—

44

Zomba - December 1895

When Alan returned to the farm he was greeted by Jess with the news that Andrew McPhail had arrived six days before. Because Alan was away at Karonga, he had arranged for McPhail to be guided to Zomba, with *machilas* arranged through Mandala.

Somewhat to Jess's surprise, she told him, he was a pleasant man, seeming older than she expected. He had taken the boys for a walk.

"What has he said?" asked Alan. "Is he determined to take them?"

"I don't know. He won't say. He wants to talk to you first. He's met with Alfred and the magistrate, but he won't discuss what was the outcome."

"He sounds rather difficult – stubborn?"

"No." She pondered. "He seems a decent man."

Alan decided that he had to be himself. There was no point in trying to be saintly or recalcitrant. When he saw McPhail walking up to the farmhouse, with the two little boys beside him, he walked out to greet them. The boys ran forward to greet him, hugging him from either side.

Andrew McPhail was of average height, and somewhat frail, like his son had been. His hair was iron grey and his eyebrows were bushy and unkempt. His skin was sallow and he was slightly stooped, which made him seem older.

They shook hands, and McPhail said, "The boys have been show-ing me round the farm. You have a fine place."

"It's coming along," said Alan. "Let's have some tea on the veran-dah – it's locally grown, you know."

They sat together while Jess brought tea and scones, then joined them. It seemed that McPhail wanted to say something to them. He waited until the boys had finished and ran off to play. Then he cleared his throat.

"Yesterday, Jessica and Alan, I made my decision, after much de-liberation. I spoke at length to the Commissioner, Mr Johnston, and to Mr Sharpe. They spoke very highly of you Alan, and of you, too, Jessica. Therefore, I have decided that I will not take the boys away. They have a good home with you, and I am confident that you will look after them well. I could offer only an inferior alternative – an elderly grandfather, with a nursemaid." He paused and wiped his brow with a handkerchief.

"I can see you are relieved, and I regret that I wrote my letter that caused you so much anxiety – please forgive me." He cleared his throat again, with a gurgling noise. "My only concern is that the boys should receive an adequate education. My interest is all the more fervent because, as you know, I was a school teacher all my life. How-ever, you are both well educated, and I know that you will do your best to make sure that the boys are properly taught."

"I aim to leave within a day or two. Perhaps I will come back again, but I fear that my poor health might not stand the rigours of another long journey. It would be nice if you could manage a trip to Edinburgh."

Jess jumped up and went to hug the old man. "We will, we will." She turned to Alan for support. "We always wanted to take the chil-dren to see Scotland and their relations there."

"Perhaps I can help you," said McPhail. "Although I was only a school teacher, I have been able to save a nest egg because my parents bequeathed to me their house in Merchiston Park, a pleasant part of Edinburgh."

———•———

Andrew McPhail stayed at *Khundalila* for Christmas, a happy family gathering, to which the two single men, Alfred Sharpe and Harry Johnston, were invited. The elderly Scot took a keen interest in the little school and Goodwill's strategy for teaching the local children to a standard that would enable them to progress to the higher school at Domasi.

"I wish I had come here as a young man, like you, Alan," he said one evening. "These young African children have such a keen interest in their lessons."

McPhail was surprised that most of the other settlers had no farm school, nor any interest in starting one. "It seems short-sighted," he said.

"I agree," said Alan. "The future ought to be a permanent labour force that has reasonable amenities, such as clean drinking water, food rations, and housing that's a step up from grass huts."

"Aye. You know, I have learned so much from talking to Goodwill. He is a fine man. I wish that our people at home could hear about his experiences – his capture and escape, and his campaigns with you. By the way, he speaks very highly of you, Alan. It was a factor in my decision to leave the boys in your care."

———•———

On the Sunday after Christmas they all walked up to Zomba plateau to visit the graves of Alistair and Nora McPhail. The donkey cart took them up to the foot of the track; they left it there with a groom, and continued on foot. Jess was concerned that the incline would be too much for Mr McPhail, but he trudged on, stopping occasionally to catch his breath. It had rained that morning and the air was clear until they were half way up the mountain, when a mist closed in on them.

327

It was at times like this that Alan felt his skin prickle. The wafts of mist were quite cold and their clothes became damp. Amanda had to be carried, but Malcolm and Andrew insisted on walking until the mist came; then Alan carried them in turn.

When they reached the summit the mist seemed to thicken. For a while Alan was afraid that he could not locate the graves. Then the cloud lifted momentarily and he was able to orient himself and move towards them.

They stood beside the graves for a long time, the old man silent with his thoughts. The boys stroked the crosses and then became restless and wanted to go back down the mountain out of the mist.

—•—

Andrew McPhail left two days later. There were tears in his eyes as he said goodbye to Jess and the boys, urging them to come to see him in Edinburgh. But he was in good spirits as he rode the mule Jenny down the track from Blantyre to Katunga, Alan rode beside him and took a lead rein from Jenny in some of the steep inclines. He was fearful that the old gentleman would fall and break a bone. Alan looked after him carefully in the camp for the one night, and helped him to board the steamer next day.

When they said goodbye, Alan promised to take Jess and the children to Scotland soon.

"Don't leave it too long," said the old man.

—•—

One day, not long after Andrew McPhail's departure, Goodwill came up to speak to Alan, who was repairing a piece of machinery and stood up, straightening his back. The African apologised for disturbing him, then said, "Sir, I think I should go in search of Musa."

It was a sombre announcement, made with deliberation, and Alan thought Goodwill must have been considering the matter for a long time.

"You mean the slaver who took you and Kawa to the coast?"

"And my sister Mary."

Alan walked to the shade of the mango tree and signalled for Goodwill to follow. They sat on the bench.

"If you found him, what would you do?"

"Bring him back here – to justice."

"That would be difficult. I mean to bring him single-handed, through hostile Yao territory?"

"Yes, that is true. But perhaps I could find out what happened to my sister."

Alan sighed. "I think you should be realistic. It happened nearly ten years ago. You have a wife and family and they need you here. Musa might not be alive. In any case you might never find him. Because slavery has been stopped here he has probably moved somewhere else. Even so, the chances of finding Mary are very slight. I know it troubles you, but you have to weigh the chances that you could find your sister against the risks that you might lose your life."

He looked at Goodwill, who was gazing into the distance. Alan continued, "You have a responsibility to your wife and your children..."

"But you went to the fighting against the slavers. You left your wife and children behind. There was real danger."

"True, my friend, but we knew that evil men were there, and it was for a short time. If you head off east into Portuguese territory looking for Musa, it will be like – like looking for an ant in a field of maize. We might never see you again. Your family – your mother and Mercy and her family – all might never see you again. You know, Goodwill, it would be different if you heard that Musa was operating somewhere east of Lake Chilwa, or if someone had heard of a woman named Mary living in some town in Portuguese territory."

Goodwill stood up. "You are right, of course, sir. I think I needed someone like you to tell me that I must stay here."

Alan stood up and put his hand on Goodwill's shoulder. "I have told you, my friend. Let us put the past behind us. There is such a good future for us to build. Stay with us."

—•—

Epilogue

There were some more battles and skirmishes with the slavers and the chiefs that traded with them, but the major campaigns ended with the hanging of Mlozi. Thereafter, the administration of the Nyasaland Protectorate was pursued in an environment of comparative law and order. For the first time in many decades the people were able to live in safety.

Alan and Jess had another daughter, named Kirsty. Their four children grew up happily at *Khundalila*. They were taught by Jess, and later in a small school in Zomba. When they were older the boys went to boarding school in Rhodesia, and the girls went to the convent school in Limbe; they all helped on the farm during their long school holidays.

Jock died on cancer in 1898 after a long and painful battle. His widow Marge employed a manager to run *Namikango,* and moved into a grandmother wing that Alan and Jess added to their farmhouse.

Goodwill had six children, one of whom died in infancy. Of those who reached adulthood, three were boys, who became, respectively, a teacher, a mechanic, and church minister; the two girls became hospital nurses. Goodwill continued working on the Spaight farm; one of his proudest possessions was a letter of commendation from Sir Harry Johnston.

Kawa continued working for Mandala, working his way up through boatswain of the *Domira*, and then chief mate of the *Ilala*. He had five children; one of his daughters married a son of Goodwill. He also received a letter of commendation from the Commissioner.

Harry Hamilton Johnston left Nyasaland in 1896 and was knighted for his services. He returned to Britain, married, and stood unsuccessfully for Parliament. He wrote several books, including his autobiography, and died in 1927. It was on his recommendation that Alan was made a Companion of the Order of the Bath.

Alan and Jess took the children to Scotland in 1897 to see their families. They visited Andrew McPhail, who died a year later and left a substantial sum of money, and his house in Edinburgh, in trust for Malcolm and Andrew, who retained the surname McPhail.

Alfred Sharpe succeeded Johnston as Commissioner, and was then appointed Nyasaland's first Governor in 1907 and knighted. He and Alan remained close friends and spent many evenings on the verandahs of their respective houses, sipping whisky and smoking cigars, reminiscing about the slave wars and discussing the state of the Protectorate.

Alan considered volunteering to fight in the Boer War that erupted in 1899. He sympathised with the Boers, so decided he could not fight against them. Equally he felt he could not fight against the British. So he remained on the farm. When the First World War started in 1914 he was one of the first to volunteer, taking Goodwill with him – but that is another story.

—•—

Abbreviated biographies

Johnston, Sir Harry Hamilton, GCMG, KCB (1858-1927), colonial administrator, explorer, artist, linguist. Met Stanley in the Congo in 1883, and led an expedition to Mount Kilimanjaro in 1884. First Commissioner of British Central Africa Protectorate (1891-1896). Author of many books. Unsuccessful candidate for the Liberal Party in 1903 and 1906.

Sharpe, Sir Alfred, KCMG, CB, FRGS (1853-1935), solicitor, colonial administrator, hunter. Second Commissioner of the British Central Africa Protectorate (1896-1907), first Governor of Nyasaland (1907-1910). He was instrumental in developing the fledgling administration of the country and tried to improve the relationships of planters and their labourers.

Buchanan, John, CMG (1855-1896), lay missionary, planter, administrator. Dismissed from Church of Scotland Mission for brutality. Acting British Consul, British Central Africa Protectorate (1887-1891). Pioneered production of tea, coffee, sugarcane and tobacco. His estates were purchased by Blantyre & East Africa Ltd. His brothers died in the Protectorate, David in 1892 and Robert in 1896.

Lugard, Frederick John Dealtry, 1st Baron Lugard, GCMG, CB, DSO, PC (1858-1945). Soldier and colonial administrator. Educated at Rossall and Sandhurst, Fought in the Afghan War (1879/80), the Sudan

Campaign (1884/85) and the 3rd Burmese War (1886/87). High Commissioner, Northern Nigeria Protectorate (1900-1906). 14th Governor of Hong Kong (1907-1912), founded University of Hong Kong. First Governor-General of Nigeria (1913-1918). Helped to organise the 1926 Slavery Convention.

Moir, John William, CMG (1851–1940), trader and explorer in Africa, recruited with his brother in 1877 to build a road from Dar-es-Salaam to Lake Tanganyika. In 1878 became joint founding manager of the Livingstonia Central Africa Company, known from 1881 as the African Lakes Company, and from 1894 as the African Lakes Corporation. Undertook early expeditions into parts of what later became northern Malawi and eastern Zambia. Actively involved, with Vice-Consul John Buchanan, in seeking to stop Portuguese expansion into the Shire highlands in 1889–90. Married (1882) and had one son and one daughter. Left Africa in March 1890 and returned to Nyasaland in 1893 and became a pioneer tea planter. A stern critic of Harry Johnston's aggressive and militaristic approach to the occupation of the country, he retired to Edinburgh in 1900.

Moir, Frederick Lewis Maitland (1852–1939), trader and explorer in Africa. Worked with his brother in Tanganyika and became joint manager of the Livingstonia Central African Company, later the African Lakes Company, later African Lakes Corporation. Married (1885), Jane Beith. Left Africa in June 1891 and did not return, becoming secretary of the company in Glasgow, later a director and chairman.

Short bibliography

Duff, Hector Livingston, *Nyasaland under the Foreign Office*, George Bell & Sons (1903).

Fotheringham, L. Monteith *Adventures in Nyassaland: A Two Years' Struggle with Arab Slave Traders in Central Africa*, Sampson Low (1891).

Good, Charles M., *The Steamer Parish*, University of Chicago Press (2004).

Hanna, A.J. *The Beginnings of Nyasaland and North-Eastern Rhodesia, 1859-95*, Oxford Clarendon Press (1956).

Johnston, Harry Hamilton, *The Story of my Life*, Chatto & Windus, (1923).

Johnston, Harry Hamilton, *British Central Africa*, Methuen & Co (1897).

Livingstone, David, *A Popular Account of Dr Livingstone's Expedition to the Zambesi and its Tributaries*, John Murray (1894).

Livingstone, David, *The Last Journals of David Livingstone, in Central Africa, from 1865 to his death, Vol 1 (1866-1868)*, John Murray (1874); Vol 2, John Murray (1874)

Lugard, Frederick, *'The Rise of our East African Empire: early efforts in Nyasaland and Uganda'*

MacDonell, Bror, *Mzee Ali; the bigraphy of an African slave-raider turned askari and scout,* 30 Degrees South Publishers (2006).

McCracken, John, *A History of Malawi: 1859-1966*, James Currey, 2012.

Ransford, Oliver, *Livingstone's Lake, The Drama of Nyasa,* John Murray, 1966.

Swann, Alfred, *Fighting the Slave-Hunters in Central Africa*

CPSIA information can be obtained at www.ICGtesting.com
Printed in the USA
BVOW03s1954060916

461308BV00021B/145/P